USA TODAY a[...]d author **Caitlin** [...] teaches her fav[...] writing classes [...] prestigious Wri[...] gets to utilise the MA and PhD in English Literature that she received from the University of York in England. She currently lives in the Pacific Northwest, with her very own hero and too many pets. Visit her at caitlincrews.com.

Margot Radcliffe lives in Columbus, Ohio, right now, but surrenders to wanderlust every couple of years, so it's hard to say where she'll end up next. Regardless of location, her apricot dog will be by her side while she writes fun romances that hopefully make readers laugh and space out for a bit. With heroines who aren't afraid to take what they want, and confident heroes who are up to a challenge, she loves creating complicated modern love stories. She can be found @margotradcliffe on Twitter and @margot_radcliffe on Instagram.

THE PLEASURE CONTRACT

CAITLIN CREWS

BRING THE HEAT

MARGOT RADCLIFFE

MILLS & BOON

First Published in Great Britain 2021
by Mills & Boon, an imprint of HarperCollins*Publishers*
1 London Bridge Street, London, SE1 9GF

The Pleasure Contract © 2021 Caitlin Crews

Bring the Heat © 2021 Terra Rogerson

ISBN: 978-0-263-29793-5

MIX
Paper from
responsible sources
FSC™ C007454

This book is produced from independently certified FSC™ paper
to ensure responsible forest management.
For more information visit www.harpercollins.co.uk/green.

Printed and bound in Spain
by CPI, Barcelona

THE PLEASURE CONTRACT

CAITLIN CREWS

MILLS & BOON

CHAPTER ONE

BRISTOL MARCH WISHED her younger sister was a little less messy, a whole lot less *languid*, and maybe the tiniest bit less free-spirited, while she was at it—but she wasn't.

Never had been and probably never would be.

Indy was two and a half years younger, liked to claim she had *a bohemian flair* in all things, and was underemployed as a deliberate life choice. This allowed her to have sex with all the pretty people she wanted without worrying overmuch about getting to work the next morning. Or paying rent. Or even cleaning up after herself when she was seized with the occasional cooking bug—but Bristol knew if she let herself start thinking like that, Indy would only laugh at her.

You don't have to *be the mom of me,* she would say, rolling her eyes. *We already have a mom, remember?*

Bristol did not plan to have that fight for the

trillionth time. Not today. She eyed her sister, currently draped over the love seat in their tiny apartment on the border of the most hipster part of Brooklyn—Indy claimed that made them *more* hipster—texting her many lovers and friends, taking the odd selfie, and also painting her toenails a shockingly bright yellow. All at the same time.

Since Indy couldn't possibly be paying attention to what she was doing or saying with so much going on, Bristol decided that she must have misheard what her sister had said.

"If your boss wants a new secretary, I'm sure there are agencies for that," she said, trying her best not to sound too academic. Indy laughed at her for hours when she got *stuffy* and, worse, *did things* to snap her out of it. Even if it had sounded like Indy had said the man was looking for *a new woman*. "Especially at his level."

"Bristol. I despair of you." Indy lifted her gaze from her banana-yellow toes. She tossed her phone aside. The spring sunshine filled their puny living room, making their long-dead plants seem almost alive again. Bristol made a mental note to get rid of the withered things and also to not forget, the way she did every single year, that she was made entirely of black thumbs. "Two things. One, Lachlan Drummond is not my boss. He is *the* boss. I've been temping in that building for two months and I've never laid eyes on him. I think he comes and goes in a rainbow of his own incredible wealth and hotness. Or possibly by helicopter."

"Fine. Your boss's boss."

"There are at least twelve more boss layers. I'm a *temp*. The man owns half of New York."

Bristol never paid that much attention to the New York glitterati who were forever flinging themselves in and out of taxis and town cars up and down Fifth Avenue or swanning about at famous functions like the Met Ball. She'd been far too busy lost in the archives and libraries she'd basically been living in over the last few years while finishing up her doctorate. But even she knew who Lachlan Drummond was.

Everyone knew who Lachlan Drummond was. Notorious for walking away from the hedge fund he'd run, giving at least three fortunes away to charity in what the papers called *his penance*—though not the fortune or four he'd inherited from his blue-blooded parents—and now famous all over again for his brand of guerilla philanthropy. Not to mention his commanding presence in otherwise deadly boring global summits filled with ancient diplomats.

Also, he was astonishingly good-looking. The kind of good-looking that made even serious-minded lifetime students like Bristol stop dead and stare from the recesses of her study carrel.

So good-looking that, actually, *mind-numbingly*

hot was a far better way to describe him. Thick blond hair and serious blue eyes, an unsmiling mouth in a great many of his pictures though those eyes always seemed to gleam, a rangy athlete's body that was always showing up in magazines that liked to feature him while he was engaged in sweaty, sporty things that often inspired him to rip off his shirt, and, of course, the intense problem that was Lachlan Drummond in formal attire.

But this was not the time to get swoony over a famous man she would never meet.

"Two," Indy was saying, "he's not looking for a secretary. He has floors of secretaries at his disposal. He's looking for a new girlfriend."

"Why do you know this if you've never even laid eyes on the man?"

It would be very like her sister to casually announce that *oh, by the way*, last month when she'd said she was camping upstate she'd actually been hooking up with *Lachlan Drummond*, no big deal.

Indy waved a hand. "You know people tell me things."

"Okay. Is there a reason you're telling *me*?"

Indy's gaze stayed steady on Bristol. "I've been working on a theory about Lachlan Drummond and I found out from one of his personal assistants that it's true."

Bristol could tell that Indy wanted her to be on the edge of her seat, so, as the older sister, she was required by all known laws to sigh and look bored instead. "It's going to be very disappointing if he's a furry."

"He is not." Indy laughed. "But he doesn't have relationships in the classic sense. He hires his girl-friends."

There was no rational reason that a notion like that should wind around inside Bristol the way it did, making her feel suddenly breathless.

And suddenly, shockingly wet between her legs.

You have spent way too much time lost in your books, she chided herself. When was the last time she'd gotten naked with someone? That she couldn't remember offhand was…worrying. Surely she should know.

"You mean escorts?" she asked.

"I wouldn't call them that. They're more long term." Indy shrugged. "He prefers to hire a woman so he gets exactly what he wants, when he wants it. No trawling around in bars. No swiping left or right. It's not like he can go out like a regular person anyway. How is he supposed to get laid?"

"So he *buys* it?" That did not fit with Bristol's image of Lachlan Drummond. "I wonder if there's an agency for *that*."

"I'm glad you asked," Indy said smugly. And there was a light in her eyes, then, that made Bristol frown. "There is. It's not an agency so much as a panel of three of Lachlan's personal assistants. They narrow down the applicants—and my friend tells me there are always way too many applicants—and then put the finalists through. Meaning, the finalists actually get to meet him."

"This sounds like the kind of reality show I don't watch."

"You watch. You just pretend you don't." Indy rolled her eyes. "He's looking for a very particular woman. She has to be beautiful, obviously, but she also has to be smart, because he doesn't want to be bored. Or embarrassed when he's out there chit-chatting with kings and statesmen, like he does."

"This woman sounds like quite the paragon," Bristol muttered.

"She has to be able to travel with him and keep up with his crazy schedule. And she has to understand that while he doesn't want a doormat, he makes the rules. All the rules. In bed and out."

"Do you really expect me to believe that people *apply* for this?"

"A lot of people. All it takes for the first round is a few pictures and a résumé. They weed all that down before offering interviews with the panel. And then there's even more weeding from there."

Bristol started to feel okay about how over-whelming she'd found the very idea of dating or dating apps or setups or anything else lately. At least she didn't have to resort to *panels* or *weeding* like poor Lachlan Drummond.

"Well," Bristol said philosophically, "if anyone can not only meet that questionable list of requirements, but actually find them exciting, it's you."

Indy laughed again, this time so hard that the silky dark hair she'd piled on top of her head fell down around her shoulders. Looking gorgeous and deliberately tousled, naturally.

"I didn't apply," she said. She smiled innocently, which set off alarm bells immediately. Bristol scowled, but that only made Indy look more *holy*. "But you did. I submitted your photos and résumé myself. You're welcome."

Bristol was outraged. Incandescent with it.

Because it was all well and good for Indy to waft through her life from party to party, sexual partner to sexual partner. Her sister had spent two years backpacking around Europe after college, had only returned after what she darkly called her *one night in Budapest, not Bangkok, but it was humbling all the same*, and liked to claim that her current lifestyle was basically still backpacking, but without the trouble of a pack.

Bristol admired her sister in many ways. Truly she did. But she'd taken an entirely different approach to life.

Their parents, Margie and Bill March—who still lived in the deeply boring Ohio town where they'd met, married, and raised their girls—had used up whatever spontaneity they possessed in naming their daughters. Though Indy liked to argue that a pair of Midwesterners naming a child *Indiana* was perhaps less an act of spontaneity than a cry of abiding sadness.

A comment their mother had never found amusing, no matter how many times Indy said it over the years.

Margie and Bill had not exactly approved of Indy's quest to do as little as possible with herself and her life, though neither one of them was much for confrontation. Bill quietly sent a weekly clippings packet to his youngest daughter, filled with job listings from all over the country, which Indy called his *pistols at dawn*.

They did not send Bristol any clippings collections, but they'd never been entirely thrilled with her obsessive need for academic achievement, either.

They were supportive, but...befuddled, really, at this child of theirs with so much drive to achieve, achieve, achieve. They'd never stood in her way, but Bristol knew that if she'd woken up one morning and announced that she was tossing it all in to live in her hometown and find a nice guy to marry, they would have found that much more understandable. But Bristol had no intention of living like that. She wanted a life of *ideas*, not Ohio. She'd gotten her scholarship to the school of her choice, had gone straight on into her master's, and had zipped through her PhD in record time. As if she had a race to win.

Now she had decisions to make. She'd been offered a postdoctoral position, which would be very prestigious and allow her to lean further into her research. Or she could pursue a position at one of the universities she'd been interviewing with.

For the first time in her life, the way forward wasn't clear.

Bristol March had no idea what to do with herself.

Something she kept trying to think her way through, though for once, *thinking* didn't seem to work. She'd finished up teaching the last of the classes that she was a teaching assistant for last week. Now there was nothing left but exam grading, and she'd long ago developed a system for that.

She was done and she didn't want to be, but that didn't make her any less done.

So when her phone rang a few days after Indy's announcement in the cluttered office she shared with two other TAs in the social science building on campus, she didn't do what she normally did—which was scowl at the offending call and switch it off. The office was empty, she still had no idea what to do with her life now that she couldn't continue on being a student as she preferred, and the loud ring jolted her out of the same old circles she was tired of traipsing around, over and over, in her head.

"Ms. March?" came the smooth voice on the other end, with the hint of a British accent.

"Dr. March," she corrected automatically, because she, by God, had earned her title.

"My apologies," came the voice with no hint of any disruption in all that smoothness. "I'm calling on behalf of Lachlan Drummond. I'm pleased to tell you that your application has been accepted."

Bristol had forgotten all about Lachlan Drummond and his *pussy panel*. Dismissed it, more like. Because it was ridiculous, and anyway, there was no possibility that a grubby, newly minted PhD would attract the attention of…a man like him, who routinely fended off the advances of gorgeous celebrities.

"I beg your pardon?" was all she could manage to get out, sounding squeaky and silly and not like herself at all.

"Interviews will take place this week," the voice on the other end of the line continued, smoothly male and confident in ways Bristol imagined she would never be. And this had to be one of Lachlan Drummond's *assistants*. "I'm going to text you a link to the interview calendar. We ask that you choose a time that works for you from the available options. This link is specifically coded to your cell phone and cannot be transferred. It is location sensitive and will work for exactly seven minutes after I terminate this phone call. Do you have any questions?"

"Does Lachlan Drummond think he's in *Mission Impossible*?" Bristol asked drily. "Is that a rich-guy thing?"

"If you choose not to pick a time," the voice continued on, plummy and still smooth, as if she hadn't spoken, "the link will expire and you will have no opportunity to reapply. Once again, do you have any questions? Do you need me to repeat anything I've just told you?"

Bristol opened her mouth, because she had nothing but questions, but nothing seemed to come out.

"Seven minutes," the voice advised. "If you miss this window, there will be no possibility of reopening it. When Mr. Drummond makes rules, he expects those rules to be followed."

"I'll bet he does," Bristol muttered, but by then, the line was already dead.

The mysterious, unidentified assistant had already hung up.

Bristol found herself staring down at her mobile. Her first response was a rush of clarifying outrage. As if it wasn't bad enough that this famous man employed hordes to do his bidding, he had to take it to truly cloak-and-dagger level. Who did he think he was?

One minute passed.

Then, against her will, Bristol found herself daydreaming about the last picture she'd accidentally seen of Lachlan Drummond. She'd been minding her own business, walking down Amsterdam on the Upper West Side, and there he'd been all over some magazine at a newsstand. It had been a typical tabloid exploration of a relationship they believed he was having with some or other famous woman, possibly a European royal, though Bristol couldn't remember which one. She'd been far too consumed with the sight of Lachlan Drummond shirtless, gleaming golden and absurdly hot on the deck of an oversize boat in a glittering bay off the coast of what looked like Italy.

She'd felt as if she could *taste* his abs. She'd *wanted* to taste them.

When she checked her phone again, a solid three minutes had gone by.

Bristol could hear her sister's voice in her head. *What do you have to lose?* Indy had demanded the night she'd brought up Lachlan in the first place. *Worst-case scenario, nothing happens.*

Or, worse-case scenario, I prostitute myself to a man who would rather hire an employee than attempt to have a relationship, Bristol had retorted.

How is that any different from being an adjunct professor? Indy had asked archly. *At least Lachlan Drummond pays well.*

That one still stung, Bristol could admit.

She heaved out a sigh and looked around the tiny little office that once upon a time, when she'd been new, she'd been delighted to call hers. Or partly hers, since it was shared. There were times when she'd loved everything about this life. Working closely with her favorite professor. The professional relationships she had with her fellow TAs and PhD students, many of whom she anticipated would be her colleagues for the rest of their careers. She loved the energy and excitement of teaching, finding that the enthusiastic students more than made up for the disenchanted or disengaged, if she made certain to concentrate on them.

But it didn't matter how much she loved it here. It was ending. She'd done it. She'd aced her oral arguments, passed her exams, logged all necessary hours, and had taken a short walk in a funny hat to collect her degree.

Whatever she chose to do next, she couldn't stay here. The academic year was winding down and one way or another, she was going to have to leave.

Two more minutes.

Without thinking it through, Bristol swiped up her cell phone, clicked that link, and entered her name into the first available time slot.

Tomorrow afternoon. Four o'clock.

And, naturally, she regretted it instantly.

But it wasn't until she was back home that night,

eating a bowl of cereal as her dinner on the love seat, with Indy off on some or other adventure, that she allowed herself to think about what she'd done. And more, allowed herself to look at the texts that had come in from that same number.

She only did it because Indy was out. If her sister had been there, there was no way Bristol would have let herself look. Indy would have made too much of it. Grabbed the phone, then started ordering Bristol around about what she should wear and what she should do.

"I'm not even going to go," Bristol assured herself, out loud.

But the following morning, she couldn't deny that she took a little extra time and care with her appearance. Just in case.

Nothing crazy, but instead of piling her hair on the back of her head, she blew it out. Instead of the usual carelessly tossed-on clothes from the part of her closet she considered professional, she chose a business-casual dress she had last worn to a department cocktail party. The time before that, she'd worn it out to dinner with a colleague when she hadn't been sure if it was a date or not, so had decided to shoot straight up the middle.

Not that she was going to keep her appointment, because of course she wasn't going to keep her appointment, but it seemed like the appropriate garment to wear for a panel meeting to decide whether or not she planned to hire herself out for billionaire sex.

A notion that made her actually giggle to herself as she caught the uptown bus to work. She usually preferred to walk, but all the extra fussing had eaten into her walking time. A dour-faced older woman stared at her and she coughed, then assumed her usual blank stare.

Bristol lost herself in her usual routine. Teaching, meetings, and attempts to avoid conversations about who was on which interview circuit with her fellow PhDs. She told herself she wasn't thinking about the silly appointment, but when her phone chimed at her to remind her, it was a relief to get away from the university.

Because everyone else was so sure about what they wanted and how to go about getting it, and Bristol wasn't. She still wasn't.

Her goal had been getting her PhD. And now that was done, she just couldn't seem to settle on a direction. The truth was, what she liked was being a student. A little bit of teaching. A lot of research. But no expectations or faculty meetings.

On the other hand, there was also no tenure or job security.

That postdoc was looking better and better, though Bristol was well aware that if she took it she would only be postponing this very same crisis for a year.

She followed the instructions she had gotten by text both the night before and this morning. The interviews were taking place in a studiously discreet brownstone on a leafy, quiet street in Murray Hill. No doubt one of the Drummond family's numerous properties, and, if she had to guess, nowhere near where Lachlan Drummond himself might be today.

Or what would be the purpose of this exercise?

She presented herself at the door, was buzzed in, and found herself in a hushed, offhandedly opulent front hall. A polite staff member ushered her into what looked to her eyes as a perfectly preserved drawing room from another time. She half expected characters from BBC costume dramas to sweep in behind her, but before she could register that she was on her own, she noticed the three immaculately dressed and obviously fashionable people in corporate business attire along one wall, studying her as she came in.

The reality of what she was doing walloped Bristol then.

She stopped dead, looking from one person to the next, waiting for…something. Any hint that they understood the magnitude of what it was they were doing.

Which was, unless she was mistaken, soliciting women for their boss.

She couldn't seem to move.

"Why don't you take a seat?" one of the assistants said, in a voice of studied blandness that she recognized from her phone call.

"You can start us off by telling us why you think Mr. Drummond should consider you," the woman next to him chimed in.

The third assistant only stared at her, stone-faced.

And it all seemed to coalesce inside her then. It rolled over her like a terrible heat. A great big flash. She thought of the pictures she'd seen of Lachlan Drummond. Of her brisk march across the stage to grab the diploma that declared her a doctor, and also that she'd done the thing she'd spent her entire adult life working toward.

She thought of her sister, draping herself across the furniture and acting as if what Bristol really needed, after all her years of study and hard work, was this.

And she couldn't help herself. She laughed.

"I'm sorry," she said when she was done, pleased despite herself that her outburst had elicited some kind of response in the wall of assistants in front of her. Even if it was clearly a negative response. "My sister signed me up for this and I don't know why I'm here. But I'm a PhD, not a prostitute, so I'll find my own way out. And I look forward to seeing who wins the opportunity to trail about after Mr. Drummond. At least until her contract runs out."

Bristol laughed again, though no one in front of her seemed to think it was amusing, and she figured that was as good a time as any to remove herself.

She started for the front door, waving off the butler who loomed there, and gulped in deep breaths when she hit the street.

One way or another, she would figure out what to do. One way or another, she would find herself and her new direction. She would. But surely selling herself was the nuclear option. There had to be a middle ground, surely.

She just had to find it.

Bristol debated whether to flag a cab—a luxury she rarely allowed herself—or let herself wander until she figured out where to go. Preferably to one of her preferred bookstores, like the Strand.

When her phone rang, she glared at it, not recognizing the number.

"This is Lachlan Drummond," came the rich, dark voice when she answered. "I'd like to meet you for dinner."

Bristol didn't ask him to prove who he was. She knew.

She could feel all that power, all that inarguable magnetism, pouring over the phone line. It rooted its way into her, making her as breathless and melting as she'd been when Indy had started this whole thing.

She ducked out of the flow of pedestrian traffic and stood there, her back against the wall of the nearest building. Maybe it was the only thing holding her up.

"Whatever for?" she managed to ask.

"I saw your video, and I—"

"My video?" She was outraged. And more than that, embarrassed. "I never consented to any recordings!"

"As a matter fact, you did." He sounded amused, and Bristol had no idea why she was clutching her mobile even tighter, pressing it against her ear as if trying to get closer to him. "I think you'll find it was in the fine print when you signed up for an interview slot."

"Oh." Now that she thought about it, there had been a rather long paragraph of legalese on that page. She'd been too busy pretending she wasn't doing what she was doing to read it. "Still."

"Dinner tonight," he said, as if it was settled. He named an excruciatingly cutting-edge new restaurant. "Eight o'clock."

Then he hung up.

And no matter how many times Bristol told herself that she obviously wasn't going to go, she also couldn't seem to put her phone away, or push off from the wall where she stood.

She was unable to do anything but stand there, holding her phone like a talisman.

Like it was her very last hope.

By the time she moved on, at least an hour had passed.

And she was already planning what she was going to wear for the dinner date she absolutely wasn't going to keep.

CHAPTER TWO

LACHLAN DRUMMOND DID not wait for anyone. He was rarely given the opportunity to try. But he waited for Dr. Bristol March in the cavernous vestibule of New York's current hottest restaurant that evening and stranger still—didn't mind.

He could have allowed the restaurant to seat him while he waited for her, as the hostess had offered to do approximately twenty-seven times already, but he wanted an untutored first impression. He wanted to see her before she expected to see him, because that was always instructive whether he was meeting someone socially or otherwise.

People liked to wear masks, especially around a man with his power and wealth. They liked to hide things, disguise things, and play pretend. Lachlan had learned long ago that it was always better to see a person's true face whenever he could.

He might carry right along as planned, but it was always better to know.

And in the case of this woman, he also wanted to see how she fit standing next to him, straight off. If her physical presence was even half as electrifying as her video had been.

If she'd make him laugh again.

Because that video had made him laugh out loud, and Lachlan couldn't recall the last time a woman he might potentially care to date had even come close. Not like that, deep and surprised and sudden. It was his own fault, he knew. He'd boiled dating down to the system his older sister, Catriona, liked to call *the squalid horror of your personal life*.

Often and to his face. While shuddering.

Lachlan couldn't help smiling at the thought of Catriona, his favorite person in the world, who had always acted as if the numerous boards she had to sit upon as one of the two remaining Drummond heirs was a terrible imposition instead of a privilege. All she'd ever wanted was what she had. What she would say she'd fought to have, given the circus of their celebrated upbringing. Her high school sweetheart, their kids, and a life as far away from any kind of spotlight as she could reasonably get when she was Catriona Drummond.

From which she liked to make a great many pronouncements about her younger brother's life choices, naturally.

Which Lachlan allowed because she was Catriona, the only person on this earth he loved unconditionally. Because they'd survived their childhood, the loss of their parents, and the constant media scrutiny that went along with both. And they were currently both surviving "Life as the Last of the Drummonds," as the papers liked to scream.

They would have been forced to get along even if they didn't, so it was lucky they always had.

We get along because you need a voice of reason in your life, and I'm the only one you've got, Catriona would have said if she was there. *Lucky you.*

But he shoved all that away, because his older sister was happily not here in this excruciatingly cutting-edge restaurant tonight. Because Dr. Bristol March wasn't like the other women who'd shown up for what his personal assistant referred to as *the casting call.* That had been obvious from the way Bristol walked into that Murray Hill brownstone with entirely too much purpose. Then had stood there, blinking around at his panel as if she had no idea what she was doing there, and had perhaps expected to find herself in a classroom.

One she was in charge of, clearly.

And then she'd laughed.

At them. At him. At the whole squalid horror of his personal life, he assumed, and how could he not follow up on that? Lachlan had felt as if he had no choice.

When he never felt that way. Because he was Lachlan Drummond. He always had a choice.

A swift glance at his watch told him she still had a minute to go before she was actually, technically late.

He didn't entertain the possibility that she might not come at all.

The restaurant was set in a self-consciously industrial space, which meant there was a long way to walk from the entrance door to the hostess stand where he waited. It was deceptively lit, with dramatic stone sconces on each side of the walkway, but even more light from above.

It meant that anyone who walked in was instantly recognizable, which was a feature or a bug depending on the person. Lachlan had entered through the private entrance out back, because he didn't need to make announcements. And as he waited, he wondered if maybe he'd seen something in the video that wasn't there. Would he even recognize the one woman who'd ever walked out of his interview process?

But the moment she stepped inside, he knew it. He felt it, as if she'd brought the slap of winter with her when he knew full well it was a lovely spring evening outside.

And he watched as she took in the long walk

ahead of her, a look on her face that told him she was equal parts dubious and curious.

He realized that he really hadn't been sure she would show, and that almost made him laugh all over again.

Because Lachlan couldn't remember the last time a woman hadn't been a sure thing.

It was a sheer accident that he'd even seen her video, much less as quickly as he had. He probably wouldn't have seen it all—because there was no way his assistants would have sent it up the food chain—but he'd happened to text his assistant about a different matter and had casually asked how the selection process was going.

Well, boss, Ryan had replied in his usual cheeky manner, the first one laughed and walked out, so take that as you wish.

That wasn't the way the selection normally went. Usually the panel had to herd the candidates out because they went on for too long. Lachlan, stuck in a car between two tedious meetings, had asked to see the woman who had broken the mold. Ryan had sent over the short video, Lachlan had laughed, and here he was.

In the video, Bristol had been dressed in an unremarkable short-sleeved, knee-length dress that he suspected was billed as the sort of thing a woman could dress up or down according to her preference. She had done neither. She'd worn no jewelry, save the utilitarian watch strapped to one wrist. She had long, dark hair, glossy and straight, that fell to the middle of her back. Her eyes were big and clever, and her *face*. It was clever, mercurial. She'd actually frowned and, more, looked as if she did so often—no regular Botox appointments to keep her muscles still and smooth.

It was her face that had captivated him, switching from something like bewildered to straight-up entertained in a heartbeat. Her laugh had been wicked.

And she'd turned and strode off without so much as a hitch in her step or a backward glance. Lachlan had been certain she would forget he existed the moment she stepped out into the street, and he'd found he...couldn't have that.

He'd expected to regret that choice.

But he didn't.

Because tonight she marched toward him wearing yet another unremarkable dress. This one was not in the sensible navy shade from before, but was a richer, darker black. And somehow he knew that both the dress and the pair of serviceable heels she wore were the one version of each she had in her closet.

He doubted very much that she had raced out to shop for this outfit. He would have sworn that if asked, practical Bristol March with her PhD in social policy had weighed the options and decided to make do with what she had.

Lachlan didn't know how he knew that. He just did.

Maybe it was that every other woman who had ever gone through his selection process had come to dinner like a trap ready to be sprung. They'd presented themselves like a living, breathing PowerPoint demonstration. Breasts out for inspection or coyly hidden, usually with an open back instead. Stunning stiletto heels, formfitting gowns, and the kind of effortless, laid-back charm that could only be achieved after a full day in the salon and a trip through the city's couture ateliers.

But not Bristol March, PhD.

Lachlan couldn't seem to keep himself from wondering where else she would present herself like this—no frills, no games, just her.

His cock was on board. Enthusiastically.

He saw the very moment she recognized that it was him, standing there waiting for her way down at the other end of the long hallway. She slowed, but only for a moment. Then she simply soldiered on.

She did not smile. She did not turn sultry. There wasn't so much as the faintest hint of slinking.

She marched up to him and Lachlan noticed that the only nod she'd given to adornment was a set of shiny studs in her ears that he doubted were real diamonds. That same watch that was clearly to tell time, possibly in several time zones, and not a piece of jewelry. No manicure and only a bit of lip gloss.

He couldn't tell, yet, if she was deliberately dressing down to appear as if she didn't care about this, or him, as some had tried—though with significantly more quiet touches of cosmetics and couture, like the one woman who had feigned surprise that she'd actually turned up with her dress on inside out. It was possible Bristol was playing that game.

It was also possible she was that rare unicorn. A woman out on a date with him who really, truly wasn't trying to impress him.

It was amazing, he thought as she stopped before him, how desperately he wanted it to be the latter.

And how much his cock didn't care either way.

"Mr. Drummond," Bristol said and thrust out her hand, as if this was a business meeting. One where she was in charge.

Then again, given his selection process, he supposed it was a business meeting. Though he'd never thought of it that way when his actual business meetings were far drier and never the least bit sexual. More to the point, the women who usually held these meetings with him acted as if they didn't think of it that way either. Because most women, in his experience, actually *wanted* to date him. Or have dinner with him. Or simply…be in his presence.

Bristol March, PhD, was clearly withholding her judgment on that.

Lachlan took her hand in his and smiled as that electricity he felt when he'd seen her video kicked through him again. Hotter and longer this time.

He estimated she was five-seven or so in her bare feet. The two-inch heels she was wearing put her chin on level with his chest, and looking down at her was no hardship. He still couldn't get over that face of hers. As if she'd been built to be wicked but had decided to be studious instead. It stirred him up.

She stirred him up.

Even when she frowned at him as if she was trying to bring him into focus.

Or maybe as if she was processing that same electrical charge.

"Dr. March," he murmured. "A pleasure to meet you in person."

He could feel it as she started to release her grip, so he held on. Just for a moment. A breath. Just to keep that electricity pumping, if only for a little longer.

And he liked it when he saw her eyes dilate.

It was a good start. Especially when she flushed slightly.

"Once again, I don't know why I'm here," she announced, forthright and to the point. "I walked out of that interview, which is the kindest description I can think of for it, for a reason. The reason hasn't changed."

"Is the reason that you find me disgusting? Actively repellent?"

"You, personally? I couldn't say. That bizarre spectacle, on the other hand…"

Again, she surprised him. Lachlan wasn't used to that. And he certainly wouldn't have imagined that, having managed it once, she would do it again. Or…repeatedly.

"You're here for dinner," he told her. "That's all. It's not a panel or any kind of audition. It's just dinner." He laughed when she only studied him, clearly unconvinced. "This is currently the most sought-after restaurant reservation in New York City. If nothing else, surely we can enjoy the experience of one of the world's most avant-garde chefs. It's widely held to be spectacular."

He released her hand, aware that he didn't want to, and that, like everything else, was new. And all her. Then he nodded at the hovering hostess to seat them at last. Walking behind Bristol, they were led to the table he'd requested. It sat on the second-floor balcony far from any other patrons, looking out over the restaurant, yet private.

So they might be seen by anyone in the restaurant, with its zero-tolerance policy for cell phone usage in a place that catered to so many celebrities, but would not be heard.

Lachlan enjoyed the view as they walked. Unlike the other women he'd dated, Bristol wasn't putting on a performance. She charged after the hostess in much the same way she'd entered the restaurant, as if she had a great many important things to do. And clearly, nowhere on that to-do list did it occur to her to vamp it up for the man who was trailing behind her.

Notably unlike the hostess, who he had seen walk crisply all over the floor of this restaurant without treating anyone to the metronome-hip action he could see before him now as she climbed the steel stairs to the second floor. It was certainly impressive, but all Lachlan was interested in tonight was the good doctor.

At the table, Bristol waved off the waiting server's offer to pull out her chair and sat herself down as briskly and matter-of-factly as she'd done everything else so far. She folded her hands on the table and gazed at him when he sat opposite her, and there wasn't a trace of anything even remotely seductive about the way she studied him.

If he didn't know better, he might have been tempted to imagine that she was the one who had invited him here. To study him. And not in a particularly flattering fashion, but as a part of her research.

"Explain to me why you do this," she said the moment the server walked away. Not waiting for him to lead their conversation. Not seeming particularly concerned with him at all, really. It was novel. "You're Lachlan Drummond. You were famous before you were born. Surely you can get a date without convening a panel."

He laughed as if winded when really, he was amused. "You seem singularly unimpressed with me."

"I had no plans to come tonight," she said, and it took him a moment to realize she was agreeing with him. "I talked myself out of it, repeatedly. But then my curiosity got the best of me, so here I am. After all, I've seen you on magazine covers and in all the papers for as long as I can remember, and that's without ever seeking you out."

"Perish the thought."

She looked as if his dry tone surprised her, which shouldn't have felt like both a rebuke and a caress. "Surely all you have to do is set foot in the street and thousands of women will flock to your side and clamor for your attention. It's not a Broadway play, so why the audition process?"

"It's more like a Broadway play than you might imagine." But maybe this wasn't the time to go over his list of strict requirements. The public events that he had to attend and the private shows he preferred to enjoy without having to worry about tending to the demands people in regular relationships inevitably had. "I've found, over time, that any woman I might meet organically comes with an emotional tax."

It was her turn to sound dry. "This already sounds healthy."

Lachlan sat back in his seat, studying her. If this was an act she was putting on, he couldn't see it and by this point in his life, he could read people all too well. Bristol March was demanding he account for himself, and if he wasn't mistaken, she actually wanted to know the answer.

She'd come for those answers, not for him.

It was a measure of how fucked up he was, clearly, that even that turned him on.

"It depends how you define *healthy*," he said.

"The usual way." She smiled faintly. "That would probably not involve panels of underlings in a creepy town house."

"The creepy town house is actually an eighteenth-century brownstone that happens to be on the National Register of Historic Places. As an aside."

"That doesn't make it *less* creepy. It makes it more likely to also be haunted."

Lachlan decided not to die on the hill of an old house some ancestor of his had built when that neighborhood, now in the middle of Manhattan's grand sprawl, had been considered "uptown" and far away from the heart of the city.

"Is it healthier to pretend that I have an emotional capacity that I lack?" he asked mildly instead. "Or to admit up front that I don't so that everybody's on the same page throughout? I happen to think that my approach is, if nothing else, kinder."

"Is that a word that you would use to describe yourself? *Kind?*" Bristol's gaze was intent on his. Unwavering. She appeared to hide nothing, and he found that almost as electrifying as her hand in his. "Are you the world's first example of a *kind* billionaire?"

That landed a bit harder and did not make him feel like laughing. Lachlan signaled one of the waiters. "I think this conversation requires wine, don't you?"

He half expected this shockingly direct woman to lecture him on remaining clearheaded for the academic exploration they were apparently taking tonight, but she didn't. Instead, she accepted the wine he ordered gratefully and took a fortifying gulp. Then another.

Much as he did.

Not as formidable as she wants to appear, he thought, and was pleased that at least he wasn't the only one having a novel experience tonight.

And as they set about ordering, which required

a small food-based performance on the part of the staff—the better to *inhabit* the chef's *vision*—Lachlan realized that he was happy to stall. To pause for a moment.

To take a breather while he sorted through the complicated tangle of emotions and pure attraction that was making him feel perilously close to off-balance here. He liked the sensation, or he didn't hate it, but it was new. He liked new. Craved it, even.

But Lachlan hadn't felt anything close to off-balance in as long as he could remember. He'd learned how to stand his ground when he was a kid and he'd viewed that as a virtue. Still did. Tonight he obviously needed to recalibrate himself. He was used to being in complete control of every interaction he had. He told himself that taking a moment to get his bearings with this woman who not only didn't follow the rules, but didn't seem to know them, was only smart.

While he did, it occurred to him that all the women who usually turned up to take part in his interview process were self-selecting in the first place. They had to want to audition for a place in his life to get invited to try. And there were precious few professional intellectuals in that set. Bristol was the first.

The professor types he met in the course of his businesses and charities were usually part of think tanks, philanthropic entities, or governments, and were certainly not interacting with him in a social manner. They wanted funding of one sort or another. They were always trying to get him interested in their research, not themselves.

And not to put too fine a point on it, but they were very rarely as pretty as Bristol.

Of course he was a little thrown. That was why he liked her.

"Why did your sister submit your application?" he asked when they were alone again. He smiled when she looked taken aback, and didn't bother pretending that he wasn't a little bit happy to see that particular shoe on the other foot. More than a little bit, even. "Or am I the only one who is expected to answer questions tonight?"

"It's very on-brand for my sister, actually, to submit applications on my behalf without asking me." Bristol rolled her eyes, but with affection. "She considers herself a free spirit in all things and would like nothing more than if I suddenly became one myself, but she gets tired of waiting for me to wake up like that one morning. So, periodically, she *does things*."

"Was she under the impression I was looking for a free spirit of some kind? If so, she's probably the first person in a long time to mistake me for some kind of hippie. Hippies don't normally have hedge funds or Yale in their past."

"You'd be surprised how many hippies turn out to have trust funds. It takes money to afford all that not doing anything."

"Not a fan, I gather. But your sister thinks *I* am?"

Bristol's gaze was shrewd. "You're looking for something that's hard to define, aren't you? The woman in question has to be free-spirited enough to take you up on your offer in the first place, which is hardly a mainstream sort of thing. She has to be able to meet your physical demands, which I've been repeatedly informed, mostly via texts from your underlings, are…"

She was obviously searching for a word, so Lachlan supplied one.

"Healthy?"

Her eyes gleamed. "Indeed. Yet you also require a certain polish and educational background, which in many ways precludes the former. I'm surprised that you ever find a single candidate, if I'm honest."

"It might surprise you to learn that many consider me a catch, Bristol. And are willing to do all kinds of things to be the one to catch me for a while. Even a night."

She picked up her wineglass but didn't raise it to her lips. "It seems to me that the only way a highly educated, appropriately polished woman would agree to serve as an escort for you would be if they needed money and were prepared to do whatever was necessary to get it. The usual reason a woman becomes an escort, I imagine. Either that or they think they'll find a way to upgrade themselves to wife. And either way, that doesn't quite sound to me like the emotion- and issue-free arrangement you're supposedly looking for. One is transactional and the other is a deliberate game of pretense. Which do you prefer?"

Lachlan felt adrenaline rush through him. He was familiar with the sensation. Notably he felt it in a business environment, right when he was about to close a major deal.

And it only occurred to him then, as she essentially laid bare his entire dating history with such ease, that he hadn't felt it in a *romantic* sense longer than he liked to admit.

"I can't say I like either," he found himself saying, which was a truth he preferred to keep to himself. Since he couldn't see how to do anything differently. Not with the life he led.

"You're too much of a catch, as you say, to like the sensation of being just a paycheck and too aware of the performance of the would-be wives to enjoy it." Bristol nodded sagely. "That is a quandary."

Lachlan had never thought of it that succinctly before. This time, he didn't have to pretend to feel winded. He felt it.

But his cock wanted nothing more than to explore all the ways she could make him feel that, in all the best ways. Less psychological profiling, more sex.

The food began to arrive then, and he found himself irritated that they were being interrupted. Even though he was well aware that this kind of self-referential dining experience was part of the package any woman who wanted to date him had to be fluent in.

He understood that it would be devastating if Bristol March could capture his interest so many ways, yet fail this test. When he normally found these dinners entertaining because, for him, they provided a checklist of ways the women he was with—though they might be marvelous in any number of ways—couldn't meet his needs to fill this role.

Bristol was right. Though there were many candidates, there were very few who were capable of making him forget what they were really after—a payday or his name.

Lachlan wasn't sure when it had become, not just amusing, but critically important to him that this woman who wanted neither pass all of the carefully constructed tests his sister had long since told him were appalling.

Try seeing if you like *her, idiot,* Catriona would say.

But Lachlan couldn't trust *likeability.* Too many people put on acts when they met him. He was too well-known. He wanted something genuine. Of course he did. Someday he would look for *genuine* when he was ready for a real relationship. When he wanted what Catriona and Ben had.

Until then, he had his dating protocol and his tests.

And though the food here was exquisite, he hardly tasted it, so busy was he watching Bristol acquit herself beautifully.

Conversation flowed easily in and around the performance art piece that was the service, and the operatic flair of the food itself. So easily that he had to remind himself to look for all the markers he usually paid such close attention to at these meetings. Like the conversation itself. Talking effortlessly to a stranger was an art that few understood and even fewer could pull off no matter their emotional state. Lachlan was a master at it. He needed his girlfriend to manage it tolerably well, because the circles he moved in required it. There was no place for a trophy in a dinner that might easily turn into the seeds of the kind of regime changes that altered the world for the better.

Bristol March, it turned out, could not only talk about any subject under the sun, but she also seemed genuinely interested in each and every one of them. She was widely read. She listened. She made fascinating connections and did not lapse into monologues or speak only of herself. She was not afraid of sharing her opinions, but had the increasingly rare quality, these days, of not seeming unduly attached to them.

His grandmother, who he and Catriona not so affectionately referred to as the Dragon Lady, would have given one of her severe nods. The sincerest form of flattery she possessed.

By the time the attentive waitstaff cleared the table, Lachlan was busier keeping his hands to himself than marking off items on a checklist. It was harder by the second to do much of anything but pay attention to that driving pulse that beat through him, that endless greedy fascination for Bristol and her frown and her clever face, making him wonder if he *could* keep his hands to himself.

"Thank you," Bristol said when their coffees had been carried off. She looked surprised. "I'll admit, this was far more pleasant than I imagined it would be."

"I'll admit that I'm used to significantly more deference and interest on the part of my dinner dates."

She tilted her head slightly to one side, which he now knew was a telltale sign she was about to be provocative. "I would have thought displays of interest and deference came *after* the audition. Once the starring role was secured."

"Some like to show that they're capable of such things, Bristol."

"Dress for the job you want, not the job you have?"

"Exactly."

"Well," she said, lifting a brow. "I did. You'll note I'm dressed like a person deciding between professorships and postdoctoral research positions at a number of highly regarded institutions. Not an actress. Or an escort."

"Is this a strategy? Do you think that if you insult me it will make me want you?" Lachlan was fascinated to find that his temper, so often dormant because he cared deeply about so very few personal things, had engaged. "I would strongly caution you against leaning too far into that."

He had his answer in the look of shock on her face. She was either the best actress he'd ever encountered…or it had literally never occurred to her to employ a strategy with him in the first place.

Lachlan wasn't sure which was more lowering.

He reached across the table, taking her delicate hand in his and feeling the kick of it. Watching, perhaps a little too closely, as her pupils dilated once again.

As her breath picked up.

It reminded him that all this architecture—all the panels and the dinners and the conversation, too—was about the chemistry between them.

These were structures he liked to put around sex, but it was still about the sex.

And that need in him, white-hot and intense.

He made rules so that he could have exactly what he wanted, precisely when he wanted it, from a woman he'd made certain, in advance, was also what and who he wanted.

And he'd never wanted a woman as much as he wanted Bristol.

"I don't have a strategy," she said quietly. Her pulse was drumming wildly in her neck. Her hand was hot in his. "I still don't know why I'm here."

"I do."

Heat poured through him, shooting out from where their hands were joined and finding its way straight to his cock. What he really wanted was to take a bite out of her. But that would come.

He was sure of it.

"Tell me, then," she invited him. Her voice was husky. "If you know."

"I have a better idea," Lachlan said. And later, maybe, he would remember this moment and worry about how far he was straying from the usual script. But right now, all he could see was Bristol. And all he could think about was getting a taste of her the way he'd wanted to do since he'd seen that video. "Why don't I show you?"

CHAPTER THREE

BRISTOL FELT AS if she was in a dream.

Though her dreams were never this exciting. She dreamed of showing up naked to her seminars. Of looking through her notes only to discover she could no longer read them. Sometimes she had very long dreams that seemed to involve a lot of travel between never-quite-identified points.

This felt a lot more like the sex dreams she'd always wished she had.

Except it was real.

Lachlan had her hand in his, and that was extraordinary all on its own. His hand was big and hard, and held hers with a matter-of-fact possessiveness that made her entire body feel as if it was melting.

Especially between her legs.

He ushered her through the restaurant again, but this time he didn't take her down the grand steel stairs. Instead, he took a different door from the second floor, leading her past the busy kitchen and then out a back entrance she hadn't known existed. There were steps and an awning, indicating that this wasn't simply the route out back for emptying the garbage and so on. It served as a subtle reminder that Lachlan Drummond wasn't like other people—not even the people who ate at a swanky place like this and delivered their status vehicles to the waiting valet, an unusual luxury in New York City.

Of course he used private entrances, Bristol thought. Because if he didn't, the paparazzi would catch him far more often than they did. She tried to imagine the measures she would have to take if she was as recognizable as he was—as famous whether she liked it or not. She probably wouldn't walk to the university. She probably wouldn't be able to teach, for that matter, if anyone could turn up. She would need significantly more security, which meant she wouldn't be able to live in her current apartment.

It had never occurred to her to wonder if the wildly famous congregated to the same secure, discreet places because those places protected them. She'd never given much thought to the idea that the wildly famous were…regular people with regular concerns, but with the money to handle those concerns differently.

Like Lachlan, who nodded at the man beneath the awning whose sole purpose appeared to be

standing guard over a sports car out in the alley.
Bristol knew less than nothing about sports cars
of any variety, but even she could see quite clearly
that whatever make and model this one was, it was
exquisite beyond the telling of it. If only because
the man who'd been guarding it eyed it as if it was
the Holy Grail before he nodded at Lachlan and
walked back into the building.

It gleamed in the lights that lit the way over the
stairs, spilling over the vehicle's sleek, low lines
and sultry curves.

Sultry curves? she asked herself. *You really do
have sex on the brain.*

But maybe that was because the back door of
the fancy restaurant slammed shut. And that left
only her and Lachlan, standing alone in the dark
night settling around them. A kind of foreboding—
or longing—danced through her then, and Bristol
had to move. Or the electricity would fry her where
she stood, she was sure of it.

She tugged her hand from his and moved down
the stairs, trying to hide the clamoring inside her.
It was so *loud*. It was shivery and bright and she
had to figure out how to breathe through it.

Then she thought of the feel of his hand in hers
and had to start all over again.

"Where are you taking me?" she asked when
she'd cleared the stairs.

The streets seemed far away. Light and noise

streaking past, all that life and commotion, while here in the alley they were practically cocooned in the kind of hush that shouldn't have been possible in New York. But brick and concrete rose high all around, hemming them in.

It should have felt claustrophobic. But instead, Bristol thought it felt like an embrace.

Her eyes adjusted to the darker stretch of alley, away from the lighted stairs—and just in time, because Lachlan was moving toward her, a look on his face that made everything inside her go still.

He backed her across the width of the alley, smiling down at her when her back came up hard against the far wall.

"Careful," he said, a hint of laughter in his voice.

But Bristol didn't want to be careful. Or she couldn't remember how.

Because the only thing she could seem to focus on was that wildfire heat that raced through her. It seemed to start in his bright blue gaze, then hum its way into her, making her flush all over. Making her bones ache.

Making her pussy melt.

And she had said, repeatedly, that she didn't know why she'd gone to that absurd panel today. Or why on earth she'd come to this dinner. But suddenly, when his hands found the wall on either side of her head and he leaned in, it all became clear.

It was this.

His heat. The stark desire on his face and the lure of his mouth, hovering close. The sudden, greedy punch of a need so hot inside her, it almost hurt.

"Where would you like me to take you, Bristol?" he asked, his voice a low rumble in the dark.

An invitation.

Worse, a temptation.

Bristol had spent so many years catering to her mind. Following each and every thought or connection down whatever rabbit hole she found, disappearing into her research, and rarely bothering to come up for air. If she thought about her body at all, it was an afterthought. As far as she'd been concerned, for years, it was a machine she kept fueled so she could keep on thinking.

Yet right here, in the back alley behind a Manhattan restaurant, she was suddenly aware of every square inch of that body and she no longer felt much like a machine.

She was too aware of her skin. Her muscles. And all the places where she was nothing at all but throbbing, delirious need.

Maybe her sister had been right all along. She really did need to get out more.

Where would you like me to take you? he'd asked.

Her body was taking over and it had a whole host of ideas.

She tipped her head back, wondering how she could feel as if she was falling from a great height when she could feel the wall at her back. "Maybe I'll be the one to take you, Lachlan. If you can handle that."

"Don't worry, Bristol," he said, his voice a dark delight. "I can handle you."

And if she already felt like she was falling, why not jump? She arched herself toward him, pushing up on her toes to find his mouth.

It felt like ignition.

A burst of a dark, intense heat. He met her with the same greed, his hard mouth claiming hers.

Claiming her.

Her heart thudded so hard she pressed herself closer to him, so if it burst straight out from her chest he could contain it.

If anything could contain it.

Because the way his palm, big and hard, gripped the back of her head to guide her mouth where he wanted it made her think it was already too late.

That heat only deepened as he tasted her, roaring into flame and fire.

His kiss was a wild thing, demanding and just this side of rough.

Bristol loved it.

He kissed her the way she'd always wanted to

be kissed. He consumed her. He devoured her and it made her clit throb to think that this man who could kiss anyone was kissing her at all, much less like this.

Like he might die if he didn't.

She let her hands roam over that celebrated chest of his, astonished that he felt even better than he looked. Everything about Lachlan Drummond, who she could admit she'd expected to find sad and faintly creepy, was *better*.

He was dressed like half of Wall Street, his suit tailored to adore him, but Bristol found that irritating. She wanted to *feel* him. She wanted to imprint his flesh into her skin so she would carry this with her, always. It took her a moment, but she found her way beneath the soft shirt he wore.

But the reward was that ridged glory of an abdomen. She could feel that V-shaped indentation that she knew led straight to that hard, hot cock pressed against her belly. She wanted to rub herself against it, to get him between her legs, but for the moment she was consumed with running her palms over his six-pack, then higher to find the heavy planes of his pectoral muscles.

And still Lachlan kissed her and kissed her, as if he couldn't decide if he was eating her alive or if he was letting her do the honors.

Bristol couldn't decide either. She forgot where she was. She forgot *who* she was.

Sensation was everything. His hard temptation of a mouth, the press of his gorgeous body, the wall at her back. And all of that bright-hot need that kept pouring through her so she was nothing more than heavy breasts and nipples pinched tight, and the greedy, hungry pussy that pulsed between her legs.

She couldn't remember wanting anything as much as she wanted this man.

And somehow, he knew.

Lachlan's free hand moved to trace down the line of her back, but then he found her ass, gripping her in a way that tugged at her clit and made everything hotter. And then he kept moving, reaching down until he could pull her dress up. And up.

She entertained the faintest thought that she should object when the cool spring air found the bare skin of her thighs. But she didn't want to. She didn't want anything to stop what was happening, because she wasn't sure she'd live through the disappointment if they stopped. If they didn't dive straight into the heart of this fire.

Then it was hard to care about anything at all because his hand found the mound of her pussy and held her there, just for a moment, while she shuddered.

And shuddered.

Before she could think about that, or analyze anything the way she liked to do, he found his way beneath the panties she wore. Then he stroked his way into her slippery heat.

His kiss grew harder, slicker, as he found his way inside her.

With the heel of his palm against her clit, he experimented with one long, broad finger, then two.

Bristol bucked against his hand while he drank every beautiful sound she made from her mouth. He ground down harder against her clit, then laughed a bit darkly when she tipped her head back and came.

Hard.

"More," she panted at him. At the alley around them. At New York. The world. "I want *more*."

Lachlan hauled her against him, drawing her legs around his waist and then holding her against the brick wall with little more than his chest pressed against her. She had to cling to his shoulders and she did, lost in that searing blue gaze of his as he reached between them.

She was panting, aftershocks still jolting through her. Possibly having a heart attack, but she didn't care. She wanted him too much. She'd just come and still, she wanted him with a desperation that should have scared her.

But he was pulling out his cock and swiftly sheathing it with the condom she hadn't even seen him pull out of thin air, and that was better than cardiac arrest. Even if it might cause it.

Then he was supporting her ass again with those big, hard hands, still pressing her against the wall.

"Move your panties out of the way for me," he ordered her, his voice another dark lick of sensation.

And Bristol would have said that she wasn't much for taking orders, but maybe she'd never heard one issued like this. Scratchy and sure, while she clung to him, her legs wrapped around him so she was wide open and ready.

God, she was ready.

She wanted him inside her. Now. She couldn't think of anything she wanted more than to obey him. Bristol reached down and grabbed the shiny fabric of her own panties, stretching them out to the side.

Then she had to bite her lip as he fit the broad, thick head of his cock to her entrance.

He was big. *So* big she thought she might come again at the thought. Deliciously hard and thick, and better still, a little bit ruthless.

"It's been a long time," she heard herself say as she felt his sleek muscles coil, telling her he was about to slam himself home.

And she didn't have words to describe the look that flashed between them then. She felt it. It was like a shock wave, possessive and bright.

It almost made her come again.

His hand returned to the wall beside her head. Lachlan pushed his way inside her, waited for her to accommodate him, then thrust a little more.

So slow it became an ache. A blistering, beautiful ache.

There was nothing but the stretch and the slide. The sound of her harsh breathing and his. In the distance, she could hear traffic, reminding her that they were outside. That anyone could happen by. For all she knew, they already had an audience from the buildings up above them.

She felt herself get wetter and hotter at the thought.

Slowly, almost mercilessly, he filled her.

And when Lachlan was finally deep inside, she thought that she might burst. She didn't want mercy. She didn't want anything but *more*.

It was the way he looked at her. It was the feel of him inside her, almost too much, so she could hardly breathe. So every breath she did take was filled with him. He was *this close* to triggering another orgasm.

But she wanted *more*, damn it. And she said so.

"Hold on," he advised her.

And then he began to fuck her.

Sure and steady, just this side of rough.

And Bristol was coming again, or still.

It was an exquisite, prolonged shattering. It was falling from on high, over and over and over. It was everything she'd ever wanted—and far more than she'd imagined.

He was so good it was almost scary.

She held on, the wild madness of it pounding through her again and again. His cock gave her no quarter, allowed no retreat. He held her away from the wall, demonstrating far more intellectual capacity than she could access—because she didn't care if the friction scraped her raw.

Some part of her wanted that.

Because she still wanted more. The tighter she gripped him with her thighs, with her ankles locked behind him, and the more he battered her, the harder she came.

Over and over again.

Until she thought maybe she'd fallen off the side of the world after all.

And she could feel it when, at last, he joined her, making a fierce groaning sound deep against her neck.

While she shattered all around him one final time.

She was aware of it when he pulled out, then made sure she could hold herself there against the wall. Even if she had to grip the bricks, hard, to stay upright.

Her dress fell back into place, which was good, because she understood dimly that she really ought to cover herself up in public. But she couldn't seem to do anything but cling to the building behind her and try to hold on to the world.

And what was left of her in the aftermath.

She was dimly aware of Lachlan stripping off the condom and tossing it in one of the garbage cans across the way. Surely the tawdry practicalities should have slapped her back down to earth. Reminded her who she was—and that she didn't do things like this.

But when Lachlan turned back toward her, Bristol felt her breath catch all over again.

He looked faintly disheveled and she had to clench down on that throbbing sensation inside her, which almost tipped her straight back over the edge.

How could he be even hotter *after* she'd sampled him? Now that he was less tailored and somehow far more dangerous? His shirt was untucked, his jacket no longer sitting quite so nicely on those shoulders of his, and he made her feel completely out of control.

More than that, she liked it.

He looked at her, his gaze dark and commanding, and appreciative, almost. As if she was a dessert and he wanted to indulge himself all over again.

This man made Bristol want things she'd never wanted in her life.

To be taken like this, instead of forced to endure endless theoretical musings about the biology of desire. To be wanted, desperately, without it having the faintest thing to do with her academic achievements or her intellect.

Sure, he wanted cocktail conversation. She understood that. But if she wasn't mistaken, Bristol thought what Lachlan Drummond really wanted was to fuck.

And because he was famous and chased after wherever he went, he needed to go to great lengths to figure out how to get what he wanted without, as Indy had said, trawling around in bars.

Even the panel made more sense to her now, still tender from the way he'd pounded them both into oblivion. It wasn't like *Lachlan Drummond* could reveal himself on a dating app. He couldn't *ask* for alley sex. It would end up on the front page of every tabloid on the planet.

Then again, maybe her sudden rush of understanding had more to do with all the orgasms she'd had.

But even thinking and analyzing connected to that blistering heat that still flared between them, it seemed. It was so bright it almost seemed like daylight, lighting her up there in a dark alley in the middle of the loud and careless city.

"Well?"

And Bristol couldn't tell if that was a taunt or an invitation. Or some combination of the two.

Maybe she should have cared about that. But she didn't.

"Well, what?" She tilted her head to one side and found herself smiling. "Are you looking for a performance review?"

And she was finding herself growing more and more addicted to that laugh of his, because he seemed so astonished that it was happening.

"I don't need you to tell me how good I am. I know."

"The kindest and most humble of billionaires," she murmured. "You are truly a Renaissance man."

"I don't believe in false humility," Lachlan said. "Especially not when you came so many times. But I do believe in contracts."

Contracts. That word rebounded around inside her, a lot like a bucket of cold water. Bristol thought she ought to be outraged. She frowned at him, but it felt as if she was trying something on. Not as if it was in any way organic.

"I don't need to sign a contract. I don't want anything from you. I don't want your money and I certainly don't want to be your wife." She shrugged. "The truth is, I don't think I'm your type."

"And that's why I like you," he agreed. And his eyes were really far bluer than was fair. "The thing is, Bristol, you want me. And there's only one way you can have me."

"I had you not five minutes ago. I'm good."

"Will that be enough, do you think?"

And she would have recoiled if he'd sounded swaggery or full of himself. But he didn't. The question sounded like a truth, and it echoed like a song.

Bristol sighed. "Contracts, then?"

"I'm afraid so."

"That will severely inhibit the new career I was thinking of starting," she told him, leaning into her frown. "I figured I'd wander about, having sex with famous men in alleyways, and selling the story to whoever would buy."

"You can have sex with one famous man wherever you want," he replied, leaning against the car of his. "And whenever I want. Which is going to be too much sex to worry about alleyways you might have known."

"Right, right." She ran her hands over her hair, pleased to find it was a mess. For some reason, it made her feel that much more beautiful. And somehow in control, that she could abandon herself so completely and then debate *contracts*. As she stood there, she braided it loosely and tossed it over her shoulder. "That's the *healthy sexual appetite* you have a panel of your assistants discuss with a field of applicants."

"I like there to be as little confusion as possible."

"What exactly does that mean, though? One man's feast is another man's famine, or so I'm told."

For a mouth she knew was hard and demanding, the way it curved looked inviting. Knowing. "This is the deal, Bristol. I like you. You seemed genuinely interested in a great variety of things instead of just playing a role to play it. I get the feeling you could talk about anything to anyone."

"Well, yes, Lachlan. That's called being a functional adult."

"You might be surprised."

He moved closer to her, but he didn't tower over her. He thrust his hands in his pockets and studied her. And it was different, now, that they both knew how hot the fire between them burned. And how it felt when he was buried deep inside her. Much, much different.

Bristol had to press her legs together. Or maybe she wanted to.

"You don't want anything from me, and strangely enough, that makes me want you more," Lachlan said with a quiet intensity. "We have insane chemistry. I can't think of anything that I'd like more than to get another taste of that, as often as possible, and with my schedule that requires a lot of effort. Or a contract."

She considered that for a moment. "So, these girlfriends of yours. *Girlfriend* being a euphemism, clearly. These are women you hire but don't call escorts. Or what they are—what I'd be. Prostitutes."

Something was obviously wrong with her that

she didn't find the very idea appalling. That here, in this alley still wet for him, that word only made her shiver. Straight down into her clit.

"If there was a word for it, I think it would be mistress," Lachlan said. "In the historic sense."

"Mistress." She laughed at that, because it struck her as such a glittering, archaic word for something that was far more prosaic. If not much discussed in polite circles, for all the strides the world had made in viewing sexuality more positively. "And these mistresses of yours all just... follow you around, making themselves available for sex on your schedule?"

He looked perfectly relaxed, standing there with that gleaming sports car behind him. Almost careless, but she could see the dark intensity in his gaze. It matched the current of fire and need that was only growing in her.

"Yes. That's pretty much the entire job description."

"Don't they have lives? Their own jobs? Things to do?"

"Some do. Some don't. It depends. And if they do, that often contributes to the length of our time together."

"What job allows time off for being a billionaire's plaything?"

"Again, you'd be surprised." She started to say something else but he shook his head. "I don't want to litigate my life, Bristol. There are far more entertaining things we could be doing, don't you think? All you have to do is sign a few documents to protect us both. It's the easiest thing in the world."

"I bet every heroin dealer in the world tells their clients the same thing."

"I promise you, I'm better than heroin."

She believed him, and that should have served as a wake-up call. Bristol opened her mouth to tell him that *of course* she couldn't do what he was suggesting. That she was an intellectual. That she didn't have a *job*, she had a career and a *body of work* and was expected to make a substantive intellectual contribution to knowledge. To social policy.

She expected these things from herself.

But she'd spent years and years doing nothing but flexing her intellectual muscles. And make no mistake, she'd loved it. She loved what she did, she loved studying, she loved teaching, and she loved writing.

But somehow in the midst of all that, Bristol had forgotten how to feel the way she did right now. A little bit battered, a little bit dazed, and wonderful.

She could still feel him inside her, thick and hard, filling her up so that she couldn't breathe without that, too, feeling like a sensual act.

And she'd gone to one extreme. Why not go to the other?

What would it hurt? a voice inside her asked.

Lachlan looked as if he could stand there, waiting for her answer, forever.

And even that stillness, that quiet ease, made him hotter.

God, but he was hot.

It was ridiculous that she was even considering this. What woman in her right mind would sign up to be a man's sex object? Not a regular one, but an articulate one if he had to have a fancy dinner before letting off some steam? Not Bristol. Because Bristol was an overeducated, deeply feminist, bone-deep believer in equality in partnerships rather than traditional gender roles.

But between her legs, she still ached.

"I can give you the summer," she told him, not even sure where the words came from. Still, she didn't take them back. "But that's all."

She expected him to gloat.

But all Lachlan Drummond did was smile, as if he'd entertained the possibility of no other outcome but this.

CHAPTER FOUR

IT WAS RAINING relentlessly in London. She should have expected that, Bristol thought, but somehow the sheets of rain and gloomy skies sat on her like a heavy stone.

Or maybe it was the new life she'd chosen for herself—but she didn't really want to think about that.

They'd arrived in England early that morning, after a swift and outrageously luxurious flight across the Atlantic in one of Lachlan's planes. One of *his planes,* she kept repeating to herself. *Just* one.

Lachlan had spent the flight locked in his office with his staff. When they'd landed, he had gone off with said staff in one set of cars, leaving Bristol on her own. In Lachlan's world, that meant Bristol had been accompanied by *her* designated assistant, Stephanie.

Though Stephanie had made it very clear that she worked for Lachlan. Handling *the girlfriend—*

a term she'd emphasized repeatedly, lest Bristol be tempted to imagine she wasn't replaceable—was her job, but she had no intention of becoming friends.

"Did I suggest we braid each other's hair?" Bristol had asked mildly. "I know I didn't, since I'm no good at braiding."

"I find it's easier to start things off with very clear boundaries," Stephanie had replied coolly. "My job is to maximize your effectiveness in your role. You might or might not thank me for that, and that's okay. As I said, I don't work for you."

"You've said it repeatedly," Bristol had agreed, in the tone she used on students who turned up with elaborate excuses for not turning in their work. "Rest assured, I am perfectly capable of maximizing my own effectiveness."

"That will be up to Mr. Drummond," Stephanie had retorted, looking stern and smug at once.

If Bristol had been asked, she would have happily taken a taxi to the hotel rather than ride with her *handler*. As if she was a show pony.

That's what happens when you sell yourself, she told herself as the gray London neighborhoods clumped together in an endless stream of low skies and rain outside the car window. *You get* handled.

The past fifteen days had been a whirlwind. Bristol had signed his contracts the morning after the alleyway. Lachlan had only driven her home that night in that sleek wonder of a sports car, then left her there in a Brooklyn neighborhood she doubted he'd ever been to before, buzzing around her apartment as if she'd chugged down a coffee plantation.

The following morning, she'd spent hours in a large conference room with his legal team and the unfriendly Stephanie, hammering out clauses, wherebys, and wherefores.

It was the least romantic, least exciting start to a relationship—even one that was as cut-and-dried as this one—that she could have possibly imagined. In a way, that was better. It made her think less about the glorious sex and more about the fact she was agreeing to have that sex on demand.

After signing the pile of documents, most of them concerning money and nondisclosure agreements, she had been ushered into Lachlan's private office.

"Are we good?" he asked her.

He looked even better than he had the night before, and she knew what he could do. She could still *feel* what he could do, and that had been outside. In public, basically. A spur-of-the-moment thing.

God help her if he actually took his time.

"I do have one question," she said, seating herself in one of the chairs set around his enormous office. The one she chose was slightly higher than the others in the small grouping nearest the big window with its view over Manhattan, and she realized when he grinned that it was his. But he came and sat across from her anyway, and she'd remembered that she liked him more than she should—because he had nothing to prove. "What if I don't feel like it?"

"That would be disappointing."

"I don't mean the whole thing." He had looked even better in the light, his eyes that astonishing blue and yet another banker's suit that he somehow made a gift to anyone looking at it. "I mean sex specifically."

Lachlan had laughed. "Why am I surprised that you want to talk about sex directly?"

"Oh. Is that not appropriate *mistress* etiquette?"

"It's certainly refreshing." He'd laughed again.

"It's a real question. You're hiring me to have sex with you. But what if I don't want to? What if I'm ill? What if I've decided I don't like you very much? What are your expectations?"

He'd shaken his head. "My expectation is that if you're not enjoying yourself, you'll leave. If you're sick, you'll get medical help. And if you don't want to have sex, you certainly don't have to. I don't have any interest in taking something you don't want to give."

"Just purchasing it."

"I like to think of it as purchasing proximity."

"How has the issue of consent never come up before?" she'd demanded, frowning at him.

"Bristol. Please."

She'd frowned harder. "You aren't seriously suggesting that no one can resist you. Do we need a safe word?"

"You can use the word *no*," he said drily. "It works like a charm."

"Not to mention the questionable power dynamics when you've *bought a woman* for the express purpose of not resisting you."

"First of all, we entered into an agreement. It's not like I picked you off a shelf at the local grocery store." Then he grinned, and all she'd been able to think about was sex. The intense glory of his cock. "Second, go ahead. Resist me."

He'd spread her out on the glass table between them and licked his way between her legs, and it didn't occur to her to resist. She didn't want to resist. And after making her come twice, he hauled her beneath him on the floor and fucked them both into sweet oblivion.

"Are you okay with the power dynamics?" he'd asked mildly enough, still lodged deep inside her.

"They seem fine," she'd replied primly, and his deep laugh had stayed with her long after she'd left his office.

But that wasn't the end of what Stephanie insisted on calling *the practicalities*. Part of what she'd signed was a promise to go get a health checkup from Lachlan's preferred physician. A battery of tests later, plus a ceremonial presentation of his own results, and they'd spent a few stolen hours between his meetings experimenting with what it felt like when he was inside her with no protection save the birth control she'd been on for years.

The answer was, she lacked the words to describe how amazing it felt.

Then all that had remained was getting her own life in order. Because Lachlan Drummond's girlfriend was there to be on hand for his needs, not to be juggling her own competing career.

Which was handy, since Bristol still had no idea what she wanted to do with hers.

"Am I hiding from my life by doing this?" she asked Indy as she packed up a small bag of personal items she intended to take with her. There was no need to pack any clothing, Stephanie had informed her coldly, as all wardrobe would be provided to make certain it was up to Drummond standards.

And as a bonus, the other woman had told her loftily, *you will be permitted to keep any wardrobe items purchased for you at the end of your association with Mr. Drummond.*

Bonus, Bristol had replied.

Perhaps more sarcastically than necessary.

"The answer is yes," Bristol had said without waiting for Indy to chime in, there in her Brooklyn bedroom that was only actually a room when the Murphy bed was closed up. Otherwise, it was just the bed. "Yes, I am absolutely running away and hiding from reality."

But Indy was Indy. All she'd done was shrug, looking entirely too pleased with herself. "You might as well hide in Lachlan Drummond's bed, then, draped in couture and riches. I don't really see the downside."

There was a downside, but Bristol had been prepared for that, too.

"Sooner or later," Stephanie had told her in one of their distinctly chilly meetings, "you will become public property because Mr. Drummond is. He prefers to keep the identity of his girlfriends under wraps for as long as possible, but there's a point at which that no longer becomes feasible. When that happens, it's my job to make sure that we have control of the narrative for as long as possible. You'll know when that happens. I'll seed a few stories and get out ahead of the more salacious ones."

"...yay?" Bristol had replied faintly.

A response that had not been appreciated, Lachlan had told her later.

With his cock in her mouth.

But that was how Bristol knew that she was

supposed to spend her free time on *maintenance*. As if she was a lawn or an obstreperous hedge.

Maintenance, she had been informed by the icy Stephanie in New York and again on the plane, was her one and only duty when she wasn't actually in Lachlan's presence. She was to attend to her exercise needs—the suggestion was that she needed this desperately. Then to her physical appearance. When she'd been sent the itinerary for this current trip of Lachlan's, her version had come with a list of gyms, spas, and private stylists if she preferred to take that route, all to make certain she didn't imagine this new life was an excuse to let herself go.

"This seems very trophy wife to me," Bristol told Stephanie in the car, when her maintenance options were raised yet again—this time in the guise of a "helpful" offer to make the appointments. "And I'm neither a trophy nor a wife, so…"

"I think you'll find the contract you signed indicated that you would maintain a reasonable level of maintenance, Ms. March."

Bristol smiled back in the exact same fake way. "That's *Dr.* March," she replied. "And I think you'll find, Tiffany—"

"Stephanie," the woman had snapped back.

"—that I can maintain just fine without your interference."

And in the spirit of rebellion, had taken herself off to the British Museum rather than explore the astonishing penthouse suite that Lachlan had booked, overlooking Hyde Park. It sprawled over the entire top floor of the five-star hotel and was stunning. The butler who came with the suite murmured, very Britishly, that he would be delighted to make arrangements at the hotel spa.

But Bristol needed a break. She made her way to one of her favorite museums of all time and engaged her mind—which as far as she was concerned was all the maintenance she required. She completely lost track of time in the exhibits and had therefore had to rush back to the hotel to change before meeting Lachlan at the formal drinks session that was to be her first appearance as his girlfriend at a function.

"You're late," Stephanie informed her sternly when she arrived at the stuffy old fortress where the drinks event was taking place.

A refrain that was repeated several more times as Bristol handed off her coat and was ushered through the crowd, including by Lachlan himself when she finally reached his side.

"Yes, yes," she said merrily. "I'm late." She turned to the man Lachlan was standing with, who she recognized along with the woman beside him thanks to the dossiers she pretended she hadn't studied when Stephanie had handed them to her at the hotel when they'd checked in. Because she was petty like that. "Ambassador, Mrs. Hargrove, I hope you'll forgive me. I lost myself in the British Museum and really, if left to my own devices, I think I could stay there forever."

"And who could blame you?" said the ambassador.

"I go there whenever I get the chance," said the ambassador's wife.

Much later, after drinks had turned into dinner and a round of after-dinner drinks besides, Bristol was feeling positively inclined toward all things British—even though it was still raining. Lachlan handed her into the car waiting for him outside the fortress and then regarded her—severely, she thought—as the driver eased into the London traffic.

"You do know you're not supposed to be late, don't you?" Lachlan asked, his voice…a dark thread between them.

Bristol could hear the warning in it. But she could also feel that warning in her clit. And though she had always been a rule follower, always a straight-A student who asked for extra projects so she could gain greater honors and distinguish herself further, Bristol couldn't seem to keep herself from smirking at him.

Maybe because she didn't like being sniped at by the assistant he'd sicced on her. Maybe because she really, really didn't like being treated like a trophy. Maybe because she still hadn't settled into how she thought she was going to *do* this.

Maybe because she knew that if she poked at him, he would do something about this addiction it seemed she already had to the things he could make her body do.

Or she hoped he would.

Especially with the partition between them and the driver shut tight and opaque for privacy.

"Then by all means," she said, "fire me for tardiness."

His blue gaze went taut, intense. His mouth curved. She could feel both like his hard mouth on her pussy, eating her alive.

"I'm not going to fire you. Yet."

"That's a tremendous relief. I don't need to set any records for longevity here, but it would be nice to last longer than a single evening." She was still smirking at him. "I can't help it if I'm competitive."

"But I'm going to need you to make it up to me, Bristol."

It was like a chain between them, this heat. She felt it snap tight, and then could think of nothing at all but that blue demand in his gaze.

She found she was holding her breath as he reached down and freed his cock from his trousers, one hand wrapping around the great, thick length of it.

"Your mouth, Bristol. It's so clever, isn't it?"

She wisely decided that didn't require an answer. "Use it."

Later, she promised herself, the weather would turn and she would resume her real life. And that would be an excellent time to question why it was she found these commands so hot. So delicious it was as if they were wired straight into her clit.

Her mouth was already watering. She slid to her knees on the floor of the car and braced herself against his rock-hard thighs. She looked up at him, letting that fierce blue fill her. Set her on fire. Make her shiver.

She was already slippery with want.

And then, holding that gaze of his, she angled herself forward and sucked him deep into her mouth.

Lachlan settled back, his eyes fierce and his magnificent body lazy. Telling her without words that this was going to take a long time.

A long, long time.

Bristol settled in and lost herself in the rhythm of it. The taste of him. He was hot and tasted male, so raw and primal it made her mouth water all the more.

She tested her own reflexes, seeing how far she could take him into her mouth and flirting with the back of her throat. Every groan he let out felt like a victory and made her ache. Her nipples were so tight they stung. Her pussy was wet and needy.

But she concentrated on the long retreat, the deep swallow. She licked her way up one side of his shaft, then down the other. She teased the wide head of his cock, sucking on it until he muttered something beneath his breath.

He wrapped his hand in her hair and took control, gently fucking her face, and that was even better.

For an endless while, she felt stretched out between the wildfire ache in her pussy and the sheer, fierce joy of taking his cock exactly the way he gave it to her. The thrust, the repeat, until she could feel moisture at the corners of her eyes from the sheer joy of it.

And when he finally came, pouring himself down her throat, the way he groaned made her clit throb.

So hard she almost came.

And in case she'd forgotten that this was a punishment for her tardiness, he did not do a single thing to ease the need she was sure was written all over her. She could hear her own breathing come perilously close to panting. She thought that she might even be able to smell her own arousal.

It only made her hunger that much sharper.

Lachlan gazed at her impassively, though his blue eyes glittered. He tucked his cock back into his trousers and zipped up, then lounged there looking faintly disheveled and with the hint of a smirk on his face.

Leaving Bristol with nothing to do but climb back into her seat.

And question, again, why she wasn't outraged. Why, instead, she felt as if this show of his, his seeming indifference with that hint of amusement at her plight, made her shiver ever closer to simply... coming, there and then.

All she would have to do was press her thighs together—but she didn't.

Because, she admitted to herself, *you want your orgasms to be his.*

Because he'd paid for them.

A notion that only there, in the dark of the car with the taste of him in her mouth, could she accept made it all so much hotter.

She had the feeling he knew it.

Back at the hotel, Bristol was left to her own frustrated devices as Lachlan was corralled by his people, then disappeared into the penthouse suite's offices for some or other important phone call.

She waited for him to come back out, but he didn't. It took her longer than it should have to understand that he wasn't going to.

That *he* had likely stepped into that office and forgotten all about her.

And she didn't want to have any more conversations with Stephanie—or any other assistant lurking about—so she took herself off to the expansive bedroom, the bed itself about twice the size of the apartment she shared with her sister. And that wasn't addressing the terraces all around with stunning views over London.

Her body was still flooded with hunger and adrenaline, her pussy still ached, but now there was something hollow inside her, besides.

Bristol didn't want to deal with that either, so she made a production out of bustling around and getting out of the outfit that had been laid out for the evening's festivities. Then she took herself into the shower stall that was the size of her neighborhood coffee shop and busied herself with the four hundred showerheads and bath products arrayed along one stone wall.

But there was only so much bustling and lathering a person could do. Soon enough she was simply standing there in a decidedly opulent shower stall in England, finally coming face-to-face not only with what had happened in his car tonight— but what she'd signed up for in the first place.

Not that he'd bought her. Not even the fact she liked that part of it, and the idea that her pussy itself was on loan.

How had she not understood the rest of it? She knew the answer to that. The last fifteen days had been a cascade of sensory input, disbelief that she was doing this in the first place, and the strangely formal practicalities of arranging a life around sex with a very busy man.

But tonight, at last, she fully understood why it was that Lachlan hired women to fill this position. Because a real girlfriend would react to what had happened tonight—that he could act as he had in the car and then ignore her when they got back to the hotel. A real girlfriend would lean into that hollow feeling inside and take it out on him.

She would not like being ignored on the flight and abandoned all day. She would argue about his rules. She would refuse to have rules, maybe, and certainly she wouldn't take his cock in the car as some kind of punishment for not catering to his demands for punctuality.

Bristol could see, clearly, all the many things she would feel if she were actually in a regular relationship with Lachlan right now.

But her feelings were exactly what he was paying not to deal with.

She stood in the water for a long time. She let the steam billow all around her, let her skin prune up, and she didn't know how much time had passed when the shower door, steamy and glassed, finally opened to show Lachlan standing there.

Her heart kicked at her, hard. And she thought she could see a certain wariness in his expression. As if he was waiting to see what her move was going to be here. Because they didn't know, did they, whether or not she could handle the job he'd hired her for.

It had all been theoretical until now.

Bristol pulled in a breath, as uncertain as he seemed to be. Was she going to yell at him? It seemed possible for a moment. She might find the way he ordered her around hot, like it or not, but she didn't like the feeling afterward—

But even as she thought that, a sense of peace settled over her.

Because she didn't have to decide what to feel. All the decisions were already made. He was the one who made them, because she'd agreed to let him. She'd literally signed papers to that effect.

Bristol felt something like liberated at that notion.

It didn't matter what she felt. She'd decided that when she'd decided to do this. She didn't have to attach her feelings to anything. She didn't have to stand up for herself or assert herself or any of the other things she might feel she had to do here if this was something else.

She could smile at him instead. She could watch the heat flaring his gaze.

She could surrender to what she wanted without worrying what it might say about who she was, or what this was.

That was already decided. They'd already agreed.

Lachlan was on her then, lifting her up as the water pounded into them, the steamy water not nearly as hot as he was. His cock was big and hard and took the same few moments it always did to fit inside her. But once he had buried himself to the hilt, he dug his fingers into her hips, tilted her back against the wall, and set up an intense, bone-rattling rhythm as he pounded into her.

It was like magic.

It really was a liberation, she thought, with what little part of her was still capable of thinking when everything else was that ache in her clit, the glory of his possession, and one fierce punch of an orgasm after the next.

All of them his.

For once she didn't have to make decisions. For once she didn't have to feel—or more to the point, she didn't have to act on her feelings.

All she had to do was this.

Again and again.

Because Lachlan was never satisfied. And all she had to do was indulge his every whim.

Finally, she thought—as he finally roared out his release and they hurtled together over the edge—something she was not only good at, but actually wanted to do.

CHAPTER FIVE

Bristol was completely different from his previous women.

And Lachlan wasn't the only one to notice.

The staff member who handled the day-to-day concerns of his girlfriends complained about her constantly. Something he might have acted upon, but *he* didn't find Bristol's refusal to slot herself into the usual role as arm candy upsetting.

"She refuses to listen, Mr. Drummond," the woman said at almost every staff meeting. Officiously, Lachlan thought. "She *insists* on doing as she pleases."

"She listens to me, Stephanie," he'd replied this morning. "Maybe it's how I ask her."

There had been other women who antagonized his staff, but all of them had also proved themselves unequal to the job. And soon enough, had antagonized Lachlan, too.

Not Bristol.

Diplomats found her charming—the minimum

requirement to appear on Lachlan's arm—but they also found her engaged. An interesting extension of Lachlan himself and, better still, his agenda. She had an uncanny knack of appearing not to pay attention only to be able to recite everything that had been said to her, usually while talking to exactly the right person at whatever party they happened to attend. More than once, over the course of that long June spent flying from city to city all over the globe, Lachlan found himself in a meeting only to have the person across from him reference a conversation they'd had with Bristol as having changed their thinking on some or other key point.

He hadn't expected that.

The question she'd asked him at that first dinner seemed to haunt him the more time passed. His previous choices had never been bimbos. That wasn't his style. But they'd tended to be either spoiled heiresses who'd relied a little too heavily on their prep school polish or sharper, more feral women who could more than hold their own but were always out for themselves. The former had always been angling for a wedding ring. The latter were more interested in the payday.

And whatever they were or wanted, none of them had ever been able to spend hours debating the finer points of contention in an initiative to bolster education in certain Third World countries with a literal think tank.

Dr. Bristol March, he realized with a measure of pride that he told himself wasn't personal but professional, was a formidable force.

"I heard that your conversation with the UN delegation grew heated," he said one early evening.

He had to check the view outside his window to figure out what country they were in. Greece, it turned out. Athens, to be precise, though it could have been anywhere. There was another black-tie function this evening and he was already dressed. Bristol, who had shrugged off the usual fawning attendants his women usually considered a perk of their position weeks back, was fastening a necklace around her neck, standing in front of a mirror so he had all the time in the world to contemplate the way the dress she wore left her lovely back open to his view.

Almost too open, he thought, with a surge of that possessiveness that had marked his response to her from the start.

But Lachlan didn't get possessive.

He told himself he was tired, that was all.

"*I* wasn't the least bit heated." She turned to face him, a wry expression on her clever face. "I'll concede that the delegation left our interaction unhappier than when they arrived. But then, they should think through the sweeping generalizations they like to make regarding their initiatives. Every wave of a hand is a life. That's all I said. If that's contentious, so be it."

"And is that up to you to decide, do you think?" he asked, lazily enough.

For a moment, she didn't respond. Her head tilted slightly to one side, but he already knew that she was unlikely to get provocative. Not anymore. And sure enough, she regarded him with that particularly opaque look in her eyes that he hated more and more. Every time he saw it, he hated it all over again as if it was new.

"I'm sure you will tell me what is or isn't up to me," she said with perfect equanimity. "I await your ruling."

Once again, she was…distinct.

The other women who'd traveled with him had responded to rebukes very differently. They would apologize, charmingly or wholeheartedly, and prettily beg his forgiveness. Or they would slink their way over to him and offer apologies in a more physical manner.

It wasn't that Bristol didn't apologize when necessary. She did. But she did so in the same forthright manner she did everything else, then looked at him as if the matter ought to have been settled.

Lachlan couldn't understand why all the ways she continued to set herself apart from the rest… lodged beneath his skin. Not enough to bother him, exactly.

But he couldn't compartmentalize her the way he'd done with all the rest. He found her on his mind at the oddest times—like in the middle of tense negotiations when he normally would have forgotten he even had a girlfriend.

"It appears that obedience is not your strong suit," he said because she was standing there, waiting for him to say something with that unreadable expression on her face. But she wasn't like the others, so he hardly knew what his point was here. The truth was she was correct in her assessment of the delegation. He agreed completely with her take on the situation. Lachlan might not have any idea what went on in her head, but everything she did in her role as his girlfriend, in public anyway, was wholly supportive of him and his aims. Why wasn't that enough? "Did you know that about yourself?"

"I suspected it," Bristol replied drily. "Hence my choice of career."

"I thought the academic life is filled with rules."

"Every life is filled with rules." She shrugged in that way she did that always made her seem *more* graceful, somehow. "But as knowledge is its own reward, thinking in new ways is always encouraged. The minutiae of a university faculty meeting aside, that part always feels...less obedient."

"But this is not an academic exercise."

He was hard again—always—when all he was

doing was sitting in a chair, studying her. The dress she wore transmitted a certain hushed elegance, but as always, Bristol undercut it by deliberately falling short of the kind of polished veneer that was expected. It should have irritated him. He knew it made the perpetually sniffy Stephanie apoplectic.

Instead of following the usual script, Bristol's manicure was clear polish only. It was such a subtle thing, but it lent her an air of capability. The understated earrings she wore, no matter how many far more riotous selections were presented for her consideration, suggested practicality. Tonight she'd pulled her hair back into a low, sleek tail instead of the dramatic sort of updo he might have expected for a dress like this, and that, too, made her look serious and even a bit determined. As if her beauty was an afterthought.

Lachlan was well aware that despite what Stephanie might have liked to believe, or liked to huff about, everything Bristol did was deliberate.

Well, of course, she'd replied when he'd said as much, one jet-lagged night in Melbourne. *I do like to excel.*

He wanted her in ways that made absolutely no sense.

"You'll have to tell me what it is that you want, Lachlan," she said quietly now. "But I should warn you, while I can try to smile and say little, that will be a stretch."

"What I want you to do is think more about obedience."

He expected to see a flash of temper then. Maybe that was what he wanted. But all she did was watch him, that enigmatic expression firmly in place.

"Have you ever asked yourself why it is you require obedience?" she asked.

Something in him seemed to kick, hard. Then that same fire that was only ever banked in her presence surged back to life.

"I know why I require obedience." His mouth curved, hard. "This is the one area of my life that I prefer...frictionless."

There was something about the way her eyes gleamed that drove him crazy. "And here I thought you were a fan of friction."

They were late to their function that night, almost unpardonably so. But Lachlan, who normally prided himself on his punctuality, couldn't bring himself to care.

He'd bent her over the bed, kicked her legs wide, and plunged deep.

Bristol had stopped wearing panties at his command, because he hated waiting even those few extra seconds to possess her. That meant only that he tortured himself throughout the evening with the knowledge that her pussy was bare. That if he reached over during one of the tedious speeches, drew up the hem of her gown, and reached beneath, he would find her wet and ready for him.

That was the thing about Bristol. She was always ready for him.

She was more challenging than he'd expected—something that was on him, clearly, since she'd given no indication that she *wouldn't* be challenging. She didn't seem to slot neatly into place, allowing him to happily forget about her when she wasn't in front of him.

He didn't like how often she was on his mind.

But he wasn't sure he'd ever been with a woman who wanted him as much as Bristol did. Voraciously. Constantly. Wildly.

He had the distinct thought later that night, when he looked over and saw her frowning intelligently in the middle of another deep conversation a bit of arm candy would never have had, that he needed to be careful with this one.

But *careful* wasn't something Lachlan knew how to do.

Because if he'd been thinking clearly, he would have known better than to take Bristol with him when he went to meet his sister and her family for a few days on the Mediterranean island off the coast of Spain their grandfather had bought a long time ago.

"You don't normally bring your girlfriends here," Catriona said within an hour of their ar-

rival, when Lachlan had only just begun to realize the enormity of the mistake he'd made. She sat
in a flowing white dress on an equally white sofa,
her too-knowing blue gaze like one of the paint-
ings on the whitewashed walls. "Did this one hit
you over the head?"

And his sister wasn't wrong. Normally he kept
his women separate from his family, because there
was no earthly reason for them to spend time together. He dropped his women in Majorca or
Ibiza—or the beach resort of their choice—for a
few days while he enjoyed his sister on his own.

But this time he hadn't been able to imagine
doing without the sex. The way he and Bristol
came together was volcanic. He found he couldn't
go too long without touching her, or he started to
lose his patience with…everything else.

"I think you'll like Bristol, Cat," he said, smiling broadly. "She's not much for sunbathing. Or
relaxing. You can buzz around the island anxiously
the way you always do, but with company."

Catriona treated him to that patented older-
sister look of hers that never failed to make him
feel like a child again. "Do *you* like her? Isn't that
what matters?"

Did he *like* Bristol?

Lachlan didn't like that word, that was for sure.
It didn't get anywhere near the complexities and
layers that made up his Bristol March problem.

But that wasn't a conversation he planned to have with his older sister. "If I didn't like her, I wouldn't be with her."

Catriona rolled her eyes. "That's a charming nonanswer that I'm sure plays well at all your very important business meetings, Lachlan."

There was the sound of a bloodcurdling scream, wafting in through one of the wide-open doors that led out toward the sea that felt like part of the decor here. The house was a sprawling, vaguely Mediterranean affair with upgrades that had been implemented when and if the current owners had felt up to it. Some parts of the house could have been lifted directly from an English manor. Others had the modern edges and crisp approach to art that reminded him more of city-based condos. Altogether, it was an eclectic monument to the passage of time and his family.

He had no idea what he'd been thinking, bringing Bristol here. Of all the women he'd dated, she was the most likely to see each and every ghost that lurked in these halls and hung on to each and every exposed beam.

Catriona was listening intently, her head tilted toward the rolling lawn outside, but waved a dismissive hand in the direction of her maniac children when the follow-up scream was less bloodcurdling and more aggrieved. "They're fine."

"Yes, I like her," Lachlan said when she fixed

that gaze of hers on him again. He disliked the fact that it took effort to sound indifferent. "If you're tempted to start getting ideas, don't. I told you a long time ago, I'm not the marrying kind."

"No one's the marrying kind until they marry," Catriona replied serenely. "I think you'll find that's pretty universal."

This was his sister, his favorite human on the planet, so Lachlan couldn't end the conversation the way he would have if it was anyone else. He stayed where he was, in her favorite room of this old, rambling villa, filled with pictures of their family. From their fierce grandmother right down to their father as a bright, happy-looking boy in the sunlight.

A far cry from who he'd become.

Catriona followed his gaze and sighed.

"Your trouble is, you insist on imagining that he was a monster." She shook her head. At Lachlan. "When the truth is that he was only a man. Like all men, he made choices. You can make choices, too, Lachlan. Different ones."

But Lachlan already had.

As far as the world was concerned, Alister and Annalisa Drummond had been unfortunate victims of a freak accident. Alister had gotten his pilot's license in his twenties and had flown from New York City to one of the family's preferred hideaways by the sea in Maine without incident hundreds of times. But that day a sudden storm had cropped up off the coast of Boston, the plane had gone down, and their bodies had never been found.

The public take on the accident was that the storm was to blame. It was a terrible tragedy, but what could have been done? Even a Drummond couldn't beat the weather, they'd said.

But Lachlan and Catriona knew better. They'd known the truth behind the placid exterior their parents liked to show to the world. He could remember, too clearly, the shouting and the drinking. Annalisa got sloppy. Alister got cruel.

Together, there was nothing they wouldn't destroy—especially each other.

Lachlan couldn't quite believe that his father had truly lost control of that plane. Not by accident, anyway.

He and Catriona had always believed that the crash hadn't been an accident, but their parents' usual game of one-upmanship taken to its logical, horrible conclusion.

It was one more reason the two of them were so close. They were the only ones left, sure—but they were also the only ones who knew.

"But what makes a man into a monster?" he asked his sister lightly, now. "I have a pretty good idea. They were toxic for each other and should have kept their distance. We wouldn't exist, but I bet they would."

"You always say that," Catriona replied with another sigh. "Yet I've managed to love Ben quite happily and without incident for the past ten years. There's no curse. There's no secret Drummond gene that turns on and makes me act like either one of them, no matter how much wine I've had. Those were choices they made, Lachlan."

"Ben isn't a Drummond," was all Lachlan said in reply. "*Mom* wasn't flying that plane."

The way he always did.

Catriona only looked at him as if he was breaking her heart. He thought she practiced it in the mirror before they saw each other. And he didn't know what she might have said then, but he was saved from having to hear it when her children came roaring in, in either high-pitched glee or murder.

While his sister sorted them out, Lachlan slipped away.

He walked through the villa, feeling the press of his family and his history on all sides. Even in the desperately chic, off-puttingly modern parts of the house, because he knew whose fingerprints were all over each room.

He'd spent so much of his childhood here. But his grandparents had both been alive then, meaning his parents had been forced to behave when they visited, at least some of the time. He had spent idyllic days in the sun, but come nightfall when the family was all together and his parents put on their act, all he'd ever seen were the lies beneath.

Lachlan didn't know if he loved this island or hated it.

By the time he made it down the long hallway to the wing he thought of as his these days, sleek and modern and scrubbed free of ghosts, there was a kind of agitation inside him. It beat at him, bright and hard.

It was nothing as simple as lust, but he called it lust all the same.

He found Bristol outside, clinging to the edge of the eternity pool. Her hair was wet and slicked back, and her gaze was trained on the horizon.

Lachlan didn't speak. He didn't know what he would say, or how.

Not when that drum in him beat like that. Jarring. Impossible.

Too much history and too much truth and he should never have let this woman come here.

She must have heard him approach, though he thought he'd been silent. Still, she turned, and he thought the sight of her slick, wet skin and the bikini halter top tied around her neck might be the undoing of him.

"Do you—" she began, but stopped.

Her eyes went wide.

And Lachlan felt it like her mouth, wet and hot while she sucked him in deep.

He prowled over to the side of the pool, bent, then hauled her up and out of the water. He didn't care in the least that holding her against his chest soaked him, too. Maybe he liked it. He felt half-blind with lust and longing, and that deeper, greedier thing that pulsed deep inside and held him in a tighter, more vicious grip.

His mouth was on hers, hard and wild, seeking and desperate.

He carried her inside, somehow finding the bed and taking her down with him, letting loose the only monster he ever allowed to take him over.

And never so out of control as with her.

He skimmed his mouth over the line of her neck, pulling the wet bikini top away from her breasts and growling a little as they were exposed to his view. Maybe it was the ceiling fan above that made those goose bumps prickle all over her skin, or maybe it was simply the same beating thing in the both of them.

Either way, Lachlan planned to devour her.

He found her stiff, hard nipples with his mouth, teasing her until she moaned. It was a broken, greedy sound and she arched up against him, offering herself in that same slick rush of surrender that he couldn't seem to get enough of.

He couldn't get *enough*.

Lachlan wanted to take his time, but he couldn't. He wanted her naked and took care of that, pulling the stretchy, soaked, irritating bathing suit bottoms off her. Only then did he find her just as he wanted her.

Wet.

Swollen with need already.

And when he set his mouth to her hard little clit, all he had to do was suck once, hard, and she screamed as she shattered.

He moved back, kneeling up to rid himself of his own clothing. Then he flipped her over in front of him, wrapping his forearm beneath her hips and hauling her into position.

Lachlan knew her body so well by now. He knew how she would brace herself, her arms flung over her head and her forehead pressed into the mattress. He knew she would arch her back and flex her hips so that he had easier access.

And when he slammed inside her, he knew the greedy, glorious little sounds she made. He reveled in how she angled herself to meet him so that each thrust was perfect.

He'd had her so many times, but it was never enough. He'd taken her in the back seat of almost every car they'd traveled in. He kept her naked on one long flight, curled up beside him on one of his jet's couches, open and longing and his for the duration. The hotels they'd stayed in blurred and the view of this or that famous city outside blended one into the next, but he remembered every sharp cry she made. The husky way she breathed his name.

The way she whispered *yes* in his ear when he lost his rhythm entirely.

Or the way she dug her nails into his back.

He could feel the way she shook, the way she stiffened, the tension radiating out from her splayed thighs and moving all over her sleek, lush body. He knew exactly how to keep her on that edge, throwing her off as he pleased and then throwing her right back into it.

Only when he couldn't take it for another moment did Lachlan follow her over.

And this time, after she'd screamed and he'd shouted, he rolled them over and pulled her to his side. Then he held her there while the ceiling fan rotated above them, washing them both with that faint breeze.

Letting the ghosts in with every turn of the blades.

He knew that as soon as he caught his breath, he could have her again. That she was always ready, always greedy.

He knew her body, but he didn't know Bristol at all.

And the more time he spent with her, the less he seemed to know himself.

It was that sharp truth that seemed to pierce him then. Straight and true while his heart kept up that drumming beat.

Until Lachlan was forced to wonder if Bristol was the one in control of the monster in him, after all.

CHAPTER SIX

"DID YOU KNOW that you're on the front page of every single tabloid there is?" Indy asked one afternoon.

Bristol had spent yet another morning in the Spanish island paradise that was entirely too easy to forget wasn't hers...at all. It was Lachlan's and she was simply aggrandized staff—but that proved difficult to remember in the most beautiful place she'd ever seen.

The villa was a patchwork of different time periods and aesthetics, jumbled altogether in a way that was somehow charming. The island itself boasted a craggy coast with limestone cliffs on one end, and gleaming white sand coves on the other. There were palm trees and pines, what was once a citrus grove, almond and olive trees. The villa was surrounded by trellises awash in violet flowers, and the soft sunshine danced over everything, as if conducting the orchestra of birdsong on the sea breeze.

Every day was the same, so achingly beautiful it should have hurt her. But didn't.

Lachlan's version of a family vacation involved waking Bristol before dawn, no matter how much of the night they might have spent driving each other mad with desire. He drove into her with what she would have called desperation, had it been anyone else. It was always a silent cascade of overwhelming need, a blistering rush of sensation and passion.

She would be half-asleep and then he would be inside her, and her dreams seemed to focus only on him anyway, so the shift always felt like coming.

And then she was.

Bristol loved it.

He went off to conduct his business while she slept more and recovered, something Lachlan never seemed to need to do. She usually met up with him later in the morning, after he'd had a few rounds of business in different time zones. And after *she'd* woken up, had fresh fruit out on the terrace with only the sea as company, and then sipped at coffee so strong and dark it made her feel like a superhero.

Sometimes she imagined she was one. Especially given the amount of sex she was currently having.

She often had more sex in a night than she'd had in the previous few years, combined.

Night after night.

Bristol loved that, too. She loved how her body felt. She loved what he did to it. She loved knowing that every need, every desire, would be explored—over and over. She loved how she felt settled into her bones and limbs in a new way, as if she was as ripe and as lush as she felt when his mouth was on her skin or his cock was deep inside her.

It couldn't be more different from her old life, which had been all about her brain and never about her body. It might as well have been night and day.

Sometimes Lachlan talked to her, always about his work. Only rarely about his sister and her family, but then, they all gathered together in the evenings for communal dinners and the polite sort of conversation that Bristol would have found difficult, had this not been a job.

Had this been a real relationship, the hollowness she sometimes felt inside might have consumed her whole.

It was better to concentrate on the flowers, the trees. The calls of the birds and the ocean breeze.

She was free from all the emotional clutter of real relationships, and that was a good thing. She could enjoy whatever Lachlan did, because none of it mattered. Their arrangement was temporary, summer could only last so long, and so she didn't need to worry if it was setting a precedent that, should she ask him why he seemed so distant when his sister spoke of family things, he replied by changing the subject.

A real girlfriend might object, but that wasn't Bristol's job.

She wasn't here to get closer to him, or get to know his sister, or do anything at all but exist in the role he'd carved out for her. Sex and conversation, one dark and deep, the other light and easy.

You can be easy, too, she liked to tell herself when she floated in the calm water of her favorite cove. *You have these few, sweet months to let someone else do the thinking.*

As a holiday for her brain, she couldn't think of anything better.

And as the days passed, Lachlan talked to her less and less when he came to find her in the bright light of another perfect Spanish morning. He preferred to pull her over his lap and move inside her again and again, letting her arch back into all that endless blue.

That didn't matter either.

If that was what he wanted, that was what she gave.

But somehow, today, the idea of this odd, breathless vacation from reality making it into the tabloids made it all feel less like a job and more like…a problem.

One she ought to have been solving, surely.

"What you mean by *every* tabloid?" she asked Indy. "I'm not comfortable with *one* tabloid."

"Then I have some bad news for you," her sister replied.

Bristol scowled at her phone. Indy liked to call and check on her older sister when she woke up. And since she'd decided New York was boring without Bristol about a week after Bristol had left, she was currently oversleeping in Europe.

She was also maddeningly vague about where, exactly, in Europe she happened to be.

And because Bristol knew Indy desperately wanted her to ask, she didn't.

"You know you have a little something called the internet at your disposal, Bristol," Indy was saying now, with so much laughter in her voice that Bristol could practically *see* her accompanying eye roll. "You can access this exciting new invention with the newfangled handheld computer you're using to talk to me, in a totally different country, *right now.*"

"I access the internet all the time, asshole," Bristol replied. "And yet, oddly enough, it's not the tabloid newspapers I look for when I do."

"Well, good news, then," Indy said brightly. "You look amazing. What else matters?"

Bristol could think of a great many things that mattered, but she had to pretend she wasn't interested for the rest of the call. For reasons. But the moment

Indy hung up—after making airy comments about where she was that managed to sound detailed without actually imparting any information—she went looking.

And sure enough, there she was.

It was the same picture on a number of tabloid covers, from one of the balls they'd been to during that first, long cycle through the capitals of Europe. Paris, she thought, if she remembered the progression of her formal dresses correctly. It was a lovely picture of the sweeping fairy tale of a dress, which she recalled had been surprisingly comfortable for a garment so fussy that it had taken two other people to get her into it.

But she wasn't named.

Lachlan Drummond and *his latest date*, as one tabloid identified her. There were several *female friends*. And a few *unnamed companions*. All featured several gushing, pseudo-journalistic paragraphs about Lachlan's philanthropic contributions to the world before segueing to several far more salacious paragraphs about all the other women he'd been seen with before Bristol.

The word *Lothario* was used. Unironically.

And Bristol congratulated herself on being his employee, not his actual girlfriend, because as an employee she had no grounds whatsoever to feel… anything.

Accordingly, she assured herself that she felt nothing at all.

She felt so much nothing, in fact, that she couldn't sit still. The open, airy terrace suddenly felt too close. Too claustrophobic. She found herself charging away from the villa for a nice long walk through the old citrus groves, down to the far cliffs and back.

Not to clear her head, which would suggest that there was some clutter in there. Which there couldn't be, because this wasn't a relationship. She wasn't *involved* with Lachlan in that way and no matter what the tabloids said, neither were any of those other women.

"I'm outside to be outside," she chanted to herself as she walked. "I'm out here to breathe deeply, that's all."

But she admitted to herself on the walk back that maybe, just maybe, she didn't know what she was doing. She saw Lachlan's sister and her oldest child from a distance and ducked back into the olive trees, pretending she wanted solitude. When what she really wanted was to avoid Catriona, with her too-direct gaze and casually incisive questions that Bristol couldn't answer.

Not the way she would have answered them if this was real.

What she did know was that she was sweating a little while she marched around the island and hid behind olive trees. And more, there was a great big ball of *mess* inside her, no matter how she tried to pretend there wasn't.

There was nothing to do about any of it but keep walking.

She'd lapped the whole island twice by the time she could finally breathe normally again. At which point it was easy enough to find her practiced smile and make her way back into the villa. And right back into her role.

The one she'd agreed to play. Legally.

"Where have you been, Bristol?"

Lachlan's voice came out of nowhere when she stepped through the ancient gate, strewn with morning glories and buzzing with cheerful bees. It made her…not quite jump, though her pulse instantly kicked into high gear. She blinked against the brightness as she looked around, eventually finding him standing in one of the wide-open arched doorways that allowed each room in the villa to flow into the next, then straight on into the sea and sky.

"I didn't see you there," Bristol said, and didn't give in to the urge to put her hand against her belly. She didn't want to draw attention to the fact that her own skin no longer seemed to fit. That she was buzzing and hollowed out and the only thing left was that same *want*.

Always that *want*, like a fire in her blood.

Sometimes when she looked at him, all she could think was that she'd let her pussy take her over. All she could do was melt, and moan, and say *more*.

It didn't help that he was even more beautiful and sensually formidable in casual clothes. Surely it should have diminished him not to be prowling around in his desperately chic corporate suits, too Wall Street to breathe. He should have looked like any random guy in his clearly very old and worn cargo shorts, a T-shirt with an obscure band on the front, and bare feet.

He did not.

His blue gaze was shadowed, but the light caught at his dark blond hair and made him gleam like gold. The rest of him was a pageant of wide shoulders, that ripped abdomen, and his narrow hips. Even his legs made her feel like swooning, when Bristol didn't think she'd ever noticed a *male leg* before in her life.

God help her, even his *feet* were sexy.

She was so busy trying not to drool over the biceps that strained against the frayed edge of his blue T-shirt sleeves that she almost missed the hard line of his mouth. The set to his jaw.

But his voice, stern and dark, reminded her where she was. And what she was here to do—which was not simply flutter about, admiring him.

Even if he did look like a dressed-down Greek statue.

Bristol reminded herself that Greece was quite a ways off to the east, give or take a few seas. And Italy.

"I came to find you, but couldn't," Lachlan said.

This was how it was now. Or maybe this was how it had always been, but Bristol hadn't realized it. This pulsing sort of undercurrent beneath whatever words they used. This dark thing inside her while she fought to keep her voice light and that smile on her face—because that was the professional thing to do, surely.

Was she only imagining it was the same for him?

"I'm sorry," she said, because apologizing was always the right move. She'd been using it on her advisers and committee members and professors for years. Coming out of the gate with an apology always put them on the back foot. "I didn't expect you to have any free time today. I would have made myself available."

There was something taut in his face then. It took her a moment to understand he was clenching his teeth enough to make a muscle flex in his jaw. "I don't think that's true, Bristol. I think you went for a walk. Catriona said she saw you down near the olive groves more than an hour ago."

"And here I thought we'd left Stephanie behind

for a while. Is your sister keeping tabs on me? You really do have eyes everywhere."

"I asked her if she'd seen you."

Bristol felt that buzzing, wanting thing shift then. Into the other thing she felt most often around him—the need to push his buttons. Hard.

Because she knew what happened when she did. He didn't betray a temper. Not Lachlan.

He fucked it out instead, and took his revenge that way.

And she loved every minute of it.

She pulled her phone out of the pocket of the flowy skirt she was wearing, then made a show of looking at it for missed calls and messages she already knew weren't there.

"I expected you to be here," he growled.

"And I've agreed I should have been. But Lachlan, you also could have called, and I would have come running."

Had she meant to use that particular tone? It wasn't bitter, exactly. But she knew that if she could hear the edge in it, he could, too.

He clearly did. "Do you have a problem with making yourself available to me, Bristol?"

And it was easier to smile then, because she could hear the dangerous note in that silky tone he used. The fine hairs on her arms and the back of her neck prickled, and her pussy was instantly slippery and achy.

Maybe he liked flirting with all the dark places between them as much as she did.

"I do not," she said, still smiling. "That's the job, isn't it?"

He didn't like that. She could see he didn't like it.

And she opted not to ask herself why she should feel it like a personal triumph when he reached over and fit his hand to the curve of her cheek. Bristol already knew the answer.

"Don't you know better than to say things like that?" His voice was still like silk, never quite concealing the power beneath. And the lick of fire that she tried not to think of as theirs. "The job is never supposed to feel like a job."

She laughed, unwisely. "To who?"

His hand tightened against her cheek and she thought he might pull her close, but he didn't. Instead, he let go and shifted back, leaving the feel of his palm against her skin. So hot she was sweating a little.

"My assistant tells me we've gotten some tabloid notice," he said. "I think we got ahead of the worst of the speculation. At least for now."

"Oh?" She shrugged carelessly. "Are we required to pay attention to those things? Is *that* part of the job? Because keeping myself abreast of the latest nasty gossip would definitely feel like a job."

"I prefer to pretend they don't exist."

Bristol told herself the sunshine was making her a little giddy, but she was fairly sure it was actually that intent blue gaze of his. It seemed to cut into her—much too deep, like everything he did. Deep and unmistakable and as dangerous to her as it was good. She wished she didn't know that.

"But they have a funny way of poisoning things. The insinuations. The gossipy, breathless tone. It's better to ignore them entirely if you can."

"I've been ignoring them entirely my whole life. I hardly plan to stop that practice now that I might see myself torn apart in them."

His mouth curved, and it made the sun seem that much brighter. "So you've seen them."

"I saw, thanks to my sister, who looks for such things, that there are some pictures of you with an *unnamed companion* who bears a striking resemblance to me."

"Trust me, they know your name."

"That is not comforting."

"See? Poison."

Bristol reminded herself that she was not here to assert herself the way she wanted to do. Or to carry on about her individuality, or cast aspersions on the sorts of "news" outlets that would choose not to name her *deliberately*. And she certainly wasn't here to make arch comments about how bracing it was to find herself anonymous when she'd spent so long making a name for herself in the first place.

The words might have been on her tongue, but she swallowed them down.

She had chosen to take this position with her eyes wide open.

Looking at him—at that impossibly beautiful face of his that sometimes, like now, made her want to cry—she found too many words tangled on her tongue, and that wasn't the deal they'd made.

Bristol made herself smile. As if this was all a joke. "Luckily for me it's a temporary poison. The antidote is waiting for me in September."

That muscle in his lean jaw flexed again. "I hope so, for your sake."

She found herself frowning at him when she normally tried hard to keep from doing that. It had been one thing back in New York. Before she'd signed up for her role as his always-available, always-amenable companion. Also, clearly, frowning gave her away. "What's that supposed to mean?"

"It's inevitable that they're going to start discussing who you are. They're probably digging around in your past as we speak."

"Terrific."

"You were counseled about this."

"I was." She should have paid closer attention to Stephanie, obviously. Or rather, she should have been prepared to feel more than she'd expected she would. "I don't have anything in my past I'm embarrassed about. Or, I suppose, the more pertinent thing is I don't have anything in my past *you* would be embarrassed about."

"I know this, Dr. March. You're not the only one who does research." He actually let out a laugh when she lifted a brow, which made her want to dance. Sing. *Something.* She refrained. "Fine. I have staff who do research."

"You were modifying my expectations about fading into blessed obscurity in the fall," she reminded him, and the gleam in his eyes warned her that she sounded…a bit tart.

She smiled to cover it.

Lachlan crossed his arms, which drew too much attention to those arms. Bristol ordered herself to pay attention to what he was saying. Or to pretend that was possible when he was looming around, too gorgeous to bear.

"Once they decide how to run at you, they'll beat that drum until the end of time. If you think of it like a game, it's better. They'll make up a character, call it you, and make sure every picture they print serves the story. You can try to fight it, but it's a war of attrition and they'll always win. It's better to ignore it."

"I remember this part," she said. But it had felt different, hadn't it, when there'd been no pictures of her anywhere. When it had all been theoretical tabloids.

To go along with all the theoretical sex at Lachlan's command and convenience.

Her clit throbbed, the greedy little thing.

"And even when we're finished, long after September, it's entirely possible they'll trot you out in every story they do like this about me, forevermore." He studied her. "Like all the exes they decided to mention today."

"Then I'm going to require combat pay," she retorted, as breezily as possible.

"Don't worry," Lachlan said lazily enough, his blue eyes glittering and his jaw still tense. "You'll be adequately compensated."

And normally conversations like this, threaded through with so much left unsaid, were solved in bed. Vigorously.

But Catriona was calling from out on the lawn, and her kids were suddenly there to demand their uncle's attention. Lachlan held Bristol's gaze a beat or so longer than he should have, and they were swept into the charming chaos of it all.

Bristol told herself it was a welcome break.

But her head was spinning, like it or not. Because it had been one thing to decide to do this thing. She couldn't deny that there were benefits. There was not having to decide what she planned to do now that she finally had her doctorate, sure. There was also the true and real freedom of surrendering herself entirely to Lachlan's sexual demands. She didn't have to think about anything. All she had to do was feel.

Feel and want and come back for more.

She didn't understand how she could love that as much as she did, yet still feel a stark sense of pure fear at the idea that this private thing of theirs was now public.

Not to mention that hollow thing, always there, where she stored the emotions she would sort out in the fall.

She'd been warned. Bristol knew that.

But being warned about the very real price of being seen with such a famous man was different from it actually happening. It was different from knowing that people she knew could see her in that dress, smiling brightly up at Lachlan. And it hadn't occurred to her to worry about the fact she would be reduced to just…one more woman gracing his arm for the moment, soon to be discarded.

They would use her name, or they wouldn't, but it didn't really matter. He was right—soon enough she would be relegated to the lower paragraphs. Sometimes with a photograph, sometimes not, but always just another footnote in the broader story that was Lachlan Drummond.

If she, a lowly academic instead of the actresses and socialites, even rated a footnote.

Again, none of that should come as a surprise. It was precisely what she'd signed up for.

But it was different now.

Maybe you're what's different now, a voice inside her suggested.

Later, he led her back to their room and she thought he would take her in a fury, the way he often did. Maybe she yearned for it.

That obliteration. That immolation.

But instead, when he stretched out over her, his gaze was intense and he kept it locked to hers.

And she found herself moving beneath him slowly. Deliberately.

Because that was what he gave her.

A slow, deep rending.

So there was no explosion, there was only this... deepening.

Until they both broke apart, together, and Bristol felt as if he'd scraped her soul raw.

Worse, that he'd meant to.

After, he held her tight against him and pushed her hair back from her face to look at her much too intently. She was afraid she knew what he could see written all over her, all too plain and obvious.

And unacceptable, given the papers she'd signed. The deal they'd made.

That hollow place inside her that only seemed to grow. All the parts of her he'd scraped raw tonight and every night.

All the things she couldn't say to him.

He's going to fire you, something in her warned.

And she couldn't tell if she wanted that desperately or if the very idea made her want to cry.

Both, she acknowledged.

"Bristol," Lachlan said. His voice was low and dark and so beautiful it hurt, and she promised herself she would remember that part. She would remember how beautiful he was and how he shined brighter than the Spanish summer outside, even at night. "I want to renegotiate terms."

CHAPTER SEVEN

BY THE TIME they made it to Hong Kong, everybody knew Bristol's name, as predicted. They not only knew it, they used it. She had to get a new phone with a private number and monitor who she gave it out to, because the old number had found its way into the hands of the tabloids. She had to suffer the indignity of "friends" she hadn't spoken to since they'd sat near each other in a high school class claim to be some kind of authority on who she was now.

Bristol no longer belonged to herself alone.

It was a remarkably strange and vulnerable feeling.

She learned quickly not to read comments sections on internet posts. And to avoid the carrion crows of Twitter like the plague.

But it was still disconcerting. Real friends and colleagues texted her, some in disbelief. Others in what seemed to her like not-so-concealed jealousy, or even condemnation.

Interesting postdoc you're doing there, one of her fellow PhDs texted. He had shared that office with her for years and yet Bristol knew, from that alone, that he was exactly the kind of man who would never take her seriously again. Because now when he looked at her or thought about her, he'd be thinking about her having sex with a man far more rich and powerful than he'd ever be.

Once again, she felt lucky that she'd actually signed binding nondisclosure agreements. Because knowing she was legally barred from commenting on what was going on between her and Lachlan made it easy to avoid telling anyone anything, even by mistake. It was a useful weapon. It also made it easy to gauge people's reactions to what little she said, and it was always illuminating.

Luckily enough for Bristol, it wasn't very surprising. Because the truth was, the years she'd spent as a doctoral student had already distanced her from old, so-called friends. To say nothing of the years she'd spent studying to get into that doctoral program in the first place. She'd always been single-minded and devoted—some might say *anal*—and her preference for studying too much and following research notions down rabbit holes even if it was a Saturday had naturally pared down her friend group.

The only person she spoke to with any degree of honesty about her relationship with Lachlan was

Indy, but Indy herself was less available as the summer wore on.

And maybe that, too, was a gift.

Because Lachlan wanted to renegotiate their terms and Bristol still didn't quite know what to make of it. How could she have discussed something she couldn't understand herself?

Not what he'd asked. She understood that perfectly. But how she felt about the possibility of making that shift.

"I want less job and more girlfriend," Lachlan had told her that night in Spain.

"Am I not doing it right?" Bristol had asked, possibly sounding more vulnerable than she'd wanted to, but what was she supposed to do? She still felt split wide open and entirely too raw. There were words she could have used to describe what happened between them in that bed that night, but she didn't dare. That was one more thing to tuck away in that hollow space inside to look at later. Like maybe in November. She'd remembered herself and cleared her throat. "All you have to do is tell me what you want, Lachlan, and I'll do it. That's what we agreed."

"That's what I'm talking about, Bristol." His hands had still been bracketing her face. He had still been lodged so deep within her she'd been tempted to imagine that was where he belonged. "I don't want that. I want a real person."

"I don't think you do." She'd felt a surge of something like panic but had tamped it down as best she could—then had offered him a smile. "Or you wouldn't have convened a panel to find one."

"The panel was meant to find me some filler," Lachlan said, his eyes so blue she'd been certain he could see every last hint of the panic she'd been trying to hide. "But you're not filler, Bristol. I want more of you."

That hollow place beneath her breastbone had felt sharp and jagged then.

"That's not what I signed up for."

"I want to know what's going on here," he'd said, gruffly. He'd tapped his finger gently against her temple, still looking at her with that intensity that had made her think that she might burst into flame after all. Some part of her had wanted nothing more. "I don't need you to agree with everything I say. I don't need you to hide away your every feeling from me."

And the part of her that might have welcomed that noted that he hadn't been promising to offer her the same in return.

"I thought the entire purpose of this was to hide my feelings from you," she'd said instead of pointing that out. "So you wouldn't have to deal with them when what you really want is sex."

"Maybe it will get messy," Lachlan had acknowledged. "But maybe that's okay."

Bristol had rolled away from him then, because when he touched her she lost her train of thought. Possibly also her mind.

"Not for me," she'd said, and had left him there to head into the shower.

They had spent a few more days on the island but Lachlan hadn't brought up renegotiation again.

Bristol hadn't tried to fool herself into believing that he'd forgotten what he'd said. If she knew anything about Lachlan Drummond after all this time, it was that he truly was ruthless. He might not enact that ruthlessness the way his ancestors had, using Wall Street like a weapon, but that didn't mean he lacked it.

Lachlan preferred to wait. As long as it took, as long as was necessary.

It was a family trait, apparently.

"You know that you're the first girlfriend Lachlan has ever introduced me to," Catriona had said on their last night on the island. Lachlan had been called into a last-minute huddle with his staff, so she'd found Bristol tucked up in one of the lesser-used sitting rooms with the big, fat book she'd been trying to finish before they left open before her. "I don't want to say that you're the first girlfriend who also reads, but…"

She'd smiled at Bristol, her face open and engaging.

Bristol knew by then that those were Catriona's sharpest and deadliest weapons.

"That's a bit harsh, surely," Bristol had replied, smiling brightly in return, even as she'd looked around for an escape. Because it felt dishonest, somehow, to have private conversations with a woman she would never see again once the summer was over. The kind of conversations real girlfriends might have with their new boyfriend's family.

She'd thought again about what Lachlan had said about wanting more of her—then shook it off. Because as much as she might have enjoyed Catriona and her family and the high-spirited banter between all of them and Lachlan at their nightly dinners, none of that was hers. Or ever could be, no matter what fantasies of *messy realness* Lachlan might harbor.

Bristol knew he didn't really want any of that. If he did, they never would have met, because he would never have created an entire system to make sure his hired companions kept their distance—up to and including the tiresome Stephanie and her *agendas*.

"It is harsh," Catriona had been saying. She'd sighed. "I suppose, Bristol, that I'm just ready for my brother to have something real."

And for a long moment, the two of them had gazed at each other across that charming room stuffed full of novels and art, a thousand things unspoken between them.

Bristol had been certain then of something she'd thought off and on throughout their stay—that Catriona knew exactly how her brother handled his intimate relationships. Just as she knew that it had been possible Catriona's oblique reference was a test to see if Bristol would disclose the nature of that relationship now she'd mentioned it, even though it was forbidden by the contracts she'd signed.

And Lachlan wasn't in the room, so Bristol couldn't look to his reaction as a guide or, better yet, allow him to handle his sister.

She'd had to go with her gut and protect him.

"Isn't that what everybody's looking for?" she'd asked softly. "If the world was better at *real*, there'd be a lot less *lonely*."

And though Catriona hadn't said anything else that night, the interaction had stayed with Bristol.

Haunting her all the way to Hong Kong.

Even flying into a city so hectic was an adventure, especially in the downpour of a humid Chinese summer. Bristol stared out the plane's windows at the bristling skyscrapers as they came in for their landing, as if Hong Kong wasn't simply a single city but every city, packed into all those endless jutting buildings. As usual, Lachlan left her after they disembarked so he could go directly into his business meetings.

Meaning Bristol was once again stranded in a car with the officious and passive-aggressive Stephanie, who had taken to reading out her lists of instructions because she knew Bristol had no intention of following them.

Outside the windows, the Hong Kong weather seemed to highlight the press of so many people, the buildings piled high. Some part of Bristol found it exhilarating. Another part of her found the tumult of it all a bit hard to process after the serenity of the island.

But it was harder and harder to tell how she felt about anything. Bristol tried her best to feel nothing at all.

"Are you listening to me?" Stephanie demanded as the car inched through traffic.

Bristol looked over at her and smiled. Serenely. "I think you know perfectly well that I'm not."

The other woman let out a huff of outrage. "This can't continue, Bristol. Do you know how many women I've seen sit where you're sitting? Here's a newsflash. Each and every one of them thought they were special, too."

"Stephanie. Look at me." Bristol waited until she did. Stephanie had to be twenty years older than she was, trim and capable and currently so tense it was surprising she didn't snap in half.

"Your itineraries are suggestions. We both know it. There's only one person who gives me orders and he's made it clear he doesn't care if I follow your agendas or not. That's just a fact, so what's the point of arguing about it, day in and day out? And what does it even matter? I'm only here for the summer. I'm sure the next one who comes along will bow to your every whim."

"These are not *my* itineraries!" Stephanie looked stung. "They're to help you do your job to the best of your abilities—and to Mr. Drummond's satisfaction."

"I admire what you do," Bristol said, soothingly. And was surprised to find she meant it. "It can't possibly be easy to corral a variety of women into this particular box, over and over. But rest assured, Lachlan is perfectly aware which one of the two of us is responsible for the way I dress and behave. If there's a price to be paid, I'll be paying it. Not you."

And for a moment, it was quiet in the car. Only the cacophony of the sprawling city outside, pressing in against the windows.

"He treats you differently," Stephanie said, and for once, Bristol could detect no trace of snideness or passive aggression in her voice. It made her blink. "To be honest, Bristol, you're the first one who makes me think I might be out of a job soon."

Despite herself, Bristol felt her pulse pick up.

Something in her stomach twisted, but not in a bad way. If she didn't know better—if she didn't know how futile it all was—she might have thought it was hope.

"There's no chance of that," she said quietly, forcing herself not to clear her throat. Because it would be much too telling. "I suspect you'll have your job for a long time to come."

And she made herself sit there for the rest of the ride across the city, imagining all the future women who would be sitting right where she was. It wasn't torture—on the contrary, she found it soothing. They would come and go like the tide. They would take up space beside her in the lower paragraphs of those tabloid articles while above, the new girlfriends would wear lovely dresses in Paris, one after the next. And she would look back on this one, long, impetuous and out-of-character summer from the safety of her ivy tower and smile.

She hoped that no matter what happened, she would smile.

Later, as the breathlessly humid day edged toward a thick, hot evening, she waited for Lachlan in the bar of the hotel where they were staying. It was a quiet place, dark and inviting, but she didn't choose one of the booths. She went instead to the dizzying sweep of windows, all offering astonishing views of the city, and found a high table there.

She almost felt as if she, too, was plump with

neon and light and bursting at the seams with all the commotion far below.

The outfit that Stephanie had chosen for her tonight—and that Bristol had decided to actually wear, only partly because she thought she ought to extend an olive branch to the woman who was, like her, just doing her job—was the kind of pantsuit she'd seen famous women wear with ease and flair, but had never attempted herself. Because she'd never understood how they made what she took to be a rather dowdy bit of work attire into elegance in the first place.

Now she knew. Everything was different when it came from instantly recognizable fashion houses and was furthermore tailored to her precise measurements. And then paired with shoes that might as well have been works of art. Shoes so high they should have hurt her feet, but that, too, was apparently only a concern at her usual price points.

She'd seen her reflection in the elevator when it had hurtled down from another opulent penthouse suite and had thought she might as well have been a stranger.

This was what came of playing games with sex, she acknowledged now, smiling faintly when the waiter brought her the drink she'd ordered from the bar on her way in. This was what happened when it turned out she might have leaned too far into that separation between emotion and action that had given her comfort, at first.

She'd thought she could hide there and unpack it all later.

Bristol suspected she'd made a terrible mistake, but the only way to fix it was to leave.

And it was already July. She had so little time left with Lachlan as it was.

She thought of the tides again, the changing of the guard, her inevitable replacements. The ebb and flow of it all. The stack of contracts she'd signed, almost merrily, in what seemed like a different life.

When she'd thought she could...just have a lot of sex with a beautiful man for a little while.

Because wasn't that what people did?

Why had she thought she could be like other people when she never had been before?

You're fine, she told herself, while outside the window, the falling dark was cut through by neon light shows all around. *You have a week off when you get back to the States and then it will be August. Why are you acting like this is a hardship?*

If it was so onerous, she'd told herself as she'd gotten ready tonight, she could always stop doing it. She and Lachlan had agreed on the summer, but she could walk away anytime she liked. As could he.

She could walk away right now and find her own way back to New York.

But she didn't move. Bristol knew that no matter what she told herself—no matter the hollowness that expanded inside her, wrecking her more and more by the day—she wasn't ready to go.

Sometimes she worried that even when September came, she still wouldn't be ready.

She sensed movement at her shoulder and knew that it was Lachlan even before she lifted her gaze to find him standing there. He was looking down at her in the way he always did now. His mouth grave. His gaze intense.

As if that hollow feeling wasn't truly hollow after all, but overfull. And both of them were stuck right there in the middle of it.

"Are you ready?" he asked, his voice that low rumble she thought she would dream about, later. When she slept alone again. When it was cold outside and she had nothing but memories to heat her up. "There's no particular rush. We're not expected for at least an hour."

He stood too close to her at that table, so it seemed as if there was a wall of him on one side and nothing but a freefall into Hong Kong's epic commotion on the other.

Bristol couldn't tell, as she gazed into those electric-blue eyes of his, if maybe she was flying after all.

"How did your meetings go?" she asked, because it only seemed polite. If a shade too domestic, maybe, for what was meant to be such a purely business arrangement.

But he didn't answer. His hair was that dark blond that she never tired of running her fingers through. They itched to do it now. He was dressed in another one of those exquisite dark suits that seemed to draw attention to the fact that he was a physically powerful man, built to move mountains, not play around with theoretical money like so many of the people they met with at these functions.

Nothing about Lachlan was theoretical. He was all action.

And the way he was looking at her made everything inside her *hum*.

"What made you how you are?" he asked, idly, as if there were no contracts between them. As if there was only heat.

Inside her, it felt like an open flame.

She tried smiling it away. "My understanding is that it's a mix of genetics and an aggressively bland childhood."

"Does aggressively bland mean...happy?"

Bristol wanted to look away, but she didn't. Why hide here when she was already wide open to him in so many other ways? Who was she kidding? "Sometimes I wonder if happy childhoods are myths we tell ourselves. It's hard to be happy if you're a child, isn't it? Your body is always changing without your input. The world around you is always changing as you become more aware of it. And no, nothing terrible happened to me. But I wouldn't say I was *happy*."

"Then you're lucky," he said, his eyes darker than before. "Because if you were unhappy, you'd know."

She opened her mouth, then closed it. "I'll give you that. I'm very lucky that what I had to complain about was mostly that I had nothing to complain about."

"And yet you're still so driven. Why?"

Bristol wished she'd gotten a stronger drink. She swirled the dregs of her soda and lime around and around, and didn't look at the man who seemed to surround her so easily. As if he was holding her in the palm of his hand.

Maybe sex was easier after all. It could feel like all of these conversations without actually having to have them.

"Pot, meet kettle," she murmured.

"My childhood had its advantages." Lachlan laughed, but it didn't reach his eyes. "I would not call it lucky. Or happy."

"I know your parents died. I'm sorry."

"In some ways the accident was a relief," he said quietly.

And Bristol was gripped by that stark look on his face. That faint hint of what might have been surprise. She knew, somehow, that this was not something he said very often.

Maybe he never had.

She whispered his name and his mouth curved, though it wasn't a smile. "I try not to say that out loud. My sister hates it when I forget and say it anyway."

"Because she feels the same...or because she disagrees?"

Lachlan shook his head as if he couldn't answer that. "Some people bring out the worst in each other. My parents started off tragic and toxic and only got worse from there. They liked to pretend, but behind closed doors, it was an endless competition to see who could cause the most damage. Catriona and I were spared the worst of it because their focus was only and ever on each other. They fought like it was to the death every time, and one day, it was."

"Lachlan. I'm so sorry."

His gaze moved over her face. "You didn't do it. They did."

"Is that what drives you?" she asked. "Losing them?"

"Not losing them." He ran a hand over his lean jaw. "Living with them. I guess you could say that after they died, that left me with a whole lot to prove. Mostly that no matter what, I wasn't going to turn into the same kind of monster. You asked me once if I was a *kind* billionaire."

"I didn't mean—"

"My father certainly wasn't. And I try, in every

way I can, to be nothing like him. Starting with the fact that I'm not actually a billionaire any longer, because most years I give away too much money to maintain that status."

Bristol's heart was beating too fast. She could feel it thundering in her chest and pulsing through her. As if she was running up a long set of stairs. As if Lachlan was deep inside her.

As if she was afraid.

Or alive, something in her whispered. *At last.*

"Why are you so driven, then?" he asked again. "What did you have to prove if your life was so bland?"

And her heart didn't slow, but she fell anyway. Not out the window to the busy streets so far below, but into his steady gaze.

Maybe she'd always been falling and only realized it now.

And the realization was like the hard thud of landing, and the impact reverberated through her, making it impossible to do anything but tell him the truth.

"I wanted to make sure they saw me," she whispered.

Her hair was tied back in a knot tonight, but a tendril fell forward on her cheek. Slowly, intently, Lachlan drew it back and tucked it behind her ear.

It made her shudder.

"Who?" he asked, hardly making a sound.

But she heard him.

And somehow, Bristol smiled, an ache made real. Right there on her face. "Everyone."

The next morning, she woke up naked and alone in the huge bed that took up the better part of yet another astonishingly vast bedroom. She was sure she would find Lachlan's fingerprints all over her but was disappointed when she looked in the nearest mirror and saw nothing.

Nothing to mark how he had held her through the night, how he had made her cry and beg.

Over and over again, until the sky behind all that light and neon began to brighten.

The man needed no sleep, as far as she could tell. She'd always thought that she was tenacious and determined, but Lachlan was a breed apart.

Especially when he was clearly trying to show her why she should let him in.

By stripping her raw. By making her sob.

Until it felt as if she was incomplete when he wasn't buried deep inside her.

As if she might never be whole again.

When her phone chimed she knew it was her sister, and ignored it. She didn't think she had it in her to talk—because once she started, she wasn't sure she would stop.

But when it beeped again, indicating a message, she swiped it up from the table where she'd left it.

Romantic, Indy had texted.

And the picture she'd sent along with her text made everything in Bristol go still.

Too still.

How had she not seen a photographer in that bar last night? But she knew the answer to that. She'd been completely swept up in Lachlan. Completely consumed.

The picture was of Lachlan tugging that dark lock of her hair back from her face and securing it at her ear. She almost couldn't bear to look at the image, but she couldn't bring herself to look away.

It was too tender. Too raw.

The look on Lachlan's face was almost too intense. And the look on her face...

Bristol looked like a woman in love.

And if that wasn't the kiss of death in this situation, she didn't know what was.

She heard herself make a small, broken sound and she tossed the phone aside, but how could that help? If Indy had seen that picture, so had the world. So would he.

Her heart was beating again, too fast. Too jarring.

Lachlan wanted her to let him in, but she knew better than to let him. She wasn't protecting herself because it was her job to maintain her distance. She was doing it because she was afraid.

She would fall in love, and much too easily. Maybe she already had.

Heedlessly. Hopelessly.

Bristol already knew the symptoms. She'd felt the same way about her research, her dissertation, and she didn't love anything by half. She threw herself in deep, losing herself completely. She disappeared into the grip of it.

That was what she was good at, loving like that, to the exclusion of all else.

But she already knew it would end the same way.

Maybe not badly, but inevitably. She would be left empty. All that focus, all that dedication, and all she would become was a footnote to a scandalous article about his next purchased girlfriend.

Last night he had held her beneath him as he'd driven them both crazy. He'd kept her on the edge as he held her face between his hands and whispered the same thing again and again.

What do you want? he'd gritted out, rough and raw. *What do you* want, *Bristol?*

And now she knew.

All she wanted was the one thing she couldn't have. Not for the world to see her. It turned out, she didn't like that at all.

What Bristol wanted was for Lachlan to see her, really and truly. She wanted to give him everything he'd asked for and more.

And then not just *see* her.

But let her stay.

CHAPTER EIGHT

THEY RETURNED TO New York on a muggy summer's day near the end of July, swollen with the threat of a thunderstorm that couldn't quite bring itself to break. A lot like the weather they'd left behind in Hong Kong, in fact, as if they were personally delivering oppressive, gray summers around the world.

It suited Lachlan's mood perfectly.

"I have you down for a few days' break," he said, almost idly, as the car took them back toward the city. Too quickly for his liking. "But you don't have to take it."

Bristol smiled at him the way she always did now, with all that distance in her gaze. Lachlan wanted to break things, but they were in an enclosed space. And also he wasn't his father.

"No, thank you," she said. Far too serenely. "I'll take it."

"Bristol..."

Her smile widened yet gave him nothing. "I'll see you in a week, Lachlan."

Though he raged and punched walls internally, externally there was nothing to be done about it. He knew what was in the contracts he'd been so insistent she sign. He'd long ago insisted on including these small, mandatory breaks following any international tour like the one they'd just taken. And it had never been for the girlfriend in question, it had always been for him. Lachlan liked the convenience of his arrangements, but he also liked his solitude. He usually needed to regroup, get his head back on straight, and deal, privately, with how the women he hired fell far short of the thing he really wanted.

But with Bristol everything was inside out.

He insisted they take her back to Brooklyn first. And he didn't simply drop her off and continue on his way. He helped her with her bags, personally. Her *bag*, that was, because she'd only brought one, single personal item with her.

And she was leaving him the same way she'd come to him, something in him acknowledged. Leaving nothing of herself behind.

She isn't leaving, he assured himself. *She's taking the mandatory break, the way they all do after a long trip. There's still August.*

But that didn't keep him from standing there in what he supposed passed for a living room, glaring at Bristol. Who, he couldn't help but notice, looked more at home in this crappy little apartment than she had in any of the spectacular five-star accommodations they'd stayed in on the road. Or even his own private island.

Why did that get under his skin? But he knew.

He didn't want her to belong anywhere but with him.

"Take a good look," she invited him, meeting his glare steadily. "I know it may come as a shock to you, but this is how real people live in New York."

"*Two* of you live here?" He didn't have to feign his astonishment. "You *and* your sister?"

"Indeed we do. And, actually, this is considered a very luxurious two-bedroom because we each have our own, genuine room. Not that you would recognize either one of them as an actual bedchamber, since I believe the bathroom on your plane is larger than both of them put together."

"Amazing."

But he was looking at her while he said it.

Bristol laughed and it was like a punch to the gut. When had she stopped laughing like that? When had she retreated into distance in those vague smiles?

But he knew the answer to that, too.

"Allow me to give you the full tour," she said. She took one step back and opened her hands wide.

"This is…the whole thing. You can view it as a kind of sociological experiment, I guess. Behold, Lachlan. This is how the common people live."

"I got the point the first time."

"It's hard to get your head around, I know," she continued in the same wildly amused tone. "No butler waiting on you. No suite of graceful, pointless rooms, lazily spread out over the top of a building with views to die for." She moved over to the window and laughed again as she looked out. "That's not Hyde Park, I'm afraid. That's my neighbor's window box and, if I'm not mistaken, that might be an illegal plant. But if you squint, you can pretend."

When she turned back toward him, he remembered that first dinner a lifetime ago now. The light in her gaze. Her laughter.

How different she'd been then.

How exciting and uncowed and…not trying to impress him at all.

He'd loved that. He'd had sex with her in an alley, for God's sake.

And then what had he done? He taken her and crushed her to fit into the same box he'd been carrying around his entire adult life. The same box where he'd put anyone who might, even accidentally, attempt to stray too close to him. What had he thought would happen?

"Bristol," he began. "I wish…"

Laughter faded from her gaze. She inclined her head toward the door.

"I'll see you in a week, Lachlan," she said with a quiet certainty that made everything in him tense. "As agreed."

He wanted to argue. He wanted to impose his will on her with a wave of his hand. Make her change her mind. Make her *understand*.

But the rules were the rules. He knew that all too well, because he was the one who'd made them.

Lachlan saw the choice before himself starkly then. It was moments like this, moments he'd never imagined he'd ever find himself in, that showed him how narrow his path really was. How no matter how he tried, he could never do enough good in the world when inside him, he was still a Drummond.

Still a monster.

He could see too well how easy it would be to be like his father, of course. Ignore any rule he didn't like, do as he pleased, and laugh about it if anyone ever tried to stand up to him.

That he could see why that was appealing, even after all these years of trying his best to be different, to be better…horrified him.

Lachlan murmured what he hoped was a neutral enough goodbye. He turned before he lost control of himself and truly became his worst nightmare. Then he let himself out, jogging down the rickety stairs, too disgusted with himself to really register any details except the need to put distance between him and the one woman he actually didn't want any distance from.

Because that was what she wanted.

When he found himself outside on the street, he waved off his driver. Then he took his waking that same old Drummond monster inside him as an opportunity. He started walking himself back into Manhattan, hoping the city would speak to him and maybe even soothe him as he moved.

It was a long walk. And a good one, even on a sweaty evening like this. He'd just crossed the Brooklyn Bridge into Lower Manhattan when the thunder started.

He could relate. It growled and rumbled up above while the air grew thicker.

By the time he made it to his building, he was soaking wet, but it still hadn't rained. The humidity was so intense it soaked him straight through, and no matter how fast he'd walked, or how furiously he let his feet eat up the blocks, Lachlan was no better off.

He was in no way *soothed*.

His head was full to bursting with Bristol March even while he had the sinking, lowering sensation that *she* was tucked up in her bed in that closet-sized apartment, sleeping blissfully and sweetly without him.

His home in Manhattan had been in his family for even more generations than that town house in Murray Hill. It was an old, much-renovated house on a cobbled street in Greenwich Village that was usually clogged with tourists snapping pictures.

But even the tourists were sheltering inside on an evening like this.

Lachlan stripped as he went inside, tossing his soaked-through clothes aside. He headed up the stairs, making his way to the roof that had long ago been converted into a private garden. *My oasis in the middle of the city,* his mother had always called it.

And for all Lachlan prided himself on his lack of sentimentality, he'd always found he could exhale better here.

Which was exactly what he did the moment he stepped outside. He could smell the flowers. He could lose himself in the potted trees and bright blossoms. The thunder muttered all around him, but he was deep in the green.

And he understood, after all these years, that the roof garden reminded him of the island. He could feel his grandparents here. He could remember those bright, brief stretches in between his parents' wars that had always smelled like this, green and sweet.

How had he missed that until now?

But that was another question he shouldn't need

to ask himself, because he knew the answer. It was Bristol. He had visited that island a thousand times, but now when he thought of it, he pictured her. He'd stood at the window in his office, too many dreary voices in his ear, and had watched her pick her way through the olive trees. The sun in her dark hair and a smile on her face that she would have contained if she knew he was watching.

He even saw her here, where she'd never been. Distance in her dark eyes and that wicked twist to her mouth.

As if she knew how futile it was for him to look for some kind of clarity no matter where he went.

Even if it was to this hidden patch of green surrounded by so much concrete.

But that was where he stood, stripped down to his boxer briefs with his head tilted up, as the rain finally began to fall.

That was where he stayed, arms open as if the storm could wash him clean.

But it didn't help.

And the next morning, Lachlan got in his car, left Manhattan behind him, and drove himself north.

Catriona and Ben lived in the Vermont countryside, closer to Canada than New York City—by design. Ben's ancestors had once farmed these rolling acres miles away from any neighbors, but now Ben, a world-renowned architect, used the converted old barn as his studio. He'd used the barn as his base for years, while Catriona had quietly made the old farmhouse into a happy, rambling, picture-perfect home for her family.

Lachlan thought about his sister's choices as he turned down the long drive that wound in and around the woods and the rolling hills and eventually ended up in front of the old farmhouse. There were no photographers here. No paparazzi waiting to sell every sighting to the tabloids. Catriona and Ben guarded their privacy. And their children got to grow up with two parents who not only doted on them but who, better still, also cared for each other.

It was nothing short of revolutionary, given how Catriona and Lachlan had grown up.

And in case he'd had any doubts about that, he saw them both come out together from Ben's barn-turned-office, holding hands as they came to see who'd pulled in.

He'd never seen his parents touch, Lachlan realized. Not casually. They'd either performed affection in public or beat on each other in private, but there had never been what he saw between his sister and her husband. *Intimacy,* he thought. Two bodies that knew each other so well, two hands clasped together because clearly that was their default position.

How had he not understood what this was? Or that he'd longed for it all this time?

"Are you all right?" Catriona asked sharply, scanning his face as she drew closer. "You look…"

"A little edgy," Ben supplied.

"I was in the neighborhood," Lachlan said, even though his grin felt forced.

"We don't have a neighborhood," Catriona retorted. "Deliberately."

Ben looked back and forth between them, then smiled at his wife. A thousand messages passed between them in another display of intimacy that really, Lachlan thought, he ought to celebrate. Given it was something neither he nor Catriona had ever witnessed in their youth.

"I think I'll leave you to it," his brother-in-law murmured, then headed back toward his office.

Catriona slid her arm through Lachlan's. Then she steered him away from the barn and the house, toward a well-worn trail toward the woods that Lachlan had taken with her before.

"Why don't you walk with me," she murmured.

This was obviously what he'd wanted or he wouldn't have come here.

And for a long while, they simply followed the trail. The path meandered in and out of the woods, gradually making its way up the side of the nearest hill. But it wasn't until they stopped at the top, with a view that made it seem as if they were the only people left on the planet, that Catriona settled herself on a big rock that might as well have been a sofa. And turned her sharp blue gaze on her brother.

"Let me guess," she said. "Bristol."

Lachlan blew out a breath.

"Bristol," he agreed.

He waited for Catriona to jump on that. To start lecturing him, so he could disagree. Or have something to fight about.

Turned out, he really wanted a fight.

But Catriona was a canny one who knew him far too well, and so all she did was wait.

"Where are the kids?" Lachlan asked.

Obviously stalling.

Catriona looked amused. "They're all at summer camp, hallelujah. Is that what you drove up here to ask me?"

It wasn't as hot this far north as it had been down in New York City, which was a good thing. It stripped away *one* of the things gnawing at him. Lachlan shoved his hands into his jean pockets and was glad he was wearing a T-shirt. That he wasn't in his usual work clothes.

But as he glared out at all those rolling Vermont hills, he couldn't help feeling that the only thing he'd accomplished yesterday, standing up on his rooftop in the rain like a lunatic, was bringing the storm into him.

He didn't feel washed clean. He didn't feel made new.

He felt sullen and low, like a brooding summer sky, when all there was before him was blue skies and sweet sunshine.

"Tell me how you do it," he muttered, though the words felt bitter on his lips.

Or not bitter, maybe. It was possible he interpreted them as bitter because they were so unfamiliar. So dangerous.

Because he'd decided, long ago, what was and wasn't possible.

But long ago, he hadn't known Bristol. And he hadn't imagined how different the world could look when someone actually got inside the way she had.

He would have said it was impossible.

He'd been certain.

"It's simple," Catriona said softly, not pretending that she didn't know what he meant. "All you have to do is decide that it's worth the risk to make yourself vulnerable. Then do it. Especially when it feels impossible."

"As easy as that, then," Lachlan scoffed.

His sister smiled. "I said it was simple. I didn't say it was easy."

Lachlan shook his head. "Maybe you and Ben have it figured out in ways that wouldn't work for anyone else. Nice and calm, no bumps in the road. Easy."

Catriona cackled. "I can't wait to tell him you said that. You've never seen us fight."

He turned, scanning her face. Then he frowned. "You fight?"

"Of course we fight, idiot. What do you think? We're real people, Lachlan. One time, and not as long ago as you might think, I was so mad at him I threw a coffee maker at his head."

She nodded when all he did was stare at her, confirming that he'd heard her correctly.

"Oh, yes. I'm sorry to inform you that you're not the only Drummond around. I have a nasty temper and, as I think you know, I never learned how to channel it appropriately. That's been a pretty steep learning curve and sometimes I revert to type."

He couldn't take that on board. Catriona had always been so solid, so stalwart when everything else around them was noise and fury.

"But you…"

"Here's the thing, Lachlan." And his sister's gaze was steady. Direct. "You've spent all these years doing your best not to end up like Dad. Because you're so sure you know what happened on that plane and you've made it your mission to make your life a monument to being anything at all but that."

"We both know what happened on that plane."

"But what you're forgetting is that Dad didn't have that relationship by himself."

Something in Lachlan stilled.

Catriona kept going, even though Lachlan was

pretty sure she knew that her words had clobbered him. "If he crashed that plane deliberately—"

"He did."

Catriona nodded, slowly. "I agree. But then you know that Mom goaded him into it. You know she picked and prodded and laughed all the way down. That's who they were, Lachlan."

Lachlan shook his head, reeling. That storm he'd taken into himself was wrecking him. Howling, raging—but his sister still wasn't done.

"Their relationship took both of them." Her gaze was intent on his, a piercing blue that rivaled the bright summer all around them. "I want you to take that on board, for once. They were both toxic. And they were both responsible."

But all he could do was shake his head. "You know Dad…"

Catriona waited as his words trailed off.

"Alone, neither one of them could have done so much damage." She held up the index finger of each of her hands, then moved them both together to make one. "Together they might as well have been napalm. They made their own tragedy. Deep down, I know you know this."

Maybe he did. Maybe it was easier to blame his father.

Because maybe it was easier to have someone to blame.

"If I blame him, it's better," he managed to get out. "Because…"

"Because if there's a villain, then they didn't race to their inevitable conclusion without a single thought for the kids they were leaving behind," Catriona finished for him. "I've thought all this myself. But they did."

Something in him shifted, big and hard like the huge boulder his sister was sitting on, surprisingly easy after all these years. As if it had been waiting all along for him to get here.

To understand that he'd wanted the anger. The fury.

He'd found it clarifying.

Because there was nothing on the other side of it but grief.

Even all these years later.

"They did," he agreed, his voice rough. "They really did."

"As for you and me? It's easy." Catriona separated her fingers. "Don't pick an atom bomb, Lachlan. Don't be an atom bomb. And you'll be fine."

"I thought that's what I was doing. What I've *been* doing. You like to call the precautions I take *squalid.*"

"Please." His sister scoffed. "You've been hiding. And how will you ever know who you really are or what you're capable of if you don't stop hiding?"

Lachlan hated that darkness in him. He hated what it told him, what truths it laid bare. "I already know what I'm capable of—what I could be capable of. We've seen it play out right in front of us."

Catriona only shook her head, as if he made her sad. "If you only let fear talk, baby brother, fear is all you'll ever hear. Soon enough, it's all you'll have. And at that point, you might as well have gone down with them."

"Jesus Christ, Catriona."

But all his older sister did was smile at him then, as if all this was worth it. As if it was heading somewhere.

"I have a better idea, Lachlan," she said softly. "Fear has taken up enough of your time. Try love."

CHAPTER NINE

BRISTOL HAD MADE it her official policy over the years to return to her hometown in Ohio as seldom as possible.

She and Indy made an appearance over the holidays, of course, when both of their schedules—meaning, Bristol's academic schedule and Indy's utter lack of any schedule at all—allowed them to spend at least a week in their childhood home. The week was the baseline. Sometimes their mother got them to stay longer, but the week was non-negotiable.

Bristol had always considered a week in frigid Amish country more than enough time back home.

So she couldn't really understand why, when she woke up that first morning back in her Murphy bed in Brooklyn, she was seized with the urge—or, really, the sudden and all-encompassing need—to go home.

Maybe it was because it was the first feeling

she'd had in a long while that she didn't have to shove down and hide. No serene smile was necessary, there in her bed, staring up at the ceiling with its leftover telltale signs of water damage from years and tenants past. Whatever the reason, Bristol embraced it.

She flew back into Cincinnati, wedged into a middle seat at the very back of the overcrowded commercial flight. It felt a whole lot like penance after the way she'd been traveling lately. No leather seats and gilded edges in the dregs of economy. She was lucky to get a minuscule bag of stale pretzels and her elbows ached after a quiet, vicious fight with her neighbor over the armrest.

At least I won, she thought darkly.

And chose not to think about why that felt like a far larger victory than it was.

She rented a car at the airport once she landed, put on some music, and then drove out into the countryside on roads she would have said she hardly remembered.

But she didn't have to look at a map. The southwestern Ohio landscape she remembered so well rolled out before her once she headed east out of Cincinnati. Green hills undulated in all directions from roads that gave her endless views of tidy farmhouses, red barns, and Amish buggies.

Maybe it was simply because her whole summer so far had been spent in cities. With the exception of her time on Lachlan's private island, it had all been skyscrapers, the crowded electric beat of Hong Kong, the proud stone chic of Paris. After all her years in New York, Bristol had come to think of herself as a city person. She would have said she longed for the concrete canyons, the snarl of traffic, the exhilaration that was always an undercurrent in big, sprawling cities.

But for some reason, the sunshine drenching all the green hills in gold seemed to soothe her today.

She didn't need a map to find her way to the small town she'd always stoutly hated when forced to live there. But when she arrived, she forced herself to slow down, look around, and ask herself why.

Why are you so driven? Lachlan had asked.

Bristol had thought she knew the answer, but it was impossible not to think that there was a clue here. In this place that had made her who she was, whether she liked to admit that or not. Much as she liked to pretend she'd sprung forth, fully formed at eighteen when she'd relocated to New York, it wasn't true.

She'd had to decide to leave this quiet little town, then make it happen. She'd had to commit to hard work to leave it in the way she wanted. And while she couldn't remember what had started those particular dominoes toppling, there was no getting around the fact the push had come from right here in Ohio. New York was the result, not the impetus.

And as she drove into town, Bristol found she couldn't quite remember why she hated this place so much.

She also couldn't remember the last time she'd been home in the summertime. All the green, the bright and happy flowers, the sunshine. She rolled down her windows and breathed in deep as the afternoon heat washed over her. She heard cicadas and crickets, lawnmowers and birds. It was so different from the intense chill of her Decembers here, all barren trees and stark storefronts. There was a lushness here today. A deep sweetness.

And to her astonishment, Bristol found herself feeling something like…nostalgic.

Her childhood home looked just as she remembered it, tucked away at the end of a dead-end street on the far side of town. As she drove toward it, she realized, with a little jolt that felt like recognition, that here on a bright July afternoon the house she'd grown up in looked the way she remembered it from her childhood.

Instead of the picture she'd superimposed over it since. The dreary, high snowbanks and barren trees like desolate exclamation points, marking the life she didn't want.

Today she drove more slowly and found that she remembered every inch of this quiet road. She'd learned to ride a bike right here. She and Indy had played elaborate games of pretend and battle in and out of the trees that lined the way. Her parents' house stood as it always had at the end, the cheerful blue shutters against the clapboard white outside, the wide front porch festooned with her mother's latest planting experiments.

Bristol pulled up out front and got out, breathing in deep. She walked toward the front door, marveling at all the summer sounds around her. At the scent of her mother's flowers, which she'd somehow forgotten bloomed so riotously this time of year, making not just the porch but the whole front lawn a pageant of bright colors.

It made her wonder if this was why she had amnesia every year and imagined that she could grow things when she couldn't.

She wasn't at all surprised when the front screen was thrown open wide, and then her mother was there.

In all her state.

"Bristol! Is it really you? Or am I having a stroke?"

"Well, I really hope you're not having a stroke, Mom," Bristol said, grinning despite herself. "That would be very upsetting."

Margie March was a literal ball of energy. She was round and bouncy and in all her days, Bristol had never met a single soul who didn't adore her.

As a sulky preteen, Bristol had found that annoying. As she'd gotten older, however, she'd come to depend on her mother's ability to light up every room she entered. Even on a summer afternoon, her smile was brighter.

At Christmastime, Margie transformed herself into Santa's most dedicated elf—the day after Thanksgiving. Literally every moment of the time Bristol and Indy spent here each year was crammed full of what Margie considered unmissable holiday activities.

To be clear, Margie considered all holiday activities unmissable.

But the fact that it wasn't the holidays today didn't slow Margie down any. She charged down the steps, swooping Bristol into a huge hug and enveloping her the way only she could. And would, Bristol knew, hold her until she was satisfied that her child was in one piece.

And not just in one piece, but a piece she approved of.

"I know it's the fashion in *New York City*, but you and your sister are far too skinny," she was already declaring, as if the red oaks were conferring with her. "At least you're not always on this or that bizarre diet the way Indy always is."

"Mom. You know she just makes up random diets to drive you crazy. I've never seen her actually *go* on one."

But there was no getting a word in edgewise. Not at first. When the hug ended, Margie was marching her up the steps, then bustling her inside, depositing her in the very same place she'd always sat at the kitchen table.

"I know what will make you feel better," Margie said then.

"I feel fine."

Margie didn't appear to hear that. She busied herself cutting Bristol a huge helping of the berry crumble she'd clearly made earlier today and fixing one for herself, too. With huge dollops of homemade whipped cream, because ice cream was saved for the evening.

Bristol had missed that, too. Crumbles and handpicked berries and Margie's belief that dessert was neither a sin nor an indulgence, but good, solid, Midwest medicine.

"Now," she said after Bristol had taken her first big bite and drifted off into a cinnamon-sugar-berry coma. Of sheer delight. "Tell me what the matter is."

Bristol pulled herself back from the bliss of her mother's crumble with great reluctance. "What makes you think there's something wrong?"

Margie laughed. "I may be a simple woman, Bristol, but I know my own child. It would have to be the end of the world for you to come home of your own volition. So. Tell me what world ended."

"You make it sound like I hate it here," Bristol said, frowning. When she would have proclaimed that she did, in fact, hate Ohio and all its works a mere twenty-four hours ago. Even twelve hours ago. "Or that I hate you. When really, it's just that—"

"Bristol." And would her name in that tone ever *not* make her shut her mouth? And sit up a little straighter? She hoped not. Margie was eyeing her with that particular *Mom* glint in her gaze. "It's not your job to make me feel secure. I've got that covered, thank you. I know who I am. But I also know who you are. And I would love nothing more than to feed you crumble and fatten you up until the cows come home, but since the day you left for college you've never turned up on the front porch out of the blue. As much as I love seeing you, we both know you would never decide to come here on the spur of a moment without a reason."

And to her great astonishment, Bristol felt that hollow cache inside her, the one she'd thought she had such a great handle on, begin to swell. It grew bigger and bigger, and more precarious as it grew, until she thought, *oh no*—

But then there was nothing to be done about it. It was happening. She broke down, right there at her mother's table, and sobbed.

For a long, long time.

Until even the crumble tasted a bit soggy when she finally ate her share.

She and her mother moved out to the backyard that rambled this way and that until it ended up in the woods. They settled down in the shade of the biggest, most majestic of the old oak trees where, Bristol could remember so clearly now, she'd spent many a long, lazy summer's day peering up at the branches thick with leaves and had tried to imagine who she would be when she grew up.

Was that where it had started?

What made you how you are? Lachlan had asked.

"I guess you probably know that I've been… dating someone," Bristol said awkwardly.

Eventually.

"No, honey," Margie murmured, her gaze up in the branches, too. "Living in Ohio is actually a kind of fugue state in which tabloids don't exist and no one ever calls to say they've seen my daughter plastered all over them."

"Ouch."

Margie only smiled serenely. Until that moment, Bristol hadn't realized where she'd gotten her version of that same smile.

It was amazing the things a person didn't see because they'd decided not to look.

Ouch, she thought again as that landed.

"I guess the point, the real truth behind all the

extraneous noise, is that I don't know what I'm doing with my life," Bristol admitted.

And it hurt, but she didn't take her words back.

"The Grand Tour, from what we can tell from here. All over Europe like the fancy ladies did it back in the day." Margie's smile grew less serene and much warmer. "Your father and I've been tracking it on a map every time you turn up in a new city."

Bristol wiped at her face. She blew out a shaky breath. Then she kicked her shoes off so she could press her toes down into the dirt between the thick roots that served as the sides of her chair.

"Everything used to be so clear to me," she confessed. "I knew, always, that I wanted to get out of this town. That Ohio wasn't good enough, that the Midwest was too confining, and for some reason I decided my ticket out had to be academics. Once I decided that I was going to be an academic star, that was all I thought about. Because you can always study more, so anything you dedicate yourself to is within reach. If you want it enough. So that's what I did. Undergraduate degree. Master's degree. Doctorate. That was the path I was on and I charged straight down it."

She was staring at her toes, pressed into the dirt the way she'd liked to do when she was little. Except her toes were pedicured now, because that was one of the parts of her *maintenance responsibilities* that she actually happily had performed regularly. Because there was something about chipped nail polish that made her feel anything but pretty. A glance at her mother's toes, the same unchipped, glossy, cherry red they always were, suggested where she might have gotten that.

"I don't know why it never occurred to me that I needed to figure out what to do after I was done with all that charging around," she said.

Margie made a supportive sort of noise, and Bristol couldn't believe she'd forgotten how comforting it was to simply *sit* with her mother. To feel the security of her presence, solid and unmistakable at her shoulder. The quiet side of Margie, not all tinsel and cider and belting out Christmas carols into the December night.

Though, if she was honest, Bristol loved her mother as an elf, too.

"I can't even remember what made me decide that I needed to push myself academically in the first place," Bristol continued now, not sure if it was all the sobbing or the sunshine that made her feel almost drunk. Hollowed out in a new way, that might as easily turn to more sobbing—or silliness. "Do you?"

"Of course I know, honey," Margie said calmly. "School was the one thing that didn't interest your sister at all. So you claimed it as yours and dug in."

Bristol blinked at that. She tried to make what

her mother had just said make some sense, but couldn't. "What do you mean?"

"You know Indy." Margie laughed. "She used to drive you crazy. When you first moved in together your father and I joked that you'd likely kill her within a week."

"I still might kill her. That's a given."

Margie drew her knees up and laughed again. "When you were little she would always follow you around, wanting to do whatever you were doing whenever you were doing it. You hated it. Anything you tried to do—any activity, any craft, any book you wanted to read—in came Hurricane Indy to do it right along with you. She wanted you to appreciate her efforts, naturally. But you did not."

"I don't remember having any kind of sibling rivalry!" Bristol frowned, thinking back. And she wasn't sure if she was shocked or if she found it all funny. "Are you sure?"

Her mother gave her a look, then laughed. "You are a very methodical thinker, Bristol. At a certain point, it must have occurred to you that you couldn't order Indy away from whatever it was you were doing. Little sisters are notoriously terrible at taking that hint. So you picked one thing after the next until you found something she didn't want to do. School."

Bristol felt her mouth drop open. "This is very

unflattering, Mom. I was sure you were going to tell me that the entirety of southwestern Ohio was struck down in wordless awe at the force of my intellect. That they *begged me* to excel, and so I did."

"There was some awe at the force of your will, maybe." Margie considered. "And your willingness to push yourself. But your sister is the fighter. You were always quieter. When Indy would blow up, it would be a big storm, but it would blow over and all would be well. But not you. You like to hold things tight and hide them away until all the fault lines are gathered inside and you feel you have no choice but to make the earth move."

And here, under the shade of her favorite tree, Bristol didn't have to hide. She didn't have to pretend. She pressed her hand to her chest, where it hurt the most. And she finally accepted that the hollow thing she'd been pretending was nothing more than an empty space tucked away in there was her heart.

"Ouch," she said again.

"Here's what I'm sure of," her mother said, and reached over to put her hand on Bristol's leg. The way she had a million times before and would a million times again. It was like an anchor. It was a version of the roots around her, tying her to the earth, to this place even if only in her memories, to her mother and to herself. "I have never known you, Bristol Marie March, not to get exactly what you want. Once you put your mind to it, that's that."

Bristol's eyes felt wet again. "What if I don't know what I want?"

"Do you not know?" Margie's gaze was as steady as her hand. "Or are you afraid that you do know?"

And it was so like her mother not to ask directly about Lachlan, Bristol thought then. Margie had employed the same strategy when Indy and Bristol were teenagers. She always seemed to know everything already and would simply gaze at them without asking until they dissolved before her, flinging out their troubles and sins and worries with careless abandon.

"I think my...dating situation is a symptom of a larger issue," Bristol said carefully. Because yes, she'd signed agreements. But this was her mom. "And it's bright and flashy and overwhelming, yes, but it's not real. And it won't last. Sooner or later, like it or not, I'm going to have to figure out what I want to do with my life."

"Here's the thing about life," Margie said after a little pause. "You never do stop thinking that you need to figure it all out. You never arrive at an age or a moment and think, how wonderful, I'm finished now."

"I don't believe you." Bristol heard her voice

crack, but she was safely tucked away in her mother's backyard in Ohio. It felt almost revolutionary to allow herself to do nothing at all to hide it. "You and Dad seem to have your lives all figured out. You've been running that high school from the secretary's desk for as long as I can remember. And he legitimately loves being a salesman. I mean, I guess you'll both retire soon—"

"Thank you, but we are in our fifties, Bristol. Not our seventies."

Bristol grinned. "All I mean is that you're happy. You're both happy. Aren't you?"

"Yes, but you would never be happy in a life like ours," her mother said with such…casual conviction that it threw Bristol a little. Okay, more than a little. "Not the way we are. Your father and I have always been good at appreciating the things we have. And better still, we've liked that we get to sink down deep into those things, year after year. There's a pleasure in a small life."

"I don't… I mean I *want* to be the kind of person who appreciates what she has, and practices gratitude, and *sinks deep*."

"Why?" Margie's voice was placid. "You've always been ambitious. I never was. I wanted…this. What I have. The boy who gave me my first Valentine, two little girls, this pretty house in the town where we both grew up. There's nothing wrong with wanting something different. We can't all be the same."

"Sometimes I wish I was happy here," Bristol confessed. She didn't say, *in a small life*, but she suspected her mother knew she meant it. "It would have made things a whole lot easier."

"But that's not you." Margie sighed a little, but in that way she often did, as if she couldn't find the right words and was finished looking. "I don't know what you're going to choose to do with yourself, but I do know this. You will always work hard, because that's who you are. And you'll need whatever you're working at to be meaningful to you, because that's your heart."

"Really? I thought you just told me that, *actually*, my heart is an angry, bitter ember. Plus earthquakes, and oh yeah, my entire academic life was aimed at Indy all along."

"That's the New Yorker in you talking," Margie said. It wasn't exactly a compliment. "Don't forget, Bristol. I know your *real* heart."

And they sat like that for a long while, while Bristol wondered if that was why it hurt so much. That her real heart had made itself known after these months of hiding. And the years of narrowly focused obsession that had come before. Her mother had somehow managed to strip all the layers away and get to that real heart with a serving of berry crumble and a trip to the backyard.

Leaving Bristol to try to figure out what the hell she was supposed to do with it, now that she could feel it beating too intensely inside her chest.

She'd been kidding herself about that hollow space. All the times she'd assured herself that she could sort it all out come fall had been like playing pretend with her sister up and down this dead-end road. She got that now.

"And not that I pay any attention to gossip, whether it's my knitting circle or those awful newspapers in the checkout line," Margie began with studied indifference.

Bristol snorted. "A bold lie from the woman half the county calls for information, Mom. Any and all information, because you gather it all."

Margie ignored that. "But I've always felt that living in a small town gives a person all the attention anyone could ever need, since I haven't walked through a grocery store without being recognized since the day I was born." She flashed that sedate smile of hers again. "Then again, you always did have higher standards. It's part of your charm."

Bristol laughed, and couldn't believe that her mother could make that happen so easily. Without even seeming to try.

She looked up at the branches spread out above her and all the green leaves. The sunshine that filtered through and the blue sky high above, filled with summer hope.

As if fall would never come.

When Bristol knew it would.

And more, that there was no point waiting around for a change of season when she already knew that this wasn't a job she could do without losing herself. Maybe other women could—and had, as tough as that was to think about. Bristol supported anyone who could play that role and be good at it. Hell, she'd march in the street for them.

But the truth she'd been trying to push off to September was that she wasn't them.

Her heart had gone hollow and she hated it.

Bristol wanted herself back, and she didn't need her collection of degrees to know that she wasn't going to find that loving a man who could never love her in return. Who had contracts drawn up to prevent it.

No matter how many times he tried to *renegotiate*, Lachlan only saw her as a clause. A business item to be handled—or replaced.

It turned out that she found the reality of that less comforting the more intense things grew between them. Or in her, anyway. Less of a lovely, soothing tide.

More of a scary riptide, hauling her out to sea.

And leaving her there to drown.

Her mother shifted next to her, and Bristol looked over. At the face she knew better than her own and that solid hand on her leg, marked with the lines and dents and years that Bristol imagined would score her own hands one day. Holding her steady, always.

That was what Margie did.

"Lachlan isn't the guy, Mom," she said softly, and was surprised how hard it was to say out loud. When she'd known that all along. "He's only temporary."

She expected an argument from the woman who had never been averse to a little matchmaking in her day, between elderly widowed neighbors and some of the high school students who found themselves in the principal's office too often.

But all Margie did was smile.

Bristol spent the rest of her week off from all things Lachlan back home in Ohio and shocked herself by loving every moment of it. She stuffed herself with all of her mother's cooking. She went fishing with her dad in the long, slow, mellow evenings down by the river. She got her feet dirty and she jumped off the old rope swing into the pond out in the woods. She let the sun make her a little crispy, she ate entirely too much hearty food, and she reconnected to the simple joys she'd long since cast aside in her pursuit of *bigger* and *better*.

When she got back to Brooklyn, she felt as if she'd taken the first real vacation she'd had in… Well, maybe since the last summer she'd spent in Ohio before she'd gone off to college.

The flight east had been crowded and delayed thanks to thunderstorms in the Midwest. By the time she landed, Bristol was heartily sick of the jeans and T-shirt she'd worn to fly in. Not to mention, it was not exactly the best choice for traipsing all over the city.

Though it did allow her to continue to feel as incognito as she had in her parents' backyard and the woods. No one was looking for Lachlan Drummond's latest girlfriend there. Or out wandering the New York streets, disheveled and anonymous.

They were looking for the *elegant academic*, as one tabloid had called her. Not an anonymous Brooklyn-bound girl in dirty, ripped jeans and a sunburned nose.

Bristol had been half-afraid that when she made it home, New York would seem as ill-fitting as everything else did these days. But instead, she felt that same rush of exhilaration she had when she'd first come here. The energy of the city, chaos and noise and soaring heights. The rush of it, the mix of drama and practicality on every street corner, in every outfit the locals wore to walk the streets, live in them, and flourish here.

And she could admit that she felt a rush of relief at that. She'd been unexpectedly moved to rediscover the place she came from—but that didn't mean she wanted to pack up and go live there.

You've always been ambitious, her mother had said.

And even on its worst and hardest day, New York City felt like an ambition realized.

Bristol rounded the corner of her block, vaguely wondering how it was that she could feel so content when she'd solved precisely nothing. But maybe that was what she'd learned. Life didn't need to be solved. All she had to do was live it.

It's time to live, *not hide,* she told herself. *At last.*

And maybe it was inevitable, then, that when she made it to the door of her walkup, she heard a car door open behind her, then slam shut. Something about the sound made her turn, and like magic, he was there.

As if she'd conjured him up, the way she had night after night tucked up in her childhood bedroom in her parents' house.

But this time, he was real.

Lachlan Drummond. The man she knew so well and didn't know at all.

And if she wasn't mistaken, he was in a temper.

She was surprised to find her own—so long shoved aside and buried beneath research or *sedate smiles*—surge to life.

"Lachlan." She ordered herself to hold on to the mellow, happy feeling that a little taste of her long-forgotten childhood summers had brought out in her. Not to jump straight into the conclusions she'd reached after her week at her parents' house. A week of remembering who she'd been long before she'd decided to become *Dr. March*. A week of reconnecting with the real Bristol, not the persona she'd apparently created to spite Indy. A week where she'd been a whole lot more than this man's *clause*. "I wasn't expecting to see you until tomorrow."

Tomorrow, when she'd intended to put an end to this.

Before it swallowed her whole.

Lachlan took the distance between his car, parked illegally at the curb, and her front door like a challenge, moving fast and low.

And the look in his blue eyes made her breath catch.

The way it always did, but this was worse. This was something much different than *drowning*.

"Where the hell have you been?" he demanded.

CHAPTER TEN

IT HAD BEEN a very long week.

Lachlan had been forced to face some things about himself that he couldn't say he liked. He was not accustomed to being kept waiting. He had driven down from Vermont the following day in a self-congratulatory haze of purpose and determination, at last, and had gone straight to Bristol's apartment to tell her all about it.

But she was nowhere to be found.

He'd tried both of the phone numbers he had for her, repeatedly, but they always went straight to voice mail. Until he was forced to conclude that she'd actually...switched her phone off. Both her phones. And unless she had hunkered down and never turned on a light that night he'd come back from Vermont, she was not holed up in that apartment of hers.

That was when he came to the unpleasant realization that for all the details he knew about her, all the facts laid out in a thousand files and all the time they'd spent together naked or at public events, it was possible he didn't really know *her* at all. Sex was telling. It was a tool—but it wasn't a personality. And cold, hard facts weren't alive and contradictory and capable of making unpredictable decisions.

Facts told him only that. Facts.

They didn't let him predict what Bristol might do when she wasn't following his schedule.

When she wasn't in the box he'd made her inhabit.

And once that got into him it rubbed viciously, like sand in his shoe, until he could think of nothing else.

Bristol was the only one of the women he'd ever dated in his own particular fashion who he'd never suspected of acting like someone she wasn't. And yet it had never occurred to him that the fact she wasn't acting like the rest had...didn't mean he knew any more than what she'd shown him.

And he had himself to blame for that, not her.

Lachlan was the one who'd set up this system, never imagining that he would also be the one to tear it down because it didn't work any longer. He understood he had no one to blame but himself— but he needed her to come home so he could burn that contract she'd signed and start over.

He'd had to talk himself down from engaging

in any truly desperate behavior—like staking out her apartment. The only reason he'd come here tonight was because this was the last day of her week's break. And he'd rationalized that, having allowed her the privacy he could grudgingly accept she was entitled to this whole long week, it made sense to come over and make sure she actually planned to return to the job.

So he could fire her and offer her something else entirely.

Lachlan was trying his best to ignore the voice inside him that told him it was all too possible that Bristol was done with him, little as he wanted to accept that. Given that she had also distinguished herself by being the only woman who had ever *wanted* the break he insisted upon.

He was inside out.

Lachlan had been contemplating the depths to which he'd fallen and what that made him when he'd seen her swing around the corner. Charging down the street as if she was anyone, as anonymous as anyone else in New York.

As if she'd never been his.

It...rankled.

"Where have I been?" she asked. And she laughed. At him, he was fairly sure, but he couldn't care about that. Not when she was *laughing* again. Because he could lose himself in Bristol's laughter. "On a vacation. You know this."

"Where?"

He recognized that her whole face had been open in a way it normally wasn't when it changed. When she disappeared, right in front of him.

"I don't remember agreeing to share my private life with you, Lachlan," she said, her voice cool and her eyes distant. That distance he couldn't stand. "My body, sure. But my private life was never part of the deal."

"Fuck the deal," he growled.

And for a moment, all she did was study him. But not the way he had grown accustomed to her doing. This reminded him, again, of the woman who had turned up to dinner with him that first night. The woman who'd walked out of his panel. The woman who wasn't convinced by him or this process or anything else.

The woman who wasn't his in any conceivable way.

"Is this really a conversation you want to have on my doorstep?" she asked in that cool tone that he'd used to like, surely. It had made her seem so... containable. Now he wanted to blow it up. "Were you lurking in your car, waiting for a confrontation? Because as far as I'm aware, I'm not required to deal with you until tomorrow."

"Is that all this is to you?" he demanded, feeling unhinged. Off-balance and completely outside himself. "A requirement?"

"Yes," she said, but her voice was too matter-of-fact. Her eyes too dark. "As laid out in the documents you insisted we sign."

"Bristol," he said, trying to pull himself back together. Trying to remember that he wasn't his father, just as Catriona had said. But that didn't mean he couldn't feel. It wasn't the feeling that was the issue, it was the execution. "Don't you understand? This isn't about contracts. I think…"

Her face was so perfect it made his heart skip a beat. Wherever she'd been, she'd spent time in the sun and it made her eyes seem brighter. Her cheeks were rosy and she'd burned her nose. Her dark hair looked careless, tossed back in a messy bun.

She wasn't dressed to impress a soul and he had never seen anything more beautiful.

He doubted it could exist.

"I don't *think*," he corrected himself before she could say anything. Because he needed to say the words that had been charging through him this whole week. He needed her to hear them. "I know."

"Lachlan," she began, her tone far too measured.

And he had to get it out. He had to *say* it. "I'm in love with you."

For a moment then, he felt suspended in thin air. New York City was on one side, and perfect, beautiful Bristol was on the other, and the wire that stretched out between the two was hope. A wild, heart-pounding hope.

But when she smiled, it was sad. She reached over and brushed her fingers over his jaw, and he had the terrible, sickening feeling that what he saw in her eyes then was pity.

"Oh, Lachlan," she said softly. "No. You're not."

And that sounded like finality.

All he could do was stare.

Bristol sighed, then fumbled in the bag over her shoulder, eventually pulling out her keys.

"You'd better come in, I guess," she said as she shoved the door open with her shoulder, which was not exactly the profession of joy and delight he'd imagined repeatedly over the course of this long week without her.

He followed her as she led him up three sets of stairs to that minuscule apartment he remembered too well. It had gotten no bigger since he'd last seen it.

Inside, she flicked on the lights. She tossed her bag on the counter that separated the tiny kitchen from the tiny living room, kicked off her shoes, and only then turned to face him. With her arms crossed and a look on her face that did not make that wire of hope inside him gleam.

Lachlan stayed where he was, with his back almost against the door, because he was entirely too tense. And he thought that if he moved any closer to her, he'd take it upon himself to remind her just why it was they were perfect for each other.

Over and over again.

Which he was guessing she would not welcome in her current mood.

"You look murderous," she pointed out. "Is that how this is going to go?"

"I'm not my parents," he managed to bite out.

She had the grace to look shamed by that. "That's not what I meant. I'm sorry."

But that didn't make it any better. "You can't really believe that I go around telling people I love them. Maybe you do believe that, but I don't. I've never said that to a woman before in my life."

Her smile was almost…bland, and he knew that meant she was getting ready to strike. "I understand that when you say things like that, Lachlan, it's meant as a very great compliment. And I appreciate that, I do. But I'm not particularly interested in winning the grand prize here."

Somehow, as he'd driven back down from Vermont with his sister's words in his head, and spent this whole week imagining how this would go, it had never been…this.

"Bristol—"

"You don't love me," she said, very distinctly, and there was nothing *bland* about her now. "You can't. We've never really been together, have we? You *hired* me and it's not the same thing. Which you should know, because that's why you do it."

"That might be how it started, but it's not where we are now."

"Maybe it's not where you are now." She shook her head. "But then, you're not the one who's had a role to play this whole time."

He didn't like that. Especially when he'd been so sure she was the one who hadn't been acting at all. He ran a hand over his face and tried to get his bearings. "Where were you this past week?"

Her eyes narrowed. "In Ohio. With my parents, not that it's any of your business. Note that I'm not asking what you were up to."

"You could. I went up to my sister's place in Vermont, then came back to the city. To wait for you."

"I didn't ask, Lachlan." And he could hear the edge in her voice. The way it raked over him. "Because that exceeds the limits of our arrangement, remember? It's not supposed to be *personal*."

"Then let's change it."

"You're proving my point."

It would take him two steps, maybe three, to cross the room and get his hands on her, but he didn't do it. Because her fists were on her hips, her eyes were blazing, and even though he had the presence of mind to understand that this was not going well for him, he couldn't help but find this version of Bristol even more beautiful. He'd never seen it before.

And as he thought that, he realized he'd never heard her voice raised before, either. Surely he shouldn't find that...exhilarating.

Confusing, maybe, but he couldn't deny that underneath the uncertainty there was nothing but adrenaline.

And that same need that had gripped him from the first moment he'd seen her on that video.

"I don't understand your point," he said when he was sure he could sound far more calm and rational than he felt. "Why is it so impossible that I might have fallen in love with you? I liked you from the start. It's why I—"

"Hired me? Yes, I know." She looked around the small space as if she was trying to conjure up an answer from the walls. "And I took your offer because I had no idea what else to do with myself."

He tamped down on his own temper. "I'm not often a last resort. I'll admit, I almost enjoy the novelty."

"I'm an academic, not an escort," Bristol shot back at him. "Though I have a lot more respect for escorts than I did before. I don't know how they do it because I'm not built for it."

"The flattery might kill me."

"Don't get me wrong. There's nothing wrong with what you do or the women you do it with. I'm not sorry I tried it." She blew out a breath. "But it's obviously not where my talents lie."

"Then don't do it anymore," Lachlan gritted out. "This is a perfect opportunity to shift into something else."

"You mean renegotiate?" But she was shaking her head as she asked that question, which he supposed was an answer. If not the one he wanted. "I mean, congratulations, Lachlan. You're not bored for once in one of these relationships. The relationships you make sure can only and ever be boring, according to your very strict rules."

"They were boring because they weren't you."

Again, she shook her head, something a little too angry to be pity on her face. But it was close enough to sting.

"If it wasn't me, it would eventually be someone else," Bristol said. Dismissively. "Because you're not actually in love. How could you be? You make all the rules. You have staff to make sure there's always distance between you and the woman currently playing the part of your girlfriend. All the conversations we have are about you. All the sex we have is about you."

That blow landed. Hard.

"You might not love me back, Bristol," he gritted out. "But don't stand here in front of me and pretend you haven't enjoyed every single second we've spent naked together. Because I know better."

"And you think that's all there is, don't you?"

She let out a sound that might have been a laugh, but not a happy one. "Naked feels a lot like vulnerability, Lachlan. But it's not. Not if sex is the only place you show it."

He didn't like that, but he couldn't let himself get caught up in how much he didn't like it. Not when there was so much at stake.

"Tell me what you want."

She laughed again, and it sounded even less happy than before. "I have spent so much time trying to answer that question. But it turns out it was right in front of me all the time. I want everything."

"You're in luck, then. Because I can give it to you."

"Can you?" He saw that she was trembling, slightly, and wanted to go to her—but the fierce look on her face stopped him. "This isn't a transaction, I'm afraid. I don't want to be in a box. I don't want contracts and rules. I want to be a whole person, and we both know that's not something you value."

Lachlan felt winded. "Bristol—"

"I quit, Lachlan," she hurled at him. "Effective immediately."

It was meant as a blow, he could see that. And it landed.

But he could take a hit.

He stayed where he was, studying her. He

watched as her belligerent chin lowered. As the fists on her hips relaxed.

"You're looking at me like you didn't hear me," she said, and she sounded…less sure, suddenly.

Lachlan didn't want her less sure of herself. He wanted her to be every part of herself, whatever that was.

She'd said she wanted everything. Well, so did he.

"I accept your resignation," he said.

Bristol blinked. Then cleared her throat. "Well. Okay. Good."

"I'll have my attorneys initiate the termination protocol." Lachlan pulled his phone out of his pocket and sent a series of texts. He waited a moment for a response, then nodded. "Our contracted relationship is over."

He could see the way she swallowed. Hard.

"All right. That's done, then." She flushed. "I'll confess I don't know the appropriate thing to say when ending something like this. Uh…thanks?"

Lachlan moved then. He crossed the room and stood before her. And waited.

Slowly, she looked up at him. Slower still, her eyes dilated, telling him that whatever her reasons were for wanting to end things with him, it wasn't because the greedy longing between them was gone.

She swayed slightly toward him, because their

bodies were that attuned to each other now, but caught herself.

"Is this…" Bristol straightened her shoulders. "Are you saying goodbye?"

Lachlan reached down and took her hands in his. She let him, and when he laced their fingers together, a small sound shuddered out of her.

He thought of his sister and Ben holding hands in all that summer light. He thought about intimacy and how he'd always assumed that any hint of it was a slippery slide to a plane plummeting from the sky.

But Bristol was holding on to him. Her pretty face was tipped up toward his and there was no trace of distance.

And he wanted to tell her all of this. He wanted to tell her what he'd learned and what she meant to him. He wanted her to know all the ways he needed her in his life. He wanted and wanted, but as she'd said already, all they'd talked about so far was him.

"Do you have a favorite restaurant in this neighborhood?" he asked.

She blinked, and he watched that brain of hers start working. "There's a Vietnamese place on the next block that's amazing. Why? Did making declarations and dissolving contracts work up an appetite?"

He decided not to tell her, then, that he was

going to spend the rest of his life hungry and only she was ever going to make a dent in it.

If he was lucky.

And Lachlan was a lot of things, but luck had never played a part before.

He was back on that high wire, holding on to hope.

Try love, Catriona had advised him.

It was the one thing even Lachlan Drummond couldn't command.

"Dr. Bristol March," he said, very carefully and deliberately, his eyes on hers like his life depended on her answer. Because it did. "Will you go on a date with me? I hear there's a great Vietnamese place nearby."

CHAPTER ELEVEN

Bristol had no intention of going out to dinner with Lachlan that night. She didn't want to *play games* with him.

And yet after saying no, with a scowl on her face while her heart galloped too wildly in her chest, she found the look on his face unbearable.

"You can call me tomorrow," she found herself saying, like a moth to the flame. "And you can ask me if I'm free next weekend. And maybe not assume that I can drop everything to please you at any instant."

He was still holding her hands and he looked down at them, his mouth curving into a smile that might almost have been bashful, had he been anyone else.

But he was Lachlan Drummond, so that curve took on a different shade altogether when she saw the look in his too-hot blue gaze.

"I can do that," he said. "But Bristol. Are you hungry?"

And that was how she found herself on her first date with Lachlan Drummond, more than two months after the first dinner they'd had in that overly precious restaurant in Manhattan. A lifetime, it seemed, since that scene in the alley and everything that came afterward.

A lifetime, maybe, but she could still remember every detail of the first time she'd tasted him.

"I'm going to call you tomorrow," he told her, almost formally, as he walked her back to the door of her apartment building. Almost formally, that was, except for the glint in his gaze that made her wet and shivery, though she would die before showing him that. "Like a gentleman."

"I may or may not take that call," she replied loftily, though what she was really doing was obsessing over whether or not he was going to kiss her. Or whether she was going to kiss him. Or if there was even going to be kissing at all after she'd quit. And he'd held her hands like that in the tiny living room that seemed to close in around him, he was so big and bright and *him*. And then he'd taken her to dinner at her favorite hole-in-the-wall place where they sat in the corner and were resolutely ignored by every other person there.

After he'd said he loved her.

More than once.

And when he didn't kiss her, or even try, Bristol couldn't decide if she was furious or grateful.

She settled on grateful sometime later that night, when midnight was a distant memory and she was once again staring at her ceiling. Lying on top of the sheets with a wet washcloth over her fan because the apartment's questionable air-conditioning was never enough in the full sweat of August.

You're lucky he didn't kiss you, she told herself sternly.

Because if Lachlan had kissed her, she really didn't know if she would have had the necessary fortitude to keep herself from kissing him back.

All the berry crumble in the world hadn't prepared her for Lachlan's...declarations.

Or the fact he apparently wanted to *date* her.

When she woke up the next morning, hot and cranky and feeling raw after a night of dreams—each and every one starring Lachlan and the many magical things that man could do with his cock—she told herself not to get her hopes up.

"You shouldn't even have hopes," she scolded herself as she made coffee. "You don't need to be a vanity project for a bored billionaire."

"But what if it's not his vanity?" Indy asked idly when she called from an undisclosed location in Europe. Bristol was too overwrought about her situation to adequately express her feelings about the term *undisclosed location.* "What if our tin-man billionaire just discovered he has a heart?"

Her own heart galloped at that. She pressed her hand to her chest and, for once, was glad her sister was across an ocean and couldn't see her do it.

"He won't," Bristol said with a brisk confidence she didn't quite feel. Or didn't want to feel. "He doesn't like not getting what he wants, that's all. Soon enough, probably before next weekend, he will grow bored and move on. He'll convene his panel and, this time, pick a more appropriately biddable woman to appear at his next function. The end."

"That's definitely his pattern," Indy agreed.

Even though she'd just said the same thing herself, Bristol found herself bristling at her sister's confirmation.

Suddenly, she could remember all the other times she'd brooded over Indy's seemingly careless comments when they were teenagers, or her tagging along to things, or her *copying* Bristol—the very worst sin of all. She found herself looking at the picture on their wall of the two of them at around eight and ten years old, giggling over something marvelous in a pile of fallen leaves beneath their favorite oak tree.

Her mother was right. She wrapped her heart in layers upon layers of armor and only grudgingly let anyone in.

Even her little sister, who adored her.

What if you controlled the earthquake for a change? she asked herself.

But Indy was still talking.

"Then again," Indy was saying, laughing softly as if she'd never been more personally delighted—which felt a lot like another indictment of Bristol's spiky, mean heart. "The whole world saw the way he was looking at you. I made sure to look at *literally every angle* in every possible tabloid, so I can confirm that the man looks fully smitten in every one of them."

Smitten, Bristol thought, and that word seemed to catch at her.

Indy sighed happily. "This might be a new era for our favorite tin man."

"Does this make me Dorothy?" Bristol asked, trying her best to sound brisk and faintly unamused and certainly not *smitten.* "Because I'm fresh out of ruby slippers."

She didn't say that she'd left all the fancy trappings of life with Lachlan behind. Dramatic shoes included. It needed to be over, she knew that, and yet she still couldn't bring herself to come out and say it. To make it real.

"And bonus," Indy said, as if she already knew. "You're already home, so no need to rely on the shoes for that."

After their call ended, Bristol couldn't get that out of her head. It was what Indy did. She seemed flighty and silly, and then she said things that should have been easily dismissed…that then lingered around instead.

You're already home, Bristol told herself. *No need to rely on the things Lachlan gave you. You're whole as you are.*

She didn't need his shoes or the wardrobe she'd been promised to do what she needed to do, which was get her life back on track. And she certainly didn't need him and his rules and his boxes.

But God help her, she missed him so much it hurt.

Lachlan called later that morning and asked Bristol out on a date, as expected.

And Bristol shocked herself when she opened her mouth to refuse, then accepted instead. Even though, when she hung up the phone, she couldn't have said why.

Why was she doing this when she already knew what would happen? How it would play out exactly as she'd told Indy it would?

In the days that followed, she tried her best not to think about Lachlan Drummond and her weakness for him. It was time to move on with her life. And while she'd felt adrift back in May, she no longer did. The kinds of meetings and conversations she'd been privy to when she was with Lachlan had given her a taste for more than the sedate academic life she'd imagined for herself.

Which was a good thing, she discovered quickly, when she reached out to some of her contacts and found almost universal disdain.

"Back from gallivanting about with Mr. Wonderful?" asked her old adviser, with a snide note in her voice that Bristol adamantly did not like. "Must be nice. And as much as we would have loved to have had you before, I can't say that the department is looking for that sort of...*notoriety*."

It turned out that none of her stuffy academic contacts was interested in her notoriety.

Bristol would have reveled in even being considered notorious in the first place, but she needed to find work. Not because she needed the money—she'd been paid exorbitantly for her service to Lachlan, after all—but because... She needed to work.

And while she hadn't understood why she was so driven, the end result was the same. She was an expert in social policy and she had every intention of using her expertise, right along with those letters she'd worked so damn hard to put behind her name.

She went on that first date with Lachlan, all on her terms and on her turf. Then it seemed she was seeing him almost every night, though she refused to think too hard about that. He was playing a game. He got to dress down like he was anyone, sneaking in and out of Brooklyn restaurants that would never make it into the pages of the tabloids. Sooner or later, she told herself, he would tire of this and go back to his penthouses and sports cars and jets.

All their dinners ended the same way. On the doorstep of her building in the hot August night, no kissing, her pussy melting and her heart beating—so hard and so long she sometimes thought it might kill her.

Maybe she only wished it would.

But a week into *dating* the man she'd already been hired to be with, she was still getting no traction whatsoever, within her academic context. So it finally occurred to her to use his.

"Do you have a problem with me reaching out to people I met only because of you?" she asked abruptly, cutting off the story he was telling her about how he was, happily and deliberately, a bad influence on Catriona's children.

They had been standing at her front door for coming up on thirty minutes, where she already knew they would stay until she tore herself away and went inside.

It took her longer and longer to do that every night.

"Not at all," he replied, so quickly that she thought he had to mean it. "Most of the people we met with would be elated to hear from you. Your résumé speaks for itself."

Bristol blinked. "How would you know what my résumé says?"

"Because I studied it," he said, grinning. "I like facts."

But she realized, as August descended into its dregs—too hot and too humid and filled with days spent in and out of interviews and nights still full of Lachlan—that it wasn't facts he was going for here.

It was details.

Every last, possible detail.

He asked her all the questions he hadn't before. He asked about her childhood in Ohio, and she found she had a lot more to say on the topic of where she'd grown up than she would have before. He asked about her sister. About every phase of her life, leading her straight on to the doctorate that had, somehow, led her to him.

"Does this go both ways?" she asked one night as they walked back from a terrible bar where they'd had to shout to be heard yet had still missed most of the conversation, there in the exhilarating press of the deliberate grimness. She'd promised him a real dive and had delivered, even though it might have deafened them both. "Do I get to ask you questions about your real life?"

"You, Bristol," Lachlan said, his gaze very blue in the dark, "can ask me anything you like."

She told herself that hadn't been a kind of vow, no matter what it sounded like.

And so they told each other stories as August fell inexorably toward September. First it felt like they were filling in the gaps. But then, as Bristol kept going on another date and another date after that, it became something else.

Less filling in gaps, more talking about who they really were. What they thought and felt. What her mother had told her in Ohio. What his sister had told him in Vermont.

But it wasn't all old paths and new beginnings. Bristol learned that the best-dressed man in New York had always hated dressing up for formal events. If it was up to him, he told her, he'd spend his life in jeans and a T-shirt far away from the public eye.

"Then why do it?" she asked, leaning in close over a rickety little table in the Vietnamese place. They kept coming back. "You can do whatever you want, can't you? I thought that was the entire point of being you."

"In order to get the kind of backing I want for my various projects, I have to know how to play the game," he replied. He shrugged. "I don't mind it as much anymore."

"But surely—"

"And besides," he said, his expression intent, "it's my responsibility to not be my father. I can't do exactly as I please. I have an obligation to use the money he made and squandered for good. If I have to wear a suit to do it, that feels like a small price to pay."

Bristol reached across the table and took his strong hands in hers. She held his gaze.

"You could never be your father. You never, ever will be."

And it was tempting to say she would be right there to make sure of it, no atom bombs in the vicinity, but she swallowed it back.

She took him to a baseball game. She took him to a crowded, raucous movie theater to see the summer blockbuster hit and to enjoy all the patrons on their phones, people talking back at the screen, and an impromptu popcorn fight.

"That was an experience," Lachlan said when they left, slinging an arm over her shoulders as they walked out into the warm, dense streets. "But I'm not sure I could tell you what that movie was about."

"The point of actually going to a movie theater to see a movie is the communal aspect," Bristol informed him. "It's not to enjoy the film so much as the crowd."

"Noted."

"Just think," she teased him, "we'll make a New Yorker out of you yet."

One night they were stuck on the subway somewhere beneath the East River. The Brooklyn-bound train was packed and quiet enough as everyone simply waited to move again. They were standing in the middle of the car and she found herself smiling up at him, up beneath the baseball hat he wore crammed down on his head to hide his face.

He was Lachlan Drummond and he could have flown them to the Maldives tonight if she'd asked but was instead on a stopped subway car like anyone else. Because she'd wanted him to do this. Whatever she asked, he did.

Like they'd flipped their entire relationship upside down.

Her stomach flipped a few times as the truth of that settled in.

But Bristol didn't want that truth. She pushed up on her toes, overwhelmed with the night they'd spent at a piano bar in the West Village, surrounded then and now by people who didn't know who he was, and kissed him.

It had been three weeks. Three long, torturous weeks, and she didn't understand how she'd done it. How she kept herself from tasting him the way she wanted to—so badly she woke up in her hot bedroom already halfway to coming, only to find herself alone.

Lachlan's hand that wasn't gripping the subway pole moved to her face as he took control of the kiss, heat and light and that same wild punch jolting between them and making her feel whole again.

How had she not understood? Kissing him—touching him—made her feel whole.

Because when the train rocked to life again, she pulled back and held on to him instead of the subway, and didn't have to pretend not to feel anything. Her own tumultuous longing or that intent look all over his face.

She just gazed up at him, mute and overwhelmed, and was nothing at all but herself.

And she could feel them both shatter. And shudder.

As if they were the same.

"It was always like this," she whispered as the conductor said something unintelligible over the loudspeaker. "But I don't want to hide it any longer."

"I don't want you to."

This time, when they got back to her apartment, she brought him inside instead of leaving him outside where a storm threatened. They climbed the stairs together and she found herself almost giddy with the notion that she was bringing Lachlan home the way she might have any other date.

When he was anything but that.

Inside, she launched herself at him and he caught her, and then they exploded, together.

First he held her against him, high in the air, taking her mouth with his while their hands smoothed and tangled and made everything worse. Or better.

Then they moved to the small couch, only to end up on the floor, everything fierce and hot, because he was far too tall for the couch.

They rolled this way and that, a pageant of hands reaching and bodies yearning.

She sat astride him, pressing herself against the hard ridge of his cock, teasing them both like they were in high school.

It was ridiculous how hot it was to roll around fully clothed with a man she had been naked with too many times to count.

But then she'd had enough. She wanted everything.

And she was astonished when Lachlan held her away from him when Bristol reached for the zipper of his jeans.

"I can't believe I'm going to say this," he said, his eyes that brilliant blue she normally saw only when he was driving deep inside her, fucking her into oblivion.

Her clit ached, but he didn't let her ease that ache against his.

"I really can't believe I'm going to say this," he muttered. "But we can't have sex."

CHAPTER TWELVE

IF HE'D ANNOUNCED he was taking holy orders, Bristol could not have been more stunned.

"What? Why not?"

Lachlan rolled with her, depositing her on her back beneath him, and she thought for a moment that it was a joke. That he would laugh and give her what she wanted, but he didn't.

Looking as if it caused him physical pain, he rolled to his feet, leaving her sprawled out on the floor with the taste of him in her mouth, her nipples so hard they hurt, and pussy soft and ready.

Damn him.

"I'm not having sex with you again, Bristol," he told her, looking something like feral. His eyes were blazing and she'd knocked that hat off, then had her hands all up in his blond hair. She'd been the one to make him look so disheveled, and that notion rocked through her like his mouth at her neck. "Not if it's just sex."

Bristol's heart kicked at her, hard. She remembered what her mother had said about earthquakes, and that was what it felt like. As if every fault line related to this man that she'd gathered up inside her was ripped wide open.

"I beg your pardon?"

He moved all the way across the room, which wasn't far at all. But it felt like an immeasurable distance. She forced herself to stand.

"I told you I want all of you, Bristol," he gritted out. "I meant it. I want everything. And I know you don't believe me."

She had never been so tempted to lie and tell him whatever he needed to hear—but she didn't.

Judging by the way his eyes narrowed, he probably knew how close she'd come.

"It's not that I don't believe you," she hedged. "I believe that you believe it. I'm aware of your pattern, that's all."

She did not say, *and so is the world*, and felt virtuous.

"In other words, you don't believe me." He smiled then, broad and confident as if she couldn't see with her own eyes how big and hard his cock was behind his fly. "No worries, baby. I can wait."

Baby.

Her heart kept going at her, harder and harder by the second. She couldn't tell what sort of pulse it was that rattled through her, lighting her up in her temples to her pussy, only that it was driving her wild.

He'd called her *baby*.

"What do you think you're waiting for?" she managed to ask. "I hate to break this to you, Lachlan, but I've already pretty much ruined you for other women."

"I'm waiting, Bristol," he said, his eyes brilliant and his tone dead serious, "for you to admit that you're in love with me, too."

That pulsing thing in her felt more like a shudder then. Her chest was so tight she was afraid she might break out in sobs, and never stop. "And if I'm not? What if what I want from you are dive-bar dates and a hot one-night stand every once in a while?"

"You can have all the dates you want." Lachlan's mouth looked particularly hard as it curved. "But the hot nights are off the table."

"That sounds suspiciously like an ultimatum."

"An ultimatum would be me insisting that you do something," he countered, almost lazily, when she could see the white-hot heat in his gaze. "But you don't have to *do* anything. I will be saving my virtue and my body for love, that's all."

Bristol laughed.

Because this was Lachlan Drummond, king of the sexual demands. She assumed, though she didn't really like to think about it, that even though he hadn't appeared anywhere with a new woman he must be doing *something* with that appetite of his. Because the last she'd counted, it was a solid month since he'd had sex with her.

No way had he actually gone that long.

Her stomach cramped and yeah, she really didn't want to think about it.

"This is specific to me, right?" she asked. "Because I know you don't think that I'm going to stand here and believe for one second that you've been abstinent for twenty-four hours. Much less, what is it? A month?"

"Thirty-three days," he said gruffly. "Actually."

And no matter how she stared at him, she couldn't see the faintest hint of a lie.

"But…" Bristol cast around, not sure she could find the words for something like this. For the way she was shaking apart where she stood. "You have no idea if I'll ever… I didn't even kiss you until tonight!"

"Because it's not about me." Lachlan held her gaze, and it undid her. "Someone pointed out to me that I'm used to everything being about me, and that's true. But not this. I'm not playing a game, Bristol. The only question is when you're going to see that."

And she was torn in two, just like that.

She wanted, so badly, to run to him. To let all the words she dared not speak out loud pour off her lips, because wasn't this what she'd wanted all along?

But she didn't. She couldn't.

"I don't believe you," she said, though her voice shook.

Though she could see it hurt him. It hurt her, too.

She didn't believe him—not until all he did was smile at her, then turn to go.

She expected him to argue, mount a defense, *something*, but he didn't. Lachlan opened the front door and then shut it quietly behind him.

And for a moment Bristol stood there, shaking, trying to make sense of what he'd told her. Trying to make sense of any of this.

Trying to keep her footing when the ground was buckling beneath her feet.

And then she was flinging open her door and racing down the stairs before she knew she meant to move. Her breath was coming too fast, laced with desperation. She heard the outside door slamming shut and made a sound a little too close to a sob as she flung herself down the last flight of stairs, then outside into the night.

The storm had settled in. There were lightning flashes overhead and the rain poured down. Bristol looked around wildly, the panic making her pant. Had he called his driver? Was he already gone? She couldn't help thinking that if he left now, he wasn't coming back—

But then she saw his unmistakable body cutting through the rain in the bright headlights of a passing truck.

She ran, seized with a kind of desperation so intense it made her want to scream.

When she reached Lachlan, she dived for his arm. He wheeled around, and the look on his face was so ferocious she actually let out a surprised sort of sound at the sight of it.

And any half-formed notion she had that his expression was for whatever stranger he thought might have grabbed him melted away, because it only intensified the longer he looked at her.

"You better be sure," he growled at her. "You're running after me in the rain and it better not be bullshit."

"How?" she demanded, and maybe she was closer to screaming than she thought. "You say you love me, but how? All we ever did was have sex."

"We didn't just have sex, Bristol," he threw right back at her, his hands on her upper arms to hold her there before him. And there was rain all around them, the commotion of the city, and it was New York. No one paid them the slightest bit of attention. It was like being alone with that *look* he was giving her. "We never *just* had sex."

"*Just sex* is what you ordered. What you paid for."

"But it wasn't us!" he shouted at her.

It was a real shout, and something in her gloried in it. This was Lachlan, uncontrolled. No more acting the part. No more putting on those suits he didn't even like.

A man, not a monster.

All man.

He gripped her arms a little more tightly, dropping his face close to hers. "I fell in love with you the moment I saw you laugh on that video. And you know it. Just like you fell in love with me long before you signed that contract. You know that, too."

"Fuck you and fuck your contract," she threw right back at him, not caring if all of Brooklyn overheard her. "Let me tell you something, Lachlan. You might have rules, but I have a heart. And you will not break it. If you want to do this, it's going to be messy. It's going to be all-consuming. You're not going to know where you end or I begin. No beginning, no end. You don't get to run away to a fancy little island when it gets too much. I want *real*, Lachlan."

"You think I can't do it." There was a kind of wondering note in the middle of all that ferocity. "You think I don't even know what you're talking about."

"Do you?"

He jerked her closer and she loved it.

She *felt* it.

She felt lit up and *alive*.

"I know you wreck me," he said, there against her mouth. "You make me feel things I've never felt. You make me do things I've never done.

You're a temptation and a torment, and I'm in love with you, Bristol. *I love you.*"

He punctuated that with a tighter grip and she wanted to laugh, wild and long and free.

But Lachlan wasn't done. "I don't *just* want to have sex with you, though I want that, constantly and desperately. I want to marry you. I want the whole big, messy deal. Ridiculous fights and screaming babies and asshole teenagers to top it off. Then you and me, in our bed, fucking our way through. All of it."

Lightning flashed. And what scared her—or thrilled her—was that she could *see* that. She could see it all too clearly.

"What about what I want?" she threw back at him, and she couldn't tell at that point if it was only rain on her face or if she'd given in to the sobs she could feel building inside her. She didn't care. "I want to be more than a dress on your arm. I want my daughters to grow up knowing they can do anything. I want them to do what they love, but not obsessively lose themselves in the only thing they're good at because they don't know what else to do."

"You can do whatever you want. Do you really not know that?"

"How would I know that?" And there was no pretending she wasn't crying then. "Don't you understand, Lachlan? I'm terrified that if I tell you I love you, I'll just lose myself in you all over again, and then what will become of me?"

He framed her face, smoothing her hair back, and her heart seemed to grow three sizes.

"I can have anything on this planet I want, except you," Lachlan said. "I tried to buy you and I still didn't get close. You only lost yourself when you weren't yourself, baby."

It was that *baby*. It was going to kill her.

She was gripping the front of his T-shirt like her life depended on it.

Lachlan didn't seem to notice. "I don't want that. I want you. I want your wild intellect and your carefree laughter. I want the way you come for me, so greedily, over and over. I want the way you scowl at me, the way you say my name when you don't agree with me, the way you scream it when I'm inside you. I want the way you wow every person you come into contact with, and I want the way you look back at me, always checking in, whether we're at a state dinner or a food truck. *I'm in love with you*, Bristol."

"I'm trying so hard not to," she whispered brokenly to him. "But I love you, too, Lachlan. I love you, too."

"See?" And again, his mouth curved, but it was different this time. His blue eyes blazed, but it was the whole world. "I told you so."

"I want to be clear about something," she said,

wiping at her eyes even though it was futile, because the rain kept coming down. "If you were only the Lachlan Drummond who robotically fucked the woman he hired and there was nothing else to you, this would never happen. I don't care about your money. And marrying you was never my goal."

"Bristol. I know your goals. I know you have offers from three different think tanks already." He shook his head at her. "Did you think the people I know wouldn't call me?"

"Maybe not so quickly," she said. A little grumpily.

"You do know that I have my own think tank, right?"

"Maybe someday," Bristol said, and she actually allowed herself to smile then. "But first, there are a great many things in social policy to take care of that have nothing to do with being…"

"Mine," Lachlan finished for her. "You're mine, Bristol. And I'm yours. As long as that's clear, who cares about all the rest of it?"

She arched into him then, this whole, mad summer whirling around inside her. She thought of all those cities they'd visited. She thought about that last night on the island, the way he'd driven into her with such slow, hot determination, sweeping away her defenses.

Signing up for sex on demand had seemed fun.

Lachlan was gorgeous. It was supposed to be a place to hide and a chance to live a little.

But she understood now that she hadn't been living. Not really. How could anyone truly live when they were hidden?

And this was far scarier. This was pure vulnerability. Placing herself in this man's hands and promising that she would hold him just the same.

Bristol looped her arms around his neck and she held his gaze the way she thought she might just keep on doing for the rest of her days.

"Lachlan Drummond," she said, very solemnly. "I love you. I'm not very good at it, but I'm planning to really take the time and get it right. And I really, really need you inside me. Now."

His smile was bright and wide and as far as she could tell, stopped the rain and called out the sun.

She would never remember it differently.

Lachlan swept her up into his arms, right there on that Brooklyn sidewalk, and then he carried her back to her building and up the stairs.

And there, finally—in a Murphy bed that barely fit the both of them in that too-hot and too-small room—they touched forever.

And this time, held on to it. Tight.

Over and over again.

* * * * *

BRING THE HEAT

MARGOT RADCLIFFE

MILLS & BOON

To Andy

Because you walk Catfish

CHAPTER ONE

AFTER A QUICK flight from New York to Miami, Oliver Kent crossed the ramp from the marina's dock onto his yacht, *Chance*. Sliding off his favorite leather Tom Ford boots, he set his bare feet down on the familiar teak with a deep sigh of relief. The simple action felt like he was not just shedding his shoes, but a part of his life he'd been waiting to jettison a long time ago, finally leaving the cold November weather behind for an endless summer.

He padded across the spacious aft deck, the wood sun-warmed under his feet and the salty breeze off the water sifting through the hair he'd let air-dry in the limo he'd taken from his condo to the airport, the first careless act of a man set on a new path.

Grinning to himself, he opened the glass doors to the aft cabin, smelling sweet, crisp air and happy that the air conditioner that he'd sprung an obscene amount of money for was doing its double

duty of keeping the boat cool but also dehumidi-
fying the air. When he'd worked on yachts after
graduating from college, he'd always hated that
inside the cabins inevitably had a stale smell to
them, and he'd been hell-bent on making sure his
own didn't. Why would he pay millions of dollars
for a yacht and yet have to put up with it smelling
like a musty sewer?

He traversed the thickly carpeted saloon that
functioned as the main living space before con-
tinuing down the hallway that led to the front, or
bow, of the boat. He took in the rest of the im-
provements and upgrades he'd made to the interior,
his thoughts drifting back to his air-conditioning
unit and the person who'd recommended the system to him in the first place. The one he was essentially waiting for and had been waiting for for
a long time. A smile tugging his lips, he glanced
back to the men following behind him with his luggage and opened a door. "This is my room," he informed them. He took a peek into the master suite
he'd designed and found it perfect, but he truly had
one destination and one destination only in mind.

Moving through the bowels of the boat, he saw
the luxury guest rooms with digital toilets and
silk duvets and the hallways lined with deep ma-
hogany wood paneling polished to a high shine.
He'd spared no expense in restoring the broken-
down motor yacht he'd purchased two years ago

on a whim and was loving seeing the final product after all this time. Loping up the stairs to the second floor, electricity sizzled in his veins as he crested the top step into the sky lounge, a place he anticipated spending a lot of time during the upcoming months, before heading farther toward the front of the boat to the bridge.

The smell here was a little different from the rest of the boat, like oiled leather and polished steel from the control board where the captain—him—operated the ship. It smelled, in short, like his freedom. The one place where he was solely in charge of where he went and when. Standing in front of the wall of windows looking out onto the open water of the Atlantic Ocean, he blew out the breath he'd been holding since, hell, he was born if he were to be technical about it. He ran his hand over the glossy steel of the wheel, the high afternoon sun glinting off the perfect circle of deluxe craftsmanship. Christ, he loved sailing.

For years, he'd waited for this moment, to be at the helm of his own ship, in charge of his destiny, to put the years of following the upper-crust edicts of his parents behind. No more stiff dinner parties with toothless smiles, no more manipulative dates set up by his scheming mother, no more endless hours on a grossly manicured golf course schmoozing with men who'd stab him in the back as soon as shake his hand. And in the space of the twenty minutes he'd been on board, it felt like that life was already thousands of miles away. Finally.

Here on the water, life was uncomplicated. Just the way he wanted it.

"I thought I'd find you here," a soft, warm voice laughed from behind him.

He turned to find Molly Madix standing in the doorway, sandy-blond hair pulled up into a ponytail that had already been blown this way and that by the wind off the water. The woman he'd loved once upon a time and had let go in an effort to protect her from the same life from which he'd only just now managed to shake loose.

Stiffening his arms straight down at his sides, he then brought his left hand up to his forehead for a dramatic salute and grinned stupidly at her. "Did I hear the words, 'o captain, my captain'?" he teased. "Since that's what you have to call me now. I'm in charge of this fine vessel, Molly, and deserve your respect when you enter my control room."

"Um, you do know that the captain dies at the end of that poem, right?" she asked, quirking a light brow.

"Always a smart-ass. Come here and give me a hug," he growled, opening his arms for her.

Crossing the small room, she stepped into his embrace and the euphoric sense that he'd made the right decision swept over him again, taking any residual doubts with it. He was where he belonged and the final piece of the puzzle was in his arms. It'd been painful all those years ago to end their relationship, but it had been for the best. His parents would have eaten her alive before sending her back home so fast they never would have had a chance. Even now the threat was there, but at least Oliver was out on his own. They no longer had a say in what he did, but it didn't mean they wouldn't try.

"I'm so glad you came," he told her, his face in her hair, the fresh scents of sun and citrus invading his nostrils.

"Me, too," she told him, leaning back to grin up at him.

Not kissing her right then was hard, but today they were just old friends. Tomorrow and the days following, he hoped to be more, but for now, however, friends. Friends who knew what the other friend looked like naked, yes, but friends, nonetheless.

He resisted the urge to brush a piece of hair out of her eyes, almost resenting it when she did it herself. "You okay?" he asked.

She nodded and he knew it was automatic, the thing people had to do to make other people feel more comfortable with their pain. "I've been better, but I'm managing. Thank you for this opportunity," she said, shaking her head. "It couldn't have come at a better time."

"Just tell me you're not going to get back together with that asshole," he said, trying to lock gazes with hers, but she looked away, unable to hide the sadness in her brown eyes.

"Of course not," she laughed, but the sound was forced to his ears.

"Molly," Oliver told her, giving her shoulders a squeeze, "he did you dirty, so don't let a little broken engagement ruin your vacation. Look at me—I've avoided three engagements myself and have never been better."

"No, I know that," she said with another little laugh, "but we were together for a long time. It's just hard." She met his eyes, a corner of her mouth quirking. "And what do you mean by vacation? You're putting me to work on this boat!"

"You know you can work as much or as little as you'd like." That was his plan, anyway.

"I knew you were going to be a good boss."

"Oh, no, I'm driving the boat, but I'm not managing people. And you're above deck now, baby," he reminded her with a grin. "We're doing this month in style."

Shaking her head at him, she planted herself in front of the wheel to gaze out onto the water just like he'd been doing when she'd entered the room.

"Damn, it's really beautiful, isn't it?" she said, her voice hushed as she took in the ocean stretched out in front of them, the sun rippling across the calm surface of the water. "I've been landlocked in Denver for so long I'd forgotten."

She turned to him then, a free and easy smile on her face that seemed erased of the bad memory of her ex. It had been the thing that inspired him to make this move now. Aimless for years and simply following his parents' directives, seeing her broken engagement on social media had rattled loose a part of him he'd buried. The part that had bought this yacht in the first place, the one that needed to finally start over on his own terms, and Molly had been the last piece of the liberation. The one who'd gotten away, if he was being honest. The lovely, caring person his family would have obliterated if given the chance.

"I didn't think I'd ever be on a yacht again," she said, her hand brushing over the control panel. "I'm ready to get greasy in the engine room again, though."

He laughed. Molly had been the boat engineer of the yachts they'd worked on after college, but he wanted this to be a vacation for her, too. She deserved it after that jerkbag of a fiancé cheated on her. Molly, who was sweet and kind and perfect, was the last person who deserved that kind of shabby treatment.

"This job will be a piece of cake for you after working on satellites and rockets."

She glanced at him from the corner of her eye. "Why do you think I'm here?"

Oliver laughed. "Come on," he urged, motioning for her to follow him out the door. "Let's check out the rest of the boat and get the provisions ordered. We sail at sunrise."

"I assume you'll be in charge of the provisions," she queried as he led her outside and back down to the aft deck toward the engine room, "or else we'll be eating out of a jar of peanut butter with only vodka to drink."

"Sounds like a great vacation to me," he shot back, grinning over his shoulder at her. "But yes, you can't be trusted with any food items."

She shook her head, knowing her reputation preceded her. "So the motor is completely redone?" she asked as he opened the door to the heart of the boat.

"Yes," he confirmed. "I did my homework and found the most reliable manufacturer in the world so I don't expect any problems."

"NavalTech?"

He nodded.

"Good boy," she teased, giving him a jovial pat on the back.

"I'm insulted that you would ever doubt me," he told her, waving her through the doorway before him.

The engine room floor was textured metal, cool

on his bare feet. Molly whistled in approval when she saw the setup—shiny fuel tanks, fuel pumps, vents, propellers, and tons of other buttons and tubes he hadn't a clue about but Molly would.

Her hands drifted over the stainless steel tanks before she checked a couple gauges, then moved on to test levers and run vents, all the things that went along with her job. "We're just doing a practice run tomorrow to sort out any possible kinks?"

He'd wanted to just get out on open water, but they weren't on a real schedule, so he could be flexible. Nodding, he asked, "So what do you think? Did I do okay?"

"You have a gorgeous vessel here, Oliver." Molly grinned and he felt himself returning it.

"I knew you'd fall in love with my big vessel," he teased.

Shaking her head, she warned, "I hope my sleeping quarters measure up or I'm going to demand repayment like the Hardwicks did before Captain Kilmartin kicked them off the boat."

Oliver groaned, shutting the engine room door before following her back across the aft deck and to the guests' quarters. "I'd blocked those people out, but what a nightmare. I'm so glad our chartering days are behind us."

"Same," Molly confirmed as they entered the main saloon again.

"It's just you and me this time," he said, waggling his eyebrows suggestively.

Molly rolled her eyes, but stopped short in the middle of the saloon, doing a three-sixty turn of the open space. "You just poured money into this thing, didn't you?"

She ran her hands over the polished cherry bar and he bit the inside of his lip. That was a thing he hadn't forgotten about Molly Madix, how tactile a person she was. She made a living working with her hands and loved touching things, feeling the way they moved, the way they worked. As a result he felt every brush of her fingers as she worked her way around the space from the leather couches that anchored each side of the room to the polished cherry bar stocked with all manner of bad liquid decisions.

"I poured a good amount," he acknowledged. It wasn't a dent in his net worth, but he'd wanted to make the boat special and he thought he'd done a good job of it. Over the two years he'd spent restoring it, he'd emailed Molly a handful of times about the engine, so when the time came for him to sail, he'd wanted her with him. And if that time happened to be on the heels of her ditching some ball-less fiancé, even better.

Finally, she grinned at him hugely, wide and open and Molly. "Definitely worth it."

He grinned back, not able to help it. Everything just felt right around Molly. "You ready to see your room?"

"I don't get my pick?" she asked, raising a playful eyebrow.

"Of course you can pick another one if you want an inferior room." She shook her head at him before following him down the hallway to the first guest room. All the guest rooms were on the main floor, two on either side of the hallway with the master suite at the end. "You might also want to consider that they're identical."

Entering the first room, Molly sighed as she took in the pale blue duvet and dark cherry furnishings. He hadn't been super involved in the guest room decor, leaving it mostly to a trained designer, but he'd approved the final product. The first two bedrooms in the hallway were identical and had two full-size beds on either wall, their own bathroom, and automatic toilets, faucets, and voice command blackout shades for when the nights in the Caribbean got a little out of hand. The rooms had everything a guest might need, but just in case they didn't, the crew were there to provide any request imaginable.

When they got to the one he'd chosen for her, fresh hydrangeas and happy daisies (because he knew she liked them) sat in an etched crystal vase on the dresser while a basket of expensive lotions and soaps waited for her in a foil-wrapped gift box on the bathroom counter. A large television was mounted on the wall and a hidden mini fridge was set into a small writing desk stocked with the artisanal liquor from a small spirits company he'd recently invested in. He'd had it delivered to the boat yesterday before he'd arrived, along with the plush robe hanging in the closet that was embroidered with her initials in green.

Molly let the fridge door close and met his eyes. "You're right, I'll keep this one."

He just shook his head. "The crew will unpack your stuff. Let's go up to the sky deck and we can start on the provisioning."

"Can I not see the master suite?" she asked, raising an eyebrow.

"My apologies, Ms. Madix," he drawled, holding his hand out for her to precede him down the hallway. "For not giving you a full tour."

"Forgiven, of course." She smiled. "But it does make me think you're hiding something in there. Did you bring a lady friend?"

Oliver raised a brow. "No." Then he opened the door and Molly inhaled audibly.

"Whoa," she breathed, her eyes darting around the room, taking in every inch of the space. The bed was raised up a step with an espresso leather headboard; pristine white carpet and mirrored ceilings enhanced the bright light shining in from the wall of windows that curved around the entire room. In a sitting area off to the side, a window seat was carved into the wall with fitted cushions for reading in front of a built-in bookshelf the same espresso color as his bed. The same pale blue duvet as the guest rooms was spread out over the king mattress, while the bathroom in all white marble felt modern and decadent.

She sat down on the window seat, her fingers running over the chocolate velvet cushion, and awareness prickled the base of his neck. Molly was beautiful and he wanted her, but it'd only been a month since her breakup; it would be a real douchebag move to go for it with her so soon, but it didn't mean the thought hadn't crossed his mind. Repeatedly. At least three times since she'd boarded the boat, but here in his bedroom where a box of condoms was stashed in his luggage it was harder to ignore.

"You like it?"

She nodded. "We've seen a lot of boats, but this window seat is a nice touch, Oliver."

She crossed the room and hoisted herself up on the bed, her bare feet dangling off the edge. She sighed and he closed his eyes at the piece of bare skin that appeared between the band of her cropped jeans and plain yellow T-shirt as her arms stretched above her head to fall onto the bed. "This is next-level comfort."

Oliver shook his head and then let himself fall

beside her, making her giggle as the force of his weight bounced her up. "You're welcome to share it," he said, wagging his eyebrows at her lasciviously.

"Always a flirt," Molly lamented with a responding smile. "You can't even help it, can you?"

Oliver shook his head. He could, of course, but being relentlessly charming was basically his most effective life skill. "I'm afraid it's a terminal condition," he said gravely.

He felt her shoulders shake before her laugh actually started. "Well, Captain, at least we'll be able to bury you at sea."

"A true sailor's death," Oliver confirmed wistfully. "I couldn't ask for more."

A small smile still on her face, Molly said, "I think we're going to have fun this month, Oliver." Then a big breath in and a sigh. "Lord knows, I need a break. I can't tell you how much this means to me. Thank you for being such a good friend."

Oliver took her hand in his and squeezed. "We're going to have the best time of our lives, Molly, and by the time we're done I promise your problems will be only memories."

Molly squeezed his hand back, her head turning to his on the mattress. This close he could see the lighter brown streaks in her eyes and wished he could take away all the hurt in them. All he could offer her was a luxury yacht voyage and companionship to let time pass by more easily.

"I know you're right," she told him. Then she looked up at the ceiling and snorted. "I should have known you'd put mirrors on the ceiling."

He shrugged, the motion invisible with his shoulders buried in the fluffy duvet. "You know I like looking at myself as I fall asleep. My beautiful face comforts me."

Molly pushed lightly at his shoulder. "You're not as vain as you want people to think."

He wasn't not vain, but she was probably right. There were a lot of things he'd worn as armor in his old life that he hoped to put away while he was on this ship.

"I'm so pretty it makes my own teeth hurt," he persisted, jumping off the bed before he did something stupid like touch her. "That's why I also did this." Then he pressed a button on the wall and the mirrors went black.

"Well, aren't you fancy?" Molly said, sitting up on the bed. "You've definitely made this boat your own. I'm proud of you, Oliver."

Those simple words so freely given clenched at his insides. Molly gave everything she had away for free and he soaked it up like a dead-inside sponge, so unused to someone offering a compliment without an ulterior motive. Hell, he rarely did it himself.

He took her through the rest of the boat before they returned to the sky lounge on the top deck and settled in. There was some business to take care of before they hit the open ocean.

"Oooh," Molly laughed, wiggling around in the lounge chair, big white sunglasses perched on her nose and the breeze gently blowing a strand of hair over her face, "this chaise is deluxe. I could definitely get used to this."

He grinned. "I think you'll like the chef, too. I've heard good things. He worked for a friend in the city so I got to sample some of his dishes and his chicken paillard was the best I've had."

"I'm really excited about it. You know how I feel about cooking," she told him, her hands stilling on the tablet in her lap.

"How could I possibly forget you endlessly burning your grilled cheese?" She'd set off the fire alarm more than once on their first boat together.

"In my defense, I'm also the person who has to fix something if it goes wrong, so no harm no foul."

"It hardly makes it more acceptable," he pointed out, taking a sip of the tequila on the rocks the chief steward had brought him. "I still don't understand why you, a woman of science, refuse to believe that cooking something on high is a bad idea."

"Things take too long to cook if they're not on high," Molly complained.

"Not if you count the number of times you have to remake everything that you burn to a crisp the first time," he said blandly.

Molly laughed, turning her head to meet his eyes where he was sitting at the bar. "Details."

He shook his head as she tapped away on the tablet, adding her requests to the provisions list. "What are you putting on there?"

"Lots of cheese and bread," she said, a goofy smile on her face.

He shook his head at her. "We'll be on the water without a chef for the first couple weeks, so I'll cook. We've also only got a skeleton crew, so only one interior steward and one deck crew person, but I'll help out where needed obviously."

"Sounds good," Molly nodded, handing him the tablet. "Your turn."

Oliver looked down at the list of items she'd requested be ordered from the grocery as well as any last-minute items from department stores they might need for an extended sail that hadn't fit in their luggage.

"You literally requested fifteen pounds of various cheeses," he said, floored. "You do understand how much cheese that is, right?"

Molly had a mischievous look on her face as she climbed off the chaise and took the seat beside him at the bar, a champagne flute in her hand. "I thought since I'll have so much free time while you're driving this ship, this will be the perfect time to experiment with flavors."

He shut his eyes and in front of her typed the words, f-i-r-e e-x-t-i-n-g-u-i-s-h-e-r.

"The boat already has them," Molly laughed.

"Not enough."

Molly gave him a playful shove, but damn if it didn't send a little stream of heat over his skin. Maybe he hadn't thought this trip through, after all. Here was a woman he'd always been attracted to, but due to life, time and distance, whatever relationship they might have had off the boat seven years ago never materialized. In its place, a casual friendship had developed, but now she was here with a broken heart and had never given him any indication that she wanted anything more than friendship. Yet he was having a difficult time remembering that as her light scent drifted over him and her pink lips closed on the delicate rim of the crystal champagne glass.

Well, he thought grimly, blue balls aside, he'd made worse decisions in his life.

"So what's your plan?" Molly asked. "I know you've got something up your sleeve and we're not just taking this puppy out for a vacation spin this month."

He quirked an eyebrow. "I don't want you to

do anything else besides keep the boat in working order, if that's what you mean."

"No, I'm not suggesting that," Molly agreed. "But as I understand it, you quit the job your parents insisted you keep."

Because people in the Kent family worked, was the refrain, even though Oliver's yearly salary was eclipsed by the monthly interest he lived on from his grandparents' trust fund and his own private investments. His father was now CEO of the largest investment firm in the country, a company that used to be owned by his father and so on, which meant Oliver had to work there, was groomed to take over the company when his father was ready to retire.

But yes, Oliver had quit. He'd walked away from his family legacy and duty. And he wasn't sorry at all.

That Molly knew he wasn't just going to drift around on the yacht indefinitely, that he had plans for something more, was nice. At least someone didn't think he was an absolute wastrel.

"I'm going to start a yacht manufacturing company," he admitted, a little hesitantly, because he'd yet to actually say the words out loud to someone.

Molly sat up straighter in her chair. "Wow," she said, mouth open, a little stunned. "That's awesome."

"I don't know about that, but it's a lucrative

market and after rebuilding this boat I have an idea of what it takes. I know all the players. And I really want to make something, you know?"

The job he'd given up was basically just moving money around and he fucking couldn't stand it. He wanted to explore the world, meet and work with different types of people, build grandiose, magnificent eco-friendly ships that would sail forever. And he wanted to do it on his own instead of riding the coattails of his family.

Molly's head tilted as she considered him and gave him a friendly pat on the shoulder. "Like I said, I'm proud of you, bud."

"So you won't mind if we take some detours to tour other boats and talk to some boat makers?"

"It'll be my pleasure to help any way I can, Oliver," she told him.

Holding up her glass, she said, "To fresh starts."

Oliver clinked his glass against hers, meeting her eyes. "To us."

CHAPTER TWO

MOLLY DIDN'T QUITE know what she was doing waking up on a yacht with Oliver Kent, of all people. The bright morning sun was streaming in the windows, and her hand brushed over the silky duvet on her bed as she thought back to when they'd been together. While working on yachts in their early twenties, Molly had fallen hard for Oliver, but even then she'd recognized that his life was far removed from anything she could have fit into once they were off the boat.

So even if she had been heartbroken that he hadn't asked her to stay together or offered to come with her to Colorado when yachting season was over, her life had gone on. And, unexpectedly, they'd kept in touch over the years and now that her gutter person of an ex-fiancé was revealed, his offer of a yacht trip felt like a miracle. She could heal after her carefully crafted life imploded.

And if sometimes she still had flashbacks of walking into her bedroom and finding her fiancé mid-thrust into their neighbor, well, that was why she was here on the water headed for the calm, sparkling blue sea of the Caribbean.

Luckily, the small team of engineers she worked with had just launched their latest satellite into space, so her current leave of absence wasn't too much of a burden to her beloved coworkers. Even they had called bullshit on the accusations Max had lobbed at her—that she was too devoted to her job and didn't have time for him, that she never wanted to hang out with his friends, that she wasn't open in bed, that she shut him out, ad infinitum. All the flimsy excuses of a man caught and unable to hold himself accountable.

But she was taking advice from her friends and was not going to start her Caribbean adventure with her ex's untrue poison in her ear. Now was her time for relaxation and renewal. With Oliver Kent, who was perhaps the single most handsome person she'd seen in real life. So yeah, total heartbreak and devastation aside, she'd definitely traded up.

Oliver had always been able to make her smile, especially back then when their superlong work-days were taken up by demanding physical labor and endlessly cranky and demanding charter guests. For a girl from a small town in Colorado, she'd been in awe of the yachting world, the interesting jobs of the guests, the exotic locations, not to mention the amount of money people threw around, the likes of which she'd never even imagined.

But Oliver hadn't been fazed by the limitless luxury. He'd always been very comfortable around the guests, charming them because he happened to be charming by nature, but also because he was *one* of them. The fact that he *owned* this yacht was astonishing. Sure, she'd known he'd been a rich kid, but his boat alone most likely cost at least ten million dollars, an amount of money she couldn't even imagine having over the course of her lifetime, and yet was merely disposable income to him.

Molly sighed and snuggled farther into the bed, not ready to start the day yet as memories of her and Oliver reemerged. Mostly good ones. But when she'd told him about her job and he'd simply hugged her congratulations, she'd taken it as a sign that things with him weren't meant to be, that maybe his reputation as a player had been true all along and she'd been another victim of a transient yacht-season romance. Regardless of what it had been, Molly had loved him fiercely, but she was nothing if not pragmatic so she'd taken the job and, ultimately, been the one to end the relationship. And what she'd known on some level back then, that she'd never truly fit into his world, was glaringly obvious to her now. She was a guest on this boat but it wasn't hers, and this month might be a fantasy version of reality, but sooner or later she would, in fact, return to her actual reality.

But until then she was going to enjoy every bit of the fantasy, because today they were setting sail and she was leaving her old life behind for a while.

Rising from the bed, she hopped into a shower that had been set to heat the water to exactly one hundred degrees before heading to the engine room. She'd given it a thorough examination yesterday and she and Oliver had started the engine without actually going anywhere just so she could get a sense of things before they headed out this morning.

Compared to the space satellites and aircraft she usually worked on, a motor yacht was somewhat less complicated, but she was responsible for essentially every moving part on the boat, from the kitchen stove to the complex fuel engine, and if the latter stopped working in the middle of the ocean they were screwed. So she didn't intend to sleep on the job even if this trip was mostly a vacation.

Satisfied that the engine room was in working order, she headed up to the kitchen to get some breakfast. She found Oliver already at the stove making eggs, the homey scent of toasted bread greeting her.

"You're cooking?" she asked, looking over his shoulder at the large skillet of fluffy scrambled eggs.

"I'd use that word loosely," he said wryly.

This morning he was wearing a pair of white linen shorts and a turquoise polo shirt, a pair of reflective silver aviators tucked into the V of his collar. Golden-haired forearms held the wooden handle of a rubber spatula as he gently ran it through a pan of eggs. The flicker of desire at watching his muscles flex and the clean, expensive scent of him wasn't surprising, but a little unwelcome. Sleeping with an ex on the heels of a breakup was a very terrible idea.

"Better than me. I would have definitely burned those eggs by now. I go for hard-boiled—less chance of screwing it up."

Oliver shook his head at the depths of her cooking ineptitude. "You wanna grab the toast? I cut up some avocado, too."

"Ooh," Molly said happily. "You know, I could really get used to starting my day this way. You might want to rethink it or you'll be tied to the oven."

He flashed her one of those charming smiles, clear green eyes and straight white teeth with a little bit of humor, that should be trademarked as his. "I'll cook you breakfast anytime, Molly. You just say the word."

Molly shook her head at the implication but couldn't totally beat back the smile forming. Taking a few steps back from him, she opened the fridge. "Can I cut some fruit?"

"Already done," he told her, nodding to a bowl beside him on the stainless steel counter. Molly whistled, impressed, as she grabbed a couple pieces of cantaloupe from the bowl. Perking up, she caught his eyes. "Did you put something on this fruit?"

"Just some lemon juice and sugar."

"It's so good," she mumbled inelegantly around the food in her mouth, digging in again for a piece of watermelon and then another. "You're a freaking genius, Oliver."

He raised a gold eyebrow at her. "What are you even eating in your normal life that fruit salad is this much of a big deal to you?"

Molly shrugged. "Mostly nutrition bars and a banana or something for breakfast. You know me, I keep it simple."

Oliver shook his head. "You're barely living, Molly."

Laughing, Molly gave him a gentle knock on the shoulder, surprised by the lack of give. "Hey, I live plenty."

He looked skeptical. "Thank God I invited you on the boat or you'd never know how good a fruit salad is."

"Oh, give me a break," she laughed. "Besides, I'm sure it's one of the many things you'll introduce me to on this boat." She'd been speaking to the luxury of the boat, but immediately regretted the words because his eyes darkened before he looked away. Yeah, there was already some sexual tension there, and the memories of what they'd done on a boat very similar to this one in the past weren't buried far enough in her subconscious right now for her peace of mind. She knew what he was like in bed, inventive and intense, which coupled with this amazing breakfast made him pretty difficult to resist. "You know what I mean, being a guest above deck with all the glamorous people."

Oliver met her eyes, his still a little heated but the intensity banked. "I knew what you meant, Molly." Then his eyes dropped down to her bare legs and back up to meet hers with a cheeky grin to ease the brewing tension. "Concerning the other, I'm sure we've both picked up some new tricks over the years we could introduce each other to."

Molly swallowed, struggling against the wave of heat flushing her skin. Not having a response, she popped a big piece of pineapple into her mouth, the juice leaking at the side of her mouth, and watched his eyes bore into hers as she licked it off. "Um," Molly finally managed, wanting to get them back to equilibrium, "so avocado toast?"

Oliver stared at her for a beat and then started laughing. His eyes were a sparkling green when they returned to hers. "Molly, I'm glad you're here. Yes, avocado toast. Why don't you quit poaching from the fruit salad and make yours how you'd like it. I chopped up some pico de gallo if you want to put that on top."

Molly nodded and went about making the toast, feeling uncomfortable and comfortable at the same time. Being around Oliver was easy. But the more she had to watch him move, cook, smile… Even with the scent of cooking eggs and the melting cheese he'd crumbled into the pan, it was already challenging.

Her sex life with Max had been good, at least at the beginning. However, even before she'd caught him cheating, she'd been so distracted by work that at least a month or two had gone by without them having sex. Which meant that she was now even further into a serious dry spell with Oliver, who had appeared back in her life like basically a sex oasis in a desert.

Making avocado toast had never required so much of her concentration.

But she was determined to stop thinking about Oliver and his enormous bed. She scooped the fresh veggies on top of the avocado Oliver had previously cut into thin and perfect slices with an inward sigh. It was as if the man wasn't bad at anything.

"Drinks!" Molly realized with a burst of inspiration. "I can make mimosas. Does that sound good?"

Oliver smiled his wide smile with crinkles in

the corners of his eyes. "It sounds perfect, Molly. But I don't want you to think you have to do anything. This trip is for you."

She nodded, but she still wanted to pull her weight, especially if he was planning on cooking all their meals. Opening the walk-in fridge, she pulled out oranges and a bottle of sparkling wine. She'd seen the stews make these drinks countless times when she'd worked on yachts.

"Oh," Oliver said, seeing the pile of fruit in her arms, "you're really going for it, then?"

"Hell, yeah," she shot back. "I'm not going to be the weakest link on this boat."

Oliver turned the heat down on the eggs and found the juicer in a cabinet for her. After juicing the oranges she had enough to make maybe too many beautifully bright mimosas, which she carried as they made their way up the stairs to the upper deck where a dining table was set up so they could eat outside in the sunshine.

Molly shook her head when she saw the places had already been set. Oversize white chargers rested on pale blue mats and a squat glass of puffy blue hydrangeas sat in the middle of the long rectangular table, soft petals strewn delicately around it.

"Chief stew did this," Oliver explained, and Molly blew out a relieved breath. She was already so much in his debt.

"It's lovely," she said. She'd grown up taking

things apart so she could put them back together and mostly getting hella dirty while she was doing it, but that didn't mean she didn't like flowers, too.

Oliver shrugged, not caring one way or another about the table setting. Molly dug into her eggs and then stared at Oliver in surprise. "No, really," she said, already digging her fork back into the fluffy yellow pile on her plate, "best eggs I've ever tasted."

Oliver snorted, but he was grinning. "I'm going to choose to believe you, but, Molly, I now feel personally responsible for your culinary education. What are you doing with your life? And why wasn't that asshole ex cooking you breakfast ever? Have you not heard of brunch, for Christ's sake?"

Molly knew he was kidding, but the words hit an unexpected soft spot. No, Max had never cooked her breakfast and maybe they'd gone out to brunch in the beginning but hadn't for years. "I guess not," she told him, keeping it vague. Oliver didn't need to know the details of her relationship, nor was she particularly keen on sharing them on the first morning of the trip.

But Oliver, ever insightful, reached out and grabbed her hand, giving it a squeeze. It was a totally innocuous, friendly gesture, but Molly felt it in her toes along with genuine gratitude that he truly cared about her. Despite the years and the miles, Oliver was a good friend.

"Hey," he said, getting her attention so she met his eyes, his green ones brilliant jade in the morning sun. "I didn't mean it like that. Brunch is stupid and overrated anyway."

Molly sent him a wan smile. "I know brunch is great, don't deny it."

"Only when I make it," Oliver allowed, a corner of his mouth quirking up.

Giving his hand a squeeze of her own, Molly said, "I look forward to eating your brunch."

"Eggs for days," he promised, the heat of his hand literally burning her skin, but he didn't let go. "But you can talk about it, you know, Molly. I know you're still processing everything, but I'm here for you. I wouldn't have invited you here if I didn't want you to be able to share what happened."

Then he picked up their hands from the table and dropped a light kiss on the back of hers, and holy hell, her pulse rocketed through her body. He let go of her hand once his head lifted, but the damage was done—he'd wrecked her. Between the kind gesture itself and the feel of his soft lips on her skin, she struggled to keep her eyes open, wanting to close them so she could relive the moment in her mind. Damn, damn, damn it, one day in and she was already hopeless.

"I appreciate that, Oliver. It means a lot," she said, holding his gaze. "All of this means a great deal to me. I hope you know that."

Oliver picked up his fork again. "There's no one I'd rather be on this boat with, so I'm the one who is thankful that you came."

The words fluttered in Molly's chest; the man knew how to compliment even if it was an exaggeration.

They fell into silence as they ate, Molly's attention being drawn to all manner of things from the seagulls swooping into the water, the different varieties of people coming and going on the dock, to the rippling waves sparkling like diamonds under the sun. She could barely believe this was her home for the next month.

"You know, two days ago it was snowing in Denver," she informed, shaking her head. "And those poor jerks are still there."

Oliver laughed. "It hasn't snowed in New York yet, but it's damn cold for sure."

"Suckers." Molly chuckled and Oliver followed.

"Another toast then, to us, for being smart enough to leave it all behind." Then he raised his mimosa and she clinked her glass against his, smiling as their eyes met once again.

They continued eating, Molly quickly working her way through the delicious eggs and toast, finally arriving back at the fruit salad.

"So we know why I'm on this trip," Molly said, swallowing a sweet strawberry. "Why now for you, Ollie?"

Oliver raised a brow at the shortened version of his name, which she knew he hated. "I knew if I didn't do this now, I never would. I was up for the promotion in the firm and the next step after that would have been the job my dad holds now and I don't want it. The chain ends with me."

"I see," Molly said, nodding. "Your parents okay with that?"

"No," Oliver said, leaving it at that.

"And you're okay with *that*?"

"No."

Molly grinned at his willfully obtuse answers. "Not giving me much to work with here, Oliver. You sure you're okay?"

"I'm a grown man, Molly," Oliver said after a moment of hesitation, as if revealing something real about himself was difficult. "I can handle my parents being angry with me. What I can't handle is spending the rest of my life on someone else's terms. So it stops now."

Molly was struck by the intensity of his voice. This time it was she who took his hand and gave it a squeeze, and she felt the same electricity she had before but something else as well. Maybe this time, unlike when they'd been younger, she might actually get to know Oliver for real. The thought sent a little bit of alarm through her because instinctively she knew that it might be dangerous. He was already breathtakingly handsome and lovely;

she didn't need him to be vulnerable as well or she was definitely going to be a goner.

"I hear you," she allowed, letting go of his hand and sitting back in the chair with her second mimosa. "So what's the plan? This trip is an exploratory mission?"

Oliver nodded. "Yes, I want to tour more boats when we go to port. I've already had meetings with the CEOs of the current US yacht companies and toured their facilities. I've offered to buy one of the companies that I know is struggling."

"Oh, so you won't start from scratch?"

Oliver shook his head. "I've run the numbers. It would be far more expensive and a time suck for me to start one up myself, purchase the equipment, find or build a brand-new facility, hire employees, et cetera. All that work has been done and I can just buy the whole thing, change the name, assess the personnel and go from there."

"Sounds like you've got a plan."

Molly said the words but she couldn't even imagine having enough money to just, poof, buy a yacht manufacturing company like it was a bag of taffy.

"Always," he said, a corner of his mouth lifting in that ornery way he had when he decided to be silly. "It'll be great and I'll need your help every step of the way. The sale will go through any day now, and I'd love it if you'd consider heading up the design team. I want my company to stand out, to make eco-luxury yachts that people can be comfortable sailing."

Molly's eyebrows rose, her chest going concave. "You want me to design yachts?"

He shrugged. "You design rockets, don't you?"

"Not actually rockets, mostly satellites and reusable crew capsules, but—"

He interrupted with, "Well, I'd think yachts would be easier."

"Well, maybe, but I'm not an expert on them. I can definitely make sure the engine on this boat is in tip-top shape, but to turn around and just design one that can compete with all the other designers out there who are formally trained is totally different."

Oliver shrugged as if this didn't matter. "You're a genius, Molly. I don't know why you're making it out like building a little fuel engine and designing an aerodynamic yacht body is some Herculean task. Maybe you haven't done it for a while, but you've sent people to space for indeterminate periods of time."

"I've worked with a team of people who did that, Oliver," she pointed out, because it was true. One person alone was not responsible for the lives of astronauts and building whatever kind of ship propelled them into the outer reaches of space.

"Well, that's what yacht manufacturing is, a team of people creating plans. You'd still be doing that, only you'd be making more money and be in charge."

She bristled at how easily he was suggesting she give up the life she'd created for herself. The life she loved. "I like the job I have."

Oliver switched gears, clearly reading her discomfort. "It's just an idea, Molly—give it some thought. You have plenty of time before it would actually happen. Buying a company isn't easy, sometimes negotiations go bad, you never know."

Molly nodded. "I appreciate your faith in me."

And as she drank her mimosa and watched his strong jaw chew a piece of honeydew melon, she thought about what it might be like to head up a team and design something different. Rockets and satellites didn't exactly invite fancy or creativity; they were built for maximum safety and storage. But yachts… She might be able to have some fun with that.

"No faith is involved," Oliver told her. "You're a dream employee. Reliable, brilliant and kind. The perfect type of person to head up my team."

Molly took a deep breath, falling under his spell once again. "I'll think about it, Oliver," she told him. "I promise."

"Good," he said, a wide grin on his face as he popped a grape into his mouth. "And if there's anything else I can do, like double your current salary, for instance, you let me know."

She just shook her head at him. "It would serve you right if I agreed to take the job and then designed all your ships to look like rockets."

Oliver's shoulders bounced with laughter and then he was fully laughing, the sound rich and deep, sending shivers up her spine. "I can only imagine the kind of clientele that sort of vessel would attract."

Molly just shook her head at him, gulping back the rest of her alcohol because she was itching to touch him. The long corded muscles of his neck were straining as he got lost in another bout of chuckling and her eyes closed. She could make it through their time together; she had to.

"We did have that charter of porn stars, if I'm not mistaken," Molly finally said, sending him into more laughter.

"Oh my God," Oliver said, a final laugh before he met her eyes. "They were a nightmare, weren't they?"

Molly nodded and he continued. "But you can design whatever you want, Molly. The world would be yours. I don't want to offer the same old thing. I want to change it up, make the yacht industry take notice, revive it. Make smaller, more affordable yachts, too, that are more energy-efficient and green. Luxury with a purpose, you know?"

She loved the idea and that he'd already put

some of those ideas into play on this boat, too. "I'll definitely think about it, Oliver."

He nodded. "I hope so. And are you going to give me a number, too? So I at least have a chance to woo you?"

Wooing her without cash was already basically happening, so she couldn't imagine what a bump in her salary might do.

So she shook her head. "There's no way I'm telling you my salary."

"I don't want you to," he reminded. "I want the number that's double it."

It was Molly's turn to laugh at his nonsense. "Thanks for making breakfast. I would say that I'd do the honors tomorrow, but I think we both know that ends with an emergency call instead of a leisurely lounge on the deck."

"We do, indeed."

Oliver met her eyes again and there was heat there, carefully controlled, but she felt it anyway and recognized it because she felt the same.

"Now," he said, folding his pale blue cloth napkin up and setting it by his plate, "are you ready to give this baby a practice run?"

"You know it."

CHAPTER THREE

OLIVER WASN'T A therapist or anything, but he knew Molly was hiding how sad she was. And while he didn't want to pry about her breakup, he did want to know why she got that lost look on her face sometimes when they were talking. Mostly he wanted to be a good friend and help her, but if he ever got two minutes with her loser ex, it'd be the worst two minutes of that guy's life. Oliver didn't have many friends he trusted and the fact that someone had broken Molly's heart infuriated him.

They'd taken the boat up the coast from Miami to West Palm Beach and back again, staying close to shore in case something went wrong, but so far it'd been, literally, smooth sailing. But the trip had given Oliver time to think. Seeing how hard she was trying to hide her sadness, he was anxious to know if that relationship was tying her to Colorado more than her job. His new company needed her vision. This venture was the biggest risk of his life and he wanted someone by his side that he could trust completely. And he trusted Molly with basically his life. She was just that kind of person.

Their first relationship had ended sooner than he'd wanted, but even if she hadn't gotten her job in Colorado he would have had to end it sooner or later. Not because he would have wanted to, but because his parents would have ruined her life like they'd nearly ruined his. They were still trying to if he was honest; he'd just become better at fending them off. Something he'd continue to do if they ever came sniffing around Molly, which was a concern. He was keeping her isolated on his boat for now so his parents wouldn't know what he was up to or how Molly fit into his new plans, because if they did they'd use her. Either pay her off to not help him, or threaten her own job, her family. He didn't put it past his family to do whatever it took to make sure he returned to the firm and married the person they'd previously approved.

His main goal had always been to protect Molly, to insulate her from his real life while being able to bask in the fantasy world they'd created together when they were younger. Those were still some of his favorite times and ever since he'd given her up, he'd been trying to get back to a place where they could have that again. Or at least some version of it.

Which meant he needed to know just how

scarred she was from her broken engagement because after two days with her, everything he'd loved about her was amplified. He was right back to wanting her, but struggling with giving her the time she needed to heal. It was just that the way she looked at him sometimes, like she wanted to jump him, he knew he couldn't hold out for very long. Not when he'd been missing her touch for years. Had cursed his parents for depriving him of the life full of laughter he could have been having with Molly all these years.

He and the deck crew member anchored the boat in open water just off the port back in Miami, and he pushed his parents to the back of his mind, reminding himself that he was on the water and life was fantastic again. When his work was done, he found Molly in the sky lounge, faint smudges of black oil on her fingers, just like he remembered from their early yacht days. She was at the bow's railing with a beer in her hand watching the sun set over Miami, the hazy pinks and yellows peeking out behind the tall buildings and waving palm trees.

"I missed this," she said when he approached.

He nodded. "We'll have countless nights watching the sunset now."

She smiled at him, the last rays of daylight painting her pale skin golden. "The sunset is lovely, but I mostly meant doing nothing. I've done more nothing in the past two days than in the past year. I didn't realize just how hard I was working, I guess."

"Um," Oliver said, picking up her hand to expose the grease and the blister she'd gotten fixing a rogue stove-top burner, "you've been working pretty damn hard on this boat."

"Not compared to real life, though."

This seemed like a good opportunity to gently ferret out what had happened with her breakup, but he had to play it just right so she didn't clam up. Molly wasn't exactly an "open up and share her feelings" sort of person. "You were working a lot?"

She nodded. "We were up against a deadline for the government, so it happens. You get busy."

"I've been there for sure, except you actually like your job so it's a little different."

"I'm glad you're doing this now," she said, her gaze meeting his. "Sometimes your texts seemed sad."

He huffed out a laugh. "Yeah, well, I probably was sad." He thought back to all the times he'd had to go to an opening of something no one cared about, to support his family's investments, to constantly push and wheedle and stay on top. He was so glad it was over.

"So yachts will make you happy?" Molly turned and met his eyes, her expression so engaged that it caught him in the chest. Had anyone ever been interested in what he had to say? He couldn't remem-

ber a single person in his life who'd ever asked him
what would make him happy.

He shook his head, trying to keep things light.
"No, building something of my own will. Being
my own boss, not living off my name. All of that."

She smiled and then her hand landed on his
shoulder, his spine stiffening as his body flared
to life under her soft touch. "I'm excited for you.
I always knew you'd do something great."

The regret in her voice, he heard, because it was
the way he'd felt, too. He hadn't wanted to break
up after that last summer, had yachted far longer
than his parents wanted him to, but there hadn't
been another choice. She hadn't been able to pass
up an amazing opportunity and his life hadn't been
his own, something he was currently trying to rec-
tify. But it gave him hope that she regretted their
breakup just as much as he did.

"You, too," he told her. "And I'm not too proud
to admit that I should have followed you to Colorado, Molly. I regret it more than anything." He left
out that even now she was in danger of his parents
finding out about her. Even if he was ready now
to fight in a way he hadn't been able to when he
was younger. If they wanted to be together now,
nothing would stand in their way.

Molly's shoulders raised. "I didn't blame you for
going back to New York. We never made promises
to each other. I'd only planned on doing a summer

of yachting and then finding a real job, but then you came along and…" She shrugged her shoulders again. "Things happened."

"So you're saying I didn't break your heart?" Oliver teased. His own had been in shreds, leaving him cursing his parents, his life, his name, the job he'd been forced to take, everything. And maybe out of spite he'd had shitty times with all the women they tried to set him up with. Until he'd announced that he was leaving the firm, him not being married was the biggest point of contention with his parents. The people who, under no circumstances, should still be married since they absolutely could not stand each other and hadn't uttered a kind word to each other since Oliver was born.

Nonetheless, the number of gorgeous and successful women they'd thrown in his path had been legion. But they'd all wanted the life his parents had and he could think of nothing worse. Not when he'd experienced how good life could be with someone he truly cared for.

"Maybe cracked it," Molly said, grinning, and he loved that he could make her smile. "But I'm an engineer. I just spackled the old girl up and she's been as good as new."

Oliver regarded her. "Is that what you're doing now? Spackling?" he asked. "Or have you suffered terminal damage?"

Molly's grin only faded a little and he was proud

of her for being tough, but honest as well. "I guess we'll see, right?"

Oliver took a drink of his own beer, looking up as the first stars appeared in the fading blue sky before returning his attention to her. "You know, I'd like to kick this guy's ass for doing that to you. I know you're fine with it, but the fact that he's just out there living and breathing like he's not a jerk pisses me off."

Her shoulders shook again in laughter and he felt like a king. "I probably feel the same," she said. "But breakups happen. No retaliation needed."

"He's the one who fucked around, so it didn't just happen, Molly," Oliver insisted, needing to know she wasn't screwed up about the facts. "He made it happen. If he had a problem with your relationship, he should have come to you like a man and told you."

"I know," Molly said, "and not that it's an excuse, but I honestly wasn't around much to even have the conversation."

"Oh, so it was hard for him to keep his dick in his pants while his fiancée was working her ass off? Give me a break. That's not the way partners operate. You pick up the slack when the other person is busy. It's the bare basics of being a decent human being. You don't go out and dip your wick into another warm body when you have one at home, and a smoking hot one at that."

Molly just stared at him and he hoped like hell he hadn't overstepped. But then she said, "Definitely. I'm not arguing with you, Oliver."

He lifted her chin with his finger so she could see how serious he was when he said, "I just feel like you're not hearing me. People don't cheat because the person isn't around. They cheat because they're assholes. Would you have cheated on him if he was working hard trying to succeed at something amazing and wasn't around to have sex with you all the time?"

"Of course not."

"Exactly. Molly, he committed to marrying you. Marriage means you weather any storm that comes along—together. A month spent with my dick in my hand would be easy compared to not being with the woman I loved for the rest of my life."

Molly's brow furrowed and he loved watching her brain work to figure out what he meant. "I know he's an asshole, Oliver, I do," she said, swallowing when he stepped closer, pulling her into his arms. "All I'm trying to say is that I'm not perfect, either. That doesn't mean he should have cheated on me, but I'm only human as well."

He wanted to tell her she *was* perfect, but that would just scare the shit out of her so he kept his mouth shut.

"I appreciate you saying that stuff," she continued when he didn't respond. Instead he was too occupied with the feel of her skin under his hand. So he did it, brushed his thumb across the slant of her jaw and watched her eyes bloom with awareness. Yeah, the heat between them was still there.

"I don't want you to appreciate it, I want you to believe it. You're a fucking catch, Molly. Don't let some jerk ever make you feel like you don't deserve to be treated well because you have a job you love. That's nonsense."

"Thank you," she said, her voice quiet, the air between them charged and electric as their eyes stayed locked on each other. "That's nice of you to say, Oliver. You're a good friend."

"I'm not saying it to be nice, I'm saying it because it's true. Not all guys cheat, Molly."

She nodded, but her expression grew uncertain. "After it happened I did kind of wonder if maybe there'd been something missing, you know? Like maybe I wasn't satisfying him. I know probably every woman thinks that who's been cheated on, so..." She stopped and shrugged. "But I know that's bullshit, too. I won't let him have that kind of power over me."

"Good. And as someone who has been with you, I can tell you with confidence that you're the best I've ever had."

He heard her little inhale of breath and his dick went stiff. Christ, this was too damn soon. She needed some time first, to get over her ex, to be ready to date again. To, hell, he didn't know—he just knew he felt like the asshole now because he couldn't stop touching her. She was looking for reassurance because some douchebag had made her feel like she wasn't Molly Madix, his walking wet dream, and he'd gone and doubled down on flirting with her. He was a different kind of bastard altogether.

"That can't be true," she told him. "You've probably slept with, like, hundreds of women."

And there went a glass of ice water on his burgeoning erection.

"Excuse me?" he asked, his thumb stilling on her chin, pressing into the skin there without his really meaning to.

"Well," she said, her eyes clouding with embarrassment as one of her hands gestured wildly to encompass his body, "look at you. Anyone would want to have sex with you."

"So what?" he pressed, cursing himself as his other arm went around her back, pulling her closer into him. "You think I just have sex with whoever wants me?"

"No, of course not," she told him, eyes apologetic and voice soft.

"Did I ever make you feel like I was looking at other girls when we were together on the boat back then?"

She shook her head.

"You just think I'm a man-whore because of my pretty face, then, or did I do something else?"

"No, I don't think that, but you left me, too, you know," Molly managed, but her breathing had turned heavy, and he knew he was affecting her just as she was doing to him. "Which leads me to believe that maybe you're exaggerating about me being the best you've ever had."

He saw the uncertainty in her eyes and gentled his hand on her face, brushing his thumb over the baby-soft skin of her jaw. "Molly, you had a job offer of a lifetime, proven by the fact that you still love it, and I wasn't going to stand in your way. If I could've gone to Colorado with you, I would have. You also didn't ask, by the way. And anyway, my parents wanted me home and right now is the first time I've truly defied them in thirty years. My life wasn't my own then, not really, anyway. If you hadn't gotten that job, I'd planned to ask you to come to New York with me." Gripping her closer to him, his thumb imprinted on her jaw as he made her meet his eyes when her gaze started to slide away. "But I remember everything about us together, Molly. Every fucking thing. And the number of nights, mornings and afternoons that I've fantasized about you with nothing but my own hand outnumbers the times I've been with other women, and that's a fact."

Her whole body went still in his arms and what

happened next was on her, because he'd been prepared to wait. Even with her soft body tight against
his, he would have let her go so they could re-
main friends until she was ready for more, but
she grabbed the front of his shirt and pulled him
down to her.

His lips met her soft, plush mouth and he fell into
a slow, searing burn. Molly had never been hesitant in bed and she wasn't now, taking control of
the kiss, her head slanting against his as her clever
tongue found the seam of his lips. Groaning, both
his hands came up to burrow into her hair, unsatisfying because it was pulled back in a ponytail, so
he quickly tugged at the band and threw it to the
floor, reveling in the mass of sandy-blond hair now
cascading over his fingers and down to her breasts.

She came up on her tiptoes then, her arms sliding behind his neck, and he gripped her hair as their
tongues tangled, licking and sucking and rediscov-
ering. A mouth had never tasted so damned good
and he bent his knees, his arms coming around
her as he picked her up and set her on top of the
railing, coming to stand between her spread legs.

Her breath sucked in at the contact, his hard
length against the place he wanted to be most,
and Oliver thanked the poor bastard who'd cheated
on her because there was no way she was getting
away from him now.

Sliding his arm around her, he held her close

even though she was perfectly balanced and wasn't going to fall into the water, but he wanted more of her. He left her mouth, pressing kisses over her jaw and down her neck as her head fell to the side, giving him more access.

"I wanted to be a gentleman and give you more time," he murmured as he got closer to her ear, "but I guess I'm not the one in charge here."

"Time for what?" she asked, her voice thready and light as her eyes struggled to stay open.

He pressed a long kiss to the cord of muscle in her neck, sucking there gently and then harder, not caring if he left a mark. "Time for you to heal," he told her, tugging on a delicate earlobe, running a tongue over it at her whimper.

Molly's brown eyes fluttered open, needing a moment before they focused on him. "I don't need you to be a gentleman, Oliver," she told him. "I just want you to be you."

"Smart-ass," he growled, sinking his teeth into her neck as his hand traveled up her abdomen to cup one of her breasts, his fingers finding the raised nipple through the thin cotton of her T-shirt.

Her gasp was followed by her legs wrapping around his back and for a moment he thought he might be getting light-headed from pleasure. It'd been so long since she'd been in his arms. To know that she'd missed him when they'd broken up, he was fucking enraged over all the lost time.

"And for the record, Molly," he said, forcing her gaze to his again, "I stayed in yachting a year more than I'd intended so I could stay with you."

Molly's eyes widened and he kissed the disbelief right off her mouth. He was done with the past, theirs and the one she had with her ex. They'd made the wrong decisions back then, but now was the time for better ones, so his hand drifted under her shirt, his eyes closing as he felt the velvet of her skin under his. Finding her nipple, he tugged gently, rolling the small point between his fingers until she was squirming against him enough that he experienced a second of alarm that she really would fall into the water.

"Why were we so dumb?" she gasped, her body arching against him as her mouth slid along his jaw.

"Young, stupid, afraid," he got out, teasing the other nipple now. "Pick one, pick them all. It doesn't fucking matter because look where we are now, Molly. It's just us. No rules, no expectations, no exes, nothing but the two of us, the ocean and this boat."

"Did you invite me here with the intention of sleeping with me?" she asked, the journey her mouth was taking along his jawline slowing as she neared his ear.

"No. I know breakups are hard," he assured her, even though he'd definitely hoped it would happen. "And I never would be doing this if you were still in love with your ex."

She met his eyes then. "I think I fell out of love with him before I found out about the cheating."

"Sounds like that was a good decision," Oliver said, not at all interested, when his dick was nestled into her soft center, in talking about her ex.

"That's why I feel so guilty, because the first thing I thought after I caught them was relief. Then of course, anger and heartbreak and the rest. I realized after I left that I hadn't been sleeping with him for such a long time because I hadn't wanted to. I'd already fallen out of love with him." Oliver slid a thumb over her bottom lip, pulling at the kiss-swollen puff, inserting his thumb into her mouth and hissing when she touched her tongue to it.

"So what I'm hearing, Molly, is that you don't want me to wait to fuck you."

Her eyes closed at the words and he knew she was struggling against the same onslaught of lust that he was.

Then she shook her head, her straight white teeth sinking into his thumb, sucking it into her mouth, her cheeks hollowing out.

"Fuck, Molly," he growled, his hips grinding against her. "Be very sure this is what you want right now because if we go any further it's going to be so damn hard to stop. And if we do this tonight, you better be prepared to keep it going for as long as we're on this boat because once you're in my bed, you're not going any-fucking-where."

Their eyes locked; her brown gaze was so warm and hazy with desire and he loved nothing more than being the one to do that to her. Efficient and brilliant Molly lay exposed and bare by his mouth. Fucking incredible.

Finally, she nodded, her tongue flicking over the pad of his thumb.

"I need the words, Molly," he told her, thrusting against her again because he couldn't help himself.

"Yes, Oliver," she gasped, and he removed his hand and replaced it with his mouth.

Permission granted, Oliver didn't waste any time. He seized her mouth in a kiss designed to take them both under. Years had passed since he'd kissed Molly and she might feel different or taste different, time might have softened some of her edges, but his body certainly hadn't forgotten how it felt to have her in his arms, the thrill, the excitement and the need to possess.

From someone who hadn't wanted to commit to more than a night at a time with a woman, it was a revelation.

They were on open water right now but close enough to the dock that they could see the people on the two or three boats anchored in the water near them, meaning that they could see the two of them as well. Even so, Oliver tugged at Molly's shirt, pulling it over her head and throwing it to the teak of the deck. He stared at her, exposed in the fading sunlight, and thought how he'd been waiting for someone to move him, and Molly with her breasts, full and round in a simple pale blue bra, was apparently what he'd been waiting for. Showers of hunger rained on him as he cupped one in his hand, squeezing, weighing, reacquainting himself to the shape of her.

"Take it off," he told her, wanting her to make the decision on her own because all the other boats on the water would be able to see her if she did.

She met his eyes and he stepped away from her to tear off his own shirt in one quick motion, dropping it to the floor beside him.

Eyes still locked, he saw her gaze shift to the other boats, to the decks full of people. Chest rising and falling, his eyes fell down to where her hands unhooked the front clasp of her bra, and he thanked some glorious deity for whatever he'd done to deserve this moment, this amazing unveiling of her breasts. She shrugged off the sheer garment, and he tossed that, too, behind him on the floor.

"Anything left on the floor of a deck is a safety hazard," she reminded him with a sly grin.

He reached out, wrapping an arm around her again, securing her against him as he took her breast in his hand. Her stomach moved as she sharply inhaled, making him smile. Brushing a thumb lightly over her soft pink nipple, he watched as the skin grew tighter. "You like being watched, Molly?" he asked as the music from another boat drifted over to them.

When she didn't answer, he leaned down and took her other nipple into his mouth and her whimper of pleasure was music to his ears, his dick responding immediately. Tugging on the unbelievably soft skin of her nipple, he felt her harden in his mouth the rougher his treatment. Teeth grazed her and she jerked against him. He responded in kind, driving her mad as he treated both nipples to the same torture.

"Does it make you wet to think about people watching us?" he murmured, drawing his hand up her thigh to where her shorts began.

Flicking at the button, he exposed the skin there, his fingers diving just below the waistband. "I don't think they can see our faces," he assured her.

And then because he was a depraved asshole, and because he had one chance to show her that she hadn't been the one with the problem in her relationship, he stepped back and slid off his own shorts and boxer briefs, letting them join the other clothes on the deck.

He stroked a hand over his erect length as he watched her. "On the other hand, I don't give a shit if they do."

CHAPTER FOUR

MOLLY WATCHED AS Oliver stroked a hand over himself, the crown glistening already with evidence of his desire. The memories of their time in bed were certainly dirty, but she'd also been too young to know that what she and Oliver had done back then had been anything but ordinary. All she'd known was that it'd been so damned good. Sex with other people had never compared and now that she was possibly baring her breasts to millionaires on neighboring yachts, she finally understood why.

"So, do you?" he said, pressing her into him as his hand splayed across her stomach. He was taking her over. Sensible and rational Molly was suddenly nowhere to be found, replaced instead by a wanton sex goddess whose only desire was more Oliver.

At her nod, he growled and pulled down her zipper. "Show me, Molly."

Oh God, she was not going to make it.

Meeting his eyes, she felt powerful because he

made absolutely no effort to hide his desire for her. Idly, he stroked himself just as he cataloged every inch of her exposed body.

Oliver was a different type of animal than her; he slid in and out of decadence, physical and material. Even the way he moved, he prowled like a leopard, showy and flashy, but no less sly or dangerous for it. His hot, beckoning gaze dared her to be bad, to forget about the circumstances that brought her on this boat and just play with him. It would be harmless if that's all it was, playing.

Scooting off the railing, locking her eyes with his, she let her own pants fall to the ground.

"Goddamn," he cursed, the words hushed on his lips. "You're so perfect."

Her gaze dropped down to where he was stroking himself. "You, too."

That grin—perfect white teeth and wide, full lips with eyes dancing—she'd never forgotten it over the years. He shouldn't be so nice and so handsome and make her feel so different than she normally did. She felt safe with him, less guarded, even though they really hadn't been close in over seven years.

"You are something else, Molly," Oliver growled, his thumb running over the head of him, slicking the moisture there around the wide head.

She shrugged, tucking her thumbs into her underwear, glancing at the other boat and feeling unsure if she should continue. "Don't chicken out now."

Looking at his eyes only, she tugged down the kelly green cotton boy shorts that weren't exactly textbook sexy but felt extremely so when his gaze went hot at the sight of them. His hand moved faster and when she straightened back up he was looking at her expectantly.

She bit her lip, pretending to consider whether or not she should take this next step, but knowing there was no way she couldn't. Her veins were vibrating with lust, just watching him; feeling his closeness even from far away as he struggled with their burgeoning attraction pulled her to him. Her fingers slid down into her folds, inhaling sharply as she encountered the sensitive bud, the welcoming wet heat to smooth her way. Her eyes fluttering closed as she began to move her finger over herself, she heard his grunt of approval on the periphery of her senses.

"Fuck," he gritted out, and she opened her eyes to see that he'd stopped stroking and was watching her.

She figured it was her turn to put on a show so she leaned back against the railing, legs splayed, head falling back as she let her own moans of pleasure float away in the breeze.

Every muscle strung tight, she was on the verge of going over when movement had her cracking her eyes open. Oliver was striding toward her, a determined look on his face.

"We're not doing this for the first time in years in front of all these assholes," he ground out before hoisting her up into his arms and heading off for the interior of the boat. He carefully maneuvered her down the narrow steps to the main deck, where he made a beeline for his master suite.

She inwardly laughed at her assumption yesterday about all the time she'd be spending alone in her own bed. That had been silly. As if she'd had no intention of sleeping with Oliver when she'd accepted this trip. As if she hadn't relived their time together over the intervening years a million times. She excelled in lying to herself.

He finally set her down at the edge of the bed, her bare feet digging into the soft, plush carpet. Her nipples beaded tightly against the cool air-conditioning and she was still wound up from touching herself. And she also wanted to touch him, so she reached out a hand and placed it flat on his chest between the raised square sections of his pectoral muscles and was shocked at the heat of him, reveled in the patch of rough hair against her palm, the racing of his heart that matched hers.

Licking her lips, she ran her fingers over his nipples, playing there for just a moment before kissing the areas her hand had greeted, licking and caressing and exploring. She wondered how he'd gotten these muscles, if he worked out in a gym every day or if he still lifted anchor chains for exercise like he'd done that summer.

"You always liked touching me," he said, eyes dark as he followed the movements of her hands.

Her fingertips drew across his collarbone down the corded hills of his biceps and beneath to the delicate skin of his triceps. She grinned when he shivered. "I like knowing the parts of something, how they all work together," she agreed, her thumb pressing into the taut muscle of his forearm before exploring the contours of his palm and fingers. "And you've got some pretty impressive parts."

Oliver laughed, interrupting her exploration by tugging her in for a quick kiss. "If you pay half as much attention to the best part as you're doing to all these others, I'll be a very happy guy."

"It's definitely my favorite part," she murmured against his lips. "And not just because I know exactly how to make it work."

"Christ, I've missed you, Molly," he sighed against her lips before taking them again in a slow, sweet kiss that she felt in the tips of her toes and in the corners of her heart.

"Me, too," she whispered back when they came up to breathe.

He stepped away from her and held his arms

out. "Well, then, I think it's time we get reac-
quainted. Go ahead and study me, Molly."

She loved that he could command without being
bossy—it was the easy way he always had about
him; nothing was too serious. Kneeling in front
of him, she started at his feet, loving the sounds
of frustration and desire he made as she ran a finger between his toes. Her face was on a level with
his straining cock so that every time she breathed
it drifted over the taut skin, and it was totally on
purpose as she busied herself with other areas. Her
fingers found the fleshy pads of his toes, some
calloused, some still soft, followed the length of
narrow bones that made up a pair of masculine
feet, large and wide and tan, up to his ankles. She
pressed in behind his knee just to see what he'd
do. He looked down at her with a wry expression,
a corner of his mouth quirked. "You sure are taking your time down there."

Shrugging, she tilted her head back so she could
meet his eyes. "I figured that we have literally
nothing but time on this boat—why not be completely thorough?"

"That's for damn sure," he told her, ripping off
his watch and throwing it carelessly onto the side
table. She'd already scoped it as a Patek Philippe that
cost more than her first car, so it meant something
that he didn't care much about it at this moment.

"I never took you for symbolic gestures," she

said, dropping a kiss on his kneecap, the hair fuzzy and strangely intimate against her lips.

"You didn't?" he asked, both eyebrows raised in surprise. "I called this boat *Chance* as in second chance, for my life and for possibly us, Molly. I'd say I'm pretty big on them. When I make the effort to make a point, I'm damn well going to make it."

She brushed slowly across the back of his thigh and he twitched. Smiling, she kissed the other knee, rubbing a thumb over the place she'd touched with her lips. "I stand corrected," she admitted, and gladly. Ignoring the second-chance-for-them remark because she knew it was just words. Oliver was so good at talking, at being amiable and telling people what they wanted to hear. It wasn't meant to be deceitful, but he wasn't promising her something. He was just talking. He'd given his boat a double meaning and that was the end of it. She wasn't going to read further into it.

With a glance at the hard length she was skipping in her journey up his leg, Molly traveled instead to kneel behind him. A curveball he hadn't anticipated that had him cursing. "Fuck, Molly, I wish you really were standing right now because I don't know how much more of this I can take."

"I think you have to take all of it, Oliver," she commanded playfully as she set her hands to both tight sides of his ass. The carved cutouts in the side where her pinkies rested were hollow and firm just like the rest of him. She caressed downward, hoping for some measure of plump fleshiness, but was to find no such thing. He was hard all over.

Dropping a kiss in one of those muscled hollows, she murmured, "You could at least acknowledge it when I kiss your ass."

She felt more than saw him shake his head. "You're treading on thin ice, Molly," he warned.

He grunted when she drew a finger down the seam of his ass. She wasn't going to breach it but she loved knowing she might have that power, loved knowing that Oliver was the type of person to put the power in her hands because he didn't feel it diminished his. She kept going up, squeezing the bottom of his cheeks as she stood, her nails digging in because touching him like this, watching his body subtly react to her, was addictive and she was drunk on his desire for her. After so many years of phoning it in during sex she felt reborn, a woman who could please and be pleased.

She ran her hands over the sides of his rib cage, over the winged span of his back, the muscles beneath the golden skin jumping and tensing with each pass of her palms, fingers and lips. Then she brought her hands up to tangle in the back of his hair, his head dipping forward as he shivered. Fingernails teased his scalp and she felt an answering tingle in her body. Tall herself, she stood only five or so inches shorter than him, and kissing his shoulder, she reached a hand around his torso to grip his length, the wetness that leaked out coating her palm as she slid it downward and up again.

His breathing was audible as he stood stock-still as she stroked like she'd watched him do earlier on the deck.

"Is this good?" she asked, knowing the mechanics were solid but seeking any special requests.

"You're back there because the angle is better?"

She nodded; she wanted to deliver maximum pleasure, and why do things the hard way when this was the most mechanically sound way to get a job like this done?

He laughed and thrust into her hand. "Well, come on, then, you've literally got me by the balls, so show me what you've got."

"Technically—"

"Molly," he growled, placing his hand over hers on his cock.

"Fine." She relented on pointing out that she was not holding his balls as such. "But hands off, this is my show." He immediately lifted his hands and she saw them fist at his sides. "Good boy," she laughed.

He grunted in response, his head shaking. So she granted him relief, slowly stroking over his length, pressing soft kisses randomly over his back as she worked him. The rough arousal she'd felt earlier on the deck hit her hard as she heard him exhale, saw his knuckles turn white as she squeezed and played.

"Is this good?" she asked, truly curious.

"Sublime perfection," he gritted.

"Are you sure there's not a certain technique you'd like me to try, no preferred way that you do this?"

"I like it any way, Molly, but if you're asking me what I do to get myself off quickly, yeah, there are some pointers I could share."

She waited for him to expound, but he didn't, just thrust forward in her hand with another audible inhale.

"Are you going to share them?"

"Wetter," he told her, then disengaged her hand and brought it to his mouth, where he licked her palm in an erotic motion, tickling and making sure to moisten the whole area. She sucked in a breath herself.

He put her hand back on his dick and sighed, then took her other hand and fastened it on his root, where the crimpy hair there tickled her skin. "Just hold that there, squeezing if you want."

She nodded against his back, kissing the top of his spine as she moved her hands again, the going easier now that her hand was wet. He liked it, too, the muted sounds he was making heating her from the inside.

"Harder," he instructed, then squeezed his hand over hers again to show her just how much pressure she should exert.

"Are you sure this doesn't hurt?" she asked, moving her hand up and down like he'd shown her.

"Positive," he gasped, his hips nearly bucking her hold off him. "It feels fucking amazing, Molly. You could give up a career in engineering and just become a professor of hand jobs."

"You told me what to do," she laughed, stroking him harder and harder as he squirmed against her, his back to her chest. She wondered if her hard nipples pressed against his back were driving him as crazy as they were her. She was so wet, so ready for him to turn around and take her, but she loved this, too. Absolutely loved being able to give him pleasure, to make him happy. He'd done so much for her by giving her this escape. She wasn't in the habit of thanking people with hand jobs, but in this instance she was more than happy to do it.

"The position was your idea," he pointed out, a little breathless. "And that made all the damned difference."

She pressed an openmouthed kiss to the ridged edge of his shoulder blade and let her hips move in time to his. It was so weird being behind a guy this way but it made her so hot, too; this was a power position. He was in *her* arms, she was giving *him* pleasure, it was new, it was delicious, it was a little dirty.

"Molly," he groaned when she pulled what she thought was too hard. "Faster, please."

She granted his request immediately, her fist flying over his erection, the pre-come leaking out, slicking her hand right up making it so smooth, so easy. Then he was bucking against her wildly grunting her name over and over again. "Move away or I'm going to come all over your hand," he warned, but she kept going. Wanted him on her, and when he went, she angled him up so he'd land on his own chest, but most of it caught on her hands, the milky white liquid coating her fingers as she continued to slowly bring him down, reveling in his little shudders against her.

"I never got to feel those when we had sex when we were younger," she told him, her voice hushed. "You were always above me or behind me and I never got to feel your whole body come."

He turned in her arms then, his eyes hot when they met hers. "Did you like it?"

She nodded. "It was nice to feel what I did to you."

That darkened his gaze even more and then it went positively black when she lifted her dripping hand to her mouth and sucked every bit of him off her fingers and hand, ending with the thumb in a smacking sound.

"Get on the bed," he ordered, his voice low and gruff and barely audible. "Get on the fucking bed right now, Molly. Jesus Christ, I can't believe you just did that. Am I supposed to be a goddamn saint?"

Apparently playtime was over.

"What?" she asked innocently. "No one's ever eaten your come before?"

He tilted his head to the side as if he was tense and stretching before a battle. "Not like that, and I hope to see you do it again sometime."

"I promise," she told him.

"Good," he said shortly. "Now get on the bed like I just told you to."

He barely gave her time to scramble over to the blue duvet before he was on her.

"You have learned some new things since last time, Molly," he said, stalking up her body on his hands and knees. He drew a fingertip through her dripping wetness. "I've never been a jealous man before, but I want to erase the memory of every person who's seen you this way," he told her, sinking down to suck a nipple into his mouth.

She arched against him as he pulled, his teeth grazing the very tip, pressing down to tease, tugging hard enough to tantalize. Her body was bellowing with want; getting him off was an extreme pleasure but had also made her desperate for him, for just his touch. He was still too far away and she wanted the weight of him against her, the roaring heat and power of his body, the smooth feel of his skin.

"I can't wait anymore," Molly breathed in a frenzied rush.

He shifted his head so he could meet her eyes, her nipple still buried in his mouth before he let it drop, and answered, "That's too bad, because I just came really fucking hard and I could spend an entire hour going down on you before I need to come again. Guess you didn't think about that before you had your way with me."

Her eyes closed because he was such an ass, but she liked it. She also could see as well as he could that he was already hard as a rock again and ready to go. He was just living to tease her.

So she raised her arm and tapped at her smartwatch.

"What are you doing?" he asked, his eyes narrowed as he dropped kisses down her abdomen to her mound.

"Setting my timer for an hour so I know how long to keep you down there," she said, scrolling to sixty minutes on her clock.

A corner of his mouth quirked as he opened her up to his gaze, his thumbs running down the insides of her folds. "You're going to regret that,

Molly," he told her, "when you're begging for me to be inside you. I'm going make you come so many times you're going to forget your name before you get what you really want."

And then he went about her destruction. His tongue found her center, applying one slow, wide-tongued lick before moving downward to lap up what getting him off had inspired in her, the sounds lewd and dirty and giving her fits of heat as she bucked against his mouth. He pushed one long finger inside her and she whimpered as he twirled it around, centering on that delicate rough patch and brushing over it relentlessly. Her breath was coming fast and sharp interspersed with moans of pleasure as he added another finger as his tongue played everywhere except where she wanted it most.

Her first orgasm hit her like a freight train; the months of celibacy and the old yearning for him that she'd neglected over the years, the memory of his touch coupled with the new reality, it all came at her at once. She shook against his mouth and he hummed his pleasure at it but kept going without much pause except his care in helping her ride through it.

His breath hot on her, he caught her eyes. "One."

And then he continued to work, his teeth grazing an already overly sensitive nub, as she squirmed against his mouth, which only made things worse. The contact intensified, his tongue stiffening to spear inside her, fucking her just as indecently without his cock even though she was desperate for it just like he'd warned. One of his hands sat at the top of her slit, not moving, but just placed there, the fingers pressing into her flesh as if he was claiming that part of her as his and his alone, protecting it against anyone else who might show up on this boat and try to take it.

His lips closed over her in one blinding suck and she gasped her climax, shuddering as he slowly licked her down from the edge, already wrung out with pleasure.

"Two," he murmured, diving back in, drinking her from her entrance, then traveling all the way to the top of her, leaving no millimeter unchecked.

By the time he sent her into her third orgasm, she couldn't stop shivering against him, overcome by sensation, her body empty of thought and purpose except to roll along with the bliss he was doling out.

"Please, Oliver," she whispered, the words coming out broken and soft. She cleared her throat and tried again. "Have some mercy."

His head rose from where he'd been slowly licking up and down the sides of her inner lips. "What's the time?"

She groaned but, hoping she could end this,

looked at her watch. "It's been one hundred and seventy-three hours since you started this."

Oliver's head lifted and his grin was so devious. "So I've made my point?"

"I never knew what your point was, but probably?" she got out, still breathing erratically.

He levered up over her in one smooth and athletic motion until they were face-to-face. His jaw and chin were a mess, but he didn't seem to care at all, wiping her away with a couple swipes of his hand before also putting his wet fingers in his mouth and licking them clean. Christ, and she thought she couldn't come again. Then his lips met hers in a hot kiss, messy and raw and on the edge. Despite his nonchalant attitude, he was just as crazy as she was.

"My point was that when your captain gives you an order, it's best to follow it."

He reached out to the nightstand and grabbed a box of condoms, sliding one on in record time.

When he was poised at her entrance, the fat head notched against her already pulsing muscles, he said, "I've been waiting a long fucking time for this."

And then he was inside her; one demanding shove and he was buried to the hilt. It wasn't easy despite how ready she was and it wasn't as if she could *be* more ready—that work was done. But her back arched as she stretched to accommodate him.

His hand came up to palm her breasts, plucking at her hard nipples as he started to move, slowly and then more quickly.

The sounds he made, the deep, unconscious grunts as he bottomed out, flared through her veins. She just loved seeing him lose control, had missed what he looked like the first time when she'd been behind him, but now she saw every flicker of sensation flit across his face along with intense concentration, the straining muscles of his arms as he supported himself. She ran a hand over the bulge of his biceps, feeling the sweat of exertion and the strength there as the muscles vibrated under the pressure of his weight and forward momentum. When she clenched him inside her, his teeth gritted and he ground against her, just on the precipice of insanity.

The hand on her breast moved down and played with her clit, lightly brushing over it before finding purchase and stroking rhythmically until she came again with a shout pulled from her gut, a release so strong for a quick second she actually wondered if she was passing out. At the very least, she'd lost a lot of oxygen to her brain, because the ability to think was gone.

"Fuck," he groaned, bucking wildly against her until he stiffened, his back a straight line as he let himself go.

Breathing hard, he eventually lowered himself down to her, foreheads touching. "Molly?"

When she caught her own breath, her hands falling limply to the bed, she managed, "Yeah?"

"Nothing. I was just making sure I was alive."

CHAPTER FIVE

OLIVER WOKE UP and felt Molly in bed next to him, smelled the light citrus of her shampoo, and couldn't help his smile as he stretched an arm above his head. Last night had been the best night on record and he had a whole month to repeat it; how could he not be happy about that? The hold his parents had on his life was already melting away. The vise of anxiety that had been gripping his insides for years was finally letting up and it was euphoric. If he could be 100 percent certain that they wouldn't use Molly as a tool to get him back in the business, that would certainly be better, but for now it was enough to be free. This was, after all, even better than what he'd anticipated it would feel like.

He felt Molly stir against his chest and ran a hand through her hair until her eyelids slowly fluttered open and he was greeted to sleepy brown eyes.

He leaned down to capture her mouth in a soft

kiss, and she felt lazy and warm as she nuzzled into him, like a kitten waking up from a nap. When he pulled away, he smiled down at her. "Hello."

A soft smile appeared on her lips as she met his eyes. "Good morning."

"The best morning," he amended, letting his hand drift down her bare back. At her shiver his inner self gave a responding ripple of satisfaction. She was so responsive, and they were so in tune. It felt like a dream he never wanted to wake from.

A faint blush stained her cheeks at his words and the fact that he was caressing the crest of her buttocks, even though, God knew, they'd been extremely intimate last night. He couldn't believe that there'd be something she'd be shy about now.

"What am I going to do with you, Molly?" he asked, running a thumb back up the delicate notches on her spine. It was an idle question, but one that had a different meaning to him than the way he said it. He didn't know yet what he was going to do with her or how he would protect her if his parents found out she meant something to him. He could always marry her—then it would be too late for them to do anything besides blow hot air—but the mere mention of that so soon would send Molly jumping overboard to get away from him. "We only have each other on this boat—how will we ever fill the time?"

She shook her head at him, dropping a kiss on

the middle of his chest as her hand moved downward over his abdomen. "I'm sure we'll be able to find something, though it might be hard." She smiled as she gently palmed his erection.

He shook his head and laughed.

"I'm learning how to be corny from you." She grinned, then let his hard length go as she climbed over his lap, straddling his hips as she looked down at him. He might as well have been dead and in heaven, that's how fucking sexy she looked on top of him, her hair in delicious tangles, her eyes still drowsy with sleep and her pale skin flushed. "First question before we sail this vessel out into the clear blue sea today, did you bring enough condoms or do we need to make a special provisioning trip?"

"Good news for you that I'm always prepared. I put more on the list yesterday so there's a jumbo pack sitting in my bathroom drawer as we speak."

"A jumbo pack, you say?" Molly's eyes looked skeptical. "What if we get stranded? I don't know if it will be enough."

Locking eyes with her, he reached out a hand to the nightstand to grab his phone and as he typed, his gaze didn't waver from her. Setting the phone back on the stand, he braced his hands on her hips. "More are on the way."

A corner of her mouth quirked. "You're a boss that gets what he wants."

His hands slid back to cup her ass cheeks, giving them a squeeze. "And I'm your captain, too," he reminded, his voice playfully stern, "so why don't you hop off me and get that jumbo pack so we can start this voyage off right."

When Molly just stared at him, playfully put out that he was giving her orders, he sat up so he could meet her eye to eye, nipping at her mouth. "You didn't seem to have this much of a problem with authority last night."

As Molly's mouth fell open, he moved her off his lap even though he really loved her being there, and took his time walking to the bathroom himself, knowing she liked to look. Which was good because he was happy to give her all the free shows she wanted. He already wanted to give her everything she wanted.

He grabbed the entire box from the cabinet and returned to his room, stopping in his tracks as he saw Molly on the bed, still kneeling with her legs spread, wetness glistening at her center.

Fuck, he should have bought this yacht years ago.

"I'm happy to see you've decided to make up for defying my explicit orders," he told her, tossing the box, minus the one condom in his hand, on the bedside table. She held his gaze before her eyes slid down to his thick, waiting cock, and she swallowed, eyes fluttering back up to his.

"You didn't ask me nicely," she scolded mildly, as

he ripped open the condom. "If you'd said, 'Molly, could you please grab the condoms from the bathroom so I can wake you up with an epic fuck,' I would have gladly gotten the condoms for you."

Then she got down on all fours, turning her head to look back at him standing dumbly by the bed, open condom in hand. "Now you're going to have to do all the work."

Getting himself together, ripping his eyes from the ripe ass just a foot away from him, he shook his head before heading over to the other side of the bed and lying down just as he'd done before he'd left to get the box. She stared at him in disbelief as he stretched out, hands propping up his head as he waited for her to straddle him again.

He couldn't wait to take her from behind, but he was interested in what Molly might do, enjoyed pressing her buttons, pushing her into a corner to see how she'd attack the problem. He just plain loved watching her mind work and if that extended to some silly games and harmless power struggles, he was all for it.

"Is this worth proving your point?" she asked, shuffling over until she was kneeling beside him.

In answer, he rolled the condom down his erect length, the contact making him suck in a breath of air.

Molly watched him, eyes hooded—he'd discovered she loved it when he touched his dick. Then a corner of her mouth quirked and his eyes widened as her hand came off her thigh, caressing upward as she found the center of her body, her middle finger disappearing into her folds.

After stroking a few times, he raised an eyebrow at her. He thought about taking the condom off and reciprocating, but instead he angled his body so he had a better view of her core and left his gaze there, riveted on that disappearing finger.

A whimper of pleasure escaped her and the muscles of his abdomen tensed, his whole body wound tight as he sat in witness to one of his favorite fantasies. On some of his lonelier nights, he'd gotten off to memories of her more times than he could count and this was just so insanely much better. The scent of their fucking from last night still lingered in the air and now it was in his nose again, firing up nerve endings and kinky corners of his brain he'd yet to explore with her. There wasn't a fetish, a position, a time of day or odd place he wouldn't explore with Molly.

"How many times do I need to say please, Molly, so you'll sit on me and let me do the work for you?"

Gasping in a breath, Molly fluttered her eyes open, then he watched below again as her hand moved underneath her and she speared two fingers inside herself. The soft suction sound as she carefully pushed them in and out of her had him nearly coming, his hips jerking off the bed as it was.

"Molly," he growled. "I'm saying please."

Another whimper as her hips began rolling faster against her own fingers.

He took himself in hand, ready to pull off the condom so he could join her because the rips of pure heat arrowing to his cock could not be denied. Sucking in a breath at the contact, he gritted out, "Molly, I'm begging you, please."

He saw three fingers disappear inside her and with a growl, he jackknifed up with the intention of pulling her on top of him, but then she opened her eyes, the look in them so hot and molten that he stuttered.

"Please, Molly," he choked, "I need to come and if I take this condom off we'll have wasted one of our precious supply for no reason."

He heard the wet sound of her fingers exiting her body and his hips jerked in response.

"You're right," she said, her eyes meeting his as her voice came out an octave lower than normal. "That would be terribly irresponsible of us."

Oliver reached out and brought her mouth to his as she pushed him back onto the bed, rising over him like a bird of prey, and he was so totally fine with being eaten.

"Recklessly irresponsible," he confirmed, his hand going back to gripping her ass like he'd done before, more firmly this time because she wasn't getting away from him again.

Then she stuck one of her fingers into her mouth, slowly licking around it before pulling it out, and he thought he might literally die from unspent orgasm.

With a warning growl, he lifted her up and centered her on his waiting cock, loving her gasp of surprise that turned to a moan of pleasure as she sank down onto him.

She leaned down to catch his mouth, and he tasted her delicious self so he sucked on her tongue, stealing all of that sweet tangy taste for himself. He started to move her on him, reveled in her intake of breath against his lips.

"You went hard last night and I think I overshot when I climbed on you earlier," she murmured in explanation for driving him nuts. "I was just making sure I was ready for you."

Then bracing on his chest, she lifted off him and started to move.

But her words pissed him off, too, and he brought a thumb to her clit, loving that she shivered as he did it. "I'll always make sure you're ready, Molly," he gritted out, trying not to be annoyed that she wouldn't think so. "This is a game. A hot, sexy fucking game I never want to stop, but you being comfortable with everything we do together is always my first goddamn concern."

"I know," she breathed. "That's not what I meant."

"It sounds like it's what you meant," he told her, bucking underneath her, her wetness sliding onto the skin of his abdomen. She was the hottest thing he'd ever encountered and even after an entire night of having her he was still too damn close to going off after such a short period of time.

She shook her head. "No, I was supposed to be doing all the work."

Oliver grinned, his fingers flexing against the plump mounds of her ass cheeks, guiding her as she rode him.

"Feeling you get wet all over my fingers is never work, Molly," he said, levering up so they were face-to-face. "That's a gift I'm always happy to get."

Then he picked up the rest of her fingers and sucked each one from knuckle to tip, his tongue swirling and tasting every bit of her until Molly was driving against him at a furious pace.

Drawing a nipple into his mouth as his thumb slid over her clit, he could tell she was close to coming apart and he loved watching it, seeing each of her features twitch and scrunch, her mouth open, breathing hard, waiting for the final release. It felt almost religious to witness her lose herself in the moment and to him.

But all too soon it was too much. Watching her move, her perfect handful-size tits bouncing with each movement, the furrow in her brow, he just wanted to watch her forever. A tightening started in his lower back and he knew he was close, his muscles tensing up as she moved over him faster, her breath quickening as he pushed her along, too wound up and close to wait much longer. They slammed into each other, his fingers finding her clit again and helping her catapult over the edge, her soft breath a warm whisper on his neck as she slumped forward. He let her recover, her hands curling against his chest.

"Keep going," she finally whispered, jiggling her hips. "I know you need to."

He took her lips then, desperate and deep and a little dangerous as a result of her directing him to take his own pleasure.

Then he lifted her off him and back to where she'd been on her hands and knees, climbing off the bed so he could stand on the floor behind her. She raised an eyebrow at him, but he shrugged. "Always a good idea."

And then he was plunging back inside her with a single decisive stroke, eyes shutting at the warm wetness of her that encased him. He fucking loved being inside Molly, never wanted to be outside her. If he could somehow attach himself to her person, it would be a great fucking day. He kept thrusting, pulling her hips back before she was ready. Her whimpers got closer, one on top of the other as he grew more forceful, her inner muscles gripping him as he left her and sucking him back in as he entered. They were in tune, together, both surging forward to that ultimate peak.

He didn't know how he'd gotten so lucky, how he'd avoided all the women his parents had wanted him to marry when this was the thing that had been waiting for him. It was so good, the pressure building in his sack, and then with a grunt he poured into the condom just as her muscles fluttered around him as she climaxed and his entire body was energized with lust before falling into complete and total bliss.

Their heavy breathing was the only sound in the room as he pulled out of her, slowly, then helped her lie on the bed. Dropping a kiss on the small of her back, he headed into the bathroom to dispose of the condom.

Once finished, he brought back a bottle of water to the bed and offered it to her. "I know you're probably exhausted after all that work," he said.

A corner of her mouth kicked up as she looked up at him. She'd turned over to her back on the bed, the lower half of her legs hanging off the side, and used her elbows to raise her torso. As she took the bottle from him and drank, he could only stare at her soft golden skin in the hushed morning light coming through the windows.

He drew a slow finger down the middle of her

chest, in between her perfect breasts, regarding her as she drank. "How am I supposed to operate this boat when I know you're somewhere aboard looking like this?" he mused, his finger making small circles on the slightly raised bump of her stomach.

"Same," she told him, recapping the water and setting it aside. "But I'm willing to at least make it out of port today so we can anchor somewhere and then do all of that again."

He laughed. "Yeah, making it off the dock will be enough."

Her head fell back on the bed, looking up at the ceiling as he continued to explore her. He thought it might be impossible for him to actually remove his hand, to stop touching her. He was already addicted to the connection.

"So we know the boat's engine is operational. I checked all the equipment yesterday including and up to hair dryers and kitchen appliances. I'd say we're ready to sail when you are, Captain."

"Sounds good."

She quirked an eyebrow at him. "Do you have plans to share where we're going during this Caribbean adventure?"

He splayed his entire hand on her stomach, watching intently at the juxtaposition of his rough hand on her smooth, flawless skin. "You want a detailed itinerary?" he asked, meeting her eyes.

Then with a shrug, "I don't have a set plan, but I'll take you anywhere you want to go, baby."

His insides warmed at her snort. Then she met his eyes, hers growing melty. "I don't need to leave this boat to have an amazing time."

Ah, fuck, this girl. His chest clenched and he leaned down to take her mouth again. The kiss was soft and sweet and he dropped another one on the tip of her nose as he broke away. "Then we'll say fuck it and sail toward the Bahamas and stay aboard. Like I said, there are a couple of ports I need to visit to look at some boats and take a meeting, but other than that it's just you and me, Molly."

"That sounds really good," she said, and he just couldn't even believe how lucky he was that her asshole fiancé cheated on her. It was a fucking miracle that she was now single after all these years and on his boat wanting to be with him.

"You mean it sounds fan-fucking-tastic," he growled, leaning down to plant a loud, messy kiss on her belly where his hand had been.

Molly laughed and tried to squirm away, but he knelt down on the bed until he was kissing back up her chest to her mouth.

"You're right," she said, grinning at him when they were nose to nose. "I'll be more careful with my superlatives in the future."

"Damn right." He smiled back. He stood, pulling her up from the bed with him. "Let's go, chief engineer, and get out of here. The sooner we set sail, the sooner we drop anchor, which means the sooner we can get back in here and do that again."

"And again?" Molly teased.

"And again," he confirmed, his hand giving her a last squeeze before heading to the bathroom for a shower.

When she stood there not coming in, he crooked a finger at her. "Don't be shy, Molly," he said. "I promise I won't seduce you."

She crossed her arms over her chest, covering her gorgeous breasts, which was a damn shame. "That's what you said in the middle of the night, and we were up for another hour."

He felt his lips curve before he even got the words out. "Sweetheart, I've been up since the moment you walked onto this boat."

Molly's eyes closed on a groan. "Oh my God," she said, her voice high with disbelief. "You are out of your mind."

"That's accurate," he agreed wryly. "Now, come on, shower with me so we can live up to the eco-conscious redesign of this boat and save some water."

Hiding a grin, Molly followed him into the bathroom and climbed into the enormous shower with him. He'd envisioned being in here with Molly, watching the clear water sluice over her body, her wet hair slicked back. He'd also imagined what he did next, which was go down on her as the hot water pelted down on her back and into his mouth as he licked at her.

"Oliver," she whispered when she was finished.

He met her mouth with a gentle kiss when he rose again. "Just a thank-you for you showering with me."

They finished washing up after she gave him the most sensuous shampoo and conditioning treatment he'd ever experienced. No one had ever handled him like that before, taking care not to get soap in his eyes or ears, massaging his scalp. It was meticulous and thorough and so Molly Madix. It also warmed his heart in a way that he couldn't even explain because he'd never felt that way before. But it finally felt like he was being *cared* for and he never wanted to let that go.

They eventually parted ways to get to work, her to the engine room and him to the cockpit at the side of the boat to take off. She'd untied the ropes harnessing them at the dock while he and the lone deck crew member communicated over the headset. Within minutes, they were in the wide-open Atlantic Ocean, pointed east toward Grand Bahama Island. It was only a two-hour sail and after about a half hour, Molly joined him back up in the bridge. Once the undocking was over, he'd come up to the main steering wheel and controls so he could see the ocean spread out in front of him.

Plus, it was much cooler in the bridge than outside, which was a plus. The sun was high in the sky already and hot. He monitored the controls as the boat glided over the water and he was so pleased by the work he'd done. No, he hadn't carved the siding or built the engine, but this boat had been his labor of love and damn if that didn't make it all the sweeter.

"What are you smiling at?" Molly asked, joining him at the wheel. She was holding a bottle of water and the tiny speck of grease on her thumb got his own engine roaring. Never had grease seemed so erotic to him.

"Just that we're an hour in on open water and this baby is purring like a jungle cat."

Molly's shoulders shook and she grinned at him. "You don't look like a silly man, but you are."

"I know my pretty face is meant to be carved in marble, but a man's got to laugh."

She shot him an amused look. "You're proud of yourself for this boat and you should be," she said. "Everything downstairs is running well. I think we're good."

"We're about an hour until we can drop anchor. I figure we'll find a shady spot in the shadow of a hill or something."

"I'm looking forward to doing not much."

"I'm looking forward to doing you," he said, already laughing at her eye roll.

"You just can't stop, can you?"

He shook his head. "It's true, though. I hope you're prepared for just how much my hands are going to be on you during this trip."

"I think I can handle it," she said, eyebrow raised. "Pun intended."

His grin was huge. "That's the spirit, Molly."

She just shook her head and directed her gaze to the blue ocean in front of them.

"Are we going to go ashore once we anchor?"

"If you want. Might be nice to have a dinner on land sometimes. Especially since we don't have a chef aboard yet. I know I'm a culinary genius, but a night off might be nice."

"You're going to cook tonight?"

He shrugged. "Who else is going to do it?"

Molly looked at him thoughtfully. "I don't know, I thought we'd just order pizza or something."

Oliver couldn't help it—he pulled her closer, into his arms. He couldn't not touch her. "I'll cook for you anytime."

She sighed in his arms. "You're just trying to make it impossible for me to ever leave this yacht, aren't you?"

"You bet." He smiled, but she had no idea just how true her statement was.

CHAPTER SIX

MOLLY WAS SITTING on the upper deck of *Chance* with an ice-cold margarita talking herself out of pinching herself as she gazed at the setting sun over the sandy white beach of Grand Bahama Island when she got the text that immediately put a crater-size dent in her euphoric mood.

Max, her ex, apparently wanted her to answer the phone calls from him that she'd been ignoring. Reading over the words a second time, she let out a pent-up breath. She didn't want to talk to Max and they most certainly didn't have anything to discuss. In fact, she was downright irritated that his text was pulling her out of the lusciously filthy thoughts she'd been having all morning about Oliver.

"No frowning on yachts," Oliver reprimanded from his place behind the bar where he was making another batch of margaritas.

"I see people cry in baseball all the time," she

told him, trying to sidestep the text she'd just gotten. She didn't want to talk about Max with Oliver anymore. Just wanted him to be a distant memory already.

"You must be thinking of soccer," he joked, coming out from behind the small chrome bar of the deck with his own refilled margarita. Looking down at her from where he stood, he took a sip and regarded her. She knew he expected her to tell him what had made her frown but she didn't want to. She wanted to enjoy being in paradise, surrounding by turquoise water, open sky and the sexiest man on earth, who hadn't put a shirt on once since anchoring the boat sometime before noon. Which meant that he'd been all day just walking around the yacht, checking his email, making calls, cooking them lunch and dinner, as if he wasn't irresistible already without the ridged expanse of his abs on full display.

"Molly," he said, taking her hand in his, letting his thumbs drift over her knuckles. Then he cursed as he saw the bit of grease she'd missed under her fingernails. "Fuck, I love it when you have grease on your hands." His eyes met hers. "Why does that turn me on so much?"

"Maybe you have an affinity for anything that could be used as lube?"

His shoulders started shaking and the corners of his eyes crinkled. He was so adorable when he laughed, so different from the cultured and sophisticated person he really was. Despite their friendship, while she was sitting on the super yacht he owned, it was literally impossible for her to forget just how wealthy he was and how far out of her depth she was. When they'd dated before, she'd been too young to really understand levels of wealth. When he'd told her his parents had family money, she'd imagined a McMansion like the ones she'd grown up around that kids whose parents were doctors or lawyers lived in. That had been her idea of wealthy and she'd still known then that she didn't belong in that world. Amazing sex aside, she knew it couldn't work.

Once she'd found out who his parents were and did an internet search on him it had become astoundingly clear. The Kents were, like, people-who-owned-sports-teams wealthy, who built stadiums and hospitals and schools, created and funded foundations and scholarship programs. She had no idea how those people lived, nor did she understand what it must have taken for Oliver to be on this yacht with her now, to walk away from running one of the largest investment firms in the world. There had to be consequences he wasn't sharing with her, repercussions he was facing to follow the path he wanted for himself. She'd never truly understand his life, but she did want to be a good friend to him, to be emotional support for him like he'd always been for her.

After one night with him, every single one of her qualms about her performance in bed with Max had been quashed. Quashed so hard the little fragments of doubt had turned into diamonds. Getting him to open up was the least she could do for him.

Oliver's thumb ran over the tip of her finger with the black mark. "I'd love to try a few items that could be used as lube with you tonight," he teased, stroking her hand. "Maybe some bacon grease?"

She dropped his hand, recoiling in disgust. "That's awful."

His eyes darkened as he seemed to consider it. "Are you sure? We could both cover our bodies head to toe in it, just slipping and sliding all over each other smelling like Sunday-morning breakfast. It could be fun, Molly."

She knew he was just being silly, but the prospect of sliding all over Oliver did send a zing of heat through her body.

Meeting his eyes, she saw the smile there and shook her head. "You're such nonsense."

He grinned, then pulled another chaise over to hers and extended out onto it, his abs rippling with the movement and his thick tanned thigh muscles standing out against the white chair cushion. "I am, but I'm also not the one staring at my phone. Talk to me, Molly. We're sleeping together now, so if there's something going on with your ex, I'd like to know."

"Nothing's going on, but he texted and he wants me to call him to clear up a few things."

Oliver's brow furrowed as he searched her expression. "You're not thinking of trying to work things out with him, are you?"

"No, of course not," she said, shaking her head vehemently. "I just don't know that I want to talk to him. I'm not good expressing what I feel out loud. I'm better at fixing things, using tools."

Setting his margarita aside, Oliver flipped over so that he was on his side facing her. "Well, you don't have to call him, but maybe it's for the best to put a bookend on it because something is happening between us on this boat, Molly. I don't know where it's going or what your expectations are, but I don't want to keep doing what we're doing if you're not ready or still want to give things a chance with him." He held her eyes then. "So if you want to talk about what you want to say more with me, I'm here. I understand he wasn't just some guy you were dating—you were going to marry him. That's a big deal."

"I know," she told him, but it was really just a statement to stall for time so she could pick and choose the right things to say after her heart had skipped a beat at his words. Something *was* happening between them but it wasn't as if they were dating for real; like last time, it was a fling, another yacht romance. Oliver wasn't going to ask her to marry him and then whisk her away to some Fifth Avenue paradise penthouse as he resumed his life as a billionaire and she went back to building spacecraft. That wasn't a likely scenario. Nor was she interested in living that life. She *liked* her life.

So she was happy to continue having fun, but after she left this boat she'd get back to her real life and while she didn't have plans to get back together with Max, she did know that she needed closure from that relationship before she moved on to another one. Whenever it might be.

"I guess it just feels weird to be hashing things out with him when I've already moved on," Molly told Oliver. "He hasn't been interested in apologizing and I don't want to hear more of his excuses, so I guess I'm just wary of what he could possibly still have to say. Maybe I actually am afraid of getting closure and moving on, after all."

Oliver ran a hand through the side of her hair, shifting her gaze to his. "I hear you. It probably won't be a super fun conversation, but do you want us to keep sleeping together?"

God help her, that was basically all she wanted right now. To drink him in like he was a magic elixir that, poof, made her life perfect. "Yeah."

His eyes glinted with satisfaction and she started to feel uneasy. "Good, so all you have to do is call him tomorrow and tell him that I'm the man in your life now and that he can go fuck off. Closure accomplished."

Was she doing an ice bucket challenge or something? Because cold water had definitely just been dumped on her head at the directive. She liked Oliver, but this was her real life she was dealing with whereas he would eventually leave her behind to return to his life in million-dollar world just like he had before. "Come again?" she asked, her voice deceptively chipper.

His eyes held hers, unwavering even though he'd picked up her change of tone. "You're sleeping with me now, so I suggested you call your shitty ex and let him know."

"You're overstepping, Oliver," she warned, her voice low but not mean.

His thumb brushed over her jaw. "I overstep, Molly, that's who I am."

"You've never overstepped with me before," she pointed out. He'd always been the perfect gentleman with her. From everything to deferring to her on boat matters, loving the grease in random places on her person, admiring how she was able to build and fix things, he'd always made her feel special and like he was proud of her.

But now he was being kind of a dick. He hadn't

even formally asked her to be exclusive, was simply demanding it and also demanding that she announce it to the man she'd been ready to marry.

"Yeah, and then you ended up engaged to some cheating loser. So I'm gonna let it all hang out now, Molly. We're not kids anymore."

She didn't know what "let it all hang out" meant, but if it meant more of him telling her what to do, she was literally not on board for it.

"Being open and honest with each other doesn't mean we can tell the other person what to do," she said, setting her empty margarita glass on the table beside her and pulling her chin from the heated grasp of his hand. "Just because we're sleeping together doesn't give you ownership of any part of me."

His eyes deepened to a dark forest as he watched her. She wanted to squirm so badly under that direct, piercing glare but she remained still.

"What does us sleeping together entitle me to, then?" he asked carefully. "Can I ask, please, Molly, that since you want to keep sleeping with me that you also not carry on a relationship with your fiancé?"

Her temper flared. "I told you that I'm not carrying on a relationship with him. You're the one encouraging the phone call. I'm just seeking closure on what was a very large and important chapter in my life before moving on."

"If you aren't still hung up on him, why do you have such a problem telling him that we're together?" he bit off. And while she wasn't afraid of him, she felt his irritation. "It sounds like maybe you're trying to have your cake and eat it, too."

She crossed her arms over her chest. "You think I want to be sleeping with both of you? Is that having my cake and eating it, too? Because that's ridiculous and something I'd never do, but I'd be willing to bet that you've eaten plenty of cakes over the years!"

"Am I the cake or the one eating it in this scenario?"

"How should I know?" she complained, throwing up her hands. "You're the one who started this!"

Her chest rising, she tried to get a handle on things. It wasn't like her to raise her voice or lose her temper, and yet with Oliver she found that it was okay to express herself. Maybe that wasn't a bad thing.

Oliver blew out a breath, the angry expression falling from his face.

"Listen," he said, bringing her hand back into his, his eyes warm with apology. "I didn't mean to push you. I'm not saying we need to go head-first into a relationship after sleeping together for a night, but I also don't want to be just some guy you sleep with, Molly, to get over your ex. That fucking sucks. I'm not some jerk you can scratch an itch with and then head out to your real life. At the very least you don't do that to a friend."

Her gaze skittered away because, of course on some level, that was exactly what she'd thought. "I guess I didn't know that it was so serious for you," Molly said, considering how to say what she needed to say without screwing up the rest of their vacation. "But this trip was meant to give me time away to clear my head. You're right that I need to talk to him because I still don't forgive him for cheating, but I need to hear him say I'm sorry and know that he at least valued what we had together, so I don't continue to believe that I'm just an insane person who thought she was in a relationship with a good person and misjudged him completely. So I do owe him a conversation, but you have to know that it has nothing to do with what's going on between us."

Oliver nodded slowly, eyes still pinning her to the chaise, his expression hurt and irritated. "I know," he finally said. "We jumped into bed too quickly and I knew I'd get fucked up about it if you hadn't worked all the shit out with this guy yet, but I couldn't help it. I just like you a lot, Molly."

"Hey," she said, leaning toward him, "I sped last night along, too, and I'm not sorry for it."

Their eyes locked and all Molly wanted to do was take that look off his face, the one that was regretting what they'd done, because it'd been amazing, the memory etched in her brain and body forever, which meant it could never be a mistake.

"Good," he said, taking a long breath. "I'm sorry I got all caveman on you."

Molly leaned back, a smile curving her lips as the tension in her shoulders from their disagreement finally eased. "Yeah, not your usual modus operandi."

He snorted. "No, it is," he disagreed. "Trust me, I've just been on my best behavior with you."

Trailing a single finger down his chest, she teased, "I'd have to agree with that."

Oliver grasped her finger in his fist, stilling her journey down his taut stomach. "I don't want to argue again, but I was also trying to point out that you haven't talked about your breakup much at all and how it made you feel. I'm your friend— unload on me. That's what I'm here for."

Molly's first inclination was to clam up. Even that first night on the boat when he'd made her tell him what happened had been difficult. She'd grown up with just a father and worked in a male-dominated profession where smiling too much made her seem unprofessional. It wasn't easy for her to admit she had emotions, let alone talk about them. More difficult still to try to sort them out in any kind of logical and useful manner. Give her an engine and she could take it apart and put it back together in no time, but asking her how she felt about her relationship, she needed a lifeline.

"I was angry at first, of course, but we were together for a long time and I loved him. Now that I'm over the anger, part of me wants to understand what went wrong from his perspective, but I'm not great at communicating how I feel back. I just clam up and agree with whatever he says."

"You did nothing wrong," Oliver assured her. "Whatever lame excuses he gives, relationships are work and he didn't want to do the work. End of story."

"Yeah, you're right," Molly agreed. "And I also want an apology. I know I deserve that."

"Damn right you do," he encouraged with one of those charming Oliver smiles. "And by the way, you're doing a great job of communicating right now."

"I can do an okay job with you," she told him, "because we're friends. And not to put a fine point on it, but you're making me do it."

Oliver's soft chuckle felt like medicine on her jumpy nerves. God, she hated this kind of stuff. Had no idea what good talking her feelings out was supposed to be doing other than making Oliver happy. Which she guessed was as good a reason as any.

Oliver let go of her hand to thread his fingers

through hers, their palms resting against each other. A flutter of pleasure rose in her.

"Can I put forth another possible reason for your reluctance to tell him that you've moved on?" he asked, his voice gentling as he squeezed her hand in his. She was already addicted to the connection, the feel of his skin against hers. "Maybe last night we discovered something really special together again and you're already looking for an escape route?"

Her heart thumped in her chest. Hell, that certainly felt like a truth bomb.

"Maybe," she admitted. "But it's not as if there's a future for us together, Oliver."

His gold brows lowered. "No?"

She shook her head, uncertain now. "You still live in New York or on this yacht and my life is in Colorado. I don't see that changing." She didn't add that essentially nothing had changed from when they'd broken up the first time. They lived in different parts of the country, but also on entirely separate planets.

Oliver searched her eyes. "You don't think I'd make changes for you? That I'd do what I'd need to do to have you in my life?"

She shrugged. He hadn't before and other than him purchasing this yacht she wasn't exactly sure what had changed between then and now. They were older, of course, but the facts of their lives were the same.

"By saying that, you're suggesting that I should make changes, too, but I love my job, Oliver, and I don't want to quit. And you can't just be an aerospace engineer anywhere. It's not exactly a robust field. So if you're saying you'd change your life around for me, it would mean moving to Colorado. Are you prepared to do that?"

He hit her gaze head-on. "Yes."

And that was all. No discussion, no request for compromise, no wish to talk about it later after they'd "see how things went," just an unequivocal agreement.

Her breath froze in her throat and she could feel her mouth suspended open in shock.

"Excuse me?" she asked, just to be sure.

"Yes, I'd move to Colorado for you."

"But you're building a yacht company and Colorado is, like, the definition of landlocked."

"So what?" he said. "Do you think I'm going run it like a floor manager or something? I hire people to do those things, Molly."

A ripple of unease stiffened her spine at the reminder of his power and of just how different they were.

"I see," she finally said, although she didn't really. Starting a company to her meant being there overseeing what was happening, feeling the boats being built, the engine humming, the line of the vessel itself. But she supposed that's why she was on this trip to explore yachts with him because she was more of a hands-on type of person.

"I don't think you do, but we'll put a pin in it for now," he said, finally and blessedly, letting his gaze fall from hers as he leaned back in the chaise.

"I do a lot of hiking in my free time, Oliver," she added. "You're telling me you'd like that? Prada doesn't make hiking boots."

"Actually, they do, sweetheart, but I hear what you're saying and I like being anywhere you are, so if you want to take a hike with me, we're good. If you want to take a hike without me, we'd be good. But this does feel like you're only proving my point that you're already putting up roadblocks between us before we begin because you know once we do begin it'll be amazing."

He took a drink of his margarita, giving her a sideways glance.

"I'm a logistics person," she pointed out. "And you and I don't make logical sense."

"Keep on going, Molly," he laughed, truly amused by her. "You can trot out a million reasons a relationship between us wouldn't work. Hell, maybe you'd be right about a lot of them." He speared her with his bright green gaze again, gilded with gold from the sunset. "But I'll be damned if I'd let a bunch of lame hypotheticals get in the way of something I want."

The intensity of his tone and the magnitude of his words did damage to her equilibrium. And they'd only had one night together.

"They're not hypotheticals if they're real," she informed. "I do like hiking."

His margarita drained, he placed the glass on the table with a decisive click before turning to her, picking her straight up into his arms and depositing her on his lap.

"I like that you like hiking," he told her, his hand going back to thread through her hair again, holding her neck steady as he held her eyes. "I like damn near everything I know about you, Molly. That's why you're the only person on this fucking boat with me. Regardless of how we move forward or don't, I'd never try to pick you apart. I like you and if I'm in something I'm in it all the way, not just if it's convenient to me. Being here is a risk for me and I've got my whole future riding on the next couple of months, but one thing I'll always be sure about is that if you want me, you've got me."

Whoa. Molly could barely breathe, definitely couldn't think, and when she opened her mouth to reply with something essential and equally important, she didn't get the chance because his lips closed over hers, demanding, and insistent, and oh, just lovely and sweet. Like he was a man trying to give her what she wanted but kept encountering resistance and was treading carefully.

Molly only knew that on day two of this trip she was already suspiciously happy to be back with her old friend. And as his tongue found hers, greeting and stroking and testing, she decided he was probably right that she was throwing up roadblocks. Oliver's hands lifted up the hem of her shirt and found bare skin, and she sucked in a breath. His touch was molten fire, the salty sweet taste of alcohol on his tongue so intimate that she pressed farther in until the kiss was so lewd she was sure she was already ready for him.

"I'll call him tomorrow," she whispered against his lips. "And maybe I'll let it drop that I've moved on with a guy who owns a super yacht. I feel like he probably deserves that."

His hands tightened on her ass. "And let him know I'm better at hiking, too."

Molly couldn't help it—she started giggling again, but that ended soon enough when Oliver captured her mouth in another soul-shattering kiss.

Yeah, a phone call was definitely in order.

CHAPTER SEVEN

OLIVER DIDN'T LOVE that Molly was currently speaking to her ex on the phone while he pretended to work, but he supposed he'd quite literally asked for it. That said, from his chair on the upper deck on the opposite side of the boat from her, he watched as she paced across the floor of the main deck and felt for the angst and heartbreak she was clearly working through.

Despite her discomfort he still liked looking at her—how the sun alighted on her sandy-blond hair, picking up the gold pieces, her lightly tanned skin brought out her big brown eyes, and her pink lips begged for him to kiss her. He'd been touching her basically nonstop and yet he still hadn't gotten enough. She gripped the railing and he wondered what the hell that fucknut was saying to her, wanting to smooth the crease in between her eyes. He'd basically given up the pretense of working to watch her even though he should be devising a plan to keep her safe in case his parents ever found out about her, and he mostly had, but as things became more serious between them, the plan had to shift to how he could have her in his life and not let his parents ruin it. Not that they'd physically hurt Molly, but they expected him to come back to his old life, one they wouldn't think she fit in. However, regardless of if he went back to his old life, he hoped Molly would be at his side. But it was obvious that even without the threat of his parents, she was uncertain about her place in his life as well.

Their conversation yesterday had been productive in cementing the fact that they were at least *in something* since she was calling Max now, but it had cost him to have it. Normally, he avoided confrontation and when the few attempted relationships he'd had had gotten to that point, he'd walked away. Jealousy was an entirely new emotion for him. He knew he'd pushed her too hard, but he couldn't handle just being another guy in her life. He needed to know that what was going on between them meant something to her, because it meant a whole hell of a lot to him, and he apparently needed to make that clear to her as well.

She was leaning against the railing now, eyes trained on her feet. He couldn't hear her conversation but he wished he could. The longer she talked, the more that thread of doubt creeping over him gained traction.

His unease increased as another half hour passed and she was still talking, now sitting on a deck chair, smiling. It was far too chummy for his liking and considering that guy had put her through so much misery. Putting the final touch on the email he'd been writing, he shut the laptop and debated his options. What he wanted to do was go down there and throw her damn phone in the ocean and drag her back to bed, but she'd most likely punch him in the face.

However much of a lovesick idiot he might already be, he truly did want to make sure she was doing all right, so he grabbed two beers from the kitchen on his way down to the main deck and held one out to her when he reached her. She accepted it with a grateful smile and took a long swig, clearly needing a drink and the alcohol.

"You okay?" he mouthed so he didn't interrupt her.

She nodded with an eye roll but didn't indicate that she'd be ending the call soon.

Hesitating, he leaned down and gave her a kiss on the cheek, just so she knew he was here for her.

Trying to put the possibility of Molly's defection from his boat out of his mind, he went back to the kitchen to start on lunch. He pulled out a bunch of stuff for sandwiches as well as the salad she'd made yesterday, put it all on a tray and took it up to the table on the sky lounge. He waited another half hour before he went ahead and ate lunch without her. It wasn't until he heard her trill of laughter that his gut clenched and he knew he was a goner because he wanted to be a good support for her, but the idea of her going back to her ex made him crazy. That laugh had him thinking maybe he had things entirely wrong. Just because he'd thought about Molly over the years didn't mean she'd felt the same way. It'd been highly foolish to assume they could just walk back into a relationship after so many years. She had an entire life he knew nothing about and the more he heard her laugh, the more this sad reality was apparent to him. A miscalculation on his part. He'd been so eager to see her, to touch her, to smell her again, that he hadn't been smart about it.

He was a mess and very much in trouble with her because while he trusted her, it was already difficult for him to imagine returning to a life without her. The new life he was forging seemed less important if she wasn't by his side.

Another fifteen minutes passed before she appeared in the doorway, a sheepish smile on her face. But it was fine because he'd composed himself, understood how he needed to proceed now. He needed to get himself together and act like a person who had control over his rampant emotional state. He wasn't just some guy with a lot of money and so few true friends that he'd created a fantasy life with a woman he'd dated years ago. Of course not.

"Hey," she said, her voice soft, "sorry that was so long."

He shrugged as if he didn't care. "It was a cold lunch anyway. No harm done."

She met his eyes, obviously reading something in his tone, but he just offered her a benign smile.

"Well, it looks delicious," she went on as if he gave a damn about what she thought about the lunch. "Thanks for putting it together."

"Eat up," he told her. "I thought we'd sail to the other side of the island and maybe go into Freeport and pick up some things."

"Oh, okay," she said, surprised. He stood and pulled out a chair for her so she could sit down.

If she expected him to ask questions about her call, she was mistaken. He was cutting himself off before he got in too deep. He liked Molly, he liked the sex, but sitting through the phone call had filled him with resolve. Being just her pal and confidant was a no-go, after all.

"Thanks," she said, scooting into the table. She took a sip of the water he'd poured earlier, the ice almost completely melted. "I didn't mean to talk so much."

"No need to apologize."

He casually watched as she took a bite of a carrot stick, as if nothing was amiss or his gut wasn't churning like a washing machine agitator.

"Would you want to take a swim after lunch?" she asked, meeting his eyes. "I was just down there looking at the water all day and thinking how we hadn't done that yet."

"Sure, Molly," he said, taking a sip of the tequila he'd been nursing. But the mescal buzz was not doing what he'd wanted, namely chilling him out to the point where he could let the length of that phone call go. Where he could be noncommittal about her talking to her ex not even an hour since he'd been inside her with her screaming his name. He could barely believe how largely he'd miscalculated how much she meant to him. For years, he'd been living in denial and in the dark about his feelings, just locking them away so he could get by, but the thought of her going back to her ex was busting the walls he'd erected around those memories open.

She searched his face. "I don't know if your scowl means you want to know about the phone call or you don't."

Fuck. He smoothed his face out, not even realizing he'd been scowling, but not at all surprised. He had a poker face for everyone but Molly. She remained the only person he ever truly let down his guard with so it made sense that he'd been unable to hide his emotions from her. Though, admittedly, he kind of thought he was doing an admirable job of it if the only evidence of his raging inner turmoil threatening to tear him from the inside out was a comparably benign scowl.

"I want you to do whatever you want to do, Molly."

She raised an eyebrow at him but he was not going to beg her for details about a phone call he just wanted to forget even though he'd tried to push her into making it. He respected her too much to put her in a position where she felt she owed him anything.

"I think it was a good talk," she told him, stopping there.

"You seemed to be having a good time at the end."

She held his eyes again and he felt her trying to ferret out his intention and meaning, but his face was a pleasant mask now. In another minute, he'd be calm enough to be the charming playboy he always was, but the heat in his stomach hadn't quite been snuffed out yet.

"I think 'good time' is overstating it," Molly said drily. "But I think we got to an amicable place. It felt good to get everything out and to tell him how I felt. Saying it all out loud made me realize that I was over it. You were right that I should call him back, to put us on the same page."

"And what page is that?"

She shrugged and he hated it. "Just that he's the one who messed up. He mentioned that the girl I'd caught him with was just a onetime thing and that he was sorry. It felt like a real apology. He didn't make excuses or anything, just really felt bad."

"He fucking should," Oliver bit off, cursing himself for the outburst.

"He does," Molly assured him. "And then we sorted some logistics about the house and what we're planning to do with it, if I want to sell it to him or if there's a chance we could try to work things out."

He didn't say anything, didn't ask the question he wanted to ask.

"So I told him I was currently seeing someone and we could proceed with selling the house."

His heart started beating again. "Do you want me to buy the house?"

Molly choked on the sip of water she'd been taking.

"Excuse me?"

"Do you want me to buy him out of the house so you can just have it now?" he asked again, slower this time so she heard him. And for the record, he knew that this offer, too, was a mistake, but he still felt compelled to offer it, to expedite this process. He'd already been waiting for her for seven years, so it would be nice if they could speed it up a bit.

Besides, if his parents did truly try to use her as leverage, it would be better for both of them if they were in a more permanent arrangement. "If you put it on the market you'll be in touch with him constantly."

"Do you think I want you to purchase a house I can afford on my own?"

"The offer wasn't made based on whether or not you could afford it on your own. I'm sure you can. The offer was made out of convenience since I can just pay him cash and have the deal be done by the end of today."

Molly shook her head. "I don't want the house, Oliver. If anything he'll buy me out."

That was still a lot of the contact he was trying to avoid. He wanted Max totally out of the picture so the pile of forty-five grand pianos would be taken off his chest and he could breathe easier.

"So he's started that process, then?"

Swallowing her bite of turkey sandwich, Molly set it down on the plate before glaring at him. "What is going on here? I thought you'd be happy that I told him I was seeing someone. Isn't that what you insisted upon yesterday?"

"It's a start," he told her.

Her eyes flashed and he wanted to smile. He liked an irritated Molly as much as he liked a naked one.

"You're just being an ass on purpose now, aren't you?"

"Maybe," he said, some of his anger dissipating at the reminder that she'd told her ex they were together. That was enough for now. Carving him completely out of her life was a project for another day.

"He's already in the past, Oliver. I promise."

At her pointed stare he just smiled, wanting to get back to normal again, wanting to believe that she was his even if it wasn't true. "Okay, you're right, let's forget about your ex. Can we go swimming now or do you want to talk more about your feelings?"

She rolled her eyes and finished up her sandwich. When she took the last bite, he made her leave the dishes there for the crew to clean up and threw his shirt off onto the chair when they reached the main deck.

"You want any of the toys?" she asked, heading toward the storage door.

"Not the water kind."

Molly just snorted and pulled out a couple rafts while he made sure they had enough water bottles.

"Do you want to do the Jet Ski?" he asked.

She shook her head. "Nah, they're a pain in the ass to get out."

His first instinct was to tell her that it wasn't their job to get them out, but he didn't want to put any more distance between them right now by bringing up the fact that he pretty much didn't do the shit he didn't want to do. He had more important stuff on his agenda at the moment.

On the aft deck, he took in the sparkling blue water around them; they were a couple miles from the shore with neighboring yachts dotting the landscape. Not in any danger of being seen, he took off his shorts and dived in naked, letting the cool water flow over him as he swam, eventually surfacing a little way from the boat. When he looked back at the boat, Molly was standing on the edge looking down at his abandoned clothes.

Then she shrugged and stripped, too, which had him doubling down on all the tumultuous emotions he'd tried to hold back since they'd talked about her ex yesterday. She could set a garage of his Ferraris on fire if she was as committed as him to abandoning propriety when it was fun to do so. This is what he'd remembered the most after they went their separate ways, that they'd just had so much damned fun, and it'd been such a long time since he could say that he'd had fun. He'd been living behind glass for so long, always watching other people living their lives and just waiting for it to be his turn. Finally, his time had come and it had definitely been worth the wait.

First, her simple coral T-shirt fell to the ground, then her yellow bathing suit top, followed by her matching bottoms and shorts, leaving her completely bare to his eyes.

"You actually coming in or just trying to work on your all-over tan?" he asked when she hesitated.

She rolled her eyes at the heckle and jumped in gracefully and swam toward him.

When she was a couple feet from him, just wading in the water, she pushed her shock of wet hair back from her face and met his eyes. "This water cooling you off?"

A muscle ticked in his jaw. "Just a little bit."

"I just don't know if us jumping into a serious relationship is the smart move, Oliver," she told him, running her hand down the exposed slope of his shoulder above the water as she voiced the reason he'd been weird about her phone conversation.

He'd made his feelings about that more than clear, so he stayed mute.

"I like you," she told him, wrapping her arms around his neck. "I'm not used to having you back in my life. I'm afraid this is all some amazing dream I'm having. I'm naked in the ocean with a guy who would make any woman drool, has promised to dedicate himself to outdoor recreational activities with me and who owns the most luxurious yacht I've ever seen. You have to know that it doesn't seem real."

He touched his lips to hers. "I'm very real, Molly," he reminded her, willing her to get over his wealth. "I'm more than just my money. It's all I've ever wanted people to know, and I hope you believe it." And then he took her mouth, pulling her into him as their legs paddled in between each other, their skin brushing silkily upon each other's. It was a weirdly sensual feeling and he'd never experienced it with anyone else.

"I know you're real," she told him, her hand finding his hard length. "It just feels like me being here isn't. I know *you're* more than your wealth, but I don't know that I belong in your real life, Oliver."

She stroked him lightly, just playing because there was no way he could fuck her like he wanted in the ocean, but he'd take her hands on him any way he could get them, and this was a different kind of intimate, the casual ownership of his dick. It didn't have to be about sex; she just knew that he was hers to do with as she pleased. For some odd reason he couldn't quite understand, that thought settled something inside him.

"My real life is shitty, Molly. That's why I'm here," he admitted, brushing barely there kisses over her sun-warmed cheek. "Whatever life we make together is the one I want." And regardless of what his parents might think or do to try to manipulate him, he was ready to defend Molly and their life together to the death.

The pebbled nubs of her nipples caressed his

chest and his breath caught as if he'd never felt the sensation before, but it was all heightened under the water, making what was already a delicious sensation even more so. "I'll believe you," she whispered against his lips. "I want to believe you so badly, Oliver."

Then she was kissing him, hard, and he gripped her head in his angling for a better way into her mouth, their tongues meeting as the need to connect rose inside them.

When he pulled back to breathe, she unexpectedly ducked down into the water, escaping from his arms. She emerged again, her head popping up with a grin, several feet away.

"What are you doing, Molly?" he asked, sensing danger.

She shrugged, then leaned back in the water until she was on her back, floating there like a goddess, the sun bright on her upturned breasts and the muscular lines of her legs.

But then she moved and he got a huge splash in the face, and it kept coming as she kicked her feet.

He growled and went after her, not able to keep the grin off his face.

"No," she called, "this is what you get for being such an overbearing ass."

Ducking under the water, he swam to her side where she wasn't expecting him and drew up and grabbed her into his arms, effectively dunking her in a crafty sneak attack.

"Oh my God," she spluttered when she came back up. "I cannot believe you did that!" she yelled when she'd pushed the hair back from her face.

"I was just trying to illustrate to you how real I was," he laughed, swimming backward as she advanced on him.

"You're going to wish you weren't by the time I'm done with you," she warned, but was also grinning, which diminished the threat in the words.

"I can't wait," he told her, then swam quickly away, knowing sooner or later he'd let her catch him.

CHAPTER EIGHT

"What do you think of it?" Oliver asked Molly as she inspected the engine room of another yacht docked in the Grand Bahama Yacht Club.

He'd dragged her to shore to tour a couple of the yachts in the port and get her thoughts on their construction. What he was really doing, however, was trying to subtly impart that by working with him she'd be completely in charge of building something from scratch, which he knew she loved. And if she was being honest with herself, if Oliver wouldn't essentially be her boss, she might love building something new for a change.

"It's pretty sleek," she told him as she ran her hands over one of the shining stainless steel hoses jutting out from the engine block. "But not as nice as yours. Since you're running liquid natural gas you're getting more bang for your buck and a cleaner ride. This is a twelve-cylinder engine while you have ten. It feels like we're talking about apples and oranges."

"So this is a dinosaur?"

She nodded, but knew he already knew it. He'd had his yacht built with cutting edge eco-technology that put it leaps and bounds beyond most boats still on the water. But this trip was how he was going to open up the conversation he wanted to have with her about building yachts.

"The market for new yachts is there, but I've been toying with devoting a portion of the business to upgrading ones already on the water. We don't make the engines, unless of course, you were to grace us with your genius for that, but what if we could design a new kind of engine that could easily exist inside the bones of an old yacht?"

"I don't know anything about yacht markets, Oliver," she said. "But I trust your judgment. I always thought there was a small market for yacht charters that cost over 600,000 a week, but it wasn't as if we ever had a free week during a charter season so my knowledge of how the one percent lives is limited. That said, with the global emissions laws ramping up, more and more yachts are going to have to comply so it's probably a good idea to start supporting that kind of change."

"I totally agree." Oliver grinned. "I guess great minds think alike. So my next question is, what would you do to make yacht engines more efficient?"

"Oliver, if you want to break into the marine manufacturing market, you need to do it without me. I told you I like my job."

"I know, I know," Oliver said, brushing her reminder aside. "But when I do hire someone, I need to know that what they're telling me is legitimate. I don't want to just build yachts, I want to build the best ones. I want shit no one has even fucking thought of before, Molly, you know? And I know you're the type of person who thinks that way. So tell me your thoughts so I know the person I hire instead of you has vision."

Molly sighed and gave him a put-upon look because he was so good at flattery and she wasn't unaffected by it. She moved farther into the room, ducking under a low light fixture to inspect an older control panel.

"Yachts are all about excess," Molly said, stating the obvious. "But engineering is about doing the most with the least amount of work, space and material. So if I were building an engine, I'd start there. But the problem is that people want what they know works. That's why the same companies in business are still in business—they're dependable—which means you can't just abandon all that has come before and start from scratch." She smiled, eyes twinkling. "But I would."

Oliver quirked an eyebrow. "Why is that?"

"Because I'm better at making things for people who dream than the people who make things for money."

There was a moment of silence as Oliver stared at her, his eyes shifting from humor, to regard, to heat, and then finally to humor again. "I like you a lot, Molly."

"Same," she told him, then scanned the engine room at large. "This is yesterday for sure, but you could make an engine that could be adjusted to fit inside a variety of spaces so that upgrades would be as painless as possible."

"What about a three-million-dollar signing bonus?" Oliver said, hoping to catch her off guard.

Molly shook her head, amused. "Nope."

"Unlimited vacation days? You make your own schedule?"

Still shaking her head, Molly crossed her arms over her chest.

"A base of operations near a mountain so you could hike at lunch?"

"Negative."

Oliver's nostrils flared and then he grinned. "My body?"

Molly snorted. "I already have that."

He shoved his hands into his pockets. "Yeah, but whenever you want it. One look and I'm naked. A snap of your fingers and I'm naked. Crook your finger and I'm naked. Ask me nicely and I'm naked and kneeling."

Molly couldn't help it—she laughed and leaned up to give him a kiss on the cheek. "This is beneath you, Oliver."

"I'm fine with that as long as you're on top of me," he shot back, pulling her into his arms. She loved how well she fit there, too. She liked it when things fit perfectly in a space, the lines and curves joining just right as her body did with his, their lips at the ideal height for her to lift an inch and for him to drop an inch and meet.

She sighed against his mouth, falling right back into the whirlwind of sex that had had them in its thrall for days now. For a person who hadn't even been on a vacation in years, this new freedom was heady and unreal. Not for a moment could she imagine waking up tomorrow and driving back to her job even though she did love it.

"If I remember correctly," she said, "I believe that it's actually your turn to be on top. So get your act together, Kent."

He made a humming sound against her lips. "I'll think of an offer you can't refuse, Molly, so I wouldn't get so comfortable."

"I have no doubt that you'll try," she told him, shivering against him as his hands gripped her bottom, pulling her into his waiting erection.

"Trying is half the fun." He grinned as his head

lowered. His tongue played at her lips, asking for entrance. She let him in and leaned into the kiss, her leg coming around his calf as they clung to each other.

Finally, he pulled back and met her eyes, his green ones dark and hooded. "We have to stop. There are people on this boat." He brushed a piece of hair that had fallen out of her ponytail behind her ear, a move that made her shiver and him grin.

"We'll tour the rest of the boat and then have dinner in town?" he asked.

She nodded and they left the engine room to return to the chief steward, who was a no-nonsense blonde woman who'd worked aboard the yacht *Windswept* for years and knew everything there was to know about the renovations to the interior and the inner workings of the boat. "So is your engineer on board now?" Molly asked her as they stood in a master suite that didn't hold a candle to Oliver's. Instead of looking contemporary, it somehow looked dated even though it had just been updated.

"No," Jane said, "it's his day off so he's on the island somewhere."

Molly nodded. It wasn't super important to speak with him, especially since she wasn't taking the job Oliver kept offering, but the engine on this particular boat was built by the only company whose engines she'd hadn't run into over the years so she was curious about his thoughts on it. Not that it meant anything; she was a curious person in general.

"I can let him know you have some questions for him, though," Jane added. "I'm sure he'd love to talk engines with someone. The other guys on this crew aren't exactly valedictorians if you know what I mean."

Molly laughed and rattled off her email address, which Jane jotted down in the small notebook she kept in the back pocket of her black pencil skirt.

Oliver's arm fell across Molly's back, lightly squeezing her shoulder, and she knew he thought he was making headway in getting her on his new venture. He could think anything he wanted; it wasn't happening, and she sent him an overly sweet smile meant to convey this, but he only shrugged. He was incorrigible.

"Do you two own a yacht?" Jane asked.

Molly shook her head. "He does."

Oliver pulled her closer into his side. "Molly is a brilliant aerospace engineer who I am trying to lure with money and favors into my company. So you've truly helped us out today on this tour, Jane," Oliver told her, that charming smile bright and playful. "She's a genius who will not be swayed but I think through your exemplary tour, I got a little closer to the negotiating table."

Then he pulled out a hefty white envelope full

of money and handed it to Jane. "Thanks again for all your help."

Jane looked down at the envelope, not surprised that she'd gotten it but at the weight of what was inside. Molly nearly rolled her eyes. Oliver literally could not help himself from being lovely. He'd tipped the driver who brought them to the boat a hundred dollars for a five-minute ride in a golf cart. Molly made a hell of a good living, but the last time she hadn't been concerned about dropping a hundred dollars like it was as disposable as a piece of toilet paper was never.

"It was absolutely my pleasure to assist you both," Jane said, her eyes focusing on Molly's, the expression in them as if to say, are you a fucking idiot for not working with this kind of man?

And hell, maybe Jane had a point. Oliver was a unicorn.

But that was also kind of the thing. Molly didn't believe in magic. She made it out of nuts and bolts and tangible things and certainly couldn't trust something she didn't truly understand.

"Enjoy your time in the Bahamas!" Jane called to them as they disembarked from the boat, Oliver's hand still on Molly's back, strangely possessive in a way he hadn't been before. On his boat, there were casual touches, flirting, but never this, him making sure everyone they met knew she was with him.

The same golf cart they'd used earlier was still waiting at the end of the dock for them and she realized that had been the reason for the big cash exchange. Oliver handed him another hundred upon their arrival in the cart and rested his arm on the back of the seat as she climbed in.

As they started off, he began playing with the end of her ponytail and Molly made a concerted effort not to shiver, but she was already becoming addicted to his touch.

"I made us reservations at a local Caribbean place if that's okay with you."

"That sounds amazing," she said. "Colorado is pretty low on seafood, high on heavy game meats."

Oliver laughed. "Not a huge fan of eating Bambi, are you?"

Molly shivered. "Not so much."

Oliver chuckled, leaning down to land a soft kiss on the top of her head. "I'm just ready for some food I don't have to cook myself."

Molly twisted away and met his eyes. "Oh, no, you don't," she warned. "I told you not to cook for me."

Oliver raised an eyebrow. "Oh, you were just going to eat peanut butter and jelly every night on a yacht?"

"I can make other things," Molly argued, offended, but her eyes slid away because it was true, her menu was limited. The favorites in her phone contacts list were all take-out places.

"You know I'm kidding," Oliver said, drawing her back into his arms. "My favorite part of this trip other than the obvious has been watching you fawn over my mediocre cooking as if I'm a Michelin-starred chef."

Molly crossed her arms over her chest, putting space between them. "You are a good cook, but I won't be eating a thing now that I know you're slaving away for my benefit alone."

Oliver's shoulders shook. "I just meant that it would be nice to have a dinner I didn't have to cook for myself as well, Molly. I've never known you to take things so personally."

"I know you don't cook in your day-to-day life," Molly explained, frowning. "So that you're doing it for me is a lot and I don't like feeling indebted to anyone."

The golf cart stopped in front of the yacht club boathouse where a town car was waiting at the curb to drive them to the restaurant. Oliver handed yet another hundred dollar bill to the driver as they exited the cart and then entered the town car.

Molly got in first, scooting over to make room for Oliver on the seat, but she could feel the tension. As they settled into the cool air-conditioning of the car, it started to move before he turned to her, his eyes locking on hers. "Listen to me right now. You are never fucking indebted to me, Molly," Oliver said, his voice deep and intense. "If I gave you my yacht, you are not in my debt because you'd deserve it. You're not in the position to dictate to another person what you think you're worth to them. So if I want to cook you dinner every night of my life, I'll damn well do it and you'll know you're worth it to me."

He brought a hand up to her jaw, trapping her gaze on his when she would have looked away at the fierce words.

"Do you get me?"

She swallowed, heart pounding against the walls of her chest. This was a different Oliver, not the devil-may-care guy on the yacht talking to Jane or the other crew members on his own boat. This was Oliver the man who bought yachts and built companies, the one she'd glimpsed during their conversation about Max. He so often played the fun and carefree rich guy that she'd failed to see the whole man.

"I don't hear you, Molly," he said, reminding her that she hadn't answered him yet. "Or are you trying to think of another way you can tell me that you don't want to be in my life?"

"That's not—" she started, but he shook his head.

"You don't want me to pay you for honest work, you don't want me to cook for you like a normal man who would share in household stuff since you are the one fucking taking care of the rest of the damned boat, so what can I do, Molly, that'll even the scales for you?" She tried to answer again, but he had more to say. "I'm always going to be rich. Unless some catastrophic tragedy happens and every stream of income I have somehow dries up, I will always be a wealthy motherfucker. I can't change it, and frankly, I don't really want to. I worked hard for the money I use, and the money I inherited will build a business that will employ thousands of people so I'm not going to be sorry for it. The real question is, we're right now at the beginning of this, so if you're going to let my money be a problem between us, let's hash it out now because what I can't do is wait until we're further into what is already the best relationship of my life and learn that you can't deal with being with me because of my money. So whatever you're thinking right now, let it out."

Molly swallowed, her throat working against the sudden nerves.

"I didn't know we were in a relationship," she finally managed, getting to the heart of the matter. The word was circling in her mind, stealing her breath by slow degrees as she considered what it actually meant. Where had the discussion been about that, by the way? Just yesterday she'd been thinking about what she'd do when she returned to her real life and now she was somehow in a relationship with someone who felt out of her reach on so many levels?

"You know what I mean," Oliver told her. "We're together and sleeping together. We're not *not* in a relationship."

"Deciding on whether or not something is a relationship takes two people, Oliver," she pointed out.

"You're deliberately focusing on the wrong part of what I said," Oliver chastised, his eyes darkening.

"I don't think so," Molly said. "Because the rest of what you said doesn't matter if we're not in a relationship. Which, we aren't."

Oliver's lips thinned and while he wasn't angry, he wasn't exactly pleased, either. Then he took her hand and his face cleared completely, a winning smile transforming his face. "Molly, will you be my girlfriend?"

An involuntary laugh flew out of her before she could grab it back. "What?" she asked, flustered despite knowing he was half goading her.

Oliver grabbed her hands in his, thumbs running over the backs of them. "You've indicated that we're not in a relationship and that we need to agree together that we're in one, so I'm telling you that I'm all for it. Let's be in one. If, of course, that is also amenable to you."

Molly felt her eyes go round as she stared first into his face and then down at their joined hands. "Um, what?"

Oliver laughed. "Are you okay, Molly?"

"Oliver, we've barely spent any time together over the last seven years, I just got unengaged, we live completely separate lives, and you want to have a relationship?"

"Well, technically, I wanted to have a conversation about your hang-up about my money to make sure the way was clear so that we could have a shot at a relationship in the future, but since you pressed the issue of my terminology instead, then yes, the answer is I'd like to be in a relationship with you. Again, Molly, because I'll remind you that we aren't strangers."

"So you don't want to be in a relationship?" Christ, she knew she was making an ass out of herself, but some weird sort of hope was blooming in her chest and she wasn't sure how to handle it.

He just raised a golden eyebrow at her bumbling.

"Why didn't you tell me how wealthy you were when we dated the first time?" And the fact that he hadn't had made her feel as if he hadn't bothered trying to make her understand or let her be a part of it because he'd known she didn't belong there.

Annoyance crept into his gaze. "I didn't think it mattered."

And, of course, it didn't—not in changing the way she felt about him as a person—but Molly dealt in boots to the ground (or in space) reality. Their lives weren't meant to mingle as they were on completely different planets and his omissions only proved it.

"It doesn't, Oliver, but I don't like feeling as if the things I have aren't good enough for you, because I've worked really hard for them. You just dropped three hundred dollars on a golf cart ride. The last time I spent three hundred dollars at once was for tires on my car. We're not living in the same space—you have to understand that."

"I do understand that, Molly, which is why I want to talk about it. What can I do to make you comfortable with it? Because I'm not letting you go, Molly, not if you feel the same way about me as I do about you. So how does this work? You know how to make things work, so help me out here. Let's communicate about these issues now, create a solid foundation and then figure out the rest, okay?"

Molly's eyes closed and she took a deep, calming breath. Oliver made sense, but she felt like she was on the precipice of something she no longer had control over. As if agreeing to date him would be a step into something unknown and from which there was no way back.

"Honestly, I don't know, Oliver," she finally said

because it was the truth. "I'm not even good at relationships, clearly, so I'm not really the authority, but I know myself enough to know that I like being on the yacht with you, but the rest of your life scares the living shit out of me. After we get off *Chance* and real life starts again, can you seriously see me at some society party? I'd stick out like a sore thumb and I have no interest in wasting my time that way."

Oliver gripped her hands. "I'm done with that shit, Molly. That's why I left."

Molly pursed her lips because she doubted that was true. Oliver was a good person and he'd defied his parents once, but eventually he'd have to be a part of their lives.

So she just went with the truth because that's who she was, too. "I want to be with you, Oliver. How about the first step is that we keep talking about this and hopefully eventually we'll come up with a solution? Not all problems are solved overnight."

A corner of Oliver's mouth kicked up in wry amusement. "So what you're saying is that I'm a big problem for you?"

Molly laughed and ran a hand up his ridged thigh to where he was growing hard in his pants. "Yeah, but I doubt you're one I can't solve."

CHAPTER NINE

OLIVER LET MOLLY pay for their dinner because after their conversation in the limo he felt a little invincible. He'd put himself and his feelings out there and she hadn't run screaming in the other direction. She hadn't picked up a bat and immediately played ball, but she hadn't completely been put off by the idea of a relationship, which was further than they'd been just a couple days ago.

He also felt like he might have a shot on the job front as well. He'd seen the spark of interest in her eyes as she contemplated how she would design an engine and hoped he could find a way around her thinking she'd be working for him instead of with him, which is what he truly intended to do. He wanted Molly as a partner, period.

Based on his progress, he was already figuring out what it would take for him to move his personal office to Denver, where she was. If she remained firm on the job, he still wanted to be in her life. And he actually liked Denver a lot, so living there

would be great. Though he'd live anywhere as long
as he was with Molly. For a guy who wasn't big
into entanglements or personal relationships, the
way he felt about her was surprisingly not scary at
all. Adjusting his life to be a part of hers felt like
the most natural thing in the world. If he could
find a way to make it more permanent and protect
her from whatever his parents would do once they
found out about her, he'd feel better about it. But
she was safe for now even if the inevitable reality
of his life threatened to press in on his happiness
bubble, including the furious texts and calls from
his parents that had been flying in at a faster pace
the longer he ignored them. But he wasn't ready
to tell them where he was or who he was with because they'd never stop hounding him and he was
determined to enjoy his time alone with Molly.

A small speedboat rode them back to the yacht,
where his deck crew person put it away. He walked
Molly back across the main deck, holding her hand
in his as he led them up to the sky lounge for
drinks. Dinner had been at a casual place, but he'd
had trouble keeping his hands off her all day. Her
ponytail exposed the long nape of her neck, and
the bright white crew neck T-shirt that outlined the
swells of her breasts so clearly paired well with the
fitted cropped jeans and cute yellow flip-flops that
were so quintessentially Molly he couldn't help but

smile. He was dressed much the same way, just happy to be off the boat for a while.

She sat down in a chaise longue and he carried over the two bottles of beer he'd grabbed from the bar's mini fridge. He waited there beside her until she got the message and scooted over so he could join her, but he shook his head and pointed at her to move forward in the seat so he could sit behind her. She complied and then she was leaning into his chest with his arms around her and it was heaven. This part, the casual way they could be with each other, it was something he'd never thought he'd have. For most of his life until he'd met Molly he'd imagined a marriage and life like his parents had, distant and cold and transactional, but she'd shown him that he could have so much more. And now that he could finally have it, it was like eating clouds or drinking a rainbow, simply too wonderful to be believed.

After setting his beer on the ground, he dropped gentle kisses up her neck, loving that she shivered at the contact. No other boats were on the water near them today and he wanted her badly out in the open air where it was just them, the wind and the water. She took a sip of her beer and he drew her earlobe into his mouth, his tongue batting the squishy pad between his teeth as she began to squirm against him. His thumb found the line of her spine and caressed down the length of it, pressing in at each delicate knob and dip. "I like you a lot, Molly," Oliver murmured as he tucked his hands under the bottom hem of her shirt and lifted it up. All that golden skin was revealed to him and he wanted to worship every inch of it. So he did, setting his lips to her spine and following the path his thumb had taken, his hands circling around her stomach to reach up and unclasp the simple white bra. He didn't think there was anything sexier than the bright white cotton against her sun-kissed skin, but he admitted he was biased, in so damn deep with Molly that she could be wearing a garbage bag and he'd think she was sexy as hell. She just *was*.

"I like you, too, Oliver," she said softly back to him, and he wondered if she also wanted to say the other, similar, words like he did, but knew it was too soon.

"You fucking better," he warned.

Her ponytail twitched as she shook her head. "Or what?" she asked, teasing but also genuinely curious.

He waited, giving her spine a little lick before her head turned back to meet his eyes. "Or I'll stop what I'm doing right now."

So he did, removing his hands from where they'd been traveling up her abdomen to her straining nipples.

Her hands found his legs, the ones bracing her

on either side, and squeezed. "I guess we're lucky I like you a hell of a lot, then," she said.

He leaned in and took her mouth in his, their tongues meeting in a sweet and luscious sweep. Her arm reached back to hold him to her while his clasped around her waist and brought her back into his chest.

"Shirt off," she instructed.

"You got it," he murmured against her mouth, holding her gaze as he leaned back and pulled off his own T-shirt.

He let out a breath of satisfaction at the skin-to-skin contact. Their lips met again and he threaded his hands through her hair, loving the small sounds of contentment she made that got lost in his own mouth. Dragging a hand up to her breast, he let his palm run over puckered pink nipples, taking one between his thumb and forefinger on the second pass, drinking in her gasp of pleasure when he pinched it.

He'd had every intention of taking things slow when he'd sat down, showing her just how much she meant to him, but she was already hot against him and the arm she had around his neck was tightening with need that echoed in his own body. He'd been hard as a goddamn rock all day as they'd acted like a real couple, that everyone they'd passed assumed they were together, were in love. And he was so fucked because he'd loved it.

He paid his regards to the other nipple and she

gasped, making him grin. There was nothing bet-ter in the world than making out with Molly under the stars in the middle of the ocean. He didn't know why he hadn't been doing it for years.

"We don't have condoms up here," she said even-tually when his hands were on the snap of her jeans.

He tugged down her jeans, her hips raising up to help him, and once they were in a pile on the floor he raised an eyebrow at her. "Do you think I'm the type of person who isn't prepared to have sex with you whenever and wherever I like?"

From his wallet he produced two condoms and flipped them onto the table beside them.

"I guess not," she got out before gasping for breath as his fingers slid into her heat. His own breathing deepened at the contact; he fucking loved touching her.

"You might be able to fix things, Molly, but I'm the guy with a plan. And my only goal most days is getting us into the position we're currently in, so yeah, so that pretty much entails having a con-dom on me at all times."

"Maybe that should be your next venture in-stead of building yachts—put things in clothing that are like secret compartments for condoms. That way you're never without them."

He grinned against her neck. "Do you mean I should invent pockets?"

She gasped and bucked against his hand when

he slid over her wet clit, stroking slowly so he could revel in every millimeter of her velvety skin. "Just shut up," she croaked out as he placed a single finger into her, crooking it against the little rough patch of skin, tormenting it over and over again until she was fairly panting, her neck straining against his shoulder.

"You don't have to tell me twice," he laughed before taking her mouth again.

Pushing another finger inside her, more blood rushed to his cock as her wetness flowed over his hand. She was close and getting closer to letting go, biting at his tongue as it mimicked what he was doing with his hands. It was messy, it was awkward and sweet, and he couldn't get enough of it.

"Oliver," she breathed as she shattered around his fingers, his thumb slowly brushing over her throbbing nub as he helped bring her back down to equilibrium.

"I'm right here," he murmured, kissing across her jaw and down her neck. "Not going anywhere."

She put her hand on his knee, leaning into his chest for a quick moment before shoving forward. Then she was twisting around in the seat so that she was straddling him, her warm, sated core up against his pulsing dick.

"Hey," she said, wrapping her arms around his neck. "You're good at that."

"Thanks." His hands came around her back and pressed her forward. "Are you going to thank me, too?"

She shrugged, lips twitching. "Didn't I just?"

"No, you complimented my skill, but didn't express appreciation."

"Well, if we're being honest about it, you have done better."

Oliver wanted to laugh. She was so full of shit, but he loved a challenge. So he stood, picking her up in his arms, and took her to the deck's metal railing, sitting her on the top rung. He covered her hands with his, securing them to the bars so she wouldn't fall over into the water below.

"Actually," he said as he considered her before him, perched on the side of the boat. He wanted her to be a little out of sorts, but not truly in danger.

So he opened a piece of the floor and pulled out a stretch of rope.

"Um, oh," Molly breathed, eyes surprised but definitely interested.

"It's just so you don't fall off, Molly," he assured her, motioning for her to stay on the railing. He pressed a kiss to her lips. "Trust me. Once I start, you're going to be glad I did this."

She clasped her hands on the railing again and watched as he tied both her hands and feet down to the metal poles until she couldn't fall backward into the water if she tried. Her legs spread wide, he stretched his neck back and forth in preparation.

"Now," he told her. "It's my turn for dessert since you ate all my cake at dinner."

"You said you didn't want it!" Molly exclaimed, her hands straining at the ropes. The material was a smooth nylon and wouldn't abrade her skin.

He sank to his knees before her, looking his fill at the prettiest, pinkest pussy he'd ever seen and feeling like every decision he'd ever made up to this point had been the right one if this was where he'd eventually ended up.

"Shh," he said as his fingers opened her wide, exposing her to the sea breeze whipping across the top deck of the boat. "This is what I was waiting for."

And then he went in, licking her entire slit in one deliciously erotic swipe, the sound of it laying him out flat. She was so wet now that she'd already come, her entrance puffed and soft, ready to take him, which she definitely would just as soon as he'd driven her to the brink of insanity. Stiffening his tongue, he speared it inside her, thrusting as she moved against his mouth, her cries already being lost across the endless ocean surrounding them. It truly felt like them against the world.

She was murmuring his name over and over again now, her knuckles white where she gripped the railing. She was a goddess, the moon illuminating her golden skin against the darkening sky behind her, and he'd worship at her feet forever like this if she'd let him. So he let himself go all in, his mouth devouring her as if it was the last thing he'd taste on earth. He sucked on her clit, her cries in his ears begging him for release, but he kept at it, taking her just to the edge and then retreating to her entrance to consume what he'd elicited, her sweet, tangy taste spurring him on.

He explored every inch of her, the lips he was spreading, every rounded secret curve of her clit, the sensitive hood, nothing was left unaccounted for as he drove her mad. And then, his own cock throbbing in pain, he sucked on her engorged, slick nub until she screamed, her inner muscles pulsing around his two fingers as he rubbed her, heightening her orgasm so she'd never forget he was the one who gave it to her.

Standing, he brushed a piece of hair out of her face, but the wind just blew it back so he tucked it behind her ear and left his hand there, his eyes searching hers.

"Do you want me to take you here while you're tied up or on the chaise?"

Her eyes widened and her lips trembled as she said, "I don't want to wait. Please."

Eyes closing, he grabbed the condom and ripped it open before stepping between her thighs again and rolling the latex down a dick that he'd never seen so hard.

"You're so damned perfect," he told her, dropping a kiss on her nose. "Thank you for this."

Just as he hitched his wide head at her entrance, she seemed to come back to herself. "I'm just thinking about next time when I do it to you."

He eased into her an inch and took her mouth, biting at her bottom lip before growling, "I can't fucking wait."

And then he surged into her waiting warmth—she opened up for him like she'd been waiting for just this moment to take his cock.

He tried to be gentle, he really did, but she was clenching him from the inside and he was barely hanging on as she gripped and thrust against him just as hard as he was going at her, as if she couldn't get enough of him. So he gave her everything, arms across her back to hold her steady against the onslaught of their joining. His balls tightened and his lower back began to twitch in warning, unspent desire brewing and bubbling in every cell of his body as he got closer to exploding.

But there was no way in hell he was going before she went again; he was already addicted to her muscles gripping him at the same time that he came, that they were together, a team in crossing the finish line and glorying in the victory together. So he dragged his thumb across her sensitive nub again, loving her jerk against him as the pleasure got too great to contain. He thrust again and again until she started to break apart, her head thrown back and her cries being carried away over the water, and that was when he let himself go, shuddering against her and missing her hands on him.

Still inside her, he pulled at the ropes, releasing them, and her arms came up behind him, holding him close against her as they both caught their breaths. When he was able to breathe normally, he undid the ropes at her feet and picked her up in his arms, carrying her over to the round lounger in the middle of the deck and laying her down on it. Picking up her clothes, he dropped them beside her before going back over to the small bar area and disposing of the condom. He procured a bottle of water and two glasses of wine and took them back over to where she'd stretched out with her gaze on the stars.

He handed her a glass of wine before lying down next to her. She immediately curled into him and he felt contentment drift over him like a warm blanket. It'd been such a long time since he'd simply held someone that being here under the stars with her was a dream. A notion that he'd pulled out and discarded over the years because it'd seemed too unrealistic. Every day kept getting better with Molly and he thanked some deity that he hadn't caved to pressure over the years and just married someone like his parents wanted, that he'd waited for something more, because nothing compared to this.

She leaned up from where her head rested on his chest to give him a kiss and he melted at the sated "mmm" sound she made against his lips. Shit, he loved that she liked touching him.

"You had a good time?" he asked, stroking the silky strands of hair pooled on his chest. "My best performance yet?"

She gave a barely there snort at the callback to her earlier challenge. "*Good* would be an understatement, I think. I didn't think sex with you could get better, but I'm not ashamed to say that I was wrong."

Oliver's eyes closed. He couldn't get enough of her honesty, her fearlessness. Knowing he never had to hide from her, too, was such a gift, and in this moment where there was so much he felt and wanted to say he still kept silent. Because if she felt like he did now, he knew she wouldn't hesitate to say it because she was brave and forthright and Molly. So he held back the words he wanted to say, words he probably should have said all those years ago before she moved to Colorado.

"And think," he told her, "we still have weeks to improve upon it as well."

The fingers roaming aimlessly on his chest stilled and her big eyes gleamed at him in the dim deck lights scattered across the floor. "Oh, I think I'll be dead in a week if it gets any better than that."

He laughed, dropping a kiss on the top of her head. "Silver lining. I can't think of a way I'd rather go."

"Fair point, well made," she told him with a grin.

They fell into silence, him sipping on his wine, letting himself indulge in his mellow a little longer. He twisted a piece of her hair in his hand while her thumb moved absently over his abdomen.

She sighed and he gave her a squeeze. "This is the best vacation ever."

Oliver tucked a finger under her chin and brought her gaze up so he could kiss her, a gentle kiss that nearly turned heated again before he broke away, pressing soft pecks to her nose, eyes, cheeks—anywhere she felt soft, he touched. "I'm glad you decided to come. To take the risk, I mean."

He pulled back, their eyes on each other now, her warm brown depths pulling him in with possibility. He wished he knew what she was thinking. "Yeah, it was worth it."

His heart clenched and he knew he was probably reading into the statement, but he needed to know that she was okay with who he was off this yacht. He could give away all his money today and he'd still be the same person and he didn't want to constantly worry that he would scare her away. He wanted her because she was strong, because she could stand up and be a partner with him, someone who walked beside him as they took on the world. That was what he intended to do and she was the only one he'd ever thought was up to the challenge. Underneath the quick smile and light conversation he offered to other people, he wasn't an easy person to be with. She could ask the string of women who'd walked straight out of his life without a backward glance. He needed one who wanted to stay even if it was difficult.

He kissed her again, this time joining her tongue with his, reminding her of what they'd just had together. "Damn right it was worth it."

She searched his eyes because his voice had turned gruff with bottled-up emotion. Now that he'd had a taste of bliss, he couldn't imagine going back to his life before Molly took a risk and came on this boat, taking a break from her job, flying across the country, sailing throughout the Caribbean all to spend time with a guy she used to date. He had to believe it meant something.

"You okay?" she asked, concern in her eyes.

"Yeah, just as long as you're not going anywhere."

She shook her head and he closed his eyes in relief.

CHAPTER TEN

MOLLY HAD WOKEN up without a blaring alarm for the nearly two weeks that she'd been on Oliver's yacht, feeling blissful. She'd fallen asleep in his arms last night, but when she reached out a hand for him she only got cool sheets instead of his warm body. Rising from the bed, she noticed that the bathroom was dark, which meant he wasn't in there, either. Quickly getting ready for the day, she made her way to the galley kitchen and found him making breakfast again, shirtless with the gray swim shorts riding low on his waist showcasing the deep ravines of his lower abs.

"Pretty sure as the boat's engineer I should tell you that you cooking shirtless is a fire hazard."

He turned to her fully, a huge grin on his face. "Fire hazard? How so?"

"Because if you get injured from some blowback grease then I might be forced to cook in your place."

Oliver shook his head and pulled her into his arms for a quick kiss. "Good morning."

"You, too," she returned, peering over his shoulder onto the griddle. "Pancakes?"

He nodded. "Sunday is for pancakes." Flipping over a row of them, he caught her as she stepped away to go get a mug of coffee. "You like them, right?"

"Of course," she said. "I'm a human being, aren't I?"

He gave her hand a squeeze before letting her go. She held back a sigh because mornings with Oliver and pancakes were amazing.

She piled the fruit, maple syrup, sausage and their coffees on a tray and followed Oliver up to the sky lounge again. It was definitely their favorite place on the boat and since it was on the same level as the bridge, he could easily check the maps and controls of the boat while still having access to the minibar, the Jacuzzi and a deck with comfy chaise longues.

They were in the middle of eating when Oliver's phone rang and she startled. Their communication with the outside world was pretty limited at this point, but the shrill ring was a loud reminder that it still existed.

Frown lines appeared on his face as he read the screen. "I have to take this," he said, sounding irritated. Then he left the table completely.

Wanting to give him privacy, she played around on her own phone, but when she got bored of waiting, she headed inside to take a shower. She didn't know where he was on the boat and thought she'd be safe using the one in the master suite, but as she got closer to the room she realized he'd gone there to have his conversation.

She would never have dreamed of eavesdropping, hated the very notion of it, but she was stopped midway down the hall by the sound of her name.

"I don't even know someone named Molly, Mother," Oliver said, his voice normal and as if he wasn't pretending she didn't exist. "So I'd say your sources aren't worth the money you're paying them."

A pause.

"Of course I know what I'm doing, and I don't give a fuck."

Silence again and then a mumbled "I apologize for the cursing but nothing else. I'm not coming back to the firm and I'm certainly not marrying Lila!"

Molly decided to leave then because he'd deliberately hidden himself to take the call, but then he continued, this time his voice angry and frustrated. "I'm not coming home anytime soon, so you can set me up on all the dates you want, Dad can threaten to promote someone else, it doesn't matter. He should have already promoted someone else because I might come visit you guys again at some point if you stop this constant hassling and threatening, but I will never step foot inside the firm again. I've already liquidated a good chunk of my assets so there's no going back. I'm out, Mom. Get used to it. You either want me in the family on my terms or you don't want me in the family. Those are your only options."

Molly bit her lip, listening to him, wondering what she'd do if her own dad only wanted her around if she did what he wanted. It was just a concept that was so foreign to her she could barely imagine it, let alone have seen that Oliver was living it.

"I don't care! I'm not fucking doing it!"

Molly jumped as she heard Oliver actually shout and knew she should leave, but her heart was breaking for him. Even if her dad hadn't shown much emotion, she'd always known that she was loved and cherished, and listening to Oliver and knowing what she knew about his life, she wondered if he'd ever felt that way. Secure in the knowledge that someone loved him just for him. She yearned for that for him—he deserved to be loved whole-heartedly.

And then, just as she knew she should leave, the door to the bedroom flung open and revealed Oliver standing there, his face red with anger.

When he saw her he took a step back, his expression going completely blank. "Molly," he said, clearing his throat. "I thought you were upstairs."

"I, uh, was going to have a shower," she explained, her voice sounding uncertain.

He sighed and ran a frustrated hand through his hair. "I'm sorry you had to hear that," he said. "But I expect it to only get worse. They're not too happy I'm not doing their bidding anymore. Recalcitrant sons get no reprieve."

"I hate that for you," Molly told him, wanting to reach out to him, but the waves of wrath emanating from him were enough to make her keep her distance. "I guess I knew you'd left the job, but I didn't realize that it was such a big deal to your family."

Oliver's shoulder lifted. "I'm the oldest child and my sister isn't too keen on working in the firm, either. It's tough for them to let it pass out of their hands. I'll still be on the board of directors, but I won't have a hand in any of the day-to-day operations like my dad currently does. But it's not like it will be in trouble—there are good people who can run it. My parents just want me under their thumb and they can be difficult when I'm not."

"I see," Molly said, wondering exactly what the word *difficult* meant in this context and if it was why he'd lied to them about knowing her.

"I had to tell them I don't know you," he explained, his expression serious as he read her mind. "Or else they'd run background checks on you and your entire family, call your bosses, the works.

They don't like it when people get in their way and if they think you are, it'll be not great. So please don't take that personally, Molly."

She nodded, but couldn't believe anyone could be so underhanded, especially someone's own parents. "Is Lila someone you dated?"

Oliver snorted. "Lila is a lovely person and they want me to marry her, but we're not dating, have never dated and will never date. It's just part of this delusional plot that my family has that once I get married I'll settle down and take the reins of the firm despite the fact that I've given no indication of ever doing that."

"So they've been wanting you to get married?"

"Yeah, that's nothing new, though," Oliver dismissed.

Molly searched his face, so many emotions for him running rampant. She knew Oliver's life, while certainly charmed, hadn't been perfect but she hadn't known exactly what that meant. That he was under that much family pressure. That the people in his life who were meant to protect him were the ones making him miserable. She wanted to smooth his scowl and make promises she might not be able to keep to make him smile.

"What did they want you to do that got you so angry at the end of the conversation?" she asked.

Oliver's nostrils flared and his fists clenched. "They threatened to vote me out of my board of directors seat, which, it's difficult to explain, but that would have some bearing on the amount of money I pull from my trusts because of the way my grandfather's will was structured."

"So what do you have to do, then?"

"The same as always, get married, do what they want, but it's not going to happen. I don't need that money." He pinned her with his gaze. "They don't understand what I've been doing for the last five years, Molly. I've been stockpiling, investing my own money using firms and businesses outside of ours because I always knew it would come to this. My family loves me, but it's with limits, and the longer I hold out, the faster I'm approaching those limits."

Molly didn't care if he didn't want her affection then—she took his hand and squeezed, raising it up to drop a kiss on his knuckles. "Well, they're going to miss out on being part of your life."

"Yeah, I don't think they're too worried about it."

"They don't deserve to know you, then," she pressed, hoping he knew that she valued him, that she cared for him regardless of what he did or how much money he had. "After all, I like Oliver the person in spite of you being a rich asshole."

He gave her a small smile then. "Thank you for that."

"I'm glad you didn't marry Lila, too." She met his eyes, giving his hand a squeeze. "I really needed this vacation."

Shoulders shaking with laughter, he pulled her into him and pressed his forehead against hers. "There was never a chance."

Scooting him back toward the bedroom, she marveled at how she needed to touch him. It was insane that she couldn't go an entire day without jumping into bed with him, but he needed that now—they both needed the connection.

She stopped near the bed and slowly pulled off his shorts, pushing them aside with her foot before taking off her own cover-up and bathing suit. She'd been ready to lounge all day in the water, but first there was the quick detour of making Oliver feel better to indulge in. Standing in front of him, totally naked, she smiled. "One time only, I'm completely at your mercy. Anything you want from me, I'll do."

A corner of his mouth quirked and it made her feel like a million dollars that after his shitty conversation she could make him feel a little lighter. "Have you been holding back things from me before?" he asked, laying a hand on her waist, his thumb caressing over the soft indentation of her rib.

"No, but—" she shrugged "—you have total domain. I'm yours to command, to do with what you will."

His gaze tracked over her body, scorching her with heat from head to toe. "You sure?"

She nodded.

"You're not nervous that I'm a little unhinged right now?" he asked, his eyes hooded.

"No, I know you wouldn't hurt me."

"No, I'd never hurt you," he confirmed. "But that doesn't mean I'm safe, Molly."

The words kicked up her pulse, the promise in them. This whole journey had been about risk and here was another one she wasn't going to pass up. She wanted to go wherever Oliver wanted to take her.

"Do you understand what that means?"

"I think so," she said.

"Good," he grunted. "At any moment if you feel uncomfortable, I'll stop."

Molly felt her eyes widen, but like she'd felt when tied to the railing of the boat, there was an element of anticipation. She'd loved every second of being exposed to him; every hot glance, every slightly shaky touch from him as he teetered on the edge of losing control felt like her having power over someone she'd never had before. In all her relationships, sex had been about sex and feeling good. It had never been about *her* the way Oliver made it feel, like he was feasting on her, couldn't let another second go by without having her. It was the passion she'd been missing for so long in her relationships and had ended up channeling into her job instead. But this, what she and Oliver had, the urgency, the tenderness, the willingness to be completely open to each other, was the best.

So when he pointed to the bed and said, "Lie down on your back," in that growly voice, tingles shot straight to her core.

She did, crossing her legs over each other to naturally hide her wet center, but he shook his head. "Legs apart."

Slowly, she slid them across the smooth duvet, her eyes locked on him as she did so. Tension still surrounded him and she'd do anything to see that classic Oliver smile on his face, all teeth and to-die-for dimples. She kept wondering what that smile had cost him over the years, what it cost him now to know that his parents only valued him for what he did for them. She wanted to show him that she valued him, trusted him. Scared, indeed, that she'd do anything for him.

"Good girl," he said, and then gave no reaction when her lips thinned.

He strode across the room to one of the large armoires and pulled out a nondescript black duffel. Dropping it next to her on the bed, his hot gaze raked up her entire body as he unzipped it.

"You look like a fucking goddess," he said, his hand stilled inside the bag. "And, yeah, I like you spread-eagled on my bed right now, but there's never a moment I don't look at you and think about how I'd go to my knees to worship you."

The words stopped her breath for a moment because she felt the same way about him. For so many years he'd been a mystical memory of a perfect boyfriend who didn't actually exist or whom she'd let get away. But now he was here in the flesh and even better than she'd remembered.

"But now, Molly," he said, pulling out a length of silken rope, "I just want to fuck. Are you okay with that?"

She nodded, but then he said, "Uh-uh, I need the words."

"Yes," she whispered, already reaching for him.

But he used the opportunity to snag both her wrists in his and pull them up over her head to tie onto a secret hook in the headboard she'd never noticed before.

Her eyes flew to his. "I had it custom-made so the hooks were hidden under the leather. You know, a classy kink."

She took a deep breath because for the first time since she got on the boat she was realizing that maybe she didn't actually know much about Oliver.

"I'm not scared," she told him.

He seemed unconcerned with this statement. "Good, Molly, but you might think differently when we're finished because these ropes will come off, but you should get used to the idea that I'm not letting you go." Those words sent a streak of adrenaline up her spine as he tied one of her ankles to another secret hook in the floorboard of the bed. Holy hell, what had she gotten herself into?

"Eventually you'll have to marry a Lila," Molly pointed out.

Oliver breathed through his nose, meeting her squarely in the eyes. "If you haven't figured out by now that I do exactly what I want when I want, Molly, then you haven't been paying fucking attention."

Then he left the room completely. What the hell? She tried to sit up, but of course, she was tied down.

"Oliver!" she shouted.

But there was no answer from the empty floor of the yacht. She knew this was all a part of the game and she was getting wetter the longer he made her wait, but at the same time, she'd never played this kind of game before and didn't know what to expect. But she trusted Oliver, knew that he'd deliver, that he could take her over the edge in a way she'd never experienced before so she took a couple deep breaths and once she'd finally settled, he reappeared in the room carrying a small tray with several different bottles on it.

"Did you need something?" he asked.

She glared at him and he grinned, running a reassuring hand down her arm, his eyebrow raising when she shivered. "You like this, don't you?"

She shrugged, which was not easy to do in her current position.

He ran a single finger down the underside of her arm and she jerked. "It's okay to admit you like it, Molly. I like it when you're in control, too, so it works both ways." The same single finger he'd used on her arm ran over her beaded nipple and she shivered. "There's never any shame in pleasure."

He leaned down and kissed the peaked point of her nipple, a single soft brush, and she thought she might die from the unfulfilling contact. She wanted so much more from him.

"Do you like it when I touch you?" he asked, his eyes following the trail of his finger over the curve of her breast, into the valley in between, and up the hill of the other breast.

"Yes," she whispered, her gaze also riveted to his finger and the sensations he was creating with that lone pad of flesh touching hers. A single millimeter of contact on her skin and it echoed over the rest of her body.

He removed his finger and met her eyes. "Do you like it when I don't touch you?"

Was this a trick question? Because it was admittedly getting difficult for her to think in her current state but she was pretty sure the answer was obvious.

"No," she said, her head motioning for him to touch her again.

"Are you sure about that?" he asked, pausing in whatever he was doing in that duffel bag again. She raised an eyebrow as he pulled out a sealed plastic package along with a pair of scissors to open it.

Her eyes were riveted to what was soon revealed to be a slender vibrator with two small prongs. "Yeah, I'm sure," she told him. "I like it when you touch me."

"That wasn't the question, though," he said. "The question was if you liked it when I didn't touch you." At her raised brow, he nodded. "I know, I know, it's confusing, but all day long when I'm not touching you and you're not touching me, I'm imagining what it would be like if you touched me."

He pulled the vibrator out of the package and left her again to go to the bathroom and her head fell back against the bed with a deep sigh. This might have been a mistake.

"So what I'm saying," he continued when he emerged from the bathroom, "is that when I finally get to actually touch you, the act of not touching you has made it all the better when I finally get to."

"Okay, fine," she said, beyond frustrated with the slow pace he was taking right now when she'd just had the promise of being thoroughly fucked thrown her way. "I like it when you don't touch me."

A corner of his wide mouth quirked. "You don't sound convinced." He vaulted up onto the bed and she gasped as she stared up at him towering over her. "It goes without saying that I would rather

touch you than not touch you, but every moment
I'm not, I'm thinking about it, wondering how
you'll feel in a certain spot, how much touching
will make you twitch, how your eyes will look. All
of those thoughts get me through any given day
and I wouldn't want to ever be without them. Perhaps what you're saying is that you never imagine
me touching you? That's too bad because I can't
tell you the number of times I've imagined you
when I got off."

"Of course I thought about you," she admitted,
waiting even now for him to actually touch her.
He looked like some kind of pornographic superhero standing on the bed, legs on either side of her
waist, with a yellow vibrator dangling in his hand.

"Good," he said. "And did you use one of these
while you did it?"

"Did what?" she asked to be contrary.

"While you fucked yourself and pretended it
was me inside you?"

Her inner muscles clutched as a new wave of
lust hit her. When he knelt down so he was straddling her, further limiting her movement, she
sucked in a deep breath.

"So Molly Madix likes dirty talk," he mused,
adjusting the vibe in his hand. "Too bad I didn't
know that before. We could have had a lot of fun
over the years." He held up the yellow plastic so

she could see it better. "You've used one of these before?"

She raised a sarcastic eyebrow.

He ignored her attitude. "And how many times did you imagine it was me?"

When she refused to answer he flipped a switch on the device and laid it against her nipple. Once again, the contact was not enough and she wanted to scream in frustration. "A lot," she finally said, hoping he'd relent and give her what she wanted.

But of course, he had his own oblique and infuriating plans and instead transferred the device to the other nipple, notching up the speed as he did so.

"What did you imagine?" he asked.

"I imagined you fucking me like you mentioned earlier," she said, letting the aggravation show.

But he just looked amused and removed the vibe completely while pulling something else out of the duffel. And then before she understood what he was doing, and because she'd been too irritated to pay attention fully, her eyes were covered and the room was dark.

And before she could even complain about her new state of affairs, he murmured, "Like this?" Then he slid the length of the vibe on full and fast vibration all the way inside her, her slick wetness easing the way.

She loved it, but just as he'd known, it was so

far from what she really wanted. The narrow glide of the vibrator only served to remind her of what she didn't have—him.

That said, the two prongs that were placed craftily over her clit were flaring all her nerve endings to life, catching her skin on fire, dragging all her intentions of letting him be completely in control out of the water. She wanted all of him inside her and she wanted it now.

"Isn't this what it's been like for you?" he asked, his voice deep as he watched her buck against him, urging him to give her more. "Not touching, not having anything but your imagination and this vibrator as a stand-in for me?"

She shook her head rapidly, anything for more.

"Imagine only having this for years. Every woman my parents tried to set me up with and I was more content with just having this, as unsatisfying and unfulfilling as it was. Because all that time it wasn't you, but hell if just the little I had wasn't enough."

Then the blindfold was gone, the vibe was removed, and he was breaching her, his wide head *finally* giving her that stretch she'd been desperate for. They came together then. He unhooked her hands so she could hold him against her as he used her body, as she did the same to him, and she knew she had all of him and she gave him all of her.

CHAPTER ELEVEN

OLIVER WOKE UP to an empty bed, which he hated after such an epic night with Molly. After that shitty phone call with his parents yesterday he'd been so enraged that he was surprised he'd pulled it together to speak at all, let alone have a coherent conversation that had ended in the hottest sex of his life.

A smile on his face, he went through his morning routine, knowing that Molly was somewhere on his yacht taking care of things. He suspected she was in the engine room as she normally was in the morning to make sure everything was functioning properly. She'd also do a run-through of the entire yacht, from the kitchen appliances, toilets, sinks, faucets, lights. He loved her thoroughness, loved watching her work. Loved her, really, which felt weird to admit to himself and not to her this morning.

But he knew he did. It had taken that conversation with his parents to realize it, to crystallize all the feelings he felt for her into one bright, beautiful thing. But if this lush lightness and simultaneous rich fullness that opened up inside him when he thought of her wasn't love, he didn't care to experience it because this was perfection enough.

Throwing on a pair of board shorts and a T-shirt, he was looking forward to today when they'd sail away from Grand Bahama Island, the chef now safely on board, for Nassau, one of his favorite places in the Caribbean.

When she wasn't in the engine room, Oliver went to the kitchen, where he found her with her head inside one of the ovens and giving directions to the wiry British chef who'd come highly recommended.

A metallic bang sounded before she popped out, grinning when she caught sight of Oliver. "The oven had low power, apparently, but I fixed it," she said, twirling a wrench in her hand. "The power from the main box was frayed so I replaced the wire. You should be good to go."

Liam, the chef, regarded Molly with stars in his eyes. "You are a genius," he beamed, and Oliver hated the stupid flip of the man's abundant brown hair. And disliked it even more when the chef turned to him. "She has already fixed the blender and the can opener. A true marvel of engineering."

"Well, she builds rockets," Oliver informed him, "so I don't think the can opener stood a chance."

And then at the error in Oliver's judgment that had been meant to communicate that he knew Molly better than the chef and didn't need the man to educate him on what a genius she was, Liam fell deeper into his effusive compliments before asking, "You build rockets?!"

"*Build* is a strong word," Molly laughed, "but I'm on the team that creates the plans for them, yes."

"Darling," Liam said, laying a hand on her arm that Oliver wanted to throw off and use to flip him over with. "What are you doing fixing ovens on a boat? You are not meant for such work."

Oliver wanted to roll his eyes. Maybe he would have been fine cooking for himself for the rest of this trip if he knew he was going to be subjected to his guy mooning over Molly the entire time.

"I'm on a sabbatical from work," Molly told him. "I'm just helping Oliver out and taking an extended vacation."

Liam's eyebrows rose. "You two are friends?"

Oliver took that moment to pull Molly into his side. "More than friends."

"But you are working on the boat, too?"

"I'm also working on the boat as captain," Oliver reminded him, his irritation growing.

"Working for my stay was really the only way I would agree to come aboard for such a long time," Molly explained. "I couldn't accept a trip of that magnitude from Oliver without giving him something in return."

Liam seemed to consider this.

"But the salient point here," Oliver clarified, "is that we are a couple, I own the boat, and Molly is a guest so she'll be treated as such."

She sent him a bland look, but as Liam looked between them both and understanding dawned, Oliver didn't much care what the consequences were, but if he found Liam flirting with her again now that he knew Molly was with him, Oliver wouldn't think twice about throwing him overboard.

"So I do not call you if I have an electrical problem?" Liam asked, worried now that he'd made a mistake.

Molly reached out to put a hand on his arm but Oliver's body stiffened, so she drew back at the last moment, frowning deeply at him. And yes, that had probably been too much, but in his defense, he hadn't even known he was doing it. It had been a purely visceral and involuntary animalistic reaction that he had no control over.

"Of course you call me," Molly assured him, a bright smile on her face. "Oliver just meant to say that you'll always be cooking for two. It's just that because he's an ass those weren't the words he used."

Oliver snorted and took her hands in his. "I apologize, Liam, if I was rude," Oliver told him, not in the habit of being surly to anyone let alone the person who was responsible for feeding him and could therefore choose to poison him at any moment. "Molly's very special to me and I didn't want there to be any confusion over the fact that she should be treated as a queen always."

Liam nodded his head. "I understand this, yes, but my food is my art, I would never not give anyone my best, sir."

Molly gave Oliver a smug smile, which he loved. "Excellent," Oliver said. "And also, if she tells you she can cook and use the oven on her own, please don't listen to her. She is officially banned from using the kitchen as the last time she did, she set it on fire."

Liam looked scandalized then, clutching the wooden spoon to his chest in horror. "Oh, no, no fires in my kitchen."

Molly spent a minute talking Liam off the ledge before they went over the menu. Eventually, Oliver and Molly left the galley for the sky lounge, where they sipped mimosas and waited for Liam to bring their breakfast.

"We're all set to sail today," she told him, her gaze on the clear, cloudless horizon. "Liam said the latest provisions are aboard, I spoke to the bosun and everything is locked down, the chief steward has everything she needs. Basically, we're ready when you are, Captain."

He enjoyed the little jolt of heat that title sent to his dick when it was on her lips. "We're going to have fun today."

"I know," Molly agreed, smiling as Liam came out with the omelets and fruit plate. They thanked him, and she continued. "I like watching you in command of this boat."

"You like watching me operate heavy machinery?" he said, half-lecherously, but mostly just kidding.

She shook her head, not about to go forward with the lewd joke and instead digging into her meal.

"Molly," he said, his tone going serious. "I do want to check in after yesterday and make sure we're good?"

"Oh, you mean after you tied me up to your bed and ravished me? Yeah, Oliver, I think I'm good with it."

"I just wanted to make sure because I'd like to do it again."

She laughed. "Well, I think we agreed that the next person in charge is going to be me."

Her eyes gleamed with mischief and heat and he couldn't wait to put himself in her hands. It would be the sweetest kind of torture.

"If you think you can handle me," he warned. "I don't go down easily."

"That's actually not my experience with you. You seem to go down more easily than most."

"If you're alluding to other guys you've been with right now that didn't eat that delicious pussy then I'm pissed off doubly, for you even mentioning it and that you accepted that kind of bullshit behavior for so long."

"Because I'm a queen?" Molly asked, smiling but also searching for something, as if she didn't quite believe that was how he thought of her.

"Yes, because you're *my* queen," he told her, dragging her into his lap and planting a kiss on her lush pink lips, tasting tangy sweet orange juice and champagne.

Her arms came around his neck and he wanted to fuck her right in this chair in broad daylight with Liam on his way up from the galley with more sausage, but he resisted. Maybe they'd do that later—he'd spread her out on the dining table after dinner like his own personal feast.

They ended the kiss, pressing short pecks as they drew back from each other reluctantly. Another stoke and the fire would be well on its way to raging out of control. They both knew there was work to be done today if they were going to make it to Nassau by lunch, which would give them the better part of the day to screw their brains out all over the rest of the yacht, which had basically been his running fantasy since he'd bought it.

Molly met his eyes, her brows drawn in concern, and he had an inkling he wasn't going to like her next words.

"Are we going to talk seriously about your parents?" she asked, her voice hesitant. And he knew why, too, because he'd been avoiding it for so long.

"I'm not going back to the firm, Molly, and I'm not marrying who they want. I don't know what else there is to say."

"So you're just going to cut them out of your life forever?"

He sighed, his shoulders tensing. "I don't know."

Her eyes, deep brown pools of worry, shifted away from his as she bit her lip. "Is not speaking to your family really sustainable, Oliver?"

"I don't really care, Molly. This is my life," he told her, the idea of not seeing his family gnawing at him. But it wasn't that he couldn't see his family anymore; he could. He was sure they'd be perfectly civilized, but the idea that what he did would affect how they felt about him gave him the strength to go on. The last weeks with Molly had shown him what it felt like for someone to just like *him* and made him realize just how nice it was to have that. So if being with her meant that his family ostracized him, so be it. He wasn't the sort of person to ever settle for second best, and that meant in love as well. "They're not kicking me out of the family," he clarified.

"They've threatened to take your trust and kick you off the company's board, Oliver," Molly reminded him. "That seems like a pretty big rift to overcome."

He knew how messed up this shit sounded to a person with a normal, loving family, that the money was just business and was separate from how his family functioned in private, but it wasn't going to fly with her. Hell, it was starting not to with him, but maybe the time for protecting her was over and he needed to be completely honest so she knew just what they might be up against if she decided to be in a serious relationship with him. But showing her his real life was running the risk that she wouldn't want to be a part of it, which was why he'd been trying like hell to keep it from her.

"The business is just the business," he told her, hoping this would explain it a little without making him sound like a totally out-of-touch nutbag. "It doesn't have anything to do with the rest of it."

Molly looked skeptical. "So you're not hurt that they want to take your money?"

He shrugged. "I don't know, I'd probably try to do the same thing."

"What?" she asked, brow furrowing, not understanding at all.

"It just means that money is a game. It's not a thing I even really think about anymore, to be honest," he said, biting back a sigh. He needed to tread carefully here but also he knew he shouldn't hide this part of his life from her anymore. "When you have so much of it, it kind of becomes a game."

She stared at him, her expression blank as she waited for him to continue. As if that would help.

"I love my family and they love me," he assured. "But the money stuff, it's how we connect and bond, how we fight, how we one-up each other."

"So, like, instead of playing Monopoly the board game, you play it in real life?"

He huffed a laugh. "Yeah, except there are a lot fewer rules with us."

Her eyes widened then. "And you like doing that stuff? Have you ever stolen money from your family?"

"Not stolen, but I've undercut them when they've tried to acquire a business, snagged people they wanted to hire, bought a competing business in the same market to see who makes more of a profit. It's just how we work. My parents are using the firm stuff as leverage because they think I'm still playing the game. But I'm not."

Molly met his eyes, considering. "But those games," she said, "that are so meaningless to you, have real consequences on the people employed in those businesses."

"To a certain degree," he allowed. "But not really. If the company is being run correctly, generally management remains the same."

Molly took a sip of her drink and shook her head. "I guess I don't know much about your actual life, Oliver."

"It's not my life anymore," he reminded gently, his voice low, wanting—needing—her to truly understand.

"It sounds like it is the same, only you're refusing to run the firm your family owns."

He shook his head. "No, it's different. I can buy and sell stuff all day, but this is my opportunity to *build* something, Molly. That's the difference. I want to actually *do* something, not just move my money around on an invisible chessboard."

"And you need me for that?" she asked, bringing up his offer for the first time on her own.

He took her hand in his, giving it a squeeze. "I want you in my life in all ways, Molly. I want you to help me build this company, I want you to build yachts, I want to build a life together. So, yes, I kind of need you for the last one for sure, but the other ones are optional."

Molly's breathing deepened and he could tell that he'd probably overshot it, but fuck it if it was too soon. The only thing he could do was try to make her love him for him and the rest of it, like his parents, they could figure out together.

"I haven't changed my mind, Oliver," Molly eventually said, carefully setting her glass back down on the table. "I don't want to leave my job."

"I know," he said. "But I'm also still waiting for you to tell me how much money would possibly tempt you away from it."

"Money doesn't matter to me."

He raised an eyebrow. "Everyone has a price, Molly. I'm not saying it's a bad thing, but if I offered you a multimillion-dollar yearly contract right now with a half million signing bonus, your head wouldn't be the least bit turned?"

Her eyes did widen, which pleased him, but then they shuttered. "Even if I wanted to take the job, which I don't, I couldn't take money or be employed by you if we were in a relationship."

"It's not as if you're going to see me in the office every day. I doubt I'll even go in at all except to see the actual yachts when they're finished being produced. There will be a chief operating officer who is actually in charge of daily operations so it's not as if you'd be reporting to me."

At her doubtful look, he took another breath and continued. "Look, I don't have all the answers, but I know that you're brilliant and I don't love the idea of you returning to the same city as that asshat ex-fiancé, and there's no one I trust more to create a new generation of boats."

Liam came out again, setting a tray of more toast, sausage and mimosas down on the table in front of them. "The oranges here cannot be beat, correct?"

"Should not the chief steward be bringing us our drinks?" Oliver enquired, jokingly, but reminding flirty-face Liam that Oliver was onto him and he was the only man Molly was interested in on this boat.

"Ah," Liam said and clapped his hands together. "But I made the bread myself so I wanted to make sure you all liked it."

Molly immediately took a large bite with butter on it and gave him a big smile. "This is outrageously good, Liam!"

Liam beamed and Oliver almost rolled his eyes, but stopped himself. And because he wasn't a total asshole, he took a bite of the bread himself and had to admit, only to himself, that it was delicious.

"It is my pleasure to serve you, my dear," Liam told her before leaving the deck with a huge smile on his face. "Do not hesitate to tell me whatever you would like me to make and I will deliver your deepest desires."

Oh, brother, Oliver thought, his lips thinning.

Molly laughed when she saw his expression, her eyes dancing. "He's fun."

"A real riot," Oliver drawled.

He ate a piece of buttered toast and watched as she did the same. "In all seriousness, Molly, have you given any thought at all to being together when we leave this boat?"

Molly met his eyes, her smile kind. "Of course I've thought about it," she laughed. "But I don't know that I fit in your life, Oliver. And I think you don't realize the implications of that."

He nearly snorted. "I've had nothing but time to think about the implications, Molly. That's why I'm here, because I've thought about all of them and I don't give a shit. You mean more to me than any of that stuff. I just want to be with you. It's as simple as that."

She drew her bottom lip into her mouth with her teeth. "I think maybe I need a little longer to believe that."

A trickle of unease slithered through him because he'd made the big romantic gesture, had left his old life behind, and had been completely honest with her about how he felt, pulled back the curtain on his parents, so he didn't know what else could convince her to believe that he was serious.

But when she climbed into his lap to deliver a kiss so sweet it turned his knees to jelly, he let it go. Waiting for her to come around was no damned hardship at all.

CHAPTER TWELVE

NASSAU WAS STUNNINGLY BEAUTIFUL. Molly had forgotten just how lovely it really was. She stood at the yacht's bow facing west toward the Gulf of Mexico, thinking back to all those times during grade school when she'd looked at places on a map and wondered what they were like. Being on this boat was a "pinch me" moment and yet it paled in comparison to Oliver telling her he wanted to build a life with her and her actually believing it this time.

But she still didn't understand how their lives could ever work together.

She could see herself building awesome boats, better ones than existed now, but the idea of working *for* Oliver gave her literal chills. It didn't matter that she wouldn't see him or he might not be her immediate boss, he would essentially *own* her because he owned the business. Nope—she shook her head—it couldn't happen.

Which meant the other option was that he come back with her to Colorado. And that seemed lovely, but just as unlikely. She tried to imagine Oliver in his two-hundred-dollar pair of socks (she'd done an internet search for them and had nearly choked on Liam's scone in the process) in the little bungalow she'd shared with Max. Not that she'd be moving back there, but even though she made a good living and loved her life it was not the same as Oliver's. Hers was not an "owning a yacht and buying companies for sport" kind of existence. And frankly, she didn't want that kind of life, either. She wanted a regular one with a guy who loved her, who liked to hike on the weekends and watch movies at night, and that was about as complicated as it got.

Except that she'd had that with a safe, reliable guy and he'd still fucked it up.

So maybe that was an argument for Oliver. She'd had more fun in the past couple weeks with him than she'd had in the entirety of her relationship with Max, but she kept going back to the fact that she was on vacation right now. This was not how she operated in her everyday life. When she was deep into a project, she rarely made it home before nine or ten o'clock at night. She worked until she couldn't work anymore; that was her work ethic and the one that had gotten her where she was in her career. She just couldn't believe that Oliver had truly considered what a life together would look like for them in Colorado.

What the hell would he even do there? Make

conference calls from a home office? Fly back and forth to the company he was buying on the coast? Sun himself on the mountains? None of it made any sense to her.

Stopping by the engine room, she took a quick look to make sure everything was functioning properly. She'd had to fix another wayward kitchen appliance for Liam this morning, a food processor with a twisted wire, but other than that life was pretty chill on the boat. The rest of the day would include lying out and reading with Oliver as usual, their casual touches and teasing revving them up for the night, when they'd let loose in the bedroom.

Smiling about what they'd done this morning with those hooks, she didn't see the woman standing with Oliver on the main deck near the stern. She stopped mid-step when she noticed the strain on Oliver's face.

"Is this her?" the girl asked, and Molly's stomach tightened. Had his parents sent down their choice for him to marry? She'd had no idea how awful this would feel, but her insides were burning with embarrassment and rage. Plus, Molly didn't exactly look like the girlfriend of a billionaire in a white T-shirt and khaki shorts, both of which, as well as her fingers, were streaked with engine grease.

Oliver sighed. "Daphne, this is Molly," he said, taking her hand in his and giving it a squeeze.

"Molly, this is my sister, Daphne, who has arrived here unannounced and unwelcome."

Daphne swatted at her brother before holding out her hand, an emerald-cut sapphire glittering on her ring finger as she did so. "It's a pleasure to meet you, Molly," she said, her voice a subdued and cultured alto.

Molly started to hold out her hand, but then swiped it back at the last second. "I'm sorry, my hands have grease on them," she said, holding them up so they could see. "I wouldn't want to get you dirty."

Daphne's eyes gleamed. "Oh, that's okay," she laughed, leaving her own hand held out. "I'm already so dirty from the trip."

Molly shook her hand and right away she wondered how she could have missed the resemblance between the two of them. They both had light hair and eyes, though Daphne's eyes were a shade or two lighter than Oliver's.

She was also lovely.

After Daphne freshened up in the room she'd be staying in, disregarding that Oliver had told her she had to stay in a hotel on the island, the three of them settled on the main deck for lunch. Liam had cooked a huge spread—mini sandwiches, sushi, salad, the works. Molly ate while she listened to Daphne chastise Oliver for leaving her in New York to deal with their parents on her own.

"Molly, would you do that to your own sister?"

"I don't have one, but I doubt it," she admitted, siding with Daphne and receiving a grateful smile for it.

Oliver rolled his eyes. "They're not going to make you take my place in the firm, Daph. You have made it quite clear that you're not interested, starting with the fact that you've never set foot inside the building."

Daphne shrugged. "Stranger things and all."

"They'll get over it," Oliver said, unconcerned.

Daphne leaned back in the chair, setting her hands on the armrests. "They'll get over being mad about it, Oliver, but they're not going to stop taking you down. If you think for one minute they're going to let you walk away easily, you're kidding yourself."

"They have no clue what I'm doing instead," he told her, confident. "I'm doing everything under multiple layers."

"It won't be enough," Daphne said, unconvinced. "Dad will use *every* avenue available to thwart you until you come back to the company. He knows who Molly is."

Molly's eyes flew to Oliver's and his face was mottled in rage, eyes dark and the flush high on his wide cheekbones. "Yeah, they called a few nights ago asking about her, Daphne," Oliver bit off. "And you were the only one who knew where I was."

"I didn't tell him, Ollie," Daphne insisted, and Molly believed her. "But I talked to you on the phone and anyone could have been listening. That's why I got a new phone after we came because I felt sure he'd track me."

Oliver shook his head. "I can't believe you brought him right to me."

"I didn't, Oliver," Daphne promised.

"It doesn't matter," he said. "You flew under your name and he'll find out from the airline where you went."

"I really don't think so," Daphne said. "I left in the middle of the night, I purposely chartered a flight under a different name and the only person who knew where I was going was the pilot."

Molly laughed. "That's a lot of subterfuge to cover what could be said on a phone call."

"And yet it still wasn't enough." Oliver grimaced, his jaw tensing.

Daphne exhaled. "I still don't know why you're even doing this anyway, Oliver," Daphne said. "It's not as if you actually have to do work at the firm. Dad has been a figurehead since Grandpa passed. Once you're at his level, you just do whatever you want to do anyway."

Oliver shook his head. "That's how you think I want to spend my life, Daph? Just half-assing a job I don't want? Do you understand how empty that sounds? Christ, I just want to do something that makes a difference."

"With all due respect, brother," Daphne said, "I

don't know how much yacht building really contributes to society, but I mean, I get what you're saying."

"I'd create a lot of jobs for people," he told her. "And I'm trying to create eco-friendly luxury. I want to build my own legacy, not live off someone else's. At least give me some credit, Daph."

"I give you a lot of credit," she insisted.

Molly watched them go back and forth, stuck on every word because it sounded as if Oliver was in the fight of his life while up until this point he'd just made it sound like he and his family played at business together. But tapping and tracing phones, trying to sabotage Oliver before he began, Daphne having to sneak out of their house during the night, seemed intense and very real. It all just sounded incredibly awful, and while she felt for Oliver to have had to deal with it for so long, she also didn't want to be a part of such a toxic world.

"They're going to use her," Daphne said, giving Molly a wan smile. "They already know where she works."

At the words, Molly got a little light-headed because her boss hadn't been thrilled when she'd asked for that much time off at once even though there were only a handful of people in the world who could do her job.

Oliver rose from his seat, the sound of the metal chair scratching loudly over the teak, tearing at her nerves. He leaned over the table to get into his sister's face. "What are they planning, Daphne?"

Daphne shook her head, giving Molly a sad look, reaching out to take her hand. "I don't know exactly, Ollie, but she's not safe."

Molly spoke then. "You mean my life is in danger?" she squeaked.

Daphne recoiled immediately. "God, no," she choked. "They would never."

Oliver pulled Molly's chair closer to his and put an arm around her, drawing her close. "They're deviants, not murderers, Molly, I promise. You're going to be just fine," he assured her, his hand warm on hers.

"Um, it doesn't actually sound that way," Molly pointed out, icy blood running through her veins. She'd known she didn't belong in Oliver's life, but damned if she was going to die for it. Good God, who in the world were these people?

Daphne was shaking her head, too. "You haven't explained the family to her, apparently?"

Oliver shrugged. "I did, but it's hard to believe unless you witness it."

Placing her chin in her hand, Daphne sighed wistfully. "That must be nice."

Molly's gaze shot to hers. "Yeah, having parents who don't want to murder your friends is a pretty big mark on the plus side as far as family goes."

"No one is going to murder you," Oliver growled.

Then he made her look at him, his expression purposeful. "But they will try to figure out your vulnerabilities. So is your father solvent?"

"You mean does he have debt?"

"Yes, or any unwise investments? Does he secretly gamble? Did he ever cheat on your mom? What are his weaknesses?"

"And you, too," Daphne continued. "Do you have any arrests, any former bosses with a grudge, bad employee reviews?"

Molly looked between both of them as they spoke. The outlandish possibilities made her head spin. The most her father ever gambled was scratch-offs he'd gotten at an office holiday gift exchange.

She shook her head, not truly comprehending what was happening or what it possibly meant for her family or career. "None of those things applies. I don't know what our weaknesses would be. We're just normal people."

"That's good," Daphne chirped brightly. "The less they have on you means the less leverage they'll have on Oliver, which is what we want."

"But we're not even together. Why would they use me as leverage?"

"Well, for example," Daphne explained, "they'll find out that Oliver wants to build yachts. And now they know he's also acquired a genius rocket scientist."

"The preferred term is actually aerospace—"

But Daphne ignored her to continue. "So what they'll probably do is try to pay you off first. Offer you double the amount Oliver is paying you."

"Oliver isn't paying me anything—I'm not working for him," Molly said, barely keeping up.

"Doesn't matter." Daphne shrugged. "Oliver doesn't have friends, so either way they'll know you're a significant piece of whatever he's doing next."

"Oliver had tons of friends when we were yachting together."

Daphne shook her head. "Oliver has acquaintances, not friends he travels extensively with."

Oliver had been silent but squeezed Molly's hand. "I'm sorry, Molly, but she's right. I'd hoped we have more time before this started, but I guess not."

"I thought you said they'd be fine with you leaving eventually."

"Yeah, emotionally, like I could go back and we could do the whole family thing. But like I said, this business stuff, they'll keep coming until they get what they want."

Molly let all of this sink in, mulling over what could be done to thwart his parents and give Oliver the life he wanted. It didn't take her long; she was a problem-solver by trade, after all.

"Well, the easy solution is for me to go back to Colorado."

CHAPTER THIRTEEN

OLIVER STALKED ACROSS his bedroom toward Molly, who was standing in front of an open suitcase placing neatly folded clothes inside, looking extremely normal as if she had no inkling whatsoever that she was ripping out his heart.

Fucking Daphne, he cursed. As if he needed her to travel to Nassau to tell him what his parents would be planning? He knew the rules of the game, had contingency plans, and then plans for those, too, if they went to shit. Her curiosity over Molly disguised as her trying to help him was so classic her, always stirring things up. She'd been on the boat for all of an hour and completely ruined his life.

"I can't believe you were serious," he said, eyes riveted on her bag.

Molly's head raised, her expression carefully easy. "Yes, this will solve the problem. If I remove myself from the equation, your parents can't do anything to me and they won't have any leverage.

You get to keep moving forward with your plans and build the company of your dreams. Problem solved."

Oliver's eyes closed and his fists clenched. He needed to get himself together and focus if he was going to keep Molly with him. He'd known she was skittish, known she had her doubts about them moving forward, and now his interfering sister had made it all worse, tipped the scales in the exact opposite direction he wanted them when he'd still had so much time left with her.

He'd been so damned good the past weeks, tiptoeing around what he wanted to say, but he couldn't let her leave now. He couldn't bear it, not when they'd gotten so close and not when he couldn't imagine waking up without her in his arms tomorrow or the next day or any day in the future.

"Molly," he said softly, reaching out a hand. "Can you please stop packing so we can discuss this?"

She shook her head. "You're just going to try to make me believe that your dream isn't in danger when I know it is, Oliver. I can't let myself be part of your downfall. So let's just take this time to be apart a little longer, and when you've got your company up and running I'll be waiting for you and we can continue this."

This calmed him a little, to know that she did

want to be together, but he still didn't want her
to go.

She turned to him then, taking his hand. "It's
probably not smart to get into another serious relationship right now anyway, Oliver. This is for
the best." Giving him a sad smile, she continued,
"And for once I'll be able to give you what you
need instead of the other way around. It means a
lot for me to be able to do that for you."

"You always—" he started, but she cut him off
with a kiss.

"Nope, it's my turn to show you how much you
mean to me," she told him. Then pointed a finger
at the bed. "It's my turn now. Get up there."

He pulled her in for a kiss that went from hot
to volcanic in three seconds as their tongues tangled and fought for dominance. She'd been talking about tying him up since he'd done it to her,
but they'd always been in too much of a hurry. But
apparently it was his turn. The thought of Molly
over him shot bullets of heat to his cock as it stiffened underneath his jeans.

"Clothes off," she ordered as she moved to the
closet and unearthed the duffel bag of toys. She
dropped it on the bed as he had and he removed his
clothes as she rummaged through the dark depths,
pulling out the ropes with a satisfied smile.

He lay on the bed, propped up against the headboard, watching intently as she slid the smooth

vinyl rope through her fingers, teasing him. "Did you buy this just for me?" she asked. "Or do you do this stuff with all the women you sleep with?"

He understood the question she was really asking and wanted nothing more than to reassure her. "It's all for you."

A light eyebrow raised. "You tied me up pretty deftly."

He grinned. "I was a bosun for years," he reminded her. "I know my knots inside and out."

This had her smiling as well and he took a deep breath, energized. She loved him, too; he knew it. All he had to do was get her to realize it and then convince her to stay with him.

"Fair point," she allowed, considering him as he lay naked and spread before her. She pulled her bottom lip between her teeth and then dropped the rope on the floor. "I'm not sure if I want you tied. I want you to obey me of your own free will."

He exhaled through his nose and met her eyes. "I will always do that."

She nodded in satisfaction before she spread his legs apart in one smooth motion, her eyes locked on the upward jut of his cock.

"You like this," she said, half question and half observation.

"I pretty much like anything you do to me, Molly."

"I thought being at your mercy would make me

feel overwhelmed or taken advantage of, but I felt powerful instead. Is that how you feel?"

"Kind of," he admitted. "I trust you enough to let you be in control so that kind of intimacy is a turn-on. I've never let a woman have that much power over me before."

She leaned down to take his mouth, her soft tongue teasing his lips open as she invaded, the shallow thrust of her tongue sensuous and loving, so much so that it nearly killed him not to be able to touch her, to show her with not touching her how much she meant to him and how much he needed her to stay.

When they disconnected, he said the truth. "With or without the ropes, you have all the power here, Molly, because I'd do absolutely anything to make you happy. Literally anything. When you frown it's like I'm being punched in the gut—that you're leaving is like you're ripping out my heart, Molly. I need you."

She met his eyes, hers dark and stormy and full of flashing emotion—pain, love, confusion, but in the end settling on determination. "That's exactly how I feel about you," she whispered, her voice urgent. "That's why you need to let me go so that I can do that for you."

Christ, he wanted to argue so badly but like an idiot he'd walked right into her trap.

"I love you, Molly," he told her, the words slipping out before he had a chance to think about the consequences. Maybe while he'd promised not to touch her wasn't exactly the best time to reveal one's love for the first time, but hell, maybe it was. He didn't have defenses or pride when it came to her. He was just a bleeding vein and when she left he'd spill out empty onto the ground, deflated and useless. "I think I've loved you for so long, and if you're really going to leave, then I need you to know."

She audibly choked back a small sob and he furiously whispered to her, begging her to let him touch her finally and she nodded her head.

Her mouth met his in a messy, tear-streaked kiss, her hands holding the sides of his face as she straddled him, still fully clothed. He could smell her subtle citrus scent, feel the smooth cotton fabric of her shorts against his throbbing dick, the gentle fall of her hair against his shoulders. He was drowning in her, the soft skin of her palms against the stubble on his chin that she'd earlier coined as vacation chic. Their tongues met, his focused on hers as it moved through his mouth, teasing, getting more intense as she took over.

Eventually, she broke away, tracing a feather-light trail of kisses down his chest, and then his leg, her deft fingers kneading the balls of his feet, the rough calluses of his toes while she murmured things he couldn't hear, but the tone was loving and warm and he couldn't believe their time together was ending already. It wasn't anywhere near the lifetime he'd aimed for.

"There are a lot of toys in that bag," she finally said, her mouth very, *very* close to his cock and yet so goddamn far away. "I thought when we got around to me being in charge, I'd have a field day with them. You know, really put you at my mercy."

He grunted when her finger grazed the root of him, teasing him. "I've been at your mercy since you stepped onto this boat."

She looked up at him and when she spoke, he felt it on the stretched skin of his head. "I like that, Oliver. You're always so good with words that for a long time I didn't believe the things you said. I thought you were too glib to actually mean anything you said."

His gaze shot to the ceiling as her hand came around his width. "Yeah, well, I like getting what I want and people generally don't respond to it when I'm an asshole."

"That's what I mean," Molly explained, her tongue ever so lightly dabbing at the liquid on top of his cock.

Jesus Christ, this was torture.

"I never knew if you were just trying to get what you wanted or if you were being honest."

On some level, Oliver knew what she was getting at. That maybe she didn't believe him when he said he loved her, or thought he was playing her. Hell, if he were her, he'd have his own doubts. "I've never had to work to be charming with you, Molly—I've always been able to be myself. That's part of the reason you're so important to me."

He guessed she liked the answer because she took him into her mouth then, her hot, wet, velvety mouth, and his hips bucked. The pleasure was so great, her tongue stroking, her hand pressing the thick root of him that wouldn't fit in her mouth. Her cheeks hollowed out as she sucked and he lost his goddamn mind when she looked up, her eyes meeting his as she did it, his glistening dick sliding in and out of her mouth. And then she went deeper and he thought he was dying, the engorged head hitting the pliant back of her throat as she swallowed.

"Christ, Molly," he cursed, the guttural sound of pleasure ripping out of his throat.

She didn't respond, just kept going, the sounds echoing in the room and driving him insane with need. His hips thrust against her, not even pulling back, and she took all of him, her lips meeting the skin of his abdomen as she stretched herself.

"I'm going to come," he panted, his voice rough and raw.

At her single nod, she kept on, her tongue running around the length of his head before taking him in again, sucking until with a final lift of his hips, he came in a sharp explosion, his whole body strung tight as all his blood and attention centered on being in her luscious mouth. As she swallowed him, the tremors continued to rule his body. Continued still as she licked him clean, completely disregarding his pleas for reprieve.

But Molly was ruthless and that in itself turned him on and by the time she'd removed every drop of him he was already fully hard again.

A satisfied smile on her face, she stepped off the bed.

"If you fucking leave now, I will lose my shit, Molly," he growled.

Instead of answering, she threw her shirt and bra off, followed by her shorts and the pale blue panties that always got him super revved up.

She climbed back on the bed, her breasts swaying with the movement. "Bring those close so I can suck them, Molly," he directed. "I'll make it so good, you'll be so wet."

"No bossing from you," she admonished. "And I'm already wet." So saying she dipped a finger into her folds and when she pulled it out it was wet with her own desire.

She leaned forward and he thought she was going to have mercy and let him have a taste, but at the last second she stuck her entire finger in her mouth, making him watch as she licked that clean, too.

"You're a cruel, cruel woman, Molly Madix," he told her, his hands fisting so he wouldn't grab her, knuckles white as she straddled him.

"I know," Molly said, her mouth red and a little puffy from going to work on him. A corner of it quirked as she met his eyes. "I'm really enjoying it."

She straddled his hips, poised directly above his cock, notching it into her crevice, the feel of all that welcoming heat sending him into the stratosphere. "Condoms are in the nightstand," he told her, wondering just how he was going to make it through this.

A flash of determination flew across her face before she met his eyes. "I'm on the pill and I trust you," she confided, her voice hushed. "Do you trust me?"

"Fuck, Molly," he said, rising from the bed to take her into his arms even as she pushed him back. "You don't just say that and then expect me to lie here and do nothing."

She shook her head, moving away from him then. "Do you not want me to?"

Damn it, it had happened; his mind was truly gone. "I would *kill* for you to do it, Molly," he groaned. "But I need to touch you. Please."

That bottom lip disappeared between her teeth again and she returned to where he was notched at her entrance, only this time she sank down.

Everyone on the damned yacht probably heard his cry of pleasure as she fully took him in, their hips meeting. His gaze held hers because he was letting go of this small connection. "I've never done this before," he admitted.

Her eyes closed and she moved her hips just a little. "Me neither," she told him.

Oliver's heart thrilled because maybe this meant he had a chance that he could change her mind and make her stay.

He held on to this hope, probably foolishly, as she moved over him, every second, every thrust, every look a miracle. She took and took without him able to give back to her, but in the end, when they came together in a rush of heat and sweat and hoarse shouts of pleasure, he knew he'd given her everything he had.

CHAPTER FOURTEEN

MOLLY DIDN'T WANT to go back to Colorado. It didn't matter that she was going to do it or that Oliver didn't want her to; she knew she had to. This whole time they'd been lazing about on the yacht cruising the Caribbean and he'd known his own parents were going to make his life a living hell just because he'd made the choice to live his own life. It broke her heart and she wasn't having it. Oliver deserved to be happy and if she had to go back to chilly Colorado in December, then that's just what she would do.

She shivered thinking about how cold it would be compared to her sun-drenched days lounging on deck, jumping into the cool water when they got too hot, then warming up together again in bed. It was going to be a harsh reality to be thrust back into, but her bags were packed and ready for her to go. Heart heavy, she did a last inspection of her original room to make sure she hadn't left anything behind. Then, so he would be safe on the next leg of his trip, she inspected the engine room one last time to make sure everything was good to go. She'd be taking the small speedboat ashore to Nassau and flying from the little airport there to Florida and then straight to Colorado.

A sigh on her lips, she swallowed as she headed up to the sky lounge, for her last meal with Oliver and the goodbye that she was dreading. She opened the glass French doors and entered the deck, her heart clenching in misery when she saw him there, sitting at the table gazing off into the ocean, the same pain she felt etched on his face.

She could feel Oliver's eyes on her as she moved to her chair, his pissed-off mood emanating from him in waves. They'd argued again this morning when she'd finished up packing and it hadn't ended how it had last night with her pouring out her heart to him in bed. Just the thought of what they'd done and then the way he'd held her against him all night, how they'd woken up in the wee hours of the morning and made love, clinging to each other in the dark silence, was almost enough to make her stay. Tears threatened because she knew she couldn't. What was a couple of months apart for him to have the life he'd dreamed about?

She took the seat beside him, brushing her hand over his knee as she did so. She wanted to soak up every last bit of him she could before she left.

He must have felt the same way, too, because he pulled her chair flush against his and put an arm around her back, pulling her into him.

"Are you really going to do this to us?" he asked Molly, his voice hushed.

She hated that she was hurting him, but her mind was made up. Daphne had been a tangible reminder of what she'd known from the beginning: Oliver's life didn't include her and the threats to what he was trying to build were legitimate. His sister had flown to the Bahamas all in the hopes of warning him of what was to come, which meant it was serious. All of Molly's fears from the beginning about how she didn't fit into his life were realized and while she believed him that he wanted to build a new life together with her, it would never happen if his parents were that threatening.

"You know I need to go." His eyes were sad and defeated, echoing the desolation she felt.

Molly speared a piece of tomato in her shrimp salad even though she had absolutely no appetite.

"I know you think that," he said. "I just wish you'd trust me. I have it handled, Molly. Your presence in my life won't make my dream impossible. You staying with me makes it all *more* possible."

Molly shook her head because she didn't believe him. She ate the meal with her gaze down, just trying to make it through without crying. The minutes were counting down until she left and she didn't want to spend them arguing, not when every breeze that blew across the deck brought back all her memories of being with Oliver; his laugh, his smile, his hungry gaze, but most of all the look on his face when he'd said he loved her, would haunt her. He'd already been resigned that she wouldn't say it back but hopeful that she would. And she hadn't—that would haunt her as well.

The moment he'd said it, she'd known. She loved him so much and knew 100 percent that while she *was* leaving to help him, she was also doing it because she was terrified of not being enough for his world. And Oliver, whose parents wanted to ruin his life through her, and his own self who was charm personified. She couldn't trust that she wouldn't be collateral damage. She couldn't trust him with her heart yet. Not in these extraordinary circumstances that she could barely wrap her head around.

The last bite of her salad eaten, she set her fork down, the metallic clink a sad sound that meant it was time for her to go.

Oliver rose, holding his hand out to her. His grip was warm and firm as he led her downstairs. Standing together on the stern, mere feet away from the speedboat that would take her to shore, Oliver drew her into his arms. Her luggage was already loaded onto the smaller vessel with a waiting bosun at the ready to take her to shore.

"What can I do to make you stay?" he murmured against her lips, his forehead resting on hers.

Her arms tightened around him and she just shook her head, not able to get words out.

He dragged her more firmly into his arms, her body pressed up against his, the last feel of his hard lines and ridges against her. She wanted to soak it all in to remember, to take out on her imminent cold winter nights alone.

"You could stay here with me, help me," he urged. "Work together with me on this. We'll be brilliant at thwarting my parents and building the best boats the world has ever seen, Molly."

It was a plea and Molly would have to be made of stone not to be affected by it. The tears came, unstoppable, because she loved the idea of being on a team with him. "You know I can't."

"Why?" he pressed, pulling back and searching her eyes. "I can handle my parents, Molly. I've known I was going to do this for years. I have it under control. You don't need to leave. And if you don't want to work for me, I'll let you buy some of the company and then we'll truly be partners."

She just shook her head, any words she might say stuck behind the lump in her throat.

"I don't know what else I can say, but know that I love you so much, Molly. These weeks have been the best of my life. There's nothing else that even comes close and it's all because you were here."

"I can't, Oliver!" she cried, much louder than she'd intended, but how was she going to get him to understand? "I have to go."

Those light eyes again, scanning her face as if memorizing it before landing on her gaze again, searching and searching. Then he was kissing her, his lips sweet and soft against her. "Trust me not to hurt you, Molly," he whispered against her lips, a final plea that ravaged her. "I won't ever lie or cheat or be anything but thankful that you're mine. Please know it's the truth."

She kissed him again, hugging him tight to her before letting him go. "I have to go." She repeated the words, choked and broken.

There were tears in his eyes, too, as he gave her hand one last squeeze before slowly releasing it, savoring the final contact between them.

"I love you, Molly," he said again when she'd stepped onto the speedboat. "At least believe that."

She nodded, then turned away as the tears threatened. The bosun in the boat gave her a commiserating smile as he started the engine and drove off toward the shore.

Finally, when she knew Oliver could no longer see her face, she let herself cry. It was embarrassing in front of another person but there was nothing to be done about it.

The worst part was that she knew Oliver was still standing there, alone on his boat, hurting just as badly as she was and she'd been the cause of it. She could go back and take the risk on love, but here she was running away, just like the scared person she'd been the first time things got serious with them. Even then, she hadn't asked him to come with her to Colorado, assuming that he wouldn't want to without really knowing. Not brave enough to take the chance and have her fears realized that it had been just another yacht romance for him.

They docked the boat at the marina and Molly helped the bosun take her luggage into the clubhouse, which was where the car was waiting to take her to the airport. But she had one more thing to do before she could go. She walked quickly to the small patch of beach near the docks to give the boat she'd had the best weeks of her life on a final look. And perhaps see a glimpse of Oliver on the yacht where she'd left him.

But when her toes dug into the soft, silky sand for the last time and she prepared to lift her hand in a final goodbye, she didn't see Oliver anywhere on the deck, which shredded any remaining pieces of her heart. With a sigh, she waved in the direction of the boat anyway, her mind unwilling to even contemplate the future without Oliver that was almost upon her as soon as she left the piece of shore.

She lifted a corner of her shirt to wipe the tears off her face so she wouldn't look like a crazy person walking through a clubhouse full of yacht owners. Having gotten hold of herself, she turned to head back to the dock but as soon as her foot left the sand, she heard shouting coming from behind her. Turning toward the boat again, she saw a speedboat slicing through the blue water, traveling far too fast in her direction.

"Molly!" a voice cried and she saw Oliver quickly approaching her in the water. "Don't go!"

She started for the water as Oliver brought the boat to a stop. Barely waiting for the other deckhand to take the boat's controls, he dived into the water and started swimming to shore. Molly's feet were moving before she even knew what she was doing and she was knee-deep in water when Oliver surfaced and walked the rest of the way toward her. They met waist-deep in the ocean, eyes locked.

"I'm sorry, but I just couldn't let you go," he choked, water dripping off his eyelashes and rivulets flowing from the drenched locks of hair down his bare neck and throat.

Molly stared at him, prepared with the same farewell speech she'd just given him on the boat but found that the words simply wouldn't leave her mouth.

"I don't want to go, either," she admitted, her lack of breath making her voice barely audible.

The waves pushed against her waist but she hardly noticed the water splashing onto her face. "But I don't want you to lose your dream just because I'm in your life."

A wet hank of hair dropping cutely over his furrowed forehead. "Molly," he groaned, his voice pleading as his eyes bored into hers. "Trust me to find a way to keep you safe, to make it work." He took a step toward her, taking her hands in his. "Jump with me, please."

When she didn't say anything, couldn't get anything past the avalanche of emotion that had her chest collapsing, she saw tears form in his eyes. "At least tell me I'm not alone here, that you have feelings for me—" He cut himself off then, his gaze downcast. "That you at least love me a little," he finished, his eyes tortured as they met hers again.

Her heart had been broken before when she'd tried to leave him, but now the weight of how she'd walked away from him without letting him know just how very much she loved him was agony.

Tears came harder now as she wrapped her arms around his neck. "Of course I love you, Oliver," she assured him, kissing his lips, his nose, his cheeks, anything she could find to make up for not being as brave as she should have been. "I love you so much. I was just too scared that I would be a disappointment to you when we left the yacht and it would kill me to know that I was the reason you couldn't have the life you wanted."

Oliver shook his head, touching his wet lips to hers, the heat from the sun beating down on them as the water sparkled all around them. This whole vacation had been like a fairy tale, and win or lose, the moment she thought she might never see him again was all she needed to know that she had to make the dream a reality.

"I love you, Molly," he told her. "You could never be a disappointment to me even if we moved back to New York and did what my parents wanted. But I don't want that anyway. I've only ever wanted a life with you, someone who just loves me for me. I've never had that before, Molly, and you've given it to me. So I hate to tell you this, but I'm never letting you go."

"Let me go?" she asked, smiling as she met his eyes. "I thought you were coming with me to Colorado."

He nodded. "Yes, because we're keeping each other forever. And if Colorado is where you're going then it's where I am, Prada hiking boots and all."

She took a deep breath and dived into her future for real. "You can skip the boots," she advised. "I'll design your boats, Oliver. We'll take on your parents and the yacht world together because I'm not leaving you to do it alone. I have a fair amount of savings to invest in the company as well. We're partners now, in everything."

Oliver brushed a thumb over her cheek, his eyes wide. "Are you sure, Molly?"

She nodded, never more sure of anything. Leaning in, she kissed him, lingering and letting all her love for him show. Finally, after the bosun had secured *Chance*'s second speedboat that Oliver had left in the water and the sun set lower in the sky, Molly came up for air, murmuring against his lips. "We definitely need to get your sister back for ruining the end of our vacation, though, right?"

Oliver shook his head. "It might be the end of our vacation, but it's the beginning of the rest of our lives together."

Molly melted and hugged him tighter. "You really know the way to a girl's heart, Oliver."

A corner of his mouth kicked up. "If that were more true, you wouldn't have left the first time and both of us wouldn't be fully clothed in the ocean right now. And besides, the truth is that I've been yours since we met, Molly, so just don't leave again or else I'll be forced into a kind of entrapment scenario to get you back, which will look really bad for the company we're creating together."

"You don't have to worry. I'm not going anywhere," she laughed, wrapping her legs around his waist as hope flared deep and enduring in her chest. "Especially since it seems like the best way to get your parents off your back and to get me out of danger is for us to get married, right?"

Oliver's eyes widened, the same hope she felt expanding her chest in rolling waves of joy reflected back at her. "Are you saying that you would?"

She shrugged. "I guess you'll have to ask to find out."

Oliver released her legs around his waist and dragged her back to shore, nearly pulling her arm out of the socket, so he could kneel on sand and not drown.

"Molly," he asked, her hand in his and water dripping off both of them to pool around their feet. "Will you marry me?"

On a vacation from her real life, Molly couldn't believe she'd ended up finding her new one with a man she'd fallen in love with so long ago, but now that she had she couldn't wait to get started.

"Maybe," she told him, laughing. "If we start this new adventure by not leaving your boat for another month."

Smiling hugely, Oliver rose and picked her up in his arms. "I thought you'd never ask."

* * * * *

COMING SOON!

We really hope you enjoyed reading this book.
If you're looking for more romance, be sure to
head to the shops when new books are
available on

Thursday 15th
April